ACTS OF THE SERVANT
Volume One

Book One of
THIS IRON RACE

By

SIR TAMBURLAINE BRYCE
MACGREGOR

THE ORIGINAL TEXT
RESTORED BY NEVIL WARBROOK

Published by

HARE & DRUM
7 Sanctuary Square, Edenborough

Copyright © this 2023 edition
The MacGregor Estate
&
Nevil Warbrook

All rights reserved. No part of this publication may be reproduced or distributed in any form without prior written permission from the authors, with the exception of non-commercial uses permitted by copyright law.

The rights of Nevil Warbrook and the MacGregor Estate to be identified as the authors of this work have been asserted by them in accordance with the Copyright, Design and Patents Act 1988.

This Iron Race

'At the height of his powers in the middle years of the nineteenth century Sir Tamburlaine Bryce MacGregor was the preeminent Scottish writer and the equal of any in Greater Britain' *Destiny McCloud, Edenborough Review*

'Mr Warbrook's restored text of Sir Tamburlaine MacGregor's late work has divided opinion. According to Sister Ethelnyd of the Iona Fellowship of Grace it is "as close to the original as we can hope for" while the noted psychic Hendryk van Zelden states that "We cannot blame the editor if Nevil Warbrook's restoration of Sir Tamburlaine MacGregor's great work ultimately disappoints; one does not send a blind man to count the stars."

'However, neither Sister Ethelnyd nor Mr van Zelden claims the slightest expertise in literature and in that regard this new edition is a small triumph. Against all odds, Nevil Warbrook has taken a minor and near-forgotten work by a neglected author and made it a great work as relevant today as the year it was written. How accurate it is to the author's ambition I cannot tell, and I sincerely doubt Sister Ethelnyd or Mr van Zelden know either. Perhaps only Mr Warbrook knows if he has come close. No matter, in undoing the butchery forced on MacGregor by his publishers he has done the reader a great service' *Diane Kane, author of A Quiet Day in Hell*

'Combining historical fact and subtle invention with the strange worlds of magick and parapsychology, the first volume of *This Iron Race* is a complex and dazzling work that occupies the boundary between what the reader knows, what he or she believes, and the realm of their imagination, yet its ambition never obstructs the reader's delight' *Benedict Greenwood, author of The Loneliest Armadillo*

'A Gothic tale of strange happenings in the Scottish Hills, clairvoyance, disembodied souls, affliction, wandering spirits, orphaned children, royal scandal, and murder' *Orson Parish, author of Rye Harvest*

'Sorcerer or not (and should we care?), MacGregor was a consummate conjuror of words' *Kate Ferne, author of Minotaur*

'Deny magick, it will destroy you: untrained it will destroy those you love'

'O'
February 11th, Avebury

The jackdaws are noisy this morning. As we approach they take flight from the linden trees with the sharp cries of scolding women. Something's upset them. Buzzard or an owl? A few settle on the thatched roof of The Red Lion. The rest circle around and fly eastwards. Miserable grey skies. Bitterly cold.

My companion is a rum sort of chap. Very tall. Only just met him and not yet caught his name. 'O' something-or-other. Eirish, perhaps? But Scots accent, from what I can make out. Wish he'd speak up. Voice like dry leaves. Still, not every day your publisher sends someone to interview you so buck up and act like a professional. Go easy on the whisky and check your flies before leaving the lavatory.

In we go. Nothing like the smell of a pub to comfort a chap. Blast. Jukebox is playing.

'Sorry about the noise,' I say over my shoulder as I turn for the parlour. 'It's Avebury's only pub so one must expect this sort of thing. There's a table by the fire. We can warm up a bit.'

My tweed jacket's smarter than my old coat but doesn't button across the tummy any more. Bloody freezing. Ah, good; he's looking at the bar. Wonder if Hare & Drum are paying expenses. Nothing ventured.

'Cropwell's Bitter is a decent pint,' I suggest. 'A whisky for me. Owl Service. No ice.'

Seems perfectly happy getting the order in. Shame it's only midday. Work beckons this afternoon. Mind you, I could have a nap first. 'Oh, you'd better make that a double,' I tell him. 'That is, assuming Hare & Drum are paying. Don't want to take liberties. We have lots to discuss. Best not to interrupt proceedings. I say, that's a fine pen you have. A writer's pen, if I'm not mistaken.'

What I know about pens wouldn't fill the back of a postage stamp, but it looks impressive. Anyway, publishers are full of failed writers. Next best thing to having a literary career is to cock up other people's literary careers. He is uncommonly tall; keep thinking he's going to bash his head on the ceiling. Ridiculous of course, but that's one's impression. Do believe I impressed him with my prognostication. At least I got a smile...

'Oh, you needn't look surprised. I can *smell* a fellow writer. I'm forever losing pens, so only buy cheap ballpoints. Is that the hardback edition you're carrying?'

It is. Must admit Hare & Drum have done a fine job of it. Looks like an old-fashioned leather cover. Fake of course, but they made an effort.

Something rattles the window. There's a jackdaw tapping the glass. Specks of rain.

'Looks like we got here just in time,' I say. 'Rain will send the tourists back to their cars.'

O looks around cluelessly. Can't believe he hasn't seen them. Must have been fifty wandering round the stones, their shiny, primary-colour cagoules like a plague of boils.

'Avebury's stone circle is world famous,' I tell him. 'Draws thousands of tourists. They treat it rather like a roundabout. Round and round they go. If you don't mind, while you do the honours at the bar I'll warm up by the fire.'

§

'Thank you, O...' I invite him to remind me of his name but he's not forthcoming. 'Whisky's just the thing on a day like this. Curious breed, the tourist. Thousands of them, rain or shine they wander around the stones...' He's tipped his head to one side and given me a quizzical look. Perhaps ought to stay on track. 'Of course, you want to know about Hendryk van Zelden and time is pressing.'

I don't much care for this story. Don't come out of it very well. Not my fault, of course. Still, give it my best shot.

'I first met Van Zelden in New Amsterdam some three years ago. I was promoting *The Deeper Well,* my history of

Gaelic poetry, on behalf of my publisher, Little Brown Johnson. Ex-publisher, I should say. It was March, I think, and late evening. The Koningin Hotel was—and I assume it still is—a brownstone on the left bank of Manhattan's third *arrondissement*.

You do know they speak French in that part of the Americas? Good. Now, perhaps not the time to say it, but never trust a publisher to know your market. Had I been among the descendants of Scots in Canada or Appalachia I'd have done good business. As it was, marooned on Manhattan Island I'd barely sold a dozen copies and had drunk one or two glasses of Californian wine when a young man in a turquoise evening suit appeared at my elbow. The world's favourite trickster knew how to make an entrance.'

That sets the scene. If I recall it was rather more than one or two, but the wine was free and, for once, a decent vintage. Can't blame a chap for taking advantage.

'*Bonsoir Monsieur Warbrook*, Van Zelden said. *Je Mappila Hendryk van Zelden*. Well, I didn't know him from Adam, but of course I shook his hand. *Does-je vous connaître?* I asked.'

Bit of a fib there. I didn't know his face from Old Mother Riley, but I'd heard that bloody name before.

'*Non*, he answered. Tell the truth, while I can read French tolerably well my accent is dreadful, and it was a relief when Van Zelden continued in rather good English. *I've done a little TV over here*, he said. *But you won't have seen it. But I know you.* And he smiled with perfect teeth. *You're Nevil Warbrook, the MacGregor expert.*'

O whatever-his-name-is raises a sceptical eyebrow. I reply sheepishly.

'I'm afraid Van Zelden's flattery worked. I agreed I probably knew more about MacGregor than anyone else in the room and he laughed, as though we were having a private joke. Which we were, except I hadn't yet realised the joke was on me. Then I asked him if he'd read MacGregor's work.'

'*This Iron Race*, Van Zelden said. *I haven't read his early stuff.*

'Not his poetry? I asked. 'He's sadly underrated.' Van Zelden shook his head and then he got the point.'

I notice that O isn't taking any notes. I don't know how he's going to remember any of this. I lean forward, inviting him into the conversation. Also, I don't want any other bugger in the pub overhearing this bit.

'*I'm more interested in his other work*, Van Zelden said. *I do stage magick, mechanical tricks; not the real thing. Not like Sir Tamburlaine.*'

O doesn't bat an eyelid. Honestly, I thought that would get a reaction. And he's not touched his pint. Waste of good bitter.

'Well, I told Van Zelden I didn't understand him, though I'm afraid I understood only too well. Then Van Zelden moved closer so we wouldn't be overheard. You, err, might want to take notes, at this point. No? Please yourself.'

Did my best. If Hare and Drum print a load of old cock, I'll know who to blame. Least I will if I ever catch his blasted name.

'*MacGregor practised magick, right?*' Van Zelden said. '*I mean, what he wrote, those insights, he must have.*'

Say something blast you. Honestly, I'm talking to a gatepost. Inscrutable, that's what O is. Effing inscrutable.

'Of course, Van Zelden gets no marks for originality. The first allegations against MacGregor came in the nineteen-thirties from socialists supporting the anti-shamanic pogroms in Russia. With no shamans of our own to torture, they turned to revisionist witch trials. Van Zelden wasn't the first to believe this nonsense. I put down my wineglass and defended MacGregor, but I'm afraid Van Zelden was a great deal more sober, and no matter how I lauded MacGregor's literary works, he brought it back to magick. Eventually, I admitted MacGregor owned books of magick.

'*Banned books*, Van Zelden said.

'Naturally, I tried to explain, but Van Zelden wouldn't be deterred.

'*The church burned them*, he insisted.'

Perfectly true, they did burn them. But Van Zelden has no flair for subtlety, then or now; transporting Stonehenge to Eireland is the act of a showman. True seers were never showmen. O still hasn't touched his pint. Queer chap. My whisky's damned inviting, though.

'Excuse me, just a sip to wet the lips.'

That's better. Better still if he was more convivial. Never known a journalist that wasn't a part-time drunk. I assume he is a journalist. Desmond, my agent, was a bit vague on the details.

'Magick books were frowned on, I said to Van Zelden, but never banned.

'*Do his books still exist?* he asked. *I read his widow sold off his library.*

'That made me rather cross. I told Van Zelden that Lady MacGregor had taken great care of her husband's legacy and his library survived intact. Of course, more fool me for Van Zelden had given me opportunity to end our conversation with a convenient lie and I did not take it! Had I done so, perhaps Van Zelden would be sane, certainly, you and I would not be seated here, and your new edition of *This Iron Race* would not exist!

'Do you know, I still wonder if Van Zelden had waited until I was worse for drink? Like a predator circling his prey. I admit I should have lied, or better still, ignored him. Ah well. Perhaps I delude myself and he would have got what he wanted anyway. As it was, thirsty from talk and eager to use *la vespasiennes*, I weakened and told him Lady MacGregor had bequeathed his entire library to King James University.

'Then Van Zelden blocked my way to the bathroom and bent to my ear with the voice of a snake.

'*Don't give me crap*, he said. *I checked their catalogue. Now tell me or stand there and piss your pants.*'

By God, O actually cracked a smile. I've had some bloody queer audiences down the years, but this chap must be the queerest.

'Well! The power of suggestion is a remarkable thing,' I

continue. 'The pain was excruciating. I was rooted to the spot. What *else* could I have done? I told him where to find MacGregor's library.'

Good, got that bit out of the way. A man's bladder is a delicate subject. Ah, an interruption from our host: Jonathan Grebe, the pub landlord.

'Don't mind me, Nevil. Put a few logs on the fire. Chilly out.'

'Certainly is, Jonathan. This is O…'

O says something and Jonathan looks like he's seen a ghost. Oddest expression. Nearly drops one of the logs he's carrying.

'From my publisher,' I tell him. 'I'm being interviewed.'

'Are you, are you, indeed? Well, as I said, don't mind me. To be honest, thought you were on your own. Brought you some pork scratchings, on the house.'

'Ah. Out of date, are they?'

'They will be tomorrow, but it's the thought that counts.' Jonathan drops a packet of scratchings on the table and throws a log on the fire.

'Indeed, the thought is good,' I tell him.

'Fine. I'll leave you and your *friend* in peace.'

Jonathan must be in a hurry. Rarely seen him move so quick. He's jiggered the fire up though. Quite toasty. O is giving me a queer look. Can't keep calling him O all the time. I get the scratchings open without tipping them everywhere for once and offer them. O looks mortified. Must be a vegetarian or something. Damn salty though and I've only got this whisky. Wonder if he's Jewish. Doesn't look Jewish. Better get back to the story.

To be continued.

Publisher's Note

In light of the seriousness of Mr Warbrook's allegations against Hendryk van Zelden, Hare & Drum were compelled to offer an opportunity for reply. That reply appears at the conclusion of this volume.

Hare & Drum, 7 Sanctuary Square, Edenborough

The Rebirth of Magick
By Sister Ethelnyd of the Iona Fellowship of Grace

Nevil Warbrook is a tireless promoter of Scotland's literary heritage: indeed, his friends wish he were less tireless for his poetic voice is equal to his father, Thomas Warbrook, and we should hear it more often.

Regarding his championing Sir Tamburlaine Bryce MacGregor, however, I fear he is overprotective. Several of Mr van Zelden's claims are entirely false, but in denying MacGregor any association with magick, other than as an informed author, Mr Warbrook does him a disservice. Speaking as a *practitioner* of magick it is my view there is more to Sir Tamburlaine than meets the eye, though it is not what Mr van Zelden supposes. Regardless of the historical facts, such as they can be ascertained, this much has become clear: while Mr Warbrook and Mr van Zelden remain opposed, all meaningful debate on Sir Tamburlaine's legacy is stifled.

For this reason, when I learned of Mr Warbrook's editorship of a revised edition of *This Iron Race*, I had misgivings. Could he set aside his prejudice against magick to produce a work worthy of the task? Happily, he has, and I believe this new edition is as close to Sir Tamburlaine's original as we can hope for, and I congratulate my friend on his achievement.

My knowledge of literature does not permit comparison of *This Iron Race* with other works of fiction; however, concerning magick I can make two observations. The lesser is to confirm its portrayal is, in the main, accurate. One might argue the characters sometimes arrive at insights for which the signs are too scant or ambiguous; but, allowing the needs of his narrative must come first, Sir Tamburlaine is faithful to the practice of magick.

My second observation is this: regardless of whether Sir Tamburlaine was its observer or practitioner, magick owes him a great debt.

In recent decades, urban authorities have begun to remove the soot from our townscapes to reveal the colours our forefathers saw. Soot was the visible, enduring stain of decades of coal burning in the furnaces and engines of industry, and the base metal of industry is iron. Iron, the ancient natural enemy of magick whose magnetic properties disrupt the etheric field, was the symbol of progress, and those threatened by its insidious power were ignored and vilified while magick retreated into the deep country, far from the railhead, far, even, from the iron plough.

In truth, iron's threat to magick was merely one chapter in a long saga. From the Holy Roman Empire of the 1600s, when many thousands were persecuted and exiled, to Russia in the 1930s when 200,000 were murdered in the Gulags, and even as recently as 1977 when its practice was illegal in much of the American Republic, magick was retreating from the world of man.

But what, you ask, has this to do with Sir Tamburlaine? It is this: for many years Sir Tamburlaine's interest in magick was thought quaint; the obsession of a man out of his times akin with the Romantic Poets who raged against the intrusion of railways through their beloved mountains. Yet, in the last few decades as we have begun to truly comprehend the damage we have wrought upon the world and upon ourselves, the younger generation has rebelled against the cold rationalism of science and turned again to spiritual values and especially a sympathetic appreciation of the natural world. As vice chancellor of the Iona Fellowship of Grace, I have witnessed this rebellion first hand, and for many of our students, their interest in magick began through reading Sir Tamburlaine's works.

Naturally, many have suggested we at Iona, Mount Dragon, and elsewhere, owe Sir Tamburlaine a debt, but I believe this greatly understates his importance. Magick is vitally different from brick and stone: it is a living thing, and its nature is capricious. It would not have waited for us to rediscover it but slipped forever into the shadows outwith the world of man. It would be as though the removers of soot from our townscape had found beneath the grime a rotten husk, fit only for the wrecker's ball. Had not Sir Tamburlaine kept the spark alive in his fiction we would have memories and relics of magick, but its vitality would have abandoned us. That *This Iron Race* cost Sir Tamburlaine his health, Nevil Warbrook and Mr van Zelden do not dispute. What other price he may have paid lies at the root of their disagreement. It is my earnest wish both gentlemen set aside their differences and acknowledge that whatever the price may have been, Sir Tamburlaine believed it worth paying.

Finally, I should like to thank Hare & Drum for inviting me to write this introduction. I hope the new edition of *This Iron Race* will persuade its readers, and its editor, to nurture whatever fragment of Grace resides in their heart.

Also by Sir Tamburlaine Bryce MacGregor

POETRY COLLECTIONS
The Border Minstrel
The Whale's Road
Roy of the Reivers
Lays of Brigadoon
A Perthshire Lass (published posthumously)

THE NOVELS
The Old Man and the Mountain
The Barra Bride
Maid of Norway
Camberwick
Wyvenhoe
There and Back Again (written for children)
Willoughby Chaste
Vortigern
Under The Pirate's Flag (written for children)
King Stephen
Edmund Pevensie

THE SAXON TRILOGY
Edwin and Morcar • Kingmaker • Dragonships

THE SCOTTISH TRILOGY
Last of the Free • House of Alpin • Brunanburh

THE ARTHURIAN CYCLE
Lady of the Lake • Sir Gawain • Launcelot du Lac • Modred • Merlin of the Woods

THIS IRON RACE
Acts of the Servant • Works of the Master • Devices & Executions

NON-FICTION
The Merchant Adventurers Company of Edenborough
Canongate Chronicles
A Basket of Balladry (as compiler and editor)
Rough Harbour: Observations of Highland Life
A History of Scottish Magick (unfinished at time of death)
Tempus Fugit (memoirs, published posthumously)

Notes on the Author and Editor

TAMBURLAINE BRYCE MACGREGOR was born in Leith in February 1811. The seventh son of a Guildsman of the Edenborough Merchant Adventurers, he was destined to enter his father's profession until, aged eleven, a near-fatal bout of polio left him permanently lame and dogged by ill health. Forced to abandon his apprenticeship with the guild and encouraged by his mother, MacGregor developed his natural gift with words and turned to poetry, finding success in his early twenties with publication in the Edenborough Review and other literary periodicals.

Two works in particular, *The Whale's Road* and *Roy of the Reivers* established MacGregor within the 'minstrel' tradition, however, his success as a poet proved short-lived. The publication of Lord Tyrone's groundbreaking *The Harrow and the Child* in 1840 heralded a new form of poetry: *dramatic realism*, and not for the last time Tamburlaine Bryce MacGregor found himself out of step with public taste. Realising his limitations as a poet, he turned to prose.

Published in 1841, MacGregor's first novel, *The Old Man and the Mountain*, showed considerable promise and over the next four years he wrote *The Barra Bride, Maid of Norway, Camberwick* and *The Saxon Trilogy*, each receiving good notices and increasing sales. His five volume *Arthurian Cycle* (1848–1851) brought him lasting success and fame and soon after came *Wyvenhoe, Willoughby Chaste* and *King Stephen*, among other works. By 1855 MacGregor was recognised as Scotland's foremost novelist with King Charles VII and the First Lord of the Treasury, Lord Wells, among his admirers, with the former having appointed MacGregor as Master of the King's Revels in June 1853. *Edmund Pevensie,* the tale of a hard-done-by Scottish nobleman who finds redemption and love in Napoleonic France, published in 1857, won MacGregor acclaim overseas and at New Year 1858 King Charles granted him the Baronetcy of Tweeddale and the Order of the Thistle in recognition of his services to

Scotland. Lauded at home and abroad, the Fates seemed to have smiled upon MacGregor, not least in his private life.

In the June of 1857 MacGregor had met Miss Madeleine Nicholson, a lady-in-waiting at Holyrood Palace and the daughter of Sir Henry Hawkins Nicholson. King Charles, always keen to impress foreign dignitaries with Scotland's culture and learning, frequently called on MacGregor to provide literary entertainments at Holyrood. MacGregor's journals show he found these duties onerous and undignified, but he could scarcely refuse the king. MacGregor met Madeleine Nicholson at a function for the Rajah of Shantipore, and despite the age difference—he was then forty-six, an old man by the standards of his times, she twenty-one—the attraction was immediate, and courtship and marriage followed in December the same year. Immediately after their wedding, Madeleine (now Lady Madeleine) joined MacGregor at Arbinger Abbey in Tweeddale, but frequent and lengthy visits to her friends and relatives back in Edenborough suggest life at Arbinger did not wholly agree with her. Even today, Tweeddale is a rural backwater and with her new husband chained to his writing desk, or away promoting his latest publication, it is not surprising Lady Madeleine found it difficult to adjust to Arbinger's isolation.

Nevertheless, she was soon with child. MacGregor wrote in his journal of his joy at becoming a father, but alas his hopes were dashed when Lady Madeleine died in childbirth, along with the son she was carrying.

Following Madeleine's death in October 1858 MacGregor abandoned Edenborough and the Royal Court and spurned all but his most trusted friends.ABandoning a part-written novel, *The Young Man of Lochnagar*, for two years he wrote only his personal journals and what he later called 'Black Books', all of which he subsequently destroyed and whose content can only be guessed at from the vague, cryptic notes in his journals. To friends and admirers, the 'Bard of Tweeddale' seemed permanently silenced.

In *Tempus Fugit*, MacGregor wrote, "There is nothing as enduring as hope, or as mutable as the spirit. Only belief is frail." He was describing events at New Year 1861 when, at the instigation of a close friend, he met Mrs Helena Northwood. She was recently widowed, and it seems each found in the other a perfect understanding of their situation. Following a brief courtship, they married in June 1861 and soon after MacGregor broke his two-year silence with 'Lays of Brigadoon'. At Christmas the same year Helena discovered she was with child and soon after MacGregor began work on *This Iron Race*.

The birth of Lorcan, MacGregor's son, passed without difficulty in August 1862, but publication of the first volume of *This Iron Race* proved troublesome. Although completed in December 1862, MacGregor's publishers objected to its content and style and he had to rewrite it several times before its eventual publication, as three volumes, in 1864. *Works of the Master* (1866) and *Devices & Executions* (1868) completed *This Iron Race* while his family increased to eight as Lady Helena bore six more sons, including two pairs of twins, and a daughter.

MacGregor had found happiness in his private life, but the first volume of *This Iron Race* and its sequels sold poorly, and he never regained his status as Scotland's foremost novelist. In *Tempus Fugit*, he claimed *This Iron Race* was intended to take magick out of the past and set it among the steamships and railways of the contemporary world, "for iron need not, and should not, be the death of magick. We must decide what we want from magick, what role it is to play in our lives." Alas, for MacGregor, public opinion determined magick, along with the divine right of kings and knights in armour, had no place in the modern world.

This Iron Race was MacGregor's final major work. Soon after publication of *Devices & Executions,* his health failed and he spent his final years working on *A History of Scottish Magick*, revising early poetical works and editing his memoirs. He died on All Hallows Eve, 1872 aged 62.

An extended account of the critical reception of the first volume of *This Iron Race* appears in the appendices.

§

Born in Oxford in 1957, Nevil Warbrook is the only son of the poet, Thomas Warbrook. He holds a first class degree in Theology and Babylonian Studies from Israel College, Oxford and lectures on the Faculty of Irrational Inquiry at Belshade College, Oxford.

Author of *The Deeper Well* and *The Wandering Minstrel* he is a respected authority on Scottish literature and, in addition to revising MacGregor's *This Iron Race*, honorary secretary of the Sir Tamburlaine Bryce MacGregor Society.

Recently divorced, he shares a house in the Wiltshire village of Avebury Trusloe with two cats and far more books than he will ever have time to read.

Publisher's Note

The following is the restored text of book one, volume one of Sir Tamburlaine Bryce MacGregor's *This Iron Race*, complete with expansive critical and explanatory notes by Nevil Warbrook.

Hare & Drum would like to place it on record that Nevil Warbrook's editorship of *This Iron Race* has been exemplary and his scholarship is not in doubt. In their opinion, however, while Nevil's commentaries have considerable merit, not all are essential to the reader's enjoyment of the narrative. Therefore, to minimise disruption, Hare & Drum have insisted only the most essential are contained within the narrative itself, while those of a scholarly, critical, or esoteric nature be consigned to an appendix.

An exception is made for biographical information shedding light on MacGregor's writing of the novel and on Nevil Warbrook's editorship.

Sir Tamburlaine Bryce
MacGregor

Author of *Edmund Pevensie*

Acts of the Servant
Volume One

Book one of
THIS IRON RACE

For now truly is a race of iron, and men never rest from labour and sorrow by day, and from perishing by night; and the gods shall lay sore trouble upon them.

Hesiod

To devise is the work of the master, to execute the act of the servant.

Leonardo da Vinci

Published by Beresford & Lucas, Edenborough

First Impression
Anno Domini
MDCCCLXIV
Lunden ~ New Amsterdam ~ Paris

Passed for publication by Authority of the
Lords Advocates, Alexander Street, Edenborough

Dedicated to Lady Helena MacGregor

&

To His Most Gracious Majesty King Charles VII
Defender of Scotland and
Champion of the Noble Race of Scots

♠

And in memoriam to

Lady Madeleine MacGregor

The chief concern of this novel is magick &
its place and purpose in the modern world.
Sir Tamburlaine Bryce MacGregor, August 1865

At such times all forget their boundaries
Prologue the First

Tower of Winchester, April 1860: The character and circumstance of CAPTAIN TITUS WOLFE, *revealing his dark secret and his part in the scandal of Prince William's death*

> The river has slipped its banks,
> Soot appals the poisoned air;
> In fog, the elements meet.
> At such times all forget their boundaries.

Begin near the end and strip the flesh from the bones; that is the way of the storyteller, and it shall be my way also… in my fashion.

'Damn this!' He pulled the scarlet cape around his shoulders. The night was not chill but fog-bound: the air thickened to that quality the locals called 'pea soup'. It burned his nostrils and he cuffed furiously at his watering eyes. It was impossible to stay clean in the city, especially in this weather.

'Damn this *place*.'

He wanted to close the guardroom door quietly, but it jammed against the frame. The beads of moisture clinging to the iron door loop would stain the leather of his gloves, but it could not be helped; he leant back and brought his weight to bear. The wood squealed and slammed home.

He held the lantern at arm's length. It could not penetrate the dark veil.

'Come now, Titus,' he encouraged himself. 'It is *only* fog.' He knew the routine well enough: he should not lose his way.

The Minster bells began announcing the hour and he took heart from a Christian sound on this unchristian of nights.

'Tonight, and always, God walk with me.'

The Great Bell struck twice as he made for Chapel Gate. He did not look back.

§

Titus. Only his mother and a succession of pretty nurses, each of whom had left in abrupt circumstances, had ever called him thus. His schoolmasters had known him as Master Wolfe, and to his school friends he was 'Wolfie', but his father had given him no name: he was always 'boy'. He sometimes wondered whether any of his bastard half-siblings would have made his father a better son.

Wolfe had been counting his steps; in part to gauge distance, but also to steady his thoughts. Yet the soft crunch of the gravel path had a restful quality, like a ticking clock, and his mind had wandered, however briefly, back to his childhood and unshackled from the present.

'Please, sir…' Something tugged his sleeve.

'Be gone!'

'Ask only for a light.'

The candlesnatcher[1] held out a stub of tallow.

'Sir,' it begged, 'be kind…'

Skin prickling with loathing, he loosened his sword and showed it the blade. The thing recoiled, dropping the candle.

'Be gone, I said!'

'Begging, sir! Ask only for a light. It is so dark…'

'Enough!' His sword sent the thing wailing into the night.

Wolfe shuddered and sword outstretched, he turned rapidly, quartering the air on all sides and above. It was a simple charm; the one form of magick he allowed himself. It would protect him, if only for a short while.

Saint Alfred's loomed from the darkness, and he reached out to caress the cold certainty of the stonework and thanked God. A few yards beyond it a light shone from a window. Wolfe raised the lantern above his head and challenged the Chapel Gate guard.

'Who speaks for the Tower?'

---

[1] Either a revenant spirit of human origin caught between this world and the next or a faerie sprite delighting in mischief. If the former it will gratefully receive a light for its candle. If the latter, it will snuff out the offered light leaving a person in darkness. *N.W.*

An iron plate opened in the door and a face peered out. 'Who asks?'

'Pengallow! I recognise your voice,' Wolfe said with forced good humour. 'Who let you east of the Tamar?'

'My countrymen said I was not fit to live among them, Captain Wolfe,' Warder Pengallow replied. 'Reckoned the English would have me. Captain, I shall want the pass.'

Wolfe grinned. Almost returned to his normal self, he allowed he was not likely to catch out the Cornishman. Pengallow was younger than most of the Tower Ward and sharp-witted. The older men, veterans all, he had found too much at ease, too slothful. They, recognising his voice, might well have forgotten the challenge and invited a charge. Warder Pengallow was not so foolish.

'Athelstan,' Wolfe said. 'Open in the name of the king.'

Bolts scraped. A lock turned. He stepped back to clear the door's outswing.

'Quickly, sir. Nice and warm in here: mean to keep it so.'

Wolfe entered. Pengallow shut the door and Warder Thomas saluted. Bald and built like a tree trunk, Thomas was one of the 'old men' of The Tower. Wolfe waved him back to his chair beside the fire.

'Only we and the bed bugs are awake,' Pengallow said. 'Coffee, Sir? It's recent brewed. This fog chills the bones.'

'Thank you, yes. Filthy weather.'

The damp had dulled his scarlet cloak to rusty red and the marks left by the soot resembled dark fingerprints. Turning to hang it on the door, he found the hook already occupied by a small figurine made of twigs bent and bound together.

'What's this?' he asked.

'Present from A'Guirre,' Warder Thomas said.

The twigs had slips of parchment woven through them and Wolfe automatically read one of them before realising it was not Latin, as he first supposed, but another, far stranger language. Resisting the urge to fling the thing on the fire, he contented himself by covering it with his cloak.

'A Guardian, she called it.' Pengallow set the coffeepot back on the stove and handed him a cup. 'She has one at every gatehouse and another at Catherine's Tower.'

'She has her ways, we have ours,' Wolfe said diplomatically. 'What have you to report?'

'Nothing, sir. Whatever concerns A'Guirre, it's not happening here. Perhaps that thing has done its job.'

'No doubt she will claim so.' Wolfe drank the coffee, then coughed a lump of phlegm into the fire. 'Damn, the air is foul tonight.'

'It'll be worse in high summer,' Pengallow said.

'I cannot imagine it; though I bow to your greater experience.'

'River brings every turd from Cheriton to the Bishop's Palace past the walls.' Pengallow had taken to a chair. 'Come July gets a bit ripe. The king, God bless him, spends the summer on Wight Island. We, sir, do not.'

'The night soil men upriver in Alresford call themselves the Royal Postmen,' Thomas added. 'On account of them sending messages...'

'*Enough.* Their crudities are of no interest to us.'

'Meant no offence, sir.'

'Then say what you mean. How long have you served at The Tower?'

'Seven years, sir.'

'You don't wish for anything more active?'

The man sucked in his belly. 'I've done my share, sir.'

'Eireland?' Wolfe asked.

'Three years,' Thomas said, as though Eireland were no more hazardous than a posting to Folkestone. 'Before that, I was with Colonel Herrick in Africa, then Flanders, and before that against Old Boney.'

Warder Thomas's tone bordered on insubordinate, but he should not have pressed the man: it was a respectable service record. The coffee finished, he reclaimed his cloak from the door, taking care nothing had broken off the doll and attached itself to the cloth.

'Pengallow, you say A'Guirre has these at every gate?
'So, I understand, sir.'
'Did she say what it's for?'
'No, sir. As you say, 'she has her ways'.'

§

The guard posts at Catherine's Gate and City Gate yielded two more of A'Guirre's dolls but no man able to tell him their purpose. What was worrying the old witch? Wolfe did not like surprises. Nor did he like A'Guirre, but that was another matter. And in God's teeth why, he asked himself for the tenth time, had he understood the queer writing? It was not Latin, nor anything like Latin, but for a second it had been clear as cogito ergo sum.

He climbed the stair at City Gate. He had still to walk the wall and call on the guard post at Catherine's Tower. Keeping his mind fully occupied was tiring and, once atop, he leant against the parapet, intending to gather his thoughts. Not one glimmer of light showed through the fog.

Winchester, capital of Anglia, lay in a fork between two valleys, making a natural basin for fog. He imagined this had always been so: the vapours slipping, dripping through the ancient oak woods of the higher valley, sliding over the water meadows, fingering the sedge and bulrush-ridden marshes and pooling above the Itchen's meandering course. From there the fog slunk downstream to meet the navigation at Blackbridge Wharf, ensnaring the rigging of the barges in its ghostly grasp, muffling the bark of the skipper's cur, snugging his cat below deck, pearling the cables holding boat to shore and cloaking the footpads in the alleys...

He shivered. The chill had crept under his cloak. He continued his round.

...Having filled the wharves with its damp-fingered grope and filtered along alleys crowded with ten-to-the-room hovels, gin houses trading in stupor and melancholy, and brothels offering five minutes' joy and years of quicksilvered madness,[1] the fog met a better class of establishment: inns and coffeehouses where gentlemen drank and gossiped, guildhalls where they won and lost their fortunes, church and chapel and Jew house where they prayed, even sanctity proving no—

'Damn this!'

His thoughts had run away; he had not imagined the city but the city drowning in fog, as he might drown. The otherworld was close tonight. Once he had delighted in the whisperings and bright colours, believing they marked him as special, but Father had beaten God's reality into him. He had learned to shut out the visions and ignore the voices: or nearly so.

Wolfe walked with the parapet at arm's length and every few seconds slapped the coping stones, using the pain to focus his thoughts.

He thought well of Warder Pengallow. True, he was a Celt, but at least the Cornish had none of the absurd pride he detested in the Gwaels. He thought rather less of Warder Thomas. Good men though they'd been, many an old soldier came to The Tower to see out their days. And too many had grown slapdash.

What was the doll guarding against?

His hand missed the parapet, upsetting his rhythm and his thoughts.

'Damn and blast. Damn this fog. Damn this night...'

He flailed an arm at the fog, as though to slice it open, but made no impression. Instead, his anger sucked the foul air into his chest. This fog put a sore in a man's throat, a cough in his children's lungs, spoiled his wife's linen, poisoned the grass and trees and rotted stonework. Everything it touched turned to mourning and God knows what it did to a man's insides. Leaning over the wall to hawk phlegm, he recalled a man might stand here and spy the sea

---

[1] A reference to syphilis which was treated with mercury and whose outcome *in extremis* was insanity and death. *N.W.*

beyond Hampton on a clear day. No such joy tonight. Only when his breathing steadied did he continue.

Colonel Herrick, another of the 'Old Men', would be sound asleep in his quarters below. Wolfe had long ago accepted higher rank was beyond him. His *disorder* had shown itself too often and he had deservedly acquired a reputation for rashness and impatience. A reputation for bravery, too, though less deserved; a man charging an enemy may only be fleeing a greater foe.

As he neared Catherine's Tower, Wolfe straightened his tunic and wiped the grit from his hand. Warders Whitemore and Jones had the unenviable task of manning this isolated post tonight. At least they would have a fire and offer a moment's company, but where, Wolfe asked himself, was their challenge? Sword drawn, he groped forward, found the guardroom entrance and hearing no sound from inside, rapped the pommel against the door.

'On guard! On guard I say!'

A chair overturned noisily within before the face of Warder Jones showed at the peephole.

'Who goes?'

'Too bloody late, man. Captain Wolfe, the pass is Athelstan. Where is your guard?'

'Sir. Apologies, sir.' The man drew the bolts and Wolfe stepped back as the door opened.

Jones saluted. 'No excuse, sir. You caught me asleep.'

To Wolfe's surprise, the man was alone.

'Whitemore's sick, sir. It's this damned fog,' Jones said.

'And his replacement?'

'Sir, he was only taken poor this last hour.'

'Unacceptable. We are warned to be extra vigilant.' He closed the door, expecting to see another of A'Guirre's dolls. The hook was bare.

'Where is it?'

'What, sir?'

'You know very well. A'Guirre's doll?'

'Whitemore, see,' Jones evaded his gaze. 'Not meaning to

shift blame, but he served in Eireland, as did you, and he has this thing about *them*. He was convinced that thing was making him poorly.' The man scratched his cheek. The stubble was grey, flecked with white.

'And?' Wolfe demanded.

'I slung it in the Navigation, sir.'

Wolfe sighed. 'My report to Colonel Herrick will recommend only a *warning* for A'Guirre's doll, but I cannot excuse sleeping on duty or failing to get a replacement for Warder Whitemore. He is in the infirmary, I assume?'

'He is, sir.'

'You can expect a charge, understand?'

'Got no complaint, sir.'

'Very well.' Wolfe drew his cloak round him and opened the door. 'I shall send someone in place of Whitemore, meantime—'

He halted, aghast. A scream of terror, rather as the cry of a vixen, but unmistakeably human in origin, had pierced the fog and entered his very being. He trembled and fell against the wall.

'Captain, are you unwell?'

Jones dragged a chair toward him.

'No, no,' he pressed himself upright. 'Did you not hear it?'

'Sir? No, sir. You took a turn, so I thought. Not your usual self.'

'I am myself,' he muttered. Fog swirled into the guardroom. Wolfe brushed it from his face, determined to see clearly. He removed a glove and delicately touched the door's ironwork. As he expected, pain, like a hot needle, lanced into his finger and his fear altered into the anger of one who lashes out with the least provocation.

'You are certain you heard nothing?'

'No, sir.'

'Then you must count yourself exceedingly deaf! A charge, in the morning: *dereliction of duty*.'

Wolfe took the steps two at a time. Halfway down, he lost his footing and fell, bruising his hip. Worse, he had instinctively grabbed the iron handrail to save himself and an intense ache now surged through the muscles to his elbow. Once recovered, he limped the remaining stairs, then drew his sword and unlocked the door into the turnyard.

Nothing broke the silence, though the scream still echoed in his head. A rat, he reasoned, for the fog did strange things to sound. But reason would not do his bidding for there was no innocent explanation: a man had screamed for his life.

'Who goes?' The fog swallowed his voice.

The Royal Apartments were four storeys above ground. From an open window, a voice would carry easily to Catherine's Tower. But who would have a window open on a night like this?

It was senseless to question: he must alert the King's Men.

He followed a drainage channel parallel to the wall. This ended in a sump and, but for the sudden stink, he would have stumbled into it. From there, he cut blindly across the open yard, making for the rear of the apartments.

'Halt!' The command came from his right. Wolfe skidded to a standstill.

'Name and business?'

The King's Men and Tower Ward seldom mixed. He did not recognise the voice.

'Captain Wolfe of the Tower Ward.'

'Tonight's pass.'

'Athelstan. Is all well in the King's Household?'

'You are armed?'

'My sword is drawn; there's a pistol at my belt.'

'Sheathe the sword. Be warned, you are surrounded.'

He did as instructed and moments later someone took his weapons.

'Move on. Speak when spoken to.'

Hands bundled him inside a small chamber. A pair of lamps either side and a heavy door in front of him. From the footsteps, he guessed three men.

'He looks genuine,' a man said.

'He does. Turn around, Captain.'

They were four, all King's Men. One was an officer: his rank of major shown by the gold crowns embroidered on his cuffs and shoulder boards. All had drawn swords.

The major held Wolfe's confiscated sword and pistol.

'I apologise for the rough treatment. What is your business?'

'A disturbance, sir. I was inspecting the guardhouse on Catherine's Tower; there was a scream from the apartments.'

'We heard nothing,' the major said. 'Fog's playing tricks on you. Down arms.'

The men sheathed their swords. Being trusted with the protection of the monarch and his family, King's Men had a casual arrogance toward other soldiers.

'It was no trick of the fog; I would swear to it, Major...?'

'Swanner, Major Swanner,' the man said. 'Exon Pullman,' a man stepped forward, 'escort Captain Wolfe to Colonel Howe. You can report to him, Captain. And Exon, take these,' Swanner handed the man the sword and pistol. My apologies, Captain; only King's Men bear arms here.'

Exon Pullman led him through into a long passageway. The leftmost wall was blank save for candle sconces and a curtained archway. The exon knocked at a small door in the rightmost wall and entered, leaving him waiting outside.

Wolfe was quite alone in the passage until he noticed a man emerge from a curtain and hurry toward him. The fellow was dressed entirely in white, and only the slap of his naked feet against the floor convinced Wolfe he was not seeing a ghost.

The exon emerged from Howe's office and asked him inside.

'Captain Wolfe of the Tower Ward, sir.'

'Sit.' Colonel Howe indicated a chair beside his desk, which was clear, save for an inkstand and a log book. The room was small, sparsely furnished, and windowless. A stove provided heat and a place to boil a kettle. In terms of comfort, it compared poorly with Herrick's office in Stonecutters Tower but Wolfe rather approved. He approved of the man also: Howe had hair the colour of gunmetal, a narrow jaw, and sharp green eyes.

'Apparently you're hearing voices,' Howe said.

'No, sir. I heard someone in distress. From the Royal Apartment, or perhaps—'

The chair was hard and upright. He had scarce sat down before a noise outside interrupted them and Exon Pullman re-entered.

'Sir, this cannot wait. Mr Panells must—'

'Out of the way.' The voice outside was frail but impassioned. The exon stepped aside. Mr Panells proved to be the gentleman he had seen moments before. He was no ghost, merely an elderly man in a nightshirt which at this moment matched the colour in his cheeks. Wolfe knew in those rheumy old eyes what had befallen and in the same sickening moment grasped the nature of that ghastly scream.

'Prince William,' the man gasped. 'There is murder!'

The news of the prince was secondary. More appalling to Wolfe was being privy to it.

'Murdered!' Panells uttered and slid to his shins.

'Exon, sound the alarm.' Howe was belting on his sword as he spoke. 'King's Men, Tower Ward, and the Fyrd. And send for A'Guirre and Dr Jennings, also.' The exon left at the double and Howe turned to him. 'Captain Wolfe, Mr Panells has greater need of that chair.'

'Of course.' Wolfe helped the old man sit.

'Mr Panells,' Howe asked, 'where was Prince William attacked?'

'The queen's Bedchamber; the king and queen are with him. The king is...'

'And William's killer?' the colonel interrupted.

'Gone. The queen saw a man flee the room.'

'But she and the king are safe?'

Panells nodded with such vigour the effort shook his frail shoulders.

Wolfe waited, wondering when the colonel would turn to him. The man was suspicious, and he must consider how he might answer. Colonel Howe continued questioning the old man.

'The guard on the Serpentine Gallery must have heard something.'

'I cannot say,' Panells hesitated. 'I informed *them*. Oh God!' the man leant forward as if to vomit.

'I see.' The colonel stared Wolfe in the eye. 'Speak plainly, Captain; what *precisely* did you hear?'

'I cannot truly say, sir.'

'Meaning you do not know or dare not admit what you know. For now, arm yourself and aid the search.' Howe returned his pistol and rapier and scribbled a dispatch order. 'Show this, if challenged. Temporarily you are a King's Man.'

Howe was at the door. Time was too short for obfuscation.

'Sir, what would you have me do?'

'Your instinct[1] brought you here. Damn well follow it.'

Howe left and Wolfe pocketed the dispatch order. Howe had seen through his pretence, and, for a moment, the knowledge paralysed him. Panells' sobs broke his preoccupation. He found a book of psalms on a shelf behind Howe's desk and pushed it into the man's hands. God's word always comforted him.

Panells' eyes were blank and watery. 'We failed him, we have all failed him,' he whispered and seized Wolfe's wrist. 'You must do what is right. Do what is *right*.'

Wolfe stepped back, breaking the man's grip. He disliked the feel of the aged flesh on his own, disliked the man's abjection.

'I will do what I can,' he said, and left.

The long passageway was deserted and silent, save for the sobbing breath of the old man behind him. 'Follow your instinct,' he repeated. It was *impossible* to even consider it, yet the dreadful scream still rang in his head as though he

---

[1] In the published edition 'instinct' becomes 'curse', indicative of Beresford & Lucas's hostility to magick. *N.W.*

were a tuning fork. He hoped the colonel would hold his counsel. Discovery would be unbearable.

This will not do, this will not do! He needed a clue, a *guide* to follow. The old man had come from the Royal Apartments... Wolfe ran to the curtained archway, finding an open door beyond the fabric and a flight of steps. They led upward and on breasting each landing he tried the doors leading off. All were locked until, at the fourth landing, one opened, revealing a gallery many yards long and elegantly furnished.

Soldiers' boots echoed down the gallery, but he ignored them; he could not follow his instinct in company and did not wish to be mistaken for the one they sought.

This was the Serpentine Gallery. He knew it by the dark green stone lining the walls. It was at the very heart of the Royal Apartments, the family's private quarters. A door lay open. There was light in the room beyond. He approached, intending to go within, but halted at the threshold.

An *expectation* surrounds a king: it comprises the ermine and velvet robes and not least the crown itself; the anticipation of the crowd and the clear path awaiting his step all play a part in gathering circumstance and drama into one personage. To see the king without those trappings is to see only the man, *a thing of flesh alone*.

No one moved and for a tiny moment, he regarded the scene the way he might a painting. The fire, banked for the night, the mound of coals glowing a dull orange-red. The king, sitting cross-legged beside the hearthstone, arms cradling his son, grieving. A bloodied cavalryman's sword, its slender curved blade catching in the light. Prince William, the fallen hero, eyes closed; scarlet cavalryman's tunic and britches contrasting with the austere whiteness of the king's nightshirt. Queen Charlotte kneeling behind and to the side of her husband, her arms around his shoulders, her nightgown trimmed with lace and pearls. The mantelpiece framing all three, its carved white marble poised like a wave about to fall.

But it was no masterpiece; there was too much inelegance: a streak of blood across the king's nightshirt; a neck too slender to bear the weight of a crown; a dark stain on Prince William's chest and his legs splayed. The queen's hair was too pale and cut too short and her nightdress had torn at the shoulder. One hand held it in place to protect her modesty. Who had torn it he could not imagine: a struggle, yes, but with whom?

Of all these, seeing the queen without her hairpiece was the most unsettling.

'He is your king, remember only that. Now go.' Her voice was quiet, but her expression utterly imperial. It was a moment before he understood she was addressing him for she had not moved from the king's side. He turned to leave, but the queen spoke again.

'You are not a King's Man?'

'No, Your Highness. I serve in the Tower Ward.'

He stared at the ground, as was proper. The king had not acknowledged his presence.

'And your name?'

'Captain Wolfe, ma'am.'

'Captain, I wish to see your face.'

'Ma'am. Yes, ma'am.'

Even bereft of her wigs and rouge, there was surprising warmth to her features: she did not deserve the "Flanders Cow" gibes of the common press. She got to her feet, not without some grace, and stood facing him. One hand rested on her husband's shoulder, the other held her torn nightdress in place.

'Ma'am, the door is unguarded. I walked in freely; another might do the same.'

The queen was unnaturally calm, and Wolfe reluctantly allowed his inner voice to question and seek but found only a chilly blankness.

'Captain, advise me. How do matters stand?'

'We have report of an attack on the prince,' he said. 'We understand there was an intruder; you saw him flee. Colonel

Howe has sent word to the Fyrd and Tower Ward. King's Men are searching the apartments. That is all I know.'

The queen looked at him as though asking the quality of horseflesh.

'What brought you? The Ward has no duties here.'

'I heard a disturbance, from the wall. I sought to alert the King's Men,' he said.

'The tower walls?' Her tone was sharp.

'I was calling on the guardpost at Catherine's Tower, ma'am. There was a cry, I believe from—'

'Impossible! There was no cry!' Her face twisted in anger, she grabbed the sword from the floor and flew at him. 'How dare you lie before your king!'

The queen had the tip of the sword pointed at his chest, but her hand was unsteady. If she lunged, he could parry the blow, but he prayed it would not go so bad. The king had still not acknowledged his presence.

'Speak plainly,' the queen said. 'What brings you here?'

'Ma'am, forgive me. I know not what I heard. It seems I am cursed to hear things no man ought.'

'More lies.' The blade trembled.

'I speak true, ma'am. Clearsight, some call it, but it goes by many names: all evil to God.'

'You are curseborn?' she said in wonderment. 'I believed soldiers cannot bear your kind.'

'*I* cannot bear my kind. Ma'am, if you will allow. I can prove what I am.'

He unbuttoned his glove and let it fall. 'Pray, hold the blade steady. You must know spaers cannot bear steel or iron.' He reached out to touch the blade. The queen, thinking he was trying to seize the weapon, pulled back and near sliced his hand open.

'I beg you, ma'am. Hold steady.'

He touched the blade and curled his hand around it. For a moment he felt nothing extraordinary: he was not always sensitive to its touch and briefly feared his display might prove nothing. Then a faint chill seeped into his palm and his fingers tightened involuntarily about the blade. His hand drained of blood, even as his heart raced and numbness spread, rapid as a flame devouring a page. His hand about the blade glowed with a strange, blue-white light, and the tendons in his wrist, each proud as a rope, conducted the cold into his arm. His heart faltered and missed a beat. He dared not bear it much longer.

'Ma'am, you see it?' He could barely breathe. His arm shook.

'Enough,' the queen said. 'Release the sword.'

He pried his fingers free with his gloved hand and cradled his injured hand. The queen stepped closer, and he showed her the vivid mark across his palm.

'Is it permanent?' the queen asked.

'It will not scar.' He gloved the hand. It was numb but when feeling returned the pain would be excruciating.

'Do your comrades know you are afflicted?'

'They do not. If it was known, they would refuse to serve with me.'

'Providence,' the queen said, her voice suddenly stronger; 'providence called you here. Captain Wolfe, a man has broken into the Tower and murdered Prince William. I command you to find him.'

'My dearest...'

The king's thin voice interrupted them, and both turned to him. He still cradled his son but now his face had lifted. The eyes were vacant, and he seemed to stare straight at Wolfe and then turn away.

'Dearest. Who...?'

The queen went to the king and kneeling beside him whispered something Wolfe could not hear. Then she returned her gaze to him.

'Captain, you have my command.'

'With respect, ma'am, men seek the intruder.'

'Understand me,' the queen insisted, 'you and you *alone* will find this murderer. Your secret is safe, for now, but by whatever means, find proof William was slain by an intruder.'

His mouth dried. If he refused, the queen would expose him. But if he accepted...?

'Ma'am, do I understand—'

'No. Do not *understand*. Serve your king; find William's killer, create him from thin air, if it is in your power, and you will not go unrewarded.'

For the first time, it struck him how strange matters were. The king and queen were in nightclothes, as was natural at this hour, yet their son was in dress uniform with his sword beside him. The meaning was plain. The prince had taken his own life.

'I am yours to command, ma'am. What of Princess Isabel?'

'She sleeps. You need not disturb her. Go now. Time is short.'

He glanced at the king and doubted he could ever again see the man without thinking of this moment.

'Ma'am,' he said, 'if I am to be rewarded, I should be a King's Man. It would make my father proud of me.'

'You would negotiate?'

'No, ma'am, I would only serve my king and queen.'

The queen lowered the sword and returned to kneel beside the king.

'A father should be proud of his son,' she said. 'Now go, or it will be in vain.'

Unable to fashion thoughts from the fog-like blur in his head, he retraced his steps. "Follow his instinct," be damned, he thought. His curse ruled him as the North Star rules the needle. Yet, as he descended the final stair, a thought did come to him, a thought so absurdly simple he could not help smiling. For the first time this dreadful night he would act of volition, and not according to his curse.

'You again?' Colonel Howe said, once more in his office.

'Permission to return to the Tower Ward, sir. I can do nothing here.'

'Very well.' Howe stood up. 'I'll see you out. The guard may not let you pass. I damn well would not.' The man smiled grimly and escorted him down the passageway.

'You discovered nothing?' Howe said.

'Nothing of use,' Wolfe said. 'Sir, has A'Guirre approached you this last week?'

'Those *damn dolls*,' Howe said. 'The queen would not allow it.'

'Colonel Herrick was more amenable. There is one in every gatehouse.'

'Then we are certain of catching the murderer,' Howe sneered.

'She knew though. We cannot doubt that,' he answered.

'Keep those thoughts to yourself,' Howe warned, 'and nor should your *instinct* show itself too often. A man gets a reputation for such things.'

'Understood, sir. And thank you.'

The guard at the door had doubled to eight men.

'Let him through,' Howe said. 'Take this, Captain.' Howe gave him a lantern. 'Damn foul night and a damn foul business. Goodnight, Captain Wolfe.'

The exon showed him out and closed the door behind him. He was alone again in the fog.

> The right man is rarely found;
> We live obliquely, hanging
> (and this man will surely hang)
> On the neighbourliness of ways and faces.

The scene will serve to set the tale in motion.

Editor's Remarks

Before passing on to the text itself, some description of the form and condition of the first draft manuscript may be useful.

Overall, given the passing of one hundred and fifty years, MacGregor's first draft is in fair condition, although that does not always translate into legibility for MacGregor was in the habit of reworking the text until he was satisfied. The leaves are quarto, being a standard sheet of machine-made paper folded twice to give four leaves approximately ten by eight inches. The colour is varying shades of light cream, slightly foxed in places, but free of significant discolouration or staining.

With the notable exception of redrafted matter, MacGregor's text is tolerably readable with letters fully formed and the words spaced evenly and regularly along the line. An exception is the dialogue where, so it appears, MacGregor strove to keep up with his characters' speech and his script deteriorates noticeably. Fortunately, context always came to the aid of your editor and at no point, in this chapter at least, was he unable to fathom the meaning.

It should be noted that in all cases the chapter titles in the restored text are taken from the first edition, as there is no reason to believe MacGregor had any preferred alternatives.

The manuscript of volume one remained as separate leaves until 1925 when it was set in two Morocco bound volumes by King James University Library, whose stamp appears at the foot of each page. Regrettably, during this process the pages were trimmed to uniform size which damaged some of MacGregor's marginalia. These are, or were, editorial comments, plot and character sketches and research notes—the spine, as it were, to the flesh of the narrative. For the literary detective enquiring into the articulation and conception of *This Iron Race* their loss is a substantial blow, and it is certain MacGregor's intentions would have been clearer, but for the guillotine.

The manuscript begins with the name "Wolfe", followed by the date, September 8,

1862. This is the date of writing: the date at which MacGregor chose to use this as the opening scene is not known. It is possible MacGregor originally conceived this as the opening scene (this is supported by the absence of earlier pagination on the pages) or that he cut the scene from Wolfe's chapter (see *This Iron Race,* volume three) to avoid having two analepsis within the same chapter. As your editor has not yet received the manuscript for volume three, he cannot speculate further.

Each page bears a partial watermark which, taken together, (none of the pages shows the full sequence of numbers) dates manufacture of the paper to 1862 and the pagination follows MacGregor's standard method for later additions to the manuscript: namely, an Arabic numeral indicating the point at which the addition is to be inserted followed by a Roman numeral for each subsequent page. Usually, the insertion follows the Arabic numbered page, but in this instance, it is clearly intended to come before.

And so to variations between the first draft of this chapter and the published text which are, with a few exceptions, confined to two scenes. The first of these is the exchange between Captain Wolfe and Warders Pengallow and Thomas whose earthy language is softened, and the obscenities removed. MacGregor protested the changes stating "these men are soldiers, not monks!" but Beresford & Lucas stood firm. While altering the tone of the scene, the changes did not affect its meaning, unlike those forced on MacGregor in the scene in the queen's bedchamber. In the published text MacGregor's naturalistic description of the king, queen, and the dead Prince William is replaced by a bloodless and sentimental tableaux: Prince William lies with his legs neatly together and his uniform unstained, the queen is bewigged and modestly dressed while the king sheds a discreet tear over his dead son. As MacGregor wrote in his journal, "I have known the devastation of grief, yet must depict it with the decorum of a letter of condolence."

Each finds his path where he least expected
Chapter One
The hills above Staffin Bay, Skye, several days later: BHEATHAIN SOMHAIRLE'S *narrative will be the weft of our tale, binding all strands together*

The eelskin welkin laments,
Breath cannot escape the hill
(four and two-legged beasts are here);
Ancient fires linger in these old crags.
The one who bears me is cursed for another's sin.

1

BHEATHAIN GLANCED DOWN the brae and shook his head, scattering the pearls of wet clinging to the lip of his bonnet. The burn was in spate, overfilling its banks. Bare rock dripped. Scree, overburdened, scarce held its weight upon the slope. Peat, soft as fresh dung, and the tussocks slippery as a trap full of eels.

It be a good ways down, he thought.

As he leant against the wind his attention wandered to his pipe. The bowl lay snugged in his waistcoat pocket, but the stem prodded the lowest rib of his heartside. He wanted only a dry stand and a smoke in the old sheep beild but, alas, the wee lamb wanted fetching before it caught chill or drowned in the milk-white waters.

A plaid covered Bheathain's shoulders and, beneath a russet-coloured coat, his waistcoat and breeches were of a coarse brown cloth. The coat had lost most of its buttons but a strand of hemp, picked from old rope, held out the wind. Sedge, plaited and tied about his shins were his gaiters, but the lower half of his breeches were wet through, and the chill went to the marrow. As he stood and gazed down the brae, he raised a hand and without thinking on it, straightened the scarf covering the lower half of his face.

His clothes linked him to the ground beneath his feet. Wool, woven by design, kept him dry not half as well as it had the sheep upon whose backs it grew. Orange scurf scraped from rocks made dye for his coat and the black of his bonnet came from oak apple. Other mosses and lichens made the yellows, greens, and purples of his plaid.

Only an amber touchpiece around his neck, his tobacco and tinderbox, along with the strand of hemp and iron for the tackits in the soles of his worn-out shoes came from off-island.

And half of himself, though he did not know it.

Blue-eyed and yellow-haired, he was taller than most on the island and might even pass for handsome, except the rain-soaked scrap of red cloth tied in outlaw manner behind his neck left too much to conjecture. The scarf covered My Lady's cursemark: a blood red stain upon his cheek, the so-called Devil's Hand, and when the cloth slipped from the bridge of his nose, as it often did, he tugged it into place with automatic gesture.

What occurred to him as he considered his path? A sheep never means to die but only tests a man's resolve to save it, certainly. That if he was to save it, he must act soon for the day was dying. That if left where it was, the lamb would be dead in a few hours. Yes, he thought all of those. Did it also occur to him none would be the wiser if he walked away and left the creature to drown or die of cold or want of its mother's milk? It would be unreasonable to say it did not reckon in his thoughts *at all* for even in the innocent wish for his pipe there was desire for something *other,* an easier if scarce easeful life. But did he consider it in all seriousness and weigh the consequences of one act against another? Did his seed of doubt leaf into open discontent against his lot? No, not then, not ever, for one thought rose above them like the tallest tree in the wood.

Here I be and this I am, is near to what he thought and, in this instance, as so often for a shepherd, there was no other to act in his stead. Spying a slab of rock beside the torrent, he kissed his amber touchpiece for luck and, seizing a clump of heather overhanging the lip of crumbling peat, swung his leg onto the slope.

The ground failed under him and, as his weight fell on the heather it broke free, leaving him with a handful of useless twigs. '*A Dia!*' The ground seized him by the ankles and in a skitter of stones he slid to the bottom of the slope where he clambered onto the slab as the loosened scree plunged past him into the torrent.

He began to laugh, as if filled with a bubble of joy. Men often do this when released from peril, real or supposed, though we shall not assume they have taken pleasure from their adventure for this laughter is only the sneeze following the itch: a release from the displeasurable and alarming and taken at one's own expense.

Daft, but alive, he thought, and as he stretched his limbs, he considered that as sheep test the resolve of man to save them, so men test the resolve of their God. He had broken nothing, not even his dignity, which was not precious to him at all, and gained no aches. However, as he laughed and gazed around him, he overlooked one small matter: the amber touchpiece about his neck hung by six strands of human hair, and of these two broke as he thrust it back beneath his shirt and a third unravelled as he flung himself upon the rock.

The burn had gathered all the noise of the rain in one place and each drop added to the tumult. A man could not hear himself shout let alone think amid the noise and here where none would see him, he looked up to a pale glimpse of sun and hauled the scrap of cloth away to show his face.

The mark on his cheek did not resemble a hand, Devil's or otherwise. It was more the mark a violent hand had wrought. Wherever he looked, it seemed to follow his gaze, which was why folks feared it. It was good to feel the wind on his face and not breathe through the sodden cloth of his scarf, but this lasted only a moment for a curious sense he was not alone came over him. He had never felt this before, not in any of the secret places where a man might stand alone and unwatched, but it compelled him to retie the scarf across his face. He did not want any seeing him without it and mayhap even a lamb might take averse to his mark for so many were convinced he also half-believed it truly gave him power to curse a man or beast. The scarf secure, his mark concealed, he trod downstream toward the lamb as the clouds closed over, leaving him shadowless once more.

The lamb, when he found it, lay trapped between the brae and the torrent. Marks in the slope showed where it had tried and failed to clamber up and the sight of him made it try again but its wee legs could not scramble fast enough, and it tumbled onto its back-ends.

'*Na dèan sin,*' Bheathain murmured, '*na goirtich thu fhéin.*'[1]

This was where he might fail. The beast would rather the water's embrace than his. He had to get downstream of it if he was to save it from itself.

A scramble up, taking him above and past the lamb, then a slide on his backside brought him round. He had chanced his luck and one foot had dipped in the water. He shook the wet from it and strode off. The lamb was still expecting him upstream and he was almost upon it, when the tackits in his soles grated on a rock. Startled, the beast leapt for the water, but diving full-length, he plunged an arm into the spate and gripped hold of its fleece.

Pain stabbed through his hand; his thumb had opened on a shard of stone. Bheathain stumbled, near falling in the water and the scarf unravelled and slid beneath his chin. Rolling clear he dragged the lamb from the stream and sat up. The lamb was a sodden rag, but a thumb pushed down its throat cleared the tongue from the throat and a good shake sparked it back to life. Whereupon it sneezed, spraying him with drool.

'*Glé mhath, glé mhath,*' he said with weary humour, for it was not so very good: the lamb was a male, a deal less valuable than a female.

'*Coma leat;*' the beast could not be blamed for what it was.

Arse cold in the wet gravel, he trapped the lamb between his knees and patiently retied the scarf about his face.

---

[1] See note on Gaelic in Appendix 2, page xlvii. *N.W.*

'Coma leat.'

He stood and brushed the stones from his backside. The lamb was soaked and blared pitifully as he did his best to squeeze the wet from its fleece before settling it under his jacket. Once trapped against his breast, the beast seemed accepting of its lot and lay quiet with its chin rested upon the lapel.

Up proved easier than down for he could now see what lay under him and he quickly met with the open, heather-clad slope and the full force once more of the wind and rain.

The flock huddled round the shelter, save one standing apart. The beast was staring at him.

'Thalla far eil do mathair.'

He let the lamb down and the instant it felt the ground it scrambled from his hand and away to its mother to suckle. The ewe bent round to sniff its infant and satisfied it was her own, turned its back on him.

There is no thanks to be had, not from a dumb creature. In another week, if the weather dried up, he'd bring the flock down to the fold. Near all the males needed nipping so they stayed longer at the tit. The longer at the tit, the bigger they grew and the better price they fetched at summer's end. Had this one a maukin stead of a wand it would give lambs and milk each twelvemonth and a fleece for spinning.

'Ach, tha mi coma dheth,' he said[1] and turned away, glad to have his back to the wind, and sucked the grit from his bloodied thumb.

Half of him was wet through and he could feel the cold seeping into his flesh, numbing his fingers and fumbling his grip. He would be chilled by the time he got home but it would not have sat right with him to let the lamb be. Staffin lay below him; the scooped hollow in the shore protected by a small island. The road to Portree ran like a bent arm about the bay with the township of Brogaig nestled in the pit of the elbow. From above, each croft seemed to lie in a little

---

[1] *Ach, tha mi coma dheth*: But it is no matter to me. N.W.

hollow, like a limpet on a rock. Few had windows and none a pane of glass. Stout wooden doors kept out the weather. This was home. Beyond the houses narrow plots of land dropped to the shore where a few skiffs lay with their hulls upturned against the rain. The storm had torn up the kelp grounds offshore and the ebb tide strewn it across the sand.

There was no sign of life at the croft Bheathain shared with his *nen*, old Manus M'Dhòmhnuill, but that meant nothing.[1] Bheathain trusted the old man would be home and tea would be brewing and tatties cleaned for the pot, with a plate of black bread and honey and a bowl of buttermilk. Rain darkened the sea beyond the bay, and eastwards the sky was falling. Soon the sheep would settle for the night. While light remained, he took a look at himself, finding the seat of his breeches wet-through and his waistcoat soaked where the lamb had pressed against it.

Nen winna be pleased, Bheathain thought as he straightened his scarf, then knowing something amiss, he felt under his shirt for the bead of amber. It wasn't there. He pulled his shirt from his breeches, but nothing fell to the ground. He ripped the gaiters from his knees and shook his legs.

'*C'àite a bheil mo grìogag omair?*' He stared at the ground and cursed the fading light. Flakes of gravel, black peat, crushed grass, heather: nothing of the small brown bead that had hung about his neck. He tore his bonnet off and wrung it in his fists. '*Mo chreach!*'

A thought and he was standing on the slope above the burn, recalling the moment he leapt for the lamb. But the bead was too small, the ground too big and if the water had it, it was truly lost. Sense won and he did not leap down the brae but gazed down the course of the burn to its joining with the river and unwinding in the bay.

'*Tha e air chall.*'

The touchpiece had hung around his neck long as he could recall, and it was hard to imagine it gone. A few times,

---

[1] *Nen* is the familiar Gaelic term for 'grandfather'. *N.W.*

as he grew, a' body had called by with a newly-plaited cord of hair to hang it about his neck. Last time it was the laird's spaer, Ethelfeyrda.

It was not long after Da drowned himself in the bay (he had drowned himself in drink long before). He had been twelve, neither child nor man. Ethelfeyrda made the cord from her own hair, so she said, and he believed her for it was the same copper-red. The woman's face, her blue eyes and red hair was one of many memories flooding on him: they were footprints leading to this moment and each was shaded now, made sorrowful, and as he thought of them, he thought of other things lost and a lump formed in his throat. The touchpiece had not only hung about his neck, it was as much a part of him as his hand or his voice. It bore a mark, like a bird's foot, and he bent to pick up a stone, scratched the rune mark on it, and slid it in his pocket.

'Is mithich a dhomh falbh.'

He tore his eyes away from the waters. The rain seemed harder now and the sky unnaturally dark; as though its colour came from his thoughts and not from the louring of the sun. Perhaps it was because of this gloom he caught sight of a solitary white stag watching him from a cloud-topped crag.

'Och-òin!'

Strange sights on the hills always had bad outcomes. A swirl of low cloud hid the creature and he shivered. It was a bad end to the day. This eve he would go down the white house;[1] he was in want of whisky and company, and he would ask after a touchpiece. He had thought little enough of it, no more than he had thought of the tongue in his head, but now he seemed to be thinking of nothing else and digging a hand into his pocket, he fidgeted with the rune stone he made and wondered what Ethelfeyrda might make of it. Not much, he reckoned. He had not one grain of Grace in his blood, and

---

[1] Officially the Staffin Inn, its local name, *An Tigh Bàn* or 'the white house' came from its limewashed walls. *N.W.*

he sensed a rune mark needed more than a scratch. But still, if he got to meet her again it would not be so bad. She had not been afraid of him; she had looked him in the eye.

§

The Staffin Inn had a warm, welcoming reek of wet plaid, pipe smoke, and bodies, mixed with the rankness of spilt ale and whisky. A peat fire flickered in the hearth, a rare feature in these parts with a breast of mortared and limewashed stone, and candles scattered across the room splashed the walls with pools of buttery brightness.

Someone had brought a newssheet in. The wind entered alongside him and flew up the pages. Eyes, dark under downdrawn brows, glanced toward him.

'*Beannachd a tha i fliuch a-muigh,*' Bheathain said[1] to all and none as he shook the wet off his oiler and shoved the door against the wind.

Hands smoothed the ruffled pages, and the patter of talk lulled a moment, like a beat missed on the pipes. Replies were long fingers tapped to foreheads and necks twitched like a ram sizing up a rival. A few mouths even unclamped their pipe stems to murmur, 'a wet night to be sure,' or, 'it is indeed,' in answer.

The 'paper would be from Glasgow or Fort James and something in it had all their eyes this evening. A man took the pipe from his mouth and jabbed the stem toward the page. Another followed a line with his finger. Neither quite brought himself to touch the sheet.

Bheathain stepped into the room and saw Manus in the corner. This was where the old sod had got to. He had gone out after tea, muttering about some "business," and vanished into the night.

---

[1] It is common, as here, for Gaelic speakers to greet each other with a remark on the weather. The same habit is found among Anglians, though less frequently. *N.W.*

The mood was quieter than usual, and none were scratching at a fiddle or tweeting on a pipe. Only the rhythmic clatter of Fionnghuala M'Aonghuis's spinning wheel accompanied the murmur of voices. Busy as always at her thread, M'Aonghuis's wife was the only woman on the premises.[1]

'*Thoir dhomh dram.*' Bheathain spilled a handful of coins in front of M'Aonghuis.

M'Aonghuis pushed most of them back across the counter. Bheathain blocked his hand.

'Wanting more than one. Cold and wet I am.'

M'Aonghuis looked him in the eye and slid the coins into his hand.

'Keeping these for the now. But you'll have what I give you, no more.'

Bheathain watched the liquid fall into the cup. It was the colour of amber, true amber, not the brown nugget he had lost. The whisky smell caught in his throat, and he muffled a cough. He'd been chilled ever since his drenching in the burn and fetched out his pipe ready to fill it.

'Cover your face and keep the tongue of civility.' M'Aonghuis stopped the bottle and added water from a brown jug. 'Bad news the night, *naidheachd dhona,* wicked business.' M'Aonghuis pointed out the crowd of dour-faced men gathered round the Glasgow Herald.

Bheathain doubted matters were bad as M'Aonghuis made out but shrugged his agreement. Matters in the Herald had little to do with Skye, unless you counted report of deaths, births and weddings, or the price of cattle at market and by the time the presses had hold of the news and passed it back to folks it would be last week's story on the island.

'Heard *The Castle* wasn't in,' Bheathain said.[2]

---

[1] Under the law of the time, only premises with a room employed solely for the consumption of alcohol required a license from the magistrate. As an unlicensed hosteller, M'Aonghuis must beware visits from the local Bailie, hence the presence of his wife. *N.W.*

[2] The *Stirling Castle* was the mail packet serving Skye and the Inner Islands. *N.W.*

'Taken shelter at Dunvegan. She isn't chancing it in this blow.' The innkeeper had drawn off the price and set the balance of the coins aside. 'You'll get back what's not spent. Sit down and no troubling folk, else out you go.'

Bheathain took his whisky and with a backward glance at the newssheet, joined his *nen* and Tòrmod M'Neis. The two men sat around a table made from the end of a barrel. A candle and a small whisky jug shared it with them. His *nen*, Manus M'Dhòmhnuill, pushed a stool over and Bheathain slid it under his backside.

'I made you good champ,' Manus M'Dhòmhnuill said, 'but little good it has done; worn out so you are.'[1]

His *nen*, the only living relative Bheathain knew of, had a narrow face with the brow climbing through a ploughfield of rucks and creases before flattening off to a smooth crown. The old man, to Bheathain's knowledge, had rarely ventured beyond Portree and his face had the look of something long-lain in one place.

'*Slàinte.*' Tòrmod M'Neis raised his cup.

'*Air do Slàinte,* Tòrmod. *Nen*, you sinful decrepit old man, come morn I'll be hale and bonny.' He downed the whisky, feeling the heat prickle his throat.

'Though I, too, risk your tongue,' Tòrmod said, 'your *nen's* not wrong. You don't look so good the night. Did you bide overlong in the wet?'

'It might be,' he admitted, for it had been a longer walk to the inn than normal. 'Had I not, the laird a lamb had lost.' He reached for the jug and hearing no protest refilled his cup 'Damned beast near drowned. I got well wet saving it. Worst of it is I lost the wee charm I had.'

'That thing!' *nen* snorted. '*Saobh-chiallach,* so it is.' The old man bent forward and stared him in the face. 'You're peaky, that's all. Tea and a sit by the fire you need. Instead, you come out here.'

---

[1] Champ is a generic Scottish dish of mashed potatoes often combined with leftovers. *N.W.*

'Alas! Did I kiss it for luck the moment before it fell in the damned water!' He slapped the table in anger. Tòrmod warned him to be easy.

'Ay, I know,' he said. 'M'Aonghuis told us. Some folks be upset the night. No knowing what of. Be too stone-tired for making trouble. Had that wee bob of amber since babe I was. Queer to have it no more. Moment there, then not.'

He shrugged and showed M'Neis the rune mark he'd made on the stone.

Tòrmod M'Neis was a good five years younger than Manus and his face was round and cherry-cheeked and he always had something to smile about. Before rheumatics got hold of his legs, he'd been the laird's gamekeeper but now he made pin money carving stags and eagles on bits of bog pine and driftwood for the tourers. His sticks leant on the back of his chair and blackened scars nicked the man's fingertips.

Tòrmod shrugged and gave him the stone back. 'Rune-scratching isn't for the likes of us. Spaer, you need for it. Someone with kenning.' Tòrmod tapped his brow.

'You can't be so worried over it,' *nen* interrupted, 'you said aught of it at supper.'

'Had no chance; you were gone as I was in,' he protested. *'C'àit an robh sibh?'*

'The big house,' *nen* answered.

'Duntulm? What took you there?'

'No business of yours.' The old man fixed him with an eye.

'News we have,' Tòrmod indicated the Herald. 'Laird's nephew is dead.'

'Dead?' The laird's nephew was no more than his age. 'And how so?'

'Murdered, it tells.'

The old man hissed. 'Doesn't say *murdered*; he's dead but gives no cause or whyfors. Is that not enough without making adventure of it?'

'Have it as ye will,' Tòrmod grumbled. 'William is dead.'

'Ach...' Bheathain struggled to undo the drawstring of his tobacco pouch, ''tis no concern of mine.'

'Hush now,' Tòrmod complained. 'Many here owe their lives to the lad's mother. Lady Maud, as well you know, begged her father, God rest his bones, to give relief during the Famine.'

'God rest his bones, indeed,' his *nen* echoed.

'True,' Bheathain admitted. 'Good woman she was.'

It was a quarter-century ago when the blight struck. Before his time, but his mama had talked of it often enough. She had shown him her sister's grave at Garafad and where, for want of aught else to eat, they had scarted limpets from the rocks. The sister died of hunger, a brother too, he recalled.

He pocketed the stone. Even if Tòrmod was right and he needed spaecraft, he was not minded to fling it just yet.

The old gamekeeper smiled kindly, saying, 'You should get another bob of amber.'

'Ay,' Bheathain agreed. 'Ethelfeyrda give it me. I'll cry on her for another.'

Tòrmod shook his head. 'You had it afore her time. Besides, she's not with the laird the now. *Seadh!*' he answered *nen's* surprise. 'Change came on her afore Christmastide.'

'She's young for the change,' Manus said. 'She's left him, eh?'

'Aye, away she's gone. Not far, though,' Tòrmod said. 'Ethelfeyrda's no age and *dreachmhor* yet, but what is the use of a spaewife when her moonblood dries?'

'What use are they at all?' Manus grumbled. 'Has laird got himself another woman, then?'

'He has,' Tòrmod said, 'though as she scarce says a word to a' body you'd not know it.'

Bheathain lit his pipe with the candle and listened to the two old men. Not all they said he grasped; a woman's moonblood was something to do with making bairns, but of spaewives he knew a deal less, though *dreachmhor* was a fair description of the flame-haired woman who gave him the cord for his touchpiece.

'Reckon Ethelfeyrda was cunt-bitten, then?' his *nen* asked.

'Poxed! Nae,' Tòrmod protested. 'Decent woman she was. *Tha i subháilceach*. Bheathain.' Tòrmod got his attention. 'That touchpiece, marked, was it?'

'*Seadh,*' Bheathain agreed, 'belike bird's foot.'

'The stag's rune,' Manus said, 'to keep him safe, or his ma and da safe from him. Can't recall now. You need call on laird's new spaer, lad.' The old man grinned, his last remaining tooth buried in his bottom lip. 'Glad sight she is, no doubt.'

Tòrmod shook his head. 'Right skinnymalink is she. Rather I,' the man's face was a cherish of smiles, 'a pair of *ciochan*, and a big fat *tòn!*' The man cupped his hands on his chest. 'If you want, I'll cry on lass. Eolhwynne's the name on her.[1] Eh, M'Aoidh, what are you looking at?'

The man whom Tòrmod addressed was standing directly behind Bheathain.

'You're ill-tongued, M'Neis. Pay some respect the night.'

Bheathain knew the voice; it had troubled his lugs many a Sabbath. Arse-about on the chair, he sighted on the bent snotter and hard little eyes of Fearghus M'Aoidh. M'Aoidh was a quarryman from Clachan[2] and as precentor at Garafad Kirk he read the lines of verse for the congregation to sing and was a keen upholder of other folk's piety. M'Aoidh owed his bent snotter to a bad-tempered cow some five years back and ever since the man's voice recalled the drones on a set of pipes.

---

[1] In the Northern Tradition a spaewife's given name was formed from two, or occasionally three, runes and conveyed something of her character or appearance. Thus, Thorwynna might describe a large and rather jolly woman, and Tyrbeithe, a woman slender as a birch tree but possessing physical strength or character. Frequently an *e* or *a* added to the name lent a degree of femininity. The correct pronunciation of Eolhwynne is Aye-yol-uh-win with the stress on the first, second and fourth syllables. *N.W.*

[2] Clachan refers to a small township or cluster of houses. When discriminating between one 'Clachan' and another (there are several upon Skye) the name of the parish or nearest settlement is appended. *N.W.*

'Keep out of this, Somhairle. M'Neis I'm striving with, not you.'

Ignoring M'Aoidh's warning, Bheathain tugged at the corner of his scarf as if to bare his mark.

'Na dèan sin,' his *nen* warned him off making trouble. But Bheathain was tired of being told what to do, tired of being cold and tired of being weary and pined for his lost touchpiece. Ignoring the old man, he cleared the scarf from his mouth and blew pipe smoke into M'Aoidh's face.

M'Aoidh jerked back, his eyes blinking from the smart and half-raised a fist before seeming to think twice and only wiped the back of it across his mouth.

'A' going you to Devil! M'Aonghuis! Get rid of this *buamastair*.'[1]

M'Aonghuis proved insistent on their leaving and as M'Aoidh yammered on—it was Tòrmod he was most upset with—Bheathain drained his cup and made certain his *nen* had the bottle off the table. As they were leaving, he saw not one cup or bottle marred the pages of the Glasgow Herald. The news was not usually given this respect.

Tòrmod, the last of them, shuffled through the door slap on his sticks and the door slammed behind them. Bheathain reckoned it was the hurt in the legs of him made Tòrmod M'Neis such a bletherer. Bheathain flung his oiler over himself, and the wind caught and clapped at its tails.

'A fair night, but did not last so long,' M'Neis said.

'It did not,' his *nen* agreed.

'Ach, well.' M'Neis turned away: his home lay across the river in Garafad. *'Slàn leat,'* he cried cheerfully and disappeared into the night.

'Fine night indeed. A thumping he'll get some day,' his *nen* said once they were alone and tramping for home.

Bheathain knew the old man was talking of him as much as Tòrmod but did not answer back. The whisky lingered in his belly, but he doubted its warmth would see him home.

---

[1] *Buamastair*: a noisy fool or practical joker. *N.W.*

He kept his hands in his pockets and clenched them into fists, but despite this his left hand, the one he'd dipped in the burn saving the lamb, remained stubbornly numb.

'Do you know where she might be?' he asked.

'Who?'

'Ethelfeyrda.'

'What of her? She's left laird's service and that's an end. Reckon you want a bit of amber?'

'I want back what I had.'

'Can't get back what's gone. Ewe was it you saved?'

'*Cha robh,*' Bheathain sighed, 'a wee lost laddie.'

He walked, matching his pace to the old man. Some nights it was an effort to walk so slow, but not tonight. The wind swirled the oiler round him, as though wanting to tangle him in its folds, and rain blew out of the darkness. A no good night at the end of a no good day. Save for the lamb he'd no kind word to say for it and fetching the lamb had cost him dear.

He peered a moment into the darkness, toward the hills invisible against the black sky and then back along the road. There was only his old *nen* beside him, but had footsteps followed them, or a voice called his name, he would not have been surprised.

'Och, lad! No night to linger,' Manus protested.

Bheathain agreed and turned back. If the white stag did prove an omen, he would know soon enough. Meantime he'd keep his thoughts to himself.

II

Five days in the week Bheathain watched over the laird's sheep and on the sixth he tended a plot of ground on the slope above the Portree road. On this he grew barley, kale and potatoes. The ground there was thin and insufficient, but digging in sea wrack did much good to the land.

Tammas M'Neis, Tòrmod's grandson and Bheathain's cousin, worked alongside him and together they raked and forked the wrack into creels for carrying off. The wrack lay heavily on the fork and half seemed to slip from the prongs before he had it lifted. The creels filled agonising slow, and his hands had chilled to lumps of gristle. It was hard work and Bheathain felt it this morning. Bending to the slither, he plucked out a strand of pink dulse, delicate as lace, and curled it into his mouth. For a moment, the brine clinging to it sucked the spit from his cheeks, but then the dulse yielded its own juices to his tongue, and he chewed slowly.

'Appetite for it the morn,' Tammas said. 'Careful now; you'll be shitten afore the jakes.'

He did not answer, being unwilling to lose the sweetness in his mouth by speaking. Dulse was a cleanser, a dose for the belly. Dried and take on a fast it rid a man of worms and other troubles. It was not worms he had, or no worse than any other fellow, but he was weary this morning and wanted cleansing. He wanted rid.

Uilleam M'Illathain's ground lay alongside Bheathain's. No boundary stone marked the division of the shore, but each man knew what was his. M'Illathain's horse, a long-toothed hand-me-down from the laird's stable, stood with head bowed and tail to the sea. M'Illathain and his two older boys emptied their creels in the cart and went straightways back to raking. They were handy at it and only took the best of the kelp for they did not look to spread it on the land but to make ash from it. Fifteen years ago, at the height of Buonoparte's blockade, kelp ash fetched twenty crowns a ton. Last twelvemonth the agent was paying two crown, eight schilling and Uilleam M'Illathain was the last kelp gatherer in Staffin. It needed a dozen tons of kelp or two hundred and fifty creels on a man's back, to make a ton of ash. It was hard work for M'Illathain and his boys, and worse since the eldest son had drowned.

Mòrag, dressed in mourning blacks, had an eye out for her two youngest, calling them back in a wind-piercing screech if they strayed too near the water. Tales of the Crimea[1] filled the

---

[1] The Crimean War of 1854–7 when France, the Austro-Hungarian Empire, the Venetian Republic and the Kingdom of Sardinia, allied with the Ottomans to defeat Russia in the Black Sea and Eastern

boy's head and he stalked the ebb for sea jellies and noisily put them to the sword with a stick. The girl was a year older and, primly ignoring the antics of her brother, gathered driftwood and stacked it beside the cart.

Once that boy had been him, save he had a scarf about his face and there only ever was his Ma and Da for company; no brothers or sisters to share the burden. Once a voice had always called him back from the wave's edge, but no more. The rain made a sharp sound against the wrack, like the patter of drumming fingers.

'See Mòrag's still in her weeds,' Tammas said.

'*Tha i*,' Bheathain agreed.

'You'd thought she'd leave off by now. While since Niall drowned.'

'Six months, it is.'

'Don't understand it. Why so long?'

Bheathain paused; he wanted to keep his answers short, mindful of the returning tide, but it seemed to him any answer not disrespectful must need more than a few words.

'Niall was the world to her,' he said. 'Betimes folk see what they've lost and not what they have.'

Tammas fell quiet and though he pretended to settle to his work, the boy was deep in thought. Bheathain thought it strange Tammas looked to him for knowledge of the world. They were only a few years apart, but Bheathain stood on the farther side of a threshold Tammas had still before him. Yet his path to manhood had been so uncommon he thought it little use to another. Tammas he had seen hand in hand with Giorsal Làman, but no lass, fair or otherwise, had slipped her hand in his, nor had any seemed to want to.

'Reckon laird was same as Mòrag,' Tammas said.

'How do you come so?' Bheathain had to drag the question out of himself, preferring the sound of weed dropping in a creel.

Mediterranean. Although events of the war were closely followed in Scotland and Anglia and the sentiment of the people and government was anti-Russian, neither country took part in the conflict. *N.W.*

'The laird lost his wife and was good time finding another.'

'Wouldn't know of that,' Bheathain said: the affairs of the laird were his own and no one else, to his mind.

'All this time without, then split-new wife he marries, and he forgets—'

'Tammas!' Bheathain cut in, 'What kind of talk is this? He isn't forgetting; do you hear me?'

'Dè dha sin?'

'The laird will not lose mind of his first wife for taking another. Such a thing never leaves you.'

'Na caill do cheann!' Tammas protested. 'My, but you're prickly the morn.'

Bheathain did not reply, and Tammas went back to raking the weed. Bheathain knew Tammas' mother was housekeeper at Duntulm and it was the boy's fancy that, while Tòrmod was out gemmering, Peigi M'Neis, back then a mere swabber in the scullery, had caught the young laird's eye and he was the outcome of their illicit union. Bheathain thought this was a wicked calumny on Peigi M'Neis, but strangely it gave Tammas a deal of pride, along with an uncalled for interest in the laird's doings. Having teased away at Tammas's story, he reckoned it founded on nothing more than a passing likeness between the boy and the laird and a hankering for the finer things in life. To Bheathain's mind Tammas and he could pass for brothers, were it not for the mark on his face.

His fork caught on a piece of wood tangled in the weed and he stooped to throw it landward. Wood would not do for burning but was handy for making pegs for holding roof thatch or a dozen other tasks. Less welcome were the sea jellies; even dead, they had a wee sting if messed with.

Each time Bheathain lifted weed into the creel he felt his eyes drawn to look for his missing touchpiece. A dozen times he had answered a false hope and picked up a likely looking stone, only to discard it. Now he had steeled himself not to heed the thought, knowing if he did there would be no end of it.

He had woken before creek o' day and when Tammas joined him, they had come down to the shore in the half-light, with the kirk bell at Garafad tolling six across the bay. Later, the sun rose behind Applecross and briefly lit up the mountains a bright, brassy yellow before cloud swallowed it.

His creel filled, he leant on his rake to watch M'Illathain's cart climb toward the trackway connecting shore to road. Mòrag, walking behind her boys, glanced back his way and jerked her head, though whether in greeting or goodbye he could not tell. He replied by dropping his bonnet for a moment. He knew, or thought he knew, what was in her glance, having seen it often enough from others: 'Why did my son drown and not you, you cursed creature?'

Tammas looked up. The lad was hopeful of a hand to fill his creel, but Bheathain ignored him.

The sea was reclaiming what it had lost, sweeping up the beach. Twice or more Bheathain had seen Mòrag's boys standing close-headed and looking out across the bay behind their mother's back. Few crofters had any love for the sea, preferring to scratch a living from the fields, but, call it blood or habit, the M'Illathains, father and sons, had a taste for fishing, always chasing the crab, herring, and ling. Since Niall drowned, their skiff had not left the strand and he fancied there would be a battle soon enough for Mòrag's boys were more venturesome than kelp gathering would satisfy, and after much greeting, the skiff would wet its keel again and Mòrag would fold away her blacks.

Tammas stood up and drove his fork in the sand. Bheathain glanced at the creel and saw the boy had not shirked.

'Let's go,' he said, '*Tha mi a chuidicheas tu a.*'

Tammas crouched with the broad strap across his chest. Bheathain got a grip on the creel and jerked it up, taking the weight as Tammas got to his feet.

'Tea and a smoke when we're done,' he said.

'Ay, sounds well by me,' Tammas murmured, 'tea and smoke.'

They followed M'Illathain's cart tracks for a while, first along the smooth sand beneath the high-water mark, then away from the shore along a track packed with stones laboriously hauled off the beach. Water ran from the hills, filling the ditches, soaking into everything not iron or stone and spilling down to the sea, and still the sky brought ever more grey cloud. To any not raised to it, it would be a dreich sight but to Bheathain it was just the way of the world. On Skye it rained, and when it wasn't raining you expected rain. That the burn running beside the track had flooded out twice and he and Tammas had water round their ankles was only to be expected. The sound of the rain hissing on the stones and pocking the weed in his creel replaced the boom of the sea, but it was not a cold rain or cold wind and he felt his flesh grow clammy with warmth and once he drew the scarf away from his face to let the air against his skin.

At a fork in the track, M'Illathain had gone south but Bheathain turned along the right-hand way past the crofts of Ruaraidh M'Aonghuis, the M'Phearsains and the Moirreachs. No one was stirring but a trickle of peat smoke spilled from the half open doors. For a brief moment in the rainy silence, he and Tammas seemed the only things crawling on the Earth. M'Aonghuis had planted oats and the green shoots showed bravely against the black ground. Much more of this and they would yellow and rot and there was not a thing M'Aonghuis might do about it. For his sake and for his own sake and the sake of the sheep and every damn beast not born to water, Bheathain hoped for the weather to break.

The track climbed to a liggat[1] by the Portree Road. Pushing the gate aside, Bheathain squeezed through; Tammas was hard at his shoulder.

'Bheathain! Mind yourself!'

A black carriage, trailed distantly by a second vehicle, sped toward them.

---

[1] A liggat is a self-closing gate. *N.W.*

'It's the laird,' Tammas said. 'And such a hurry!'

Black pennants fluttered on the roof and a black plume tossed on the horse's head.

'Where's he hurrying?' Bheathain asked. 'Burying, is it?'

'It's the car he takes,' Tammas agreed, 'Ach! Bheathain, *A' Prionnsa*. The laird's off to Anglia for burying of the prince!'

Bheathain tucked his bonnet under his arm in respect and recalled his words at the inn. "No concern of mine," he had said. He regretted the mean spirit now.

'Be all the talk at the inn, yestreen,' he said.

'Da told us,' Tammas said. 'Reckons the prince was killed. Though my da loves making *boiream* of such.'[1]

Mud and grit sprayed up from the wheels and horse's hooves, and Bheathain protected his face, expecting a buffeting, but abruptly the coachman reined in and slowed up.

'Heh! The laird draws up for us!' Tammas cried.

It was true, or nearly so, for the coachman brought his horse to a trot and then, so Bheathain thought, lifted his whipstaff in greeting; though as it was only the curtest of motions, he could not be sure. He raised a hand in return and would have bowed his head, save for the weight of the creel on his shoulders. Thus, stood almost upright but with his chin against his collar bones, he was briefly eye-to-eye with the occupant of the carriage. The laird, black coated, had leant to the window. Why, Bheathain could not tell, but for a second their eyes were either side of a pane of glass and though there was not time to blink it was as if the laird had looked into his deepest thoughts.

---

[1] According to *The Gael's Dictionary* (Glasgow Press, 2009) "A *boiream* can refer to any form of news but especially to rumour of an excitable and gossipy nature. Those among us who regard such matters as the prerequisite of the female of the species might draw comfort from its similarity with the Gaelic word for woman '*boireannach*'. However, as Gaelic offers *boir*, meaning elephant, *boirche* for elk, buffalo and the thick edge of any item, and *boireal* meaning a joiner's brace in similar juxtaposition, we suggest the similarity is one of coincidence <u>not</u> significance." *N.W.*

The carriage went on, leaving him view of the coachman's hatted head and the spinning irons of the wheels. There was a curious smell, half sweet and half rank, which did not belong and for a moment he had the sense of being in two places at once, as happens sometimes on waking from a dream. The sense and the smell lasted only a moment before the wind took one and he shook himself free of the other.

Out of habit, he patted his chest, thinking to feel the reassurance of his touchpiece, but his hand faltered, finding it missing as he absently stepped into the road.

'Bheathain!' Tammas hauled him back as a pair-horse and drag thundered by, spraying him with mud and grit.

'Woe!' Bheathain fell back against the wall and wiped the filth from his face.

'Surprise, it is. I mean, not you were near killed, but the laird seems in good humour,' Tammas said.

Shaking the mud off his coat, Bheathain stepped forward. The laird's carriage had now gone from sight and moments later the drag followed it, turning east toward Garafad and Portree.

'You reckon so, Tammas?' The laird had not seemed cheery to him; quite the opposite.

'He took care to pay us his attention,' Tammas squeezed through the liggat onto the road. 'Heh, reckon he knew us as his ain?'

Bheathain laughed. It was as though some hitherto undetected weight had been lifted from him, leaving his feet light on the ground. He did not think the lad's reasoning up to much and besides, it was he the laird's eye seemed to catch.

'*A' prionnsa* was the laird's nephew?'

'Aye,' Tammas agreed, 'son of Lady Maud, the laird's sister.'

'Then you'll be mourning him yourself, will you not, seeing he was your cousin!'

Bheathain stepped clear as Tammas threw a fist.

'Quit your mocking. I'll be proving it someday, so I will.'

'Seadh, seadh,' Bheathain pretended to agree, 'but reckon this scarf of mine caught the laird's blinkers, eh?' He tugged at the cloth, as though to pull it from his face.

Tammas scuttled away from him, holding his fork like a soldier's pike. 'Leave it be; you big child, so you are. My mother holds with magick, and I'll not chance your queer face. Manus M'Dhòmhnuill can take his chances, but he's an old *bodach*. I have my life afore me, so I have.'

Bheathain laughed and tucked the scarf in place. 'Get along now! Sooner we shall have these creels off our backs. You're near worn out from the carrying!'

'Na gabh cùram!' Tammas hollered. 'Don't follow too close, you hear.' Tammas skipped across the road and down the track toward the field, always keeping a distance ahead of Bheathain.

'And I'm fit and hale,' Tammas carried on, 'not weary at all, not bit of it.' The lad tried to kick up his heels to show his fitness and near fell on his backside. 'Keep mind I'm not so grown as you, big lump you are.'

'So you are, wee Tammas,' he called after the boy. 'And shall I be saying to Giorsal Làman? "Ah, but Tammas is just a lad," eh?'

'You'd never,' Tammas yelled, 'is jealous you be.'

Bheathain crossed the road and sauntered after the boy. Giorsal had a sweet smile, but she'd never turn it his way.

'Aye,' he murmured. 'Jealous I am.'

§

Climbing toward the sheep beild that afternoon he sensed something awry. He could not put his finger on it, but it was the same as when a fellow tells you a crock of falsehoods or the sky cannot decide if it's to blow foul or fair. As he walked, he could not keep his hands still or fix his mind on any one thing.

The morning's rain had passed, leaving a pale watery sun in its place. Light streamed across the hills, catching on the crags and darkening the fissures and cracks. Wind brushed the heather, sending deep shadows rippling across the new green growth. Some days the land was as changeable as the sea and a man might never knowingly stand on the same earth twice. Clouds across the sky, the shaping of the wind on the heather, the colour of light, it would change the look of the land so much. Even the naked rock, immovable and resilient, altered hour to hour as the sun passaged from east to west, becoming smooth, then deep-riven as the light took it, then dull pink by evening.

There were few deer in these hills and a white stag would have caught folks' attention. The longer he stared up at the rocks, the more he thought the beast only a trick on the eye or a chance eddy in the mist.

An hour he spent cutting the brush off the heather and fitting out the beild with fresh bedding. His scarf kept the muck off his face. A candle glimmered in a cranny, but he'd put it there more for company than the use of it. The door faced east, and no sun fell within. What light there was had a pale, bluish quality that changed slowly as clouds passed over. Once or twice, he thought a shadow had fallen across the doorway, but each time he was mistaken and put it down to a passing cloud. Nevertheless, he wished he still had his touchpiece for the sense he was not alone would not abate.

There was nothing wrong with the roof timbers; a blessing as they would be trouble to replace. The thatch was not bad, either. Heather thatch lasted a good long time. The worry was the ropes holding the anchor stones. These were made of lengths of heather twisted together and a good few had unravelled, and the stones lay pitched about. Without anchors a gale might strip the roof bare overnight. Walking around the beild he found the anchor stones and piled them together, then worked out how much rope was needed and noted it on a scrap of paper he'd brought along and thus found comfort in labour. It was then the queer sense he had of being watched overwhelmed him.

'Foghnaidh sin!' he said and glanced about. A few sheep

had broken off grazing to watch him, but it was not their eyes he felt upon him.

'*Cò th' agam?*' he shouted at the emptiness. '*Dè do ghnothach rium?*'

The sheep tore at the grass. Lambs hunkered out of the wind or skipped like thistledown. A dozen crows squabbled up the brae. Nothing was out of place and though he shaded his eyes and scanned the high hills, nothing was amiss.

The wind carried a strong, sweet scent he could not place but as soon as he dwelt on it, it had gone, and the smell of heather and sheep and the sea prevailed. He buried his face in his baccy bag and breathed in its familiarity, then filled his pipe and smoked a while with a glance toward the gully where he'd lost his amber touchpiece and a scratch at his chest where it had lain.

It was not all he had lost, for he had lost peace of mind as well. He knew the very moment he had lost the touchpiece for he had the cut on his thumb for proof and the nagging chill in his left hand. He had the bit of stone he scratched a rune mark on, and as he smoked, he wrapped a hand around it to keep it safe in his pocket.

The other loss he could not place. Yesterday had been a no good day all round but he'd not felt this out of sorts last evening and nor this morning gathering weed with Tammas. Why had the laird's carriage slowed when neither he nor Tammas were obstructing the way? There was a mystery. He finished his pipe and knocked the ash out on a stone.

It was late in the afternoon when he left off. The sky was clear, but the wind had chilled, and he looked forward to his tea, but once home he found the kettle cold beside the remains of the fire and no sign of his *nen*.

'*C'ait am bheil e?* Manus! Are you about?'

Silence welcomed his cries. Crouching by the hearth he reached in among the seemingly cold peats and broke one apart to expose the bright pink glow within. He blew on it to excite the flame then set it down and gathered the peats against it until the air trembled and warmed his fingers.

He filled the kettle in the darkening yard and called out again for his grandfather. Silence answered. The thought he might be making his own supper displeased him and with each step and motion his body grew more resistant and his thoughts more sluggish, like water crusting-over as it freezes. Only when he had the kettle on the swee had he shuffled off his shoes and settled to do nothing but listen to the water boil.

Even leaning to the fire, the chill air crawled over him like a spider. The day had been bleak, but no worse than yesterday and he'd not worked harder than the day before or the day before that, but he was weary to the bone. No going down the inn tonight; something to eat and then bed would do him. With the kettle boiled, he made tea and left it to steep by the fire and found a scrap of strength to make a supper of mutton bones and barley broth. The iron cook pot was a deal smaller than the kettle, and as he lowered the swee to bring it closer to the fire the hot chain swung back and burned his hand. He sucked on the reddened flesh.

He had grown up in this house. Every stone and every stick of furniture he had known all his life. Longer than it was wide, the sides of the room were bare stone and the ends planked with timber. The roof space was open, end-to-end and the peat reek drifted into every corner. Doors in the partition walls led to a small room where Manus slept and an entranceway leading to the yard and the old byre. Bheathain's own bed was an alcove beside the door to Manus' room. A bit of sacking curtained it off from the living space. The fire burned in the centre of the room, its smoke escaping through the thatch as best it could and a chain hung down from the roof for holding kettle and cooking pots.[1] Decorations were few: a plain cross upon the wall, a china

---

[1] A passage in MacGregor's journal written during his stay at Dunvegan describes this exact scene, but the exact location of the hovel and the name of its occupant are omitted. A further note suggests Lord MacLeod thought MacGregor's interest in the blackhouses and their occupants more than a little eccentric. *N.W.*

figure of Jesus on the dresser, and a pair of bills, stained dark with the smoke, advertising emigrant sailings. His grandfather had pinned them to the wall. Bheathain supposed they brightened the place, or reminded a man there was worse luck at sea.

He drank his tea with a splash of milk. It was well sitten, but the bitter taste was how he liked it. The broth seeming heated through, he ate slowly and though each mouthful warmed his tongue the heat failed inside him, and he felt no benefit, as though his belly was a cold and bottomless hole, and no goodness would fill it. He thought of his ma and how she had sickened, and no amount of care and good eating did any good, and wondered, in a vague groping in the dark way, if he was sickening for something. Since he'd never known himself to sicken of anything the feeling had a curious novelty, for how might a man know something for the first time? The bowl wiped with a bit of bread and put back on the dresser, he took out his mother's Bible. If fire and food could not warm him, then God's Word might as it had once warmed Mama. Pouring the last of the tea, he added a drop of milk and sat down to read in the candlelight. A black mark on the cover left dirt on his hand; the Bible had been mother's comfort and drink had been his da's and one hungry night Da had ripped the Book from mother's hands and flung it on the fire. Ignoring his blows and vile utterances, she saved it before the pages burned, but not before the flames scorched the cover.

How long he read he could not rightly tell for his reading laboured, as though the words were knots and tangles his fists could not unbind. Hearing a slam at the door, he called out, 'Manus, is it ye?' but was answered only by the wind. He got his mawd and wrapped it around him. It was damp still, but he didn't care. The fire smouldered but gave no heat, though it seemed to warm the kettle well enough. He made tea again, but like his supper it only warmed the extremities of him and not his belly.

'*Dè fo ghrian tha cearr ort?*' he muttered and leant forward into the pool of candlelight, seeking like a moth. The holy words swam in the yellow gloom. The morn was the Lord's Day; he'd be hearing these words from Father Peabody at kirk. The Lord's Day, the day of rest. He would not stir, save to haul his bones to chapel. Where in damnation was Manus when he wanted him?

Fidgeting, he brought the book closer to his eyes, but it seemed to make no difference. It was as if something lay between him and the light, casting a shadow. Putting the book down, he rubbed his eyes. His cheek was tender, as though he had caught the sun, and his hand came away bloodied.

Taking the candle to the dresser he stared into the mirror mounted between the shelves. His mark was bleeding. A line of blood trickled to the side of his mouth. It tasted foul and he spat on the floor.[1]

'God in heaven,' he muttered and turned away.

He was alone. No sense trying to raise a' body. Whatever was wrong with him would keep till *nen* got home. Weary, he slumped at the table and stared at the Bible until the words ran like blood in water. Candle fat dripped on the white paper, then ran down the stub and burnt his thumb. He pushed the book and candle away and peeled the cooled tallow from his skin. As it came loose it took on the shape of his hand, ghostly pale and shimmering in the candlelight.

Something hammered at the door, as though seeking entry.

'Manus, *An tus' a th'ann?* Is it you?'

It was no night to leave a stranger at the door. The latch proved stiff, but the door opened easy enough when the wind caught the planks and flung it back on the leather hinges.

'*Cò tha sin?*'

---

[1] The 1864 published text has Bheathain retreating to his bed at this point with the rest of the scene narrated as a dream, rather than taking place in Bheathain's wakeful reality. See Text Note on variations between first draft and published text. *N.W.*

Only the wind answered him as he stared into the blackness.

'Manus, is it you?'

Rain chilled his face. The clouded sky admitted nothing of moon or star and no neighbour's light shone. The only light came from within the house he'd left and, half-turned, he glanced within to the peat fire and the candle flickering in the draught from the door. A man at the table had his back to him. He seemed familiar.

Something moved in the darkness. He knew it as well he knew the presence of the Lord when bowed in prayer at the Kirk, but it was not Manus.

'Ciod tha dhìth ort?'

Then he saw it; a shimmer, like distant lightning as the white stag stepped into the narrow entry of the yard. He knew it was the same creature he saw on the hills, but now he knew it was no ordinary beast. It came within the yard, seeming to fill it with light. It held its head high, antlers spread like the crown of a tree.

He clung to the doorframe, his pale, ghostly hand barely holding him against the wind. The man sat within at the table was himself. *Was* himself, for he was no more. This pale ghost was all that was of him. And this bright creature was also himself; familiar as the reek of his own bed. His time on Earth was done: his soul had come for him.

'*O Iosa Crìosd! O Dia!*'

And yet why, if his corpse was cooling, did the wind keen his face? And if a man faced death naked as he came into the world, why was he clothed? No man met his soul and lived; yet this was his soul, and he was not dead.

He found the stone he'd marked and held it out, like a penny for the alms plate at kirk.

'You've come for us?' he asked.

He did not know if it heard him. Did not know if he spoke aloud or only into the echo of his head, yet the stag came and stood over him.

''*S mise mharbh?*'

The creature dipped its head, surrounding him with the points of its crown, and nuzzled his cheek. Its breath was musk and hill-damp, with the sweetness of heather and honey, and the sound of it was the wind through the long grass in summer. He breathed, knowing it was air from the Far Country. It circled in his chest, warmer than any liquor, warmer than any August day.

He would have breathed that air forever, but the stag nudged his face aside and dropped one prong beneath his arm. Its strength lifted him off his feet and, suddenly fearful, he slipped and stumbled against the doorway. The stag bowed and tried to cage him in its crown, pressing him against the stone. It was playful, like a father with his child, but he was wary of its strength. He had a hand against its muzzle, but it was too strong for him and pressed him back. An antler caught his ankle, unbalancing him. He fell and the bright crown closed around him and then he was scrambling for a hold on the creature's back.

'Bitheam 'pasgadh!'

But it did not let him be and he could only let it carry him down the track toward the sea. The full force of the wind was on him now. It seemed to flow through him, like ice through water. He closed his eyes and held them closed, save for glimpses. Waves licked his feet, clouds dewed his face and hair. Sheep scattered. A dog gave chase, barking and crazed. Mountains and crags reared out of the darkness.

There was no telling how long the dizzying ride lasted before the creature settled, seemingly weary, upon a shore, and lowered him to walk beside it. Waves fell, thunderous in the dark. Sea spray flicked his face, bringing salt. They walked parallel to the waves with no sign or sight of where this was, save beside Ocean. Presently, when he had grown easeful with his new condition, he caught hold of the creature's antler and it responded to him, bowing its head to one side like a horse following the rein. He swung his legs across its back to ride, and antler in hand turned the creature away from the sea.

'Dh'achaidh,' he said: 'Homeward.'

§

The Bible still lay in his hand. A grease stain and a drop of blood spoiled the page. Had he been dreaming?

He could remember nothing, save a smell of honey and lavender.

His cheek was ember hot, and his hand came away bloodied. There was wind out and silence within.

'*Nen? Cò tha sin?*'

His throat rasped like iron. He could not wait up. A ball of candle fat squashed beneath his hand as he raised himself up by the table. Its legs protested his weight, but he could scarcely stand. His left arm was weak and cold to touch, its flesh bone-white. He could not leave the fire be. It would burn out untended. He bent and covered it for the night, but then could not stand again. So, he crawled, the floor hard through the knees of his breeches. Grit bedded itself in his palms. He did not dress for bed but shucked his boots before crawling beneath the blankets and thrusting the curtain across. His bed reek welcomed him, and he folded into a ball of flesh more dead than alive.

> Green Lanes lead between the worlds,
> Unmarked, no road stone paves them
> And no footprints bruise their grass;
> Each finds his path where he least expected.
> *His soul did not mark his death, but the death of who he was.*

Editor's Remarks

With chapter one of MacGregor's first draft the quality of the paper subtly alters, and examination of the watermark shows it was manufactured in 1858. This supports the generally-held opinion that MacGregor wrote nothing apart from his journals, (which were readymade stationer's notebooks purchased from Rutherford Printmakers and Stationery

Supplies on Edenborough's Lawnmarket) together with whatever constituted his 'black books', in the period between Madeleine's death and commencing 'Lays of Brigadoon' in the late summer of 1861.

There is also a marked changed in the character of MacGregor's script which averages thirty lines per page (two more than in the First Prologue) and there is noticeable compression between the individual words, suggesting MacGregor was in haste to capture his ideas. The first page is numbered 1, supporting your editor's view that this was the first scene conceived by MacGregor, and though undated, MacGregor's journal indicates it was begun on, or shortly after, Christmas, 1861, with, if one allows a little dramatisation, news of Lady Helena's pregnancy fresh in his ears.

It is not clear how far he advanced before New Year celebrations interrupted. He had resigned as Master of The King's Revels following Lady Madeleine's death and had no official duties, but, eager to re-establish his place in society, he and Lady Helena accepted the king's invitation to the Christmas Eve Ball at Holyrood. On the same visit to Edenborough, he handed Beresford and Lucas the fair copy of 'Lays of Brigadoon', and called at the offices of James Ludd, whom he had commissioned the previous October with building a "fitting memorial to my first wife where I may grieve for her in private." (Letter dated 3 October 1861. MacGregor Archive, box xxxv 1861–62 King James University, Edenborough). Whatever the substance of James Ludd's work, MacGregor reported it as "disappointing", though he did not elaborate whether it was lack of progress or the design itself that disappointed. After a brief delay waiting out a snowstorm, the MacGregors arrived home in time for the traditional Scottish New Year celebrations on January the sixth.

Despite the compression and haste, the writing in chapter one is fluid and assured and in large passages there are no significant differences between the original text and that of the published edition. Those differences that occur mainly concern the dialogue which is noticeably saltier in the first draft. Quite apart from betraying MacGregor's intention to depict people as they were, the harm done by the excision of dialogue was more egregious than many readers might suppose, for it subtly altered MacGregor's depiction of Tòrmod M'Neis.

In the first draft, M'Neis is portrayed ambivalently, his crudities distancing the reader and contrasting with the relative kindness he shows to Bheathain. Thus, the reader is uncertain whether Bheathain should side with M'Neis or not, which has the effect of further isolating Bheathain from those around him. In the published edition M'Neis is too obviously going to be Bheathain's ally in events to come.

That M'Neis speaks as men have always spoken in the male-dominated world of drinking houses—a world Sir Sidney was certainly familiar with even if the devout John Lucas was not—reflects MacGregor's concern to show as he found, but it is clear he sometimes used the frankness of his characters for narrative reasons, as well as capturing verisimilitude.

There are two more notable variations between the first draft and published edition. The first, though relatively minor, is rather curious: no mention of the castration of lambs survived into the published text. Quite why Sir Sidney, or John Lucas (they were not always in accord with their criticisms) objected to MacGregor's reference to the commonplace procedure of castrating male sheep (the same procedure was and is carried out on male cattle and horses) is puzzling. It would be understandable had MacGregor described the bloody business, as it is enough to make any man weep with empathy for the beast concerned, but it seems one or other, or both, of the publishing partners ruled out even a reference to castration.

The effect of this alteration was minor, since, while it alludes to wider themes in the novel, it is not indispensable (as we shall see in a moment); however, the other alteration forced on MacGregor was much more serious. Essentially, in the published text Bheathain's soul appears within a dream—making it a product of Bheathain's fevered mind—rather than the undeniably supernatural phenomenon portrayed in the first draft.

Belief that the soul can appear at times of great change in people's lives—as opposed to solely at their death—is at odds with the teaching of the Alban Church, of which John Lucas was a major benefactor, and my supposition is that this alteration was at his insistence. It is the first of many instances in *This Iron Race* where Sir Sidney and/or John Lucas attempted to push the supernatural into the margins of MacGregor's novel.

At sunset the rooks murder on the hill
Prologue the Second
Winchester, one generation before our present: THE CURSE, our intangible, nay bodiless, narrator reveals the motive of its maker and its present intentions

> She drew water from the well,
> Lit a candle for a flame:
> Her breath trembled on the air.
> At sunset the rooks murder on the hill.
> *My Lady summoned me from wind and stone...*

A BURST OF air chilled the dampness on My Lady's face and her sight dimmed as though a great abyss had opened beneath her feet. The feeling lasted but a second and with her grip firm upon the bronze knife she cut into the bark of the holly tree, once, twice, to expose the living wood and make the mark complete.

She knew her craft and made me well; what she had sensed was not fear, for, unlike her hand her heart did not tremble, but only me entering her being, just as she desired. Stone-dark and ice-wind, she welcomed me despite the shiver in her flesh and this is what I found. Love received is the scent of the rose, but spurned, disregarded, mocked, it is the flesher's knife and within her breast My Lady felt only a semblance of life, for where the life should be the knife had done its work and she was empty, save for desire to be revenged. Her throat ached, cruel as a pinch, and she sniffed and cuffed her dripping nose. Her eyes, at least, were dry now but two salt streaks showed the path of tears.

And I? I knew her desire for vengeance would pass, leaving me unwanted and orphaned. From my birth I knew life was indifferent to those to whom it gives and those from whom it takes, and a just God is but a necessary dream.

Through My Lady's eyes, I saw a city suspended in a bowl of hills. Beyond it, the sun dipped to the horizon. Windows glowed, carriage lamps made darting runs like fireflies, and a ship's lantern crawled seaward on the navigation. There was shadow pricked by flame, while about My Lady the walls of the ruined chapel and the oak trees blazed in the saffron of the dying sun. Yet in her heart was darkness: she was falling and could not help herself from falling; the physicality of her act, slight as it was, the cutting of runes and bloodmarking, lay out of her will. She did not truly desire this moment but supped, knowingly, from the poisoned cup for she could not endure her thirst.

I heard, through her ears, only the shriek of rooks circling the hill and the tolling of a street crier's bell. I find the name of things in her thoughts. The city is Winchester; there is the Minster's spire, the many-towered building is The Tower, there is the Merchant Hall, the Bishop's Palace, Saint Cross Road, and this hill is St Catherine's, this ruin St Catherine's Chapel.

And her name? Her own name is denied her for she hears it still upon his lips, so I shall call her My Lady of Remorse.

Those of ordinary means seek to build a wall against their hurt and troubles, but that was not My Lady's way. As any heartbroken, spurned through another's act or lack of act, she had resorted to her strongest suit and with My Lady, this was enchantment, gramarye, magick, and she conjured not a wall but a weapon of revenge: Me.

Yet these thoughts lay behind her deed; they were the storms casting the wave, not the wave itself, and in the moment of its breaking, in the moment of my making, what filled her mind had but one overwhelming force:

'I cannot live, I cannot breathe—unless by this.'

The mark she cut is in the shadow cast by the tree and My Lady lit a candle stub to examine her work. Each cut she measured with the back of her knife and compared it to a drawing in her book. As she worked, she did not notice the book's worn, irregular type, or the machine-sewn binding or the flimsiness of the paper, though she did recall the hooked face of the bookseller from whom she stole it. Then she opened a white silk kerchief. Stained only with her tears, one corner had in blue embroidery two initials coiled like serpents. In this she gathered the strands of bark cut from the tree and tied them into a bundle.

The instructions clear in her mind, My Lady reached into her bag, drew out a bottle of dark green glass and removed its stopper. She poured half the wine-dark contents over the handkerchief and the remainder across the runestaves. Sealed with moonblood, nothing could unbind these runes: cut the tree down, burn it, scatter the ashes, the runes had summoned the curse. She would be the vessel of the curse, the poisoned cup, she would pass it to the one who betrayed her, and in time, he would pass it to his firstborn son. An innocent would suffer but she was blind, thinking only the guilty must suffer for the hurt he caused. In a hollow scraped between the roots, My Lady buried the handkerchief with its fragments of bark concealed within.[1]

The act was irredeemable as murder, and perhaps she was aware of this as she gathered the book and the now empty bottle into her bag, for removing her tools from sight she was also one part removed from what they had made, and she would hide that also, hide the mark upon the tree. Working quickly now, she scribed Mann, the holly stave above the bindrune and Beorc, the concealment stave, below, whereupon the marks faded to leave only a dark stain on the trunk. She had chosen the tree with care. Its roots tunnelled into a crack in the rock, drawing strength from the purest form of earth and each green spike of leaf wove power from the wind. She took one of its whip-thin branches in hand and stood at the edge of the cliff, swaying gently. The ground below called to her, its song a lullaby, an enchantment offering perpetual sleep, but she would not give it satisfaction, not yet. Clouds hung grey and violet against the azure of the evening and overhead the first stars

---

[1] It is a common misconception that when engraving marks of power only the finished article is significant while the removed material is waste. In fact, it is of equal and diametrically opposite power and must be disposed of with care. *N.W.*

disturbed the heavens. The rooks had ceased their chatter and settled for the night and from a square down in the city My Lady heard a band playing marching music: either 'Napoleon's Retreat', or 'Hussar's Hurrah', for the tune came only to her in fragments, and the foolish rhythm and discordant horns made her smile even though her heart wanted silence.

Later, when the sky had darkened to a violet bruise, and the Minster bell tolled nine and the band returned to their barracks, My Lady's thoughts turned to leaving. Though she carried me in her breast, a weight had lifted from her as though she had climbed to a great height and from it seen the farther view and thought it sweet. She knew the path home even in the dark, but doubted she would need the knowledge again. She could not see herself returning to this place, not ever, and her back turned upon the dusk, she walked into the darkling wood.

> Those ruins were frequented
> By sore pilgrims long ago
> Who made this path their habit.[1]
> This day, My Lady chose the harder road.

What My Lady made of the remainder of her life need not detain us now. I am what she summoned from wind and stone: a curse laid upon an innocent son. In part this story is the story of that son and in lesser part it is the story of the many among whom I searched for one I might bless and thereby end my misbegotten existence; but above all, it is my story, and if I choose to share it, it is on my terms.

Editor's Remarks
The first draft of this scene follows directly on
the page from the previous, with only a blank

---

[1] A reference to the ruined chapel on St Catherine's Hill, Winchester, once a resting place on the Pilgrim's Way to Canterbury. *N.W.*

line and a single word in block capitals, "LADY" followed by a question mark and the date, January 4, 1862. From the content of the previous chapter, it seems probable that MacGregor anticipated taking up Lord MacDonald's narrative after his meeting Bheathain (see chapter two) but realised he must address the origin of his narrator first.

Notes in the margins indicate an interruption between completion of Bheathain Somhairle's chapter and starting the second prologue. He and Lady Helena were still in Edenborough on the fourth, their return home having been delayed by bad weather, but as MacGregor always travelled with a portable writing table that seems unlikely to be the cause. More probably it reinforces the version of the novel's genesis MacGregor gives in "The Nature of the Tale"—following chapter seven in volume one—stating he was uncertain of the novel's direction.

Several of his early novels were begun without a preconceived plan or plot, but it had been increasingly his habit to sketch out ideas before commencing the main task of writing. With the first volume of *This Iron Race* MacGregor reverts to his earlier methods, squirrelling ideas and plot points in the margin as he writes, rather than following a plan. As mentioned earlier, many of these notes were damaged when the pages were bound by King James University in 1925 and it is not always possible to follow his thoughts.

For such a short chapter there are significant differences between the first draft and published text, primarily concerning the depiction of runecraft, much of which is either missing or rendered impressionistically in the published edition. It could be argued the publishers were concerned a reader might attempt to practise what MacGregor describes, however Sister Ethelnyd of the Iona Fellowship of Grace advises your editor that this is not a reasonable concern. It seems the very worst that might happen to anyone copying the charm portrayed in the text is a bloodied thumb. Moreover, MacGregor's publishers would be well aware of this. Magick, according to Sister Ethelnyd, is akin to turning a clay pot upon a wheel: no amount of reading or observation is the slightest use and the only way to master it is to have the gift of Grace and to endlessly practise. It is certain, then, that the curtailment of the description of runecraft was simply one more example of Sir Sidney and John Lucas pushing magick into the background of MacGregor's novel.

Although this was the most obvious change between the first draft and published text, it was not the most egregious: that was to the character of the girl-woman at the centre of the scene who was portrayed as a vindictive Jezebel in the published text on par with the wicked Salome, or indeed Jezebel herself from the Old Testament Book of Kings. Completely lost is any suggestion of her provocation by a faithless lover or that she acts out of desperation, rather than malice. The reason for Sir Sidney and John Lucas insisting on the change must remain unsaid for the time being, as it would disclose too much of the story. It is enough to say that it will become obvious in due course. This new edition offers, for the first time, the sympathetic portrayal of My

Lady of Remorse that MacGregor intended. First and foremost, she is a young woman who has been wronged by a man and though we do not have the full account—his voice is absent here—we understand her revenge is an act of desperation made when she is not in full control of herself. This was a crucial alteration since it undermined the justification for her soubriquet, "My Lady of Remorse", and with it the logic of the story which depends on her regretting what she did when her mind was disturbed. In this sense, hers is an act of the servant because we are all servants of our passions.

The thief of delight
Chapter Two
Portree Road, Skye, the present returns: The character of LORD MACDONALD of Skye, shewing his domestic life & responsibilities and the onerous task he undertakes

    The narrow road to the south
    Bears away from his estate
    (whose ruin he must carry);
    Obligation is the thief of delight.
Wishing only my extinction, I sent a shadow into the world to seek one I might bless and redress the wrong My Lady wrought. My journey began with a glance through the window of a carriage.

I

HIS LIMBS ANGULAR as the forks of a tree, Lord MacDonald leant back against the worn plush and sighed the formless expression of his inchoate thoughts.

    The air was foul; an evil mix of polish, mildew, and thyme: the last a gift from his wife as he was leaving. His head throbbed miserably, and he took advantage of an abrupt slowing of their pace to lean forward in his seat to lower the droplight and admit a little air. And thus, quite by chance, for a fleeting moment he found himself eye-to-eye with the young man standing at the roadside whose presence had occasioned the brief hiatus.

    The man's face was chiefly notable for being half-hidden by a red scarf, as worn by the reivers of old, but also because it was in some sense—and in this he could only rely on that part visible, comprising the bridge of the nose, the eyes, and brow—familiar, as of a scent teasing at memory.

    Indeed, so startling was this brief, if incomplete recognition, he scarce noticed I had joined him and with a frown at the spits of rain flying through the dropped light and a tensing of his fingers, MacDonald settled in his seat to contemplate the day ahead in ignorance of my presence.

§

An hour earlier, his entire household had gathered beneath an awning in the courtyard to see him away. His groom, Finlay McNeil, had held the carriage door open against the wind when his wife, Clara, whom, MacDonald noted was not properly attired for the weather, suddenly stepped forward as though to board. Fearing a scene, for his wife had only reluctantly accepted her journeying with him was out of the question, he nearly ordered McNeil to close the door in her face, but Clara had halted, recoiled sharply, and clasped one hand over her nose, and the other across their unborn child.

'But my dear, it smells appalling! Emily,' she turned to her maid. 'Kitchen garden, quickly now, a clutch of thyme.'

'Yes, m'lady.'

'Clara, I cannot delay,' he protested.

'Oh Pish! Darling, what does a few minutes matter? Two days with that foul smell and you will be ill. Don't you agree, McNeil?'

The groom, plainly startled, coughed slightly before speaking. 'I canna speak fer the laird, m'lady, but a wudna find it 'greeable mysel.'

'Thank you: you see my dear; even the servants think it too bad.'

'Very well. I suspect it was not properly aired. Matters have been rushed.'

He stepped back under the awning. He might insist on leaving without his wife's gift, but it would leave a sour taste and he conceded the smell inside the carriage was not pleasant. No sun shone through the cloud and the courtyard had an atmosphere of gloom, not improved by the darkness of the stone. An irregular quadrangle, its longest side accommodated the main part of the house with the servants' quarters at right angle to it. The shortest side consisted of the gatehouse, coach house and stables, while a wall overlooking the sea bound the fourth side of the courtyard.

This had been rebuilt repeatedly over the last decades as rock falls from the cliffs below ate away the land.

Outside the coach house, a large drag, painted in a deep shade of maroon, stood waiting. Its passengers were Gillanders Neave and his newly-appointed spaewife who would both accompany him to Winchester. McNeil would ride with them once he had seen MacDonald aboard the black chariot. The drag, drawn by a pair horse, was also carrying the bulk of the baggage.

'Clara, we must return inside. You may catch a chill,' MacDonald said.

'I have a fire to return to, and I do believe fresh air is restorative.'

The air was decidedly too fresh, and MacDonald glanced sympathetically at his coachman. John Duff had a miserable day ahead; likewise, the man's son, Iain, who had charge of the drag.

The maid returned with her hair flying loose.

'Emily, my dear, where is your bonnet?' Clara asked.

'Wind did took it m'lady. I'd nae time for running after. I have the thyme ye wanted.'

Emily gathered her hair and as she handed Clara the herb, he noticed the girl glance coyly toward the coachman's son. It was an open secret at Duntulm that Emily and Iain were walking out together, and he wondered how much, if any effort she had made to retrieve the bonnet.

Clara gathered the stems and produced from some pocket or recess women always seem to have at hand, a pink ribbon to yoke them together.

'Thank you,' he said and cautiously sniffed the posy. It stung the upper reaches of his nostrils but was preferable to the rank smell in his carriage.

'And this is for you as well,' Clara thrust a book in his hand. 'You really must have something agreeable to read. No, you cannot protest.'

He stared at the thing in his hand. 'I have *The Times*,' he said, 'which I have barely glanced at since yesterday, and a mining report to study,' his wife's eyes narrowed dangerously, 'but I will certainly consider,' he glanced at the novel's spine, '*Edwin and Morcar*, I believe I have not read it.'[1]

So, saying, he dropped the book on the seat and quite intended leaving it there, having never read or considered reading, anything by MacGregor, or Copperfield, or Thaxstead, or any other manufacturer of novels.[2]

'I shall pray for you; you will take all care?'

Her voice was plaintive; he knew her request was part question, but chiefly a requirement she laid on him. Clara had, in his opinion, somewhat elaborated the dangers of his journey and particular purpose.

He leant forward and kissed his wife decorously on the cheek.

'Mind you do not overtire yourself, my dear,' he said. 'Pray for me, as you wish, but do so from the comfort of the fire.'

Clara preferred the chapel—she thought prayers offered in it had more value than those committed at the bedside—but it was wholly too damp and chill.

'Hurry home soon as you may and I shall weary myself still less,' she said.

He refrained from sighing but reminded her to heed the advice of Dr Ramsay.

'He would wrap me in wool and never let me leave the fireside,' Clara protested.

'Then the good doctor is a man after my own heart,' he said. 'Well, my dear, now will you let me go?'

Her hand squeezed the soft flesh above his elbow, and he

---

[1] It is the first of MacGregor's *Saxon Trilogy* published by Beresford & Lucas in 1843. *Kingmaker* and *Dragonships* are the subsequent volumes. *N.W.*

[2] James Copperfield has lately fallen from favour as his caricatured depiction of ethnic minorities is no longer acceptable, however Charles Thaxstead remains a fixture on school syllabuses and several of his works have been successfully adapted into feature films. *N.W.*

felt her lips brush his ear. 'If you must. If you truly must.'

'Truly, I must,' he rested a foot on the carriage step.

'Then God speed your return, my darling.'

He thought to kiss her properly, but instead bent into the small cabin with a silent imprecation against whatever whims of God or nature sent him north of the six-foot mark in a world built for Adams of lesser stature. Seated, his knees upward of his hipbones, he leant back and unfurled his arms with the caution of a new-made butterfly.

Clara was instantly at the window, her pert mouth close against the glass, breath quivering the beads of wet clinging to the surface. McNeil swung the door to and Clara, ignoring the swirling rain, gave him the sweetest of smiles before inscribing a heart, a little smaller than a goose egg, upon the misted glass.

Impulsively, a sudden, uncharacteristic rapture thrilling through him, MacDonald touched his hand to its centre.

At the same moment, she stepped back from the carriage and lowering her head a fraction, gazed solemnly at him from beneath the pale arches of her brows. Her hair foamed from beneath her bonnet and fell about her cheeks, and he took in her blue eyes and bright smile; the fall of hair to her shoulders, bare beneath a white shawl framing her décolletage, and, below again, his eyes reached the fullness of her belly where his child lay.

The carriage swayed. John Duff had readied himself. Lifting a hand in goodbye, MacDonald glanced in turn at all those gathered to see him off. Emily's dress had trailed in the earth, but someone had found her a fresh bonnet. He would miss the wholesome cooking of Mrs M'Neis, and James McMurray welcoming him at the door. The names and offices of the others of his household need not delay us now, save to say all are well known and valued by their master and all, save his young wife on whose unborn child it would call ill luck, wore a black sash in honour of Prince William.

Returning his gaze to Clara, MacDonald tapped the doorframe with his cane, signalling the coachman.

The carriage lurched, its wheels juddering on the wet gravel, and turned to exit through the gatehouse. He had a glimpse through the arch of his wife and servants until the drag, following close behind, blocked the view.

Leaning back against the seat he settled his hands upon the silver top of his cane and puffed out his cheeks. He did not like goodbyes, nor did he much enjoy journeys. Thinking it would be his last sight of home for some weeks, he stared out at the pine and birch trees overarching the road.

Among them clumps of Indian rhododendrons were swathed with white and pink buds and abruptly, having forgotten such simple pleasures in the last few days, he realised he would miss their flowering.[1]

'Damn you, William,' he cursed under his breath and was at once ashamed of speaking ill of his nephew and of the dead. 'Damn,' MacDonald paused and glanced from the window to the copy of The Times and this time spoke aloud, 'Damn whoever spilt your blood, for I will know their name.'

§

He had only a moment to compose himself after his encounter with the young man before the carriage drew up sharply. A voice hailed them and glancing out, MacDonald found they were alongside a cart laden with seaware. William MacLean stood upon it and supposing it was he who hailed them MacDonald dropped the window to enquire.

'MacDonald, sir,' MacLean addressed him the way all Gaels addressed their clan chief. 'River's washed oot footings o' bridge, it has.'

'How badly?' he asked. 'Will it bear us and the drag?'

This had now drawn up behind them.

---

[1] MacGregor's stay on Skye did not coincide with rhododendron flowering; however his journal records a conversation with Lord MacLeod describing the gardens at Dunvegan in these exact words. Rhododendrons had been brought to Scotland from Iberia some sixty years previously. *N.W.*

'I canna say, sir. Yersel, ay, like it will, but,' MacLean glanced at the heavier drag, 'that I canna say.'

Would not say; the man did not want to be held liable. MacDonald called for John Duff. It was possible to return to Duntulm and make for Portree via Uig and Loch Snizort, but not if he intended to be at his cousin's by nightfall.

'We'll be there, sir,' Duff said with confidence. 'See how the bridge stands. If needs be we kin lighten oursels. As ye say, we canna make Dornie by way of Uig, not by the night.'

'Very well; it is to be expected in this,' he glanced at the sky. 'MacLean, if you would show Duff the situation.'

'Sir, ye could cry on Eolhwynne,' Duff said.[1]

'Indeed, have her assist you. Only have us across the bridge in one piece. If need be, I shall dismount, and those in the drag must do likewise. Go to it.'

MacDonald retreated to his seat and raised the window, cursing the weather whose vicissitudes tore up so much of the country with gale and rain. To add expenditure to delay, this was a district road and its upkeep fell upon the estate.[2]

Mulling on this, he took out his pipe and tobacco while keeping an eye and ear on the scene outside, first overhearing Duff speaking to Eolhwynne and then seeing them walk with MacLean toward the stricken bridge. The woman had wrapped a dark red cloak about her against the rain but left herself bareheaded. One hand she had clamped to her hair to prevent the wind blowing it while the other held the pouch with her runes. His instinct was to trust the pragmatic Duff rather than magick and he hoped the woman was not long in satisfying whatever gods or spirits guarded their way, or at least no longer than it took Duff to appraise the state of the bridge.

Meantime, the MacLeans had not let this interruption delay unloading their cart. The eldest son, MacDonald

---

[1] To 'cry on' someone is to ask them to perform a service. *N.W.*
[2] As opposed to a parliamentary road which was built and maintained from the public purse. *N.W.*

recalled, had drowned the previous fall—the funeral was the last occasion he had made use of the chariot—and he was surprised to see the boy's mother still wore mourning blacks. In the absence of their father, a pair of brothers, themselves nearly men, stood in the back of the cart and busily pitched the sodden seaware into the drying yard while their crow-garbed mother held the horse's bridle, though he thought the skinny beast more likely to drop dead from fatigue than upset the cart behind it. Several seconds of vague attention sparked recollection it had once dwelt in his stables at Duntulm and most probably had hauled the very carriage in which he now sat.

Among this scene, and in between his own carriage and the drag, a boy and girl, both barefoot, darted with shrieks and grimaces and generally made themselves a nuisance.

After ten minutes of this diverting scene and with his pipe well alight, MacDonald saw Duff and Eolhwynne return with MacLean. Duff and MacLean looked no different, but Eolhwynne's wet skirts suggested she had been in the water. Duff approached and he lowered the window.

'How is it?'

'Well enough, sir, but best have ye oot here fer the while. I'll take the horse over w' yer car, then give lad a hand with drag. Eolhwynne reckons likewise.'

The woman had joined Duff at the window. Rain flecked her hair, but despite the inclement conditions, she seemed in her element and her cheeks had a rosy glow.

'What say you?' MacDonald expected to hear little of use, but he should be considerate.

'The river is very forceful, my Lord. I cannot tell what damage it has done.'

'But we are safe?' he pushed.

'I believe so, though I do not think the bridge will stand much longer.'

Repairs and a bill: at least it would provide work for some. He gritted his teeth and, taking his coat with him, stepped down. The ridge was black against the sky but seemed to offer no protection from wind or rain. Everything ran with water, and he felt the damp reach in through his layers of clothing, like prying fingers. Duff led the horse and carriage across the bridge without alarm and seeing them safely crossed he instantly followed and retook his seat. Presently, with the drag also across, the journey continued and taking out his watch he calculated they had lost perhaps forty minutes of the day.

MacLean's industry was admirable, but kelp was better on the land than burnt for ash. What might it fetch? Two and one half crowns a ton, a pittance, he reckoned, and settling into a familiar line of thought, he recalled his grandfather, glass in hand and back to the fire, one hand slicing the air like a rapier as he berated Buonoparte's evil ways.

The fire was in an Edenborough town house bought on the proceeds from kelp for, as was then the fashion, Grandfather had hired a tacksman to run the estate and only visited Duntulm in the season for grouse shoots and deer stalking with his expensive city friends. While they sported in the hills, men laboured on the shore to cut the best of the weed, launching their little boats even in appalling weather. Grandfather and his tacksmen brought settlers to the island and encouraged early marriage to bring big families, eager for ever more men to cut the kelp and greater profit on the scaleyard at Portree. Ricks piled high all summer and as the skies yellowed with smoke, the MacDonalds departed for Edenborough without a backward glance at the coming winter.

For him, it was always a time of sadness, for Arthur's Seat seemed poor exchange for the wonders of the Quiraing. Both Grandfather and Father blamed his melancholy and love of wild places on too much poetry. Maud, his elder sister, had understood, but then Maud had understood everyone; that was her gift.

The war with Buonoparte over, peace brought imports of Spanish *barilla* and the beginning of the end for the kelp.

Superior to kelp ash and a fraction the price, overnight, or so it seemed, the kelp market collapsed from twenty crowns to barely five. A tariff on *barilla* helped kelp survive another decade, but the soap and glass manufacturers who were its chief customers, forced repeal and the price halved again. Except for a few holdfasts like the MacLeans, kelp was finished and thus had a celebrated victory over the French led to famine, penury, and hopelessness at home. A shipowner now rented the Edenborough town house and Grandfather's grouse had long ago filled the crofter's cook pots. Only the deer remained to wander the lonely hills.[1]

Grandfather, for all his faults, had been good company, at least until his final chair-bound years. Duntulm was a glum place nowadays and he wondered how Clara bore it. At least he would be meeting Georgie at Inverness. Sometimes he regretted persuading George that Aberdeen was the best Catholic university in Scotland.

The thought of his son brought to mind the boy's face. Those deep brown eyes and a habit of compressing his mouth into a moue during rare moments of seriousness, George took from Rebecca, his first wife. Since her death, he had been ten years alone at Duntulm, a grave mistake, he now saw, for solitude had not suited him half as well as he thought and was cruel on the boy. Thank God for Clara, and he had to thank God for he could see no quality in himself to win her favour, for this last year, even when loneliness seemed an unbreakable habit, her sweet nature and unguarded affections had lifted his spirits. All the more bitter this foul business called him away at such a time.

---

[1] Lord MacLeod of Dunvegan is known to have been critical of the management of his estates during his father and grandfather's tenure and it is likely MacGregor based much of this passage on MacLeod's opinions. MacGregor's journals show he and Lady Helena greatly enjoyed their stay at Dunvegan, however, there was one subject where he and Lord MacLeod agreed to differ: MacLeod was a firm supporter of the clearances while MacGregor thought them inhumane and degrading. *N.W.*

He had been inattentive and allowed his pipe to go out. Relighting it, MacDonald sat back and pulled his coat about him for warmth. Shuffling through *The Times* and the surveyor's report, he picked up the novel and, damned if he was going to be constrained by MacGregor's contrivances, opened a page at random and began reading, but his thoughts continued to stray.

He had inherited the estate and title in eighteen-thirty-eight, the year Georgie was born and five years after the death of his own father who fell in the Dutch wars. Peace had come, but Grandfather, distrustful of politics, urged him to clear land for sheep. Sheep, the old man calculated, would profit the estate twice what it would receive through rent, should parliament rescind the duty on *barilla*.

Of course, Grandfather was not the only laird to see the future in sheep and thousands of evicted tenants had taken to emigrant ships for Labrador or Quebeck. Nevertheless, the old man put few of his plans into effect: "Change," he had said, "is for the young, not an old invalid." Instead, he pointed to deficiencies at Duntulm: the roof of the Great Hall and the inadequacy of the kitchens and their distance from the dining room, leading food to arrive cold at the table. All these, Grandfather said, would benefit from the profit from sheep, though why they had not benefited from kelp was never made clear.

Twenty years after Grandfather's death, there were no more sheep than the uplands could support and none of his tenants had lost their lands. The sag in the Great Hall's roof remained, but the old morning room now served as family dining room and, with a hoist to the kitchens below, MacDonald enjoyed his dinners hot. He was content with his stewardship of the estate.

§

They stopped to water the horses at Lealt Bridge, and in a little over one hour arrived at the Royal Hotel, Portree, where a boy approached the carriage. MacDonald recognised Dixon's runner.

'MacDonald, sir, Mr Dixon was speirin if ye had time t'see him afore ye gae.'

'I do,' MacDonald replied. 'He is at the house?'

'Be so, sir. Shall I run fetch him?'

'Indeed. But quick, I do not expect to be above an hour.'

There would be such matters, MacDonald thought, there always were. The lad was fleet-footed and should take five minutes to get to Portree House. Murdo Dixon would need rather more to return. He trusted there was no delay. Meantime, Duff and McNeil had his horse out of the shafts and a stable boy stood by with a decent looking post horse.[1]

'John, where is Eolhwynne?'

'Inby, sir,' Duff said. 'They'd a room set fer her.'[2]

'Good. I expect to be a while with Mr Dixon. You have time for a dram. God knows you must need it today,' the man's coat was dark with rain. 'You too, McNeil. My account, naturally.'

'Gracious of ye, sir,' Duff said. 'An' the laddie?'

MacDonald smiled. 'I leave to your conscience.'

'If I warrant it, dis he as well. I'll look oot fer him.'

Splashing back to the hotel entrance MacDonald let himself in, finding the snug empty and its fire lit. Neave took away his hat and coat for drying and McNair, the hotel's license-keeper, came to see him.

'Greetings, yer lordship; a whisky, is it?'

'Thank you, yes.'

He sat down and leant toward the fire. From the saloon, he heard Gaelic, English, German and possibly Norwegian or Danish. Sips often refuged at Portree.

McNair brought him whisky and a jug of warm water.

'You have a crowd in this morning,' MacDonald said.

---

[1] A horse kept for private hire at an inn or coaching station. *N.W.*

[2] Respectable women rarely entered the public rooms of licensed premises and for the laird's spaewife to have done so would be highly inappropriate. *N.W.*

'Blow-ins,' McNair said, 'we're thranged the day; three boats storm-sted. Got one frae Bergen, a Hansard.[1] They were after a slate fer the officers: och, I tauld they, "Silver, or gae dry",' McNair tapped the bar top for emphasis. 'Whit dae they take me fer? Weather clears,' he pointed a finger skywards, 'they'll be aff wi' oot a care.'

'That flag brings out the worst in men,' he agreed.

The flag was the red and white of the Hanseatic Company. Hansard was the common name for them, though 'Jews of the Sea' was also popular and reflected their business practices. Feeling the welcome heat of the spirit in his chest, MacDonald glanced at his watch, finding the time a quarter after ten and stretched his legs toward the fire. Circulation returned to his feet.

Murdoch Dixon arrived in some quarter of an hour, leather bag in one hand and walking cane in the other. Setting the bag on the table and his cane against the chair, Dixon shook his hand and sat opposite him.

'You were delayed.' Dixon said.

'Both leaving Duntulm and again at Brogaig,' he replied.

Dixon adjusted his spectacles and opened a notebook.

'At Brogaig,' MacDonald continued, 'have the road inspector look at the bridge.'

'Repairs?' Dixon asked.

'Most likely, agree to whatever he decides. We are obliged to maintain the road and cannot argue against him. Now to business: I shall be away at least three weeks. Confidentially, the funeral is set for the twelfth but that has not yet been made public.'

Dixon scribbled away attentively.

'How soon I can return after that date, is uncertain,' he concluded.

---

[1] Norway in 1860 remained a dependency of Denmark (it gained independence in 1923) and Bergen housed one of the four great kontore of the Hanseatic Company (the others being at Bruges, St Petersburg, and Winchester). The company's dominance of Bergen led to it being known colloquially as Little Germany. *N.W.*

Dixon glanced up. 'I did not think you would delay returning. What of Clara?'

'I appreciate your concern, and I have not forgotten her condition; quite the contrary, in idle moments I think of nothing else, but I find William's death troubling, don't you agree?'

However informally he might speak to them, relations with almost all his people were those of master and servant. The exception was his factor, Murdoch Dixon, a man he regarded as a friend.

'It does seem unnatural,' Dixon said, 'healthy young men rarely drop dead without reason.'

'You understand, then?'

'I do.' Dixon paused. 'There will be an official investigation,' he said in mollifying tone.

'Which will reveal what is 'officially' acceptable,' he said dismissively. 'I learned enough about the Royal Court from Maud when she was with us. A Royal House always protects itself, even from its sons;[1] or should I say, especially from its sons, since they are the most likely to bring it disrepute.'

Dixon did not argue, though neither did he appear wholly convinced.

'In any event,' MacDonald continued, 'William was half MacDonald, and as clan chief I have the right to know how he died. You have sent notice to the shipping company at Inverness?'

'For an additional cabin, yes,' Dixon was clearly anxious for a change of subject. 'I hired a post-boy. He assures me he handed it to the mail coach at Lochalsh. You could confirm by postrider when you reach Invermoriston tomorrow evening; they make regular passage through the glen.'

MacDonald nodded. 'Well, what have you for me?'

Dixon took a sheaf of letters from the bag. 'These are

---

[1] MacDonald's maxim is borrowed from Kristoffer Møller's *Tamerlane the Tyrant*, first performed at the Kugleteater, Roskilde in 1632. MacGregor was happy to acknowledge the plot for *This Iron Race* owed a good deal to the 'Great Dane'. *N.W.*

received yesterday and this morning. Condolences, in the main, though this one is curious.' Dixon showed it him. The letter had a drawing attached. 'Robert Lockhart proposes a memorial, in stone, for the prince.'

MacDonald did not understand.

'You recall Lockhart has part share in the Cill Chriosd Quarry,' Dixon said.

'Good God. The boy's not even cold,' he took the letter. 'What are these numbers?'

'Dimensions and costs, I haven't studied it carefully.'

'There is a Hansard weather-bound here. Lockhart would do well with them, I fancy,' MacDonald said.

Dixon gathered the letters together and handed them over the table. There must be thirty in number, he thought, and each must have a reply.

'Any other matters?' he asked.

'The Emigration Society,'[1] the factor handed him a letter with several pages attached. 'I need your authorisation to release the monies.'

Settling himself, MacDonald glanced at the names, then, bitten by guilt, read more slowly. Some he could put a face to, others he recalled the land they rented; a few, to his shame, he could not place at all. Each crofter required his permission to vacate the land and would receive ten crown, five schilling, as agreed between the estate and the Society, plus the cost of passage at steerage rate for the man and his dependants.

He paid closest attention to the ship's particulars, given in at the foot of the document: "*Hector,*" he read, "of the Blue Star Company, Liverpool: three-masted brig with auxiliary engine: Master Joseph Watkins, First Mate Uriah Copper. Crew of forty-five, all temperate and reliable men."

---

[1] Despite their benevolent-seeming name, the Emigration Societies were parliamentary bodies with a remit to reduce expenditure on Poor Relief in the so-called 'congested' areas by encouraging emigration and assisting landlords to forcibly clear their lands. Three societies covered Scotland with similar bodies appointed by Lunden operating in Eireland and parts of Gwalia. *N.W.*

The ship would vittle at Portree and leave on the fourteenth for Arcadia[1] and Quebeck.

'Next Wednesday,' he mused. 'Is she a good ship?'

'Three crossings,' Dixon said, 'a few losses in steerage but no contagions. I would not put faith in 'temperate'.'

'Perhaps not. Call on her captain: see he runs a good ship. Your pen.'

There were always losses. Reluctant to leave the land they had known all their lives, many were half-starved even before the rigours of the passage. His grandfather would have dismissed the sentiment, but the MacDonalds had failed these wretches.

He signed the papers and returned them to Dixon.

'That's it, then?'

'Apart from my personal condolences, sir; though you might persuade Lord Egan to tax Spanish *barilla*.'

He smiled. 'I will try; though doubt he'll be swayed.'

The snug door opened, and Duff entered.

'Sir, we kin gae when yer ready.'

'Thank you. Inform McNair.'

Duff left and Dixon removed his spectacles and closed the leather bag. He looked as though he had bitten an apple and found it sour. MacDonald sympathised and took his hand.

'Thank you, Murdoch. Thank you indeed. Not a word to any of my concerns regarding William.'

'Clara knows of your intentions?'

'She does.'

'I wondered why Eolhwynne is with you,' Dixon said. 'She may be useful to you.'

'You believe so?' he asked. 'Spacing is a mystery to me, always has been. Ethelfeyrda, I might have trusted, but Eolhwynne's damnably young. Frankly, I would have her remain at Duntulm, but Clara insisted she go with me. It was the price for taking her into my confidence.'

---

[1] Now the Canadian Province of Newfoundland. *N.W.*

McNair joined them, followed by Gillanders Neave with his hat and coat, both clean and certainly drier.

'Make the most of your blow-ins, McNair. I must be off.'

Neave helped him into the coat.

'It was a good day fer hostellers when Hansards gave up temperance,' McNair said. 'God speed an' preserve ye, sir.'

Murdoch Dixon came with him to the roadside. The rain had increased, and McNeil stood ready to open the carriage door with a cape over his head and shoulders.

'If *He* wished me speed, Murdoch, He would have sent fair weather. Goodbye, friend, and take care of my people. I do not care for this business at Winchester, not at all. One final thought: the emigrants, how many were employed at Lockhart's quarry?'

'Two or three,' Dixon said, 'I can confirm and write you at Winchester.'

'Do so, and tell Mr Lockhart I am considering his offer, with conditions.'

He nodded for McNeil to open the door and leapt aboard.

II

William of Normandy's fleet lay in ruins; destroyed by storm before reaching Anglia's shore. Now steeped in blood, the brothers Edwin and Morcar, earls of Mercia and Northumberland, sought to overthrow the power of Wessex and plotted the death of Harold Godwinsson...[1]

An hour into the novel, he found MacGregor had the curious ability to bring the past to vigorous life and tell it as though truths, other than the historical, might prevail, but despite the author's skill, the whisky and the regular motion of the carriage proved stronger, and closing the book, MacDonald leant against the seat back and closed his eyes.

---

[1] King Harold II, 1066–1072, the last of the Saxon kings. His defeat at Lincoln in October 1072 by Sweyn Hardarcnut, began six centuries of Danish rule in Anglia. *N.W.*

The inn at Broadford arrived quickly. As at the Royal, he found a fire lit and his rightful dram quickly offered. Food was simple fare, but agreeable: mutton broth followed by cold venison with juniper sauce and potato mashed with butter. Several glasses of port washed it down. Except to serve the food, the hosteller said little, and no one disturbed him. Immediately on retaking his carriage MacDonald fell into a profound slumber and remained thus until woken by a jarring motion. Seeing they were arrived at Kyleakin, the violent shaking arising from the granite setts of the quayside, MacDonald opened his pocket glass and smoothed his hair and straightened his collar before the carriage drew up at the Kyle Inn: Kyleakin's only hostelry of note.

Once halted, John Duff opened the door for him.

'Cobbles are wet, sir. Have care, noo.'

His vantage in the carriage doorway gave MacDonald an unusual view of his head coachman: the dome of a tweed hat above a foreshortened face seemingly all brow and cheekbones. He thought it an honest face, save for the luxuriant moustache and beard concealing the man's mouth and jaw. Collecting his hat and cane from the seat, he exited backward and noted the rain had ceased and streaks of blue now broke up the cloud.

'The ferry?' he asked.

'Nar ready fer us,' Duff answered.

Lord MacDonald saw Neave descending from the drag which had pulled up behind them.

'Gill, get to the ferry and see all is in order.'

'Ay, sir.'

The wind was damnably cold. Wanting exercise to restore his limbs, MacDonald walked along the quay where a line of boats waited out the bad weather. A few miserable looking gulls stood sentinel on their masts. Farther off, where the beach met the surf, Calum MacAuley and his son, Alasdair, were readying the ferryboat for them.

Beyond the harbour mouth, a beam of sunlight lit up the mountains, but the sea remained forbidding.

'My Lord?'

He turned to find Eolhwynne and her peregrine falcon. A leather cap covered its eyes and the bird sat absolutely still on the woman's arm: a leather gauntlet protecting her from the talons. In addition to the gauntlet, the woman had replaced her red travelling cloak with a broad strap worn diagonally over the left shoulder. Of black leather and decorated with various designs, he had no idea of its function, except she always wore it when handling the bird.

'I trust the journey has not been unpleasant,' he said.

'I do not look to my own comfort, my Lord,' she said. 'I must be certain of your crossing.'

'Is that necessary? There is our destination.' He gestured to the huddle of houses across the strait.

'I am advised there are dangerous currents, and the wind has changed. Can you not feel it, my Lord?' Her eyes were dark and serious.

'It's got colder, I grant you,' he said.

Eolhwynne removed the cover from the bird, and it looked around with a rapid motion alternated with stillness. Watching the wind ruffle its feathers, it occurred to him the woman must be cold. Her dress, of the same dark red as her cloak, seemed scant protection.

'Your bird seems eager, and a little spacing can do no harm,' he said.

'Thank you, my Lord. May I ask which our ship is?'

'I should not call it a ship.' He indicated the ferry. 'Though it is safer than it seems,' he added, sensing her alarm. 'Though more suited to cattle and sheep than ourselves.'

He would have caught John Duff's eye for a moment's shared scepticism, but the coachman was busy and did not see him.

Eolhwynne's expression had not changed, nor that of her bird, whose gaze was disconcerting.

'Please continue. Act as you see fit.'

'Thank you, my Lord.' Eolhwynne curtsied and turned away. He watched as she slipped the jesses from her wrist and cast the falcon into the air. It needed only to flick its wings to take it soaring into the air above the harbour.

Having long ago decided spaewifery and all matters drùidheachd were beyond him, MacDonald turned away and sought escape from the wind.

Kyleakin only existed to serve those passing to and from the mainland and offered little to detain them, save a scrabble of houses and one decent inn.[1]

Plainly, Duff believed he would prefer to wait at the inn, but he had had his fill of such places today. One other building stood out from its neighbours, a small stone chapel with its door propped open with a stone. Inside it followed the custom of the Free Kirk, with limewashed walls and a central aisle paved in red tiles. 'The path of faith is paved in blood', he recalled.

To the sides of the aisle were the plain wooden tables and benches where the congregation sat and between them at the farther end a table dressed in white cloth bearing a pair of iron candleholders. There was no altar, only a pulpit of raw oak and a wooden cross.

It was too austere for his Catholic sensibilities, but God was present here, no less than He was in the Chapel of St Mary in Portree.

Taking a Gaelic Society prayer book,[2] MacDonald sat at a bench to read but soon found himself struggling, for though he could speak and understand Gaelic well enough, he had little use for the written language and the disparity between pronunciation and spelling proved beyond him.

---

[1] According to his journal, MacGregor and Lady Helena passed through Kyleakin on October 23, two days after receiving news of his father's final illness. *N.W.*

[2] Formed in 1837, the Gaelic Society printed Bibles and other religious texts and distributed them freely throughout Highland Scotland to encourage retention of the 'auld tongue'. It was dissolved in 1868 under pressure from parliament in Edenborough who regarded both it and Gaelic speaking in general as encouraging sedition. *N.W.*

Presently a tall man entered from a side door. An unbuttoned coat revealed vestments and MacDonald made to stand.

'Please, there is no need,' the churchman said.

'You would be Father Dobie.'

MacDonald did not know the man directly but knew of him. Father Dobie had not been on the island more than six months, and the Free Kirk itself was something of a newcomer. The man was certainly striking, with pale grey hair worn almost to the shoulder and piercing deep-set eyes. He wondered if Father Dobie recalled his family were Catholic.

'My condolences on your loss,' Father Dobie's tone was reassuring. 'Though, if I may be candid, a man soon tires of that phrase. He who tells it, tells it once, he who hears, hears it many times.'

Father Dobie leant across the table to put fresh candles in the holders.

'I have not tired of it yet,' MacDonald said. 'The simple matter is I did not know my nephew as well as I ought. Perhaps when I am at Winchester I shall feel more.'

The minister began sweeping the floor. 'Your son is not travelling with you?'

'I meet him at Inverness, he is a scholar there. You do not object to my waiting? I saw the door open.'

Dobie smiled. 'There are those who would object, but God does not bar the door to His house, and nor shall I. However, this particular door is open because I have a less welcome guest,' the man pointed to the roof where a pigeon squatted on one of the beams.

'Leviticus, is it not?' MacDonald asked.

'For childbirth, indeed so. "A pigeon unto the door of the tabernacle, unto the priest".[1] But this is no wild bird, only a messenger idling on its task.'

MacDonald saw the canister on the bird's leg. Like him, it had taken refuge from the wind.

---

[1] Leviticus Ch. V. *N.W.*

'You keep a spaewife,' Father Dobie said. He had stopped at the outer door from where he had view of the quayside.

'I do. It is a family tradition,' MacDonald replied. Many in the church were hostile to spaers and magick of all kind, but to his surprise Father Dobie smiled agreeably.

'You need not fear my wrath; I have no quarrel with spaers any more than I have with the Church of Rome.'

'I am relieved to hear it,' MacDonald said. 'My family has employed spaers for near five hundred years. I am not one to abandon tradition, though I doubt their usefulness. Eolhwynne is ensuring I have *safe* passage.'

'You're a sceptic,' Father Dobie returned his broom to the vestry. 'Perhaps I should have you leave after all.' The man's humour took the menace from the words. 'Spaers are a curious breed, but accepting it is God's wisdom to deny to a few those gifts he naturally gives to the many; I refer to the deaf and blind among us, we should allow it is also in his power to grant exceptional gifts to a rare few.'

An uncommon opinion, MacDonald thought. At best, the Free Church tolerated spaewives.

Father Dobie glanced around the room, and apparently satisfied with his work, came over to shake his hand. The man's grip was as reassuring as his gaze.

'I must be away. May I wish you safe journey and if you would leave the door as you found it. Hopefully the bird will take the hint.'

'I shall. And thank you.'

Father Dobie left by the side door and in the silence, MacDonald found his eyes drawn up to the pigeon.

Sometime later, not long surely, he thought, though time in a church moves differently to time without, Eolhwynne returned.

'We have safe passage I trust?'

'Fàidh saw dark cloud to the west,' Eolhwynne said and closed the door behind her. 'We must expect more rain.'

'More rain,' he said without interest, 'well, it has not delayed us thus far.' She had not re-hooded her bird and its gaze had fixed on him in a way he found quite disconcerting.

'May I ask when you last made use of the ferry?'

'What?' he turned his attention back to the spaewife, 'Oh, Christmas, I believe. Clara and I visited Sir David, the gentleman with whom we are staying this evening. I assure you, it is quite safe.'

The woman's gaze was intense under the black arch of her brows. Her apparent eagerness to please, irritated him but he allowed her concern was genuine, if misguided. He was, though, intrigued by the bird perched on her wrist and particularly its eyes, which shone like black pearls within a halo of vivid yellow. Staring at them he had the curious impression he was addressed by two individuals and not one. It unsettled him and his reaction was to take a step back and pick up the prayer book once more.

'If that is all, you should rejoin Neave and McNeil,' he said.

'Sir, I must ask, you know of no losses from it? No—'

'Heavens no! Now stop troubling me with these things.' His voice echoed off the walls and his cheeks flushed. 'Please,' he tried to sound reasonable. 'I have enough concerns without these fancies. I know the ferry to be reliable and that is an end of it.'

He returned the prayer book to its shelf.

'I apologise,' Eolhwynne's voice had lost its insistence. 'I only sought—*Fàidh!*'

Air brushed his face, and a sharp ringing noise troubled his ears. The falcon had flown after the pigeon. Alert to its peril, the bird scurried to a gap between the wall plate and the roof beams where the falcon could not pounce. Unable to dive and take its prey, the falcon landed on a crossbeam, its head bobbed as it stared at the pigeon. The traces dangled about its legs and Eolhwynne leapt onto one of the tables to reach but the pigeon darted across the room with the falcon following.

'Fàidh. Come!'

Eolhwynne stood beneath the bird, holding her

gauntleted hand up. Tears streaked her face, and her cheeks were scarlet, but the falcon had eyes only for the pigeon. The ringing came from a small bell attached to the falcon's traces and each trace ended in a silver ring, about the size of a one crown piece.[1] Apart from the bell, the bird's flight was silent while the pigeon's wingtips met with a sharp noise, like a pistol shot. The falcon had speed, but could not use it in a confined space, while the pigeon had agility. Repeatedly, the falcon closed on the bird, but each time could not turn swiftly enough to grasp it.

Eventually the falcon settled on the ledge of the west window. Its beak gaped and its tail twitched in agitation as it caught its breath.

'Is there anything I might do?' he asked.

'She will come,' Eolhwynne said. 'I trust her.'

He could not tell if she believed what she said. Footsteps sounded and Father Dobie entered noisily from the vestry.

'Faith, who asks for faith?' The minister acknowledged him and then turned to Eolhwynne, before he caught sight of the pigeon upon the communion cloth.

'Blasted creature!'

'Pray, Father, let it be,' MacDonald said.

Father Dobie glanced from him to Eolhwynne.

'It was ye,' he said. 'Ye asked for faith?'

'No,' Eolhwynne said. 'Fàidh is the name of my familiar.' She pointed at the falcon.[2]

'Bless me!' the minister said.

'We have a battle on our hands,' MacDonald said.

'I am truly sorry, I did not leash her.'

'Father, this is Eolhwynne, my spaewife. Eolhwynne, Father Dobie,' MacDonald crossed the chapel and glanced into the vestry. 'We must close this,' he pushed the door to, 'and open the outer door. Eolhwynne, if you would, please. I

---

[1] The bell allows the falconer to locate the bird after it has made a kill. *N.W.*

[2] The name is Gaelic with the meaning of 'prophet'. *N.W.*

believe your bird will return only when she has won or lost her prize.'

Eolhwynne nodded but as she went to open the main door she suddenly recoiled.

'The latch is iron,' Father Dobie murmured. 'Child, leave it to me.'

Dobie pushed the door back against the wall as far as it would go, letting in wind and light.

Eolhwynne was rubbing her hand; he had forgotten spaewives could not bear the touch of iron.

'Now we wait,' MacDonald said. 'I trust, Father, you are not a sporting man.'

They had tipped the odds in the falcon's favour. The pigeon, seeing the open door, fluttered across the room. The falcon waited its chance. Eolhwynne's gaze was fixed on her bird.

They did not wait long. The pigeon swooped almost to the floor, then climbed as though about to land on a table. The falcon followed a yard behind but the last moment, the pigeon jinked and flew out the door. The falcon overshot and had to circle the room. Eolhwynne flung herself across the doorway, and for a moment, the bird appeared to hesitate, torn between instinct and training. Inevitably, to his mind, instinct prevailed. Eolhwynne did not move and as the bird swooped through the door one of the silver rings struck her across the face.

'Quickly now!' He ran to the door with Father Dobie following. Eolhwynne was outside on the quay wiping her forehead. The pigeon flew up over the harbour, but the falcon was plummeting after it. There was no escape and after a final, desperate turn, the pigeon stalled in the air and the bird took it.

The bird circled. Its prize limp in its talons.

'Extraordinary,' Father Dobie said.

Eolhwynne waited for the bird at the quayside. The wind caught the woman's red dress, pressing the material against her waist and hip and she continually had to push her hair clear of her face. This time the bird came to her, landing on the quayside and instinctively spreading its wings to cover the pigeon. Eolhwynne knelt, took the bird onto her gauntlet, and looped the jesses around her wrist.

'She will be mortified,' Father Dobie said.

Eolhwynne stood and walked away. MacDonald called after her and she turned and wiped her eyes.

'I must go. I am a disgrace. I apologise to you also, Father, forgive me.' The woman turned and hurried away leaving both men staring at her back. Father Dobie spoke first.

'When she is herself again would you be so good to tell her this escapade has quite cheered my day. It may even have given me an idea for a sermon.'

'I shall, but I will give you my apologies also: should you find any damage, Murdoch Dixon in Portree will see it right.'

'I cannot think there will be any need. Your spaewife is young and with much to learn. Now, the bird carried a message, and we are its recipients.'

Dobie picked up the bird and held it as MacDonald removed the roll of waxed paper.

'It has a seal upon it,' he said, 'but I cannot make it out.' He slipped a fingernail under the seal and unrolled the message while Father Dobie tossed the pigeon into the harbour. Several gulls immediately descended to investigate.

'Your coachman is coming for you,' Father Dobie said.

'He will tell me we are ready to depart.'

The paper was flimsy, and he cupped his hand to shelter it from the wind.

'German,' he said. '"Attn. CNn. *Goldenbusse*, Weatherbound, Portree. Expect 2 days delay. Yrs. Kpt. Hausmann." There is a Hansard weatherbound at Portree.'

'Their bird did not get far,' Father Dobie said.

'No matter, we owe them no favours.' He let the wind take the fragment of paper and shook Father Dobie's hand. 'Now I must go.'

'The lass intends well,' Father Dobie said, 'Doubtless, she will learn caution.'

'One hopes so. Thank you.'

The Minister turned back to the kirk and as he left, he saw gulls fighting over the dead pigeon. The ugliness of their gaping yellow beaks and angry cries was at odds with their beauty in the air.

'MacAuley's set fer us, sir,' Duff said. The coachman fell in beside him. 'Yon Eolhwynne is tishied.' It was both statement and enquiry.

'Her falcon got loose in the kirk, chased a pigeon out,' he said. 'I don't think she wants everyone to know.'

'I fancy we all saw what came o' pigeon,' Duff said.

'Where is she now?'

'In the drag, sir. No certain she wants tae come oot.'

'Lord MacDonald!'

It was Calum MacAuley calling him from beneath the harbour wall. 'Mr Duff reckons ye'll no wait on the drag.'

'Agreed, Gill will ride up with you,' he said to Duff. 'I shall need him with me at Dornie. Finlay and Eolhwynne will remain with the drag.'

The carriage had been hauled up planks laid over the boat's transom and made secure.

'I shall be with you presently, Mr MacAuley.'

'This bit o' weather winna wait on, sir.'

'I know,' he said without thinking, 'we are due more rain.'

MacAuley nodded. 'Yon spaer's bird will have seen it.'

He had Neave remove those items from the drag he would have immediate need of at Dornie, then spoke to Iain Duff, saying, 'Your father is taking me directly on when we land. How many times have you driven the Dornie Road?'

'Twice, sir, but I've ridden it wi ma father often enough.'

'Good. Mr McNeil, ride up with him. It will be dark soon and two sets of eyes are better than one.'

'Ay, sir.'

'Milord, I reckon Eolhwynne cud put up bird t' watch oot fer us.' Iain grinned.

'I think not young man,' he knew the boy was jesting, 'but take care on the road.'

The trickiest assignation he left to last. Having knocked on the door of the drag, he did not wait for reply before opening it. The falcon's cage sat on the floor with a cloth over it. There was no sound from within, but something stirred inside a wicker basket.

'I am truly sorry, Lord MacDonald,' Eolhwynne leant forward into the light, her hand clasping a handkerchief. 'Fàidh had been caged all day and I could not bear to restrain her so soon. It was foolish of me.'

'These things happen,' he said and smiled, in a manner he hoped reassuring. 'The adventure has been the highlight of a miserable day. You have a fine bird.'

'Thank you, sir. I do not deserve your kindness.'

'My cousin will make provision for you at Dornie. I am taking the boat with Mr Duff and Mr Neave. McNeil will ride with Iain. I would have you travel with me, but,' he indicated the basket and the bird cage. 'I fear there is not room.'

The woman wiped her eyes.

'My Lord, I fear I must ask... rather, I would prefer not to travel by your carriage, if that is acceptable.'

'Very well,' he said, frowning at the request, 'I shall see you at Dornie.'

Matters magickal were beyond him, but so, he had often found, were women.

Beyond the harbour, the swell took hold of the boat, pitching and rolling them unpleasantly. Sat in the bows exposed them to the worst of the motion and Lord MacDonald was glad of his coat to ward off the spray. Gillanders Neave was filling his pipe, his only distress the wind plucking the baccy from his fingers. John Duff sat peaceably next to Neave. He too had taken to his pipe.

Part of the boat's starboard rail was new wood and the frames below it repaired.

'Gill, that is recent, is it not?'

'I speired MacAuley of 't,' Neave said. 'They'd a wee bash month last.'

'Any losses?' he asked.

Neave took out his pipe. 'I dinna get yer meaning, sir.'

'Loss of life,' MacDonald explained.

'Oh, ay. If ye can call it that. Two sheep, so he says.'

The carriage rested on planks roped across the thwarts, amidships. Ropes about the axles and frame made all secure, and MacAuley's son, Alasdair, was checking the ropes. He went to speak to the boy.

'It's fast, sir,' Alasdair said.

'Glad of it. I am given to understand you had a collision a month back.'

The boy's face darkened. 'Ay, an' me da's not let us lose mind of 't. I was over keen tae get us in. Muckle swell was runnin', but nae excuse,' the boy ducked behind the carriage out of his father's sight. 'Da's taken price o' sheep out what he gives us. It's a muckle bit, sir an' I was for helpin' out the drovers. They wanted to be at Broadford by the night.'

'Skye is full of sheep. Too many, I feel,' MacDonald took the boy by the shoulder and led him away. 'Tell me of the repair.'

'Ye want t' ken of boatwright'n, sir?'

He would indulge the boy until he knew the true extent of the "wee bash." Gillanders and John Duff shifted over to give space as he and Alasdair studied the repaired timber.

'See, we doubled the ribs where they'd broken an' clinked it up. I fixed it, see'n as I broke it, like. It's good work, but no so good as it was.'

'No, I imagine not, thank you. I'll not delay you further.'

He returned to his seat in the bow.

'Eolhwynne saw it wasna right,' Neave said. 'Alasdair's got they clinks over-close. Weakened the frame.'

'Does his father know?'

'Oh ay,' Neave said, 'he kens it right enough. It's like this,' Neave leant closer and lowered his voice. 'If the laddie's all doon in the mouth he may get thinkin of elsewheres. Alasdair's a guid head on him an' a 'prentership down south wud suit him; but, if he gaes Calum's naebodie t' gie a hand wi ferry. That's truth of 't, sir.'

'And Eolhwynne knew the repair was poor?'

'Did she no tell ye, sir?'

'She tried to. I did not take her concern seriously.'

'Can I speak free, sir?' John Duff leant around Neave. Duff rarely spoke his mind and he readily agreed.

'Clearsight's strong in the lass. I ken there's times she seems off wi the faeries, but them as take time t' lissen to her hark what she says, if ye get ma meanin.'

'I do. I have been preoccupied of late.' MacDonald glanced at the damaged timbers. 'Away with the faeries? That is indeed what I thought of her. I shall take your advice John and thank you. Thank you both.'

A bright shaft of sunlight broke through the cloud and sparkled the waters. Eolhwynne might previously have known of MacAuley's accident: servant at Duntulm overhearing it from a drover, perhaps. Or she might have seen the recent repair work and assumed it the result of some mishap. Yet, if it had been some attempt to impress him, she had been curiously reticent and uncertain. No, the rational explanation would not do. It offended his ability to judge character. Spaewifery was vague, uncertain, hedged with maybes and suppositions, all things he was uncomfortable with, but he knew enough not to dismiss it as smoke and mirrors. When making travel arrangements he had intended for Eolhwynne to remain at Duntulm, believing Clara would welcome the girl's company in his absence, particularly in her condition. Instead, throwing his plans into disarray, Clara had insisted he take the spaer with him. He was grateful now. The girl had something, and he should not have dismissed her concern so lightly. He would make amends.

§

Some two hours later an insistent knocking on the roof woke him from deep sleep. It could only mean one thing, but he leant forward and dropped the window.

'Dornie, sir. Ye've a few minutes yet.'

Correctly, John Duff had alerted him to their arrival. He rapped his cane on the roof in acknowledgement and let the window down. The night air was refreshing. He repaired his hair from the disturbance of sleep and straightened out his sleeves. Neave would find fault, but it had been a trying day and he need only find his way through his cousin's welcome to whatever had been prepared for him. Eilean Donan seemed in perpetual rebuilding to suit fashion and he had no idea where and in what fashion he would spend the night.

He rubbed his eyes and smoothed out the sagging flesh below the lids. The carriage slowed and turned right. A hollow sound beneath the wheels told they were crossing the wooden bridge. He sat back and adjusted his hat. MacGregor's novel lay open, cover upwards on the seat. He had read a little until bad light made it impossible. He closed it now and set it aside. He had other plans for tomorrow and doubted he would be reading on. The carriage turned again and abruptly the noise redoubled, thrown back by the gatehouse walls. He leant forward in anticipation. A lantern swung in the dark courtyard.

They halted and a hand grasped the door from outside.

'Greetings cousin; how goes it? We have expected you this last three hours.'

> She spoke as he desired her;
> The gift of forgiving wives
> Can fill a man with sorrow.
> And smiling, concealed her fears with thyme.

He is one who bruises on the inside. As to my quest, I found in Lord MacDonald naught to redress, no cause to bless, and sought another. I found him with a lantern at Eilean Donan.

Editor's Remarks

The manuscript continues in the same shade of ink, suggesting he did not break off after completing the previous scene but rather left a line blank and noted the name 'MacDonald' to indicate the new chapter, along with the date, January 7, 1862. A note suggests he considered writing the chapter chronologically before deciding to begin with MacDonald's encounter with Bheathain and then backtrack to show his departure from Duntulm.

The date indicates his eagerness to return to work as soon as the Christmas celebrations were done with. Although he did not yet have children of his own to celebrate Christmas with, the Arbinger estate included the village and a number of farms, counting some two dozen families, all of whom were invited to the tenant's hall for a good dinner, music and storytelling. January 1862 was a resumption of this tradition after a lapse of three years and MacGregor was keen to celebrate in style, perhaps buoyed by news of Lady Helena's pregnancy, albeit there was no announcement at the gathering. According to Lady Helena's diary the children were given miniature hares made of white, green or pink sugar.

The text of chapter two is little altered between MacGregor's first draft and the first edition. There are a handful of alterations to the dialogue at the Royal Hotel which lessen MacDonald's criticism of The Clearances, and the portrayal of Eolhwynne's character in the first edition is notably less sympathetic, especially during the scene at the church in Kyleakin, but otherwise there are no omissions. MacGregor's writing throughout the chapter is fluid and there are relatively few corrections. That said, the character of a good-hearted laird struggling to adapt to changing economics had appeared under various names in a few of

MacGregor's earlier novels, so it is not surprising if Lord MacDonald presented him with few problems.

Esteem reflected in the eyes of those he loves
Chapter Three
Eilean Donan, evening of the day: The circumstances of Sir David Mackenzie, shewing faults in his character and the regrettable effects thereof

> A man warming feet and hands
> By his hearth keeps his heart in
> Winter and sees his esteem
> Reflected in the eyes of those he loves.

The journey ended and from the dark a lantern shone. Was this a man I would bless?

I

Sir David stepped back as his cousin emerged.

'All the better for seeing you, David. 'What hour is it?'

'Coming on seven.' He helped MacDonald down from the carriage: a shabby old thing of antique style. 'What kept you?'

'Business in Portree,' MacDonald shrugged aside his help. 'I have come straight from Kyle. The drag follows; it will not be here for some hours.'

'No matter; the kitchen will arrange supper for your people. We should have you inside. The evening is chill.'

Regretting he had come outside without a coat, Sir David ushered MacDonald past the servants and into the entrance hall where ancient pikes and war axes glimmered in the lamplight.[1] These were relics of the past, now anchored permanently to the walls; the rack of muskets beside the door spoke of more recent troubles.

---

[1] MacGregor returned overland from Skye to Edenborough in haste, considerably alarmed at news of his father's illness. He did not delay his journey at Dornie and except for a note regarding "a tower upon an island, much-restored and spoilt," (written, apparently in his carriage for the writing is near-illegible) he relied on imagination for his depiction of Eilean Donan. *N.W.*

Sir David's footman closed the door behind them and took MacDonald's hat and cane.

'The wind has turned to the north. With luck it will bring clear weather. Miserable day's travelling.'

'Allow me, Kel.' Sir David helped MacDonald out of his coat and handed it to the doorman.

'I planned for us to dine at eight,' he said. 'I could delay if it is too soon, but would prefer not, frankly. You are not my only guest; three fellows from the Emigration Commission[1] are with us.'

MacDonald frowned. 'What is their business?'

'Numbers and quotas: they tell me our colonies may fall to the French if we do not increase our numbers and Scots make good colonists.' He snuffed out the lantern.

'For the sake of politeness, I hope they will not find my position unreasonable,' MacDonald said. 'I signed papers for ninety emigrants this morning. However, as you are aware, I will not compel any man to leave. Eight for dinner is quite acceptable.'

The footman returned from hanging his cousin's coat and Sir David instructed him to show MacDonald to his room.

'I near forgot,' MacDonald said halfway up the stair. 'My spaewife is travelling with me. I believe I did not include her in my letter.'

'No trouble,' Sir David said. 'Ethelfeyrda can lodge with Sigel'inge tonight, she has a spare cot in her quarters.'

'Her name is Eolhwynne,' MacDonald said, 'if you recall, Ethelfeyrda left me at Christmas. I intended leaving the girl at Duntulm, but Clara insisted I take her with me.'

'Is there disagreement between them?'

'A little,' he admitted. 'My wife has listened to too many priests. I do not think she wishes Eolhwynne gone; rather she believes I have more use for her. Unexpectedly, I am

---

[1] A government body quite separate from the Emigration Societies which provided an overview on all aspects of emigration in the so-called 'Congested Districts' of Highland Scotland and report directly to the Secretary of Trade in Edenborough. *N.W.*

beginning to agree with her. But later, David, we must talk.'

Sir David saw MacDonald up the stair then left for the Great Hall. This was by some margin the largest room in his house and the least friendly. A small fire took the chill from the air but not from the judgemental glower of the portraits lining the walls. A few of the glum-faced men and unhappy women he had known in life, but most were dead long before he was born and they gazed down on the present with varying degrees of disapproval, or so he thought. Among 'the family', as he called his ancestors, were a few Royals, but while the family portraits were competent hackwork, the royal portraits were crude copies; however, they had served to advertise Mackenzie loyalties for the half and one century since the Union of the Crowns. Passing through an archway beneath the salmon-pink face of George I, he began to climb the spiral staircase to the upper floor. Voices came through a door, the hectoring tone of the Bishop of Stirling loudest among them. He would far rather be spending the evening with MacDonald; however, the Emigration Commission was influential in Edenborough and even now a Mackenzie man must take care to show his loyalty.

Lord Dundee caught his eye the moment he entered.

'Your cousin is well, we trust?'

'He is, and will join us for dinner, which will be at eight.'

'Most excellent,' said Sir Gordon. 'Highland air gives one an appetite.'

Brightly lit, the drawing room was a sharp contrast to the Great Hall below. Three men sat in wingback chairs about the hearth. Two were dressed in formal eveningwear and the third, the bishop, in black frockcoat with lace collar and cuffs. A fourth chair awaited his return to the party.

'Excellent, indeed,' said Lord Dundee, secretary of the Commission and the senior of the three.

Sir David filled his glass, a French crystal goblet engraved with the Mackenzie Arms, at the side table. Behind the table was his favourite picture in the room, a Dutch *vanitas*. It had once hung in full view, but Margaret detested the thing and to please her he had it lowered until one could only appreciate it while pouring oneself a drink.[1]

Replacing the decanter on the tray, Sir David tugged the bell pull beside the door and returned to his seat.

'My apologies for leaving you, gentlemen,' he said. 'I propose a toast in mind of my cousin's journey. I give you 'God save the King!''

'God save the King!' repeated all three.

'And Prince Alexander,' added Sir Gordon, 'now, he alone stands between us and Prince Oswald.'

Prince Oswald was Alexander's stepbrother; his mother was the king's second wife, Princess Charlotte of Bruges, sometimes known as the Flanders Cow. He was, by most accounts, a spoilt, ungracious creature.

They drank to Prince Alexander and lowered their glasses. The bishop coughed apologetically.

'I confess I do not hold Prince Oswald in such low opinion,' the bishop said. 'The Flemish are a sensible people, unlike the backward-looking Danes. This country ought to reconsider its loyalties: if Flanders leads the way in industry, we must follow.'

'Wherever it goes, Thomas, wherever it goes,' Sir Gordon said.

The bishop, one Thomas Waldegrave, did not reply.

Gifford entered to answer his call.

'My cousin is settling?' he asked.

'He is, sir. His manservant attends him.'

'Good. You recall he spoke of a spaewife?'

'I do, sir. I gi'en word on Sigel'inge. She'll make arrangements as suit.'

'Good. Pass on my apologies to Sigel'inge for the late notice.'

'Aye, sir.' The servant left and Sir David returned to the company.

'Difficulty, Sir David?' Dundee asked.

---

[1] A genre of still life painting popular in the 1600s emphasising the temporality of life and inevitability of death. *N.W.*

'A late addition to my cousin's party,' he said. 'His spaewife. It is no matter.'

'That is your opinion, Sir David,' the bishop said. 'The power of those women is unholy. A gentleman would have nothing to do with the dark arts.'

'Come now, Thomas,' Dundee said, 'we are guests here.'

'I must uphold the views of the church on this matter,' the bishop insisted.

'Indeed, you must,' Sir David said, 'though I find them at odds with my experience; my own spaewife is on good terms with the local minister. I am certain he regards her skills as neither unholy nor dark.'

'I can only speak for the Alban Church;[1] they are clear on the matter.'

'Please, gentlemen,' Sir Gordon said, 'this is unsavoury. I agree with you, Dundee. We are guests of Sir David and must respect his domestic arrangements and those of his cousin.'

'My point exactly,' Dundee said. 'Thomas, I believe you must apologise to our host.'

The bishop glared at his colleagues and kissed the crucifix around his neck.

'Very well; I meant no offence against your person, Sir David, or against your cousin. I apologise if any was taken.'

'I assure you I took no offence,' Sir David said.

'In any event spaewives are not within the remit of the Emigration Board,' Dundee said.

'One small matter.' Sir Gordon's face creased in thought. 'Sir David, did you not say your cousin's wife is with child?'

'I did. Why do you ask?'

'I am surprised your cousin has not left his spaewife with her. They are, quite apart from any other abilities, excellent midwives, are they not?'

'A good enquiry,' Dundee said, 'I recall were it not for my father's spaewife I would not have survived my first night on this earth!'

---

[1] Named after Albany, the ancient name for Scotland. *N.W.*

'Their nursing skills are admirable,' the bishop allowed.

'Apparently my cousin's wife persuaded him his need for a spaewife was greater than hers.'

'How curious,' Dundee said. 'Why might your cousin want her at Winchester?'

'Would he be open to our enquiring?' Sir Gordon asked.

'I trust so,' he said, 'I fully intend to discover it for myself.'

'Ah! Aha. Well put,' Sir Gordon said, 'in any event we have our own enquiry with Lord MacDonald.'

'Indeed?'

'Sir Gordon confirmed it while you were downstairs,' Dundee said. 'Your cousin's lands are congested[1] but rather than oblige his tenants to leave he is too easy with the poor relief. He should learn from you, Sir David. I doubt his family is so finely provided for.'

Sir Gordon nodded vigorously. 'We have noted on our travels that where a man has sheep, he has wealth and where he has tenants, he has none. That is the nub of it.'

'Indeed so,' agreed the bishop; 'it is not for us to morally approve or disapprove, merely to record the facts.'

'Wealth begets wealth, Sir David, poverty leads to despair,' Dundee added.

Poor Kel, what will these men do to you, Sir David thought.

Someone knocked at the door. He called 'enter' and Megan, the children's nurse, leant into the room. Small faces and suppressed voices huddled behind her.

'Sir, the children wish to say goodnight.'

'Of course.'

The nurse opened the door and the children filed in and stood eldest to youngest. Philip and Duncan bowed in turn to Lord Dundee, Sir Gordon, and the bishop, each trying to outdo the other in dignity. At twelve and eleven, there was a whole year between them, but it was not obvious, and

---

[1] Land with a greater population than it can profitably support. *N.W.*

Duncan was proud they could be mistaken for twins. Philip had determined on the army and Duncan had inevitably declared for the navy. Eight-year-old Briget curtsied while six-year-old Joseph fidgeted and glanced about.

'Goodnight, father,' Philip said.
'Goodnight, father,' Duncan echoed.
'Goodnight, boys.'
'Goodnight, father.'
'Goodnight, Briget.'
Joseph was staring at the bishop.
'Joseph?' The boy dragged his eyes away. To a child, Sir David imagined the bishop's black coat and long face were a little unnerving.
'Goodnight, Joseph.'
The boy muttered his reply and returned into line with his elder sister.

Hannah, five a week ago and still clutching her favourite doll, broke from the line and clambered up the side of his chair. Surrendering, he reached down and plucked his daughter onto his lap.

'Kiss dolly,' she whispered.
'I'm not sure I want to kiss dolly.'
'Dolly wants you to kiss her goodnight.' Hannah buried her face in his ear.
'Very well,' he said. Hannah held the doll for him, and he kissed its red cheek, finding the porcelain cold against his lips.

Megan had remained at the door and now called the children to her ready to lead them to bed: 'Little ones; leave Papa wi' his friends.' The children began to file out obediently and Hannah slid off his lap to hurry after her sister. Joseph, turning round in the doorway, stumbled on the hem of his nightgown and Megan scolded him as she closed the door.

The doll had left a stale taste on his lips and he finished his sherry to cleanse it.

'And there is the man's true wealth,' Dundee said to his companions. 'And you have another, so you were telling me.'

'Lorcan, my eldest: he is schooling at Glasgow,' Sir David said. 'I admit I am blessed. My family is my greatest joy.'

'A toast then,' Sir Gordon said and raised his glass.

'A moment please; mine is empty,' Sir David protested.

'Mine also,' said Dundee.

He refilled both glasses at the side table and once every man had a glass in hand, they raised them.

'Gentlemen,' Sir Gordon said, 'to a man's greatest joy: his children.'

§

Within the half hour, Sir David had retired to his chamber to dress for dinner; the Commission men and his cousin doing likewise in their guest rooms. McCandles, his valet, having laid out fresh clothes and set a bowl of hot water on the washstand with his shaving paraphernalia, Sir David unbuttoned his collar and pulled it loose with a discouraged sigh, then undressed to his undergarments. He was about to shave when a knock at the door interrupted him. Before he could answer it, Margaret entered.

'My dear, I will be down presently,' he said.

Margaret closed the door and leant back against it with her arms folded. She had gathered her hair under a black silk scarf and a jet necklace hung from her throat. It was a moment before he realised she was showing respect for Prince William, and belatedly decided on a black silk tie instead of the green he had intended to wear at dinner.

'You asked of Clara?' Margaret said with the air of one not easily moved.

'Kelso tells me she is well.' He brushed soap onto his face.

'It is too bad,' Margaret said. 'And he takes his spaewife with him. Who is Clara to confide in?'

'They have acquaintances in Portree and there are the McLeods at Dunvegan.' He shrugged. 'According to Kelso it was Clara's idea he take Eolhwynne.'

'You mean Ethelfeyrda, surely?'

He took up his razor and scraped from cheek to jawbone.

'No longer, so he tells me. Eolhwynne has been with him a few months. A pretty thing, rather young though.'

Margaret pursed her lips and stepped close behind him. 'Darling, do not tease me by pretending to notice other women.' Her hands were around his waist.

'My dear, you know I never tease.'

'Good,' she said and pinched the fold of flesh above his hipbone.

The razor nicked the skin near his ear lobe, and he anxiously checked in the mirror. It had not drawn blood.

'Besides,' Margaret continued, 'I know full well the woman has not yet arrived so you cannot possibly know if she is pretty or not.'

'Kel told me.'

'Liar. Your cousin would not notice such a thing.' She laughed. 'But Georgie might, I wonder if Kelso has thought of that. But my dear, though I agree he is impoverished by choice, I beg let us have no talk of sheep.'

'I will do my best,' he said, rinsing the razor in the bowl. 'However; the matter is not in my command.'

Margaret sighed. 'Those men are so disagreeable. Do you know, this morning I am certain I saw the bishop throw a stone at Sigel'inge's cat.'

'You loathe that cat.'

'Beside the point; fortunately, his aim is as bad as his manners. I must reconcile myself to a dull evening, then?'

'I fear so. Kelso intimated he wishes to speak to me privately, but it will have to wait 'til the others give us some peace.'

'You will forgive me if I retire early.'

'Of course, I only wish I might retire with you. Alas, I must stay, if only to defend Kel from the emigrationists.'

'Which you will do admirably,' Margaret said and kissed him on the shoulder before leaving.

Alone again, he finished his toilet and began dressing.

He was not blind to the injustice of the Clearances, but

they were not inherently cruel. He knew of many who, having taken to the ships, now had greater acreage and better quality of land than they could have dreamt of at home. Moreover, there were many other opportunities in the New World: vast tracts of timber; waters teeming with fish, beaver pelts and other furs; cities where a dozen, nay a hundred trades awaited a man prepared to learn. An unlucky few were lost on the passage, and some fell on hard times in their new land, but others wrote home to praise their fortune and entreat their family and loved ones to join them.

He called McCandles in: 'The tie, black is more suitable; and black cufflinks also.'

'Onyx or jet, sir?'

'I should prefer silk,' he said.

'Silk for the tie, Sir David; I was askin' o' cufflinks.'

He wished the fellow would show an ounce of wit but every one of his servants was meek as sheep.

'The jet will be fine, thank you.' McCandles left.

There had been shameful episodes, it was undeniable. Families evicted, houses torched; but such were common to all great endeavours. Nevertheless, Kelso regarded *inaction* as a virtue in itself. One had only to walk around Duntulm to see change was inexorable for the sea was destroying the very rock beneath. And if change was inevitable, Sir David averred, it must be directed. Chaos serves no one.

McCandles reappeared with cufflinks and tie. The cufflinks proved a fiddle and he had to ask the servant to assist him. Dismissing the man, Sir David turned to the mirror to straighten the end of his cuffs and brush a fallen hair from his shoulder before declaring himself presentable.

II

'I understand you travel with your spaer,' Sir Gordon said to Lord MacDonald across the dinner table.

The servants were presenting an entrée of beef consommé. Margaret had been served first, followed by the bishop and Lords MacDonald and Dundee. Sir Gordon would follow them. As custom demanded, he would be served last.

'I am, yes,' MacDonald replied.

Margaret gave his cousin a frosty look, but to Sir David's relief said nothing contrary.

'Forgive my interest,' Dundee said, 'but what purpose might she serve at Winchester?'

MacDonald seemed amused by the question. 'She has only recently entered service with me and is very young still. At Winchester, she will meet with spaewives from other schools. It will be a great benefit to her.'

'Ah.' Dundee leant forward and examined the content of his bowl before sniffing loudly and reclining in his chair. 'Indeed, yes, most sensible of you, MacDonald.'

Himself served, the servants departed, and they began eating. The smell from the consommé was appetising but all was not as it should be. The liquid should be a clear, light colour and this was cloudy with a faint sheen of beef fat obscuring the surface. It was impossible to get decent staff in the Highlands and harder to invest a Highlander with the subtler arts of cooking. He imagined Margaret must have noted the cloudiness too, and perhaps Lord Dundee and Sir Gordon, both educated men. A glance at the Bishop of Stirling showed he need not consider his opinion for he was busily shredding a square of bread into the consommé even as he replied to MacDonald, saying, 'You may not find as many as you hope. The tradition of spaewives is passing.'

'In France and the Habsburg Empire perhaps,' Sir Gordon argued, 'but you will find them at the Danish, and Swedish courts, and Bourbon Spain and the Moors of Granada employ them.'

'None of whom are at the forefront of European power.' The bishop dug a spoon into the glutinous mass now filling his bowl. 'And you forget Lazarus. He *will* be there no doubt. What might your spaewife learn from him, MacDonald?'

The words left a chilly silence, perhaps as the man intended.

'You disapprove of spaewives?' MacDonald asked.

'My personal opinions are not at issue: I defend the edicts of the church.'

'As you must; but tradition should also be defended. When Eolhwynne's predecessor left my employ, I gave serious thought to not replacing her, believing I might save on the expenditure. Ethelfeyrda had served my family well for near twenty years and it was she reminded me the MacDonalds have retained a spaewife for over five hundred years *without break*. I did know, naturally, but I had not thought of it in such a light. I dare say she had the interests of her calling at heart, but as a man of the church, you surely appreciate the importance of tradition and uncertainty of change.'

The bishop frowned, as though he had found a frog paddling in the consommé. 'You refer to the dispute with the Dissenters?'[1]

'I do.'

'Then I agree there is a deal to be said for tradition.'

Dundee cleared his throat. 'Of course, change is sometimes called for.'

'Patently true,' MacDonald said.

'We agree then?'

'In principle, yes; but pray continue.'

'In *principle*,' Dundee agreed, 'but have you considered our position in the Americas lately?'

'I note the colonies have an appetite for Scottish blood,' MacDonald said with a hint of weariness. 'And money, also. My grandfather invested in the Scottish Canadian Company and got not a penny for it.'

'My father also lost money on that enterprise, but you should not hold the present administration accountable for the hubris of its predecessor,' Dundee said. 'Sir David, I spied a globe in your drawing room. Would you permit it brought to table?'

---

[1] The Alban Church did not formally recognise the Free Church of Scotland until 1884. *N.W.*

'Of course. It is not of recent manufacture; it was my father's.'

'I am certain it will suffice,' Dundee said. 'Man alters; geography endures.'

Margaret gave him a forlorn glance to which he could only offer a shrugged apology even as he called Gifford and gave instructions.

It was not an auspicious start to the evening. The bishop's show of being a plain and simple man of plain and simple tastes merely made him appear ignorant. Sir Gordon was continually dabbing his beard clean while Dundee had more interest in politics—a subject Margaret and MacDonald detested—than dining. He did not suppose the consommé so bad as to be unpalatable but trusted cook had better fortune with the main course.

'Ah, the world,' Dundee applauded as Gifford and a lad assisting brought the globe in and placed it at his elbow.

'I trust you shall not require it long,' Margaret said in mock horror, for it was nearly three feet across and entirely hid her behind its northern regions.

'Forgive me, Lady Margaret. I shall be minutes only.' Dundee spun the globe to display the Americas to MacDonald. 'The situation of the colonies: New Gothenburg, Nova Dania, and Christiania, our particular concern, in the middle. Bordered to the north by Republican French and the Hanseats and to the south by Louisiana[1] and Mexico, all with expansionist ambitions. In the government's view our colony must grow if it is to prosper.'

---

[1] Louisiana nominally claimed allegiance to the French Royalists but was effectively an independent nation, as was Mexico. Hanseatic possessions focused on the trading stations on Wittemborg Bay in the modern-day Manitoba. Unlike the other colonisers and fledgling states of the New World who introduced European law and culture, the Hanseatic Company had no interest in civilising and simply plundered the land's natural resources. The western seaboard from San Diego to Vancouver Island was under Spanish control. *N.W.*

MacDonald nodded, 'And for growth you need *Scottish* blood?'

'Any blood, providing it is loyal to the crown,' Dundee said. 'It is sensible in congested areas to encourage emigration and clearance of land for sheepwalks.'

The bishop interrupted his eating. 'The caveat applies to the Eirish; their loyalty cannot be trusted.'

'I accept the logic,' MacDonald said, 'but not its justice. Today, I signed papers for ninety emigrants, but I will not and will never force people from their homes.'

'Ninety you say; what is their destination?'

'Arcadia and Quebeck.[1]

'Too north for our concerns,' Dundee cavilled, 'we need them in Christiania.' His finger moved south. 'We must push our territory westward.'

This was startling news and forced Sir David into the conversation. 'Into the Tribal Lands?' he asked.

'Indeed, unavoidably, so. We must protect our interests.' Dundee tapped the globe for emphasis. 'The French and the *Hanseats* do not honour treaties with the natives, therefore neither can we.'

'In any event, one is not concerned for the skraelings,' the bishop said. 'They were savages when Thorfinn Karlsefni landed and savages they remain.'[2]

'Then you expropriate men from the only land they have ever known and send them overseas to force another from his,' MacDonald said, not hiding his disapproval.

---

[1] Together with the provinces of Buonopartia and Montreal, Quebeck was governed directly from Paris. *N.W.*

[2] A part historical, part legendary Norse adventurer, Thorfinn Karlsefni with Leif and Thorvald Ericsson, was the first European to settle on the American mainland. From the descriptions in the Vinland Saga, the *skraelings* they encountered were probably ancestors of the now extinct Beothuk who, from the custom of painting themselves and their belongings with red ochre, gave rise to the name 'Indien Rouge' or 'Peau Rouge' which was subsequently applied (in a derogatory sense) to all native Americans. *N.W.*

'If one were a Christian and the other a Heathen, indeed I would,' the bishop replied.

'Gentlemen, let us not be heated,' Dundee said. 'Some arrangement will be made with the tribes. In any event, I can assure you the ninety you spoke of would have found a more equable climate in Christiania than they will in Arcadia. It is a pretty name for a harsh land.'

'I think they will prefer what they are used to,' MacDonald said. 'It is attested that when a bullock is taken from Skye for fattening on the mainland the herdsman must prevent the creature eating itself to death inside a week. They are not used to rich pasture.'

'You suggest a man who knows only *want* does not learn *moderation*,' the bishop said.

'He does not learn what he has no use for. Moderation, gentlemen,' MacDonald addressed them all, 'is for those who suspect they have too much. The soup is excellent, cousin, most warming.'

Sir David laughed. 'Thank you, Kelso, thank you indeed. Your point is taken.'

'Ah. Aha,' barked Sir Gordon, 'you have a dry wit, sir. I believe we shall enjoy your company.'

'And I yours,' MacDonald said, 'but I fear not for long.'

'But till Monday, surely,' Sir Gordon protested.

'Alas, no: I must be in Inverness for Monday's sailing.'

'You break the Sabbath,' the bishop grumbled.

'To do otherwise would jeopardise the purpose of my journey: the next sailing is not for three days.'

'He has time for chapel in the morning, is that not so, cousin?'

'Naturally. Provided, Your Grace, you will accept one from the Church of Rome. Will you be reading the sermon?'

'Indeed,' the bishop answered. 'And I expect observance from all who travel with you, whatever church, or *none*, they hold to.'

'Of course.'

Dundee raised a hand. 'If we may move on. There is

another matter MacDonald may aid us with. You, Thomas, brought it to mind.'

The bishop inclined his head to listen.

'Lazarus,' Dundee continued, 'after the shambles in the Crimea does the new tsar trust his late father's archimage?[1] The French bloodied Russia's nose, but I do not believe for one moment she is done: she is blessed with immense riches but with the Bosporus barred to her fleet, she has no certain access to the world's oceans.'

'There is Saint Petersburg,' Sir Gordon said.

'It is a *great* city, I know for I have been there; but the Gulf of Finland is icebound five months of the year and Russia needs a *warm water* port. No: having failed to escape the Black Sea, she must improve her situation in the Baltic by gaining territory westwards, beyond the winter ice. I expect Russia to move against the Courland[2] or even the Hanseat cities this year or next, that is,' Dundee raised a hand signalling his main point, 'if Alexander listens to rational men; but if the unholy fool guides the son as he did the father, there is no telling what he may do.'

He could not see Margaret's face, but it took no effort to imagine its expression was several degrees cooler than the polar regions obscuring her from his view. Russia was clearly a hobby horse for Lord Dundee.

Sir Gordon had now emptied his bowl and what he had not eaten he began cleaning from his beard while continuing to talk. 'I believe I understand my colleague: mere observation might reveal the depth of the man's influence on the

---

[1] Male practitioners of magick were largely unrecognised in the Northern Tradition of magick (albeit they certainly existed and were expected to control their abilities) but in the Eastern Tradition males dominated and were known locally as shaman or koldun. The west, being unfamiliar with them and their practices, referred to them as wizards, sorcerers and mages, none of which is strictly accurate. Archimage describes a wizard of particularly marked ability. *N.W.*

[2] A region on the Baltic now part of modern Poland. *N.W.*

tsar; perhaps your spaer may even be of use in the matter.'

'I fear you overstep the mark.' The bishop had cleared his bowl also. 'I have no affection for any spaer, but I should keep her well away from Lazarus. An *archimage*, indeed. He is a diabolist, and the devil himself around any woman.'

'I will heed your advice,' MacDonald said. Nevertheless, why might Russia not move against Copenhagen? It controls the Baltic as surely as Constantinople does the Black Sea.'

'The odds against success are too great,' Dundee said.

The bishop disagreed. 'The Danish fleet is modern, but few in number. Copenhagen could be taken.'

'But not held,' Dundee argued. 'Sweden will not stand Russia guarding the Baltic, nor will Flanders or the Hanseats and treaty binds us to defend Denmark as if she were our own; Russia will not take on so many at once. France may even join against the tsar if they see profit in it. No. I hazard Russia will strike at Lübeck. If few care for the Poles none at all care for the Hanseats.'

'Russian ships will still be liable for passage dues at Öresund,' the bishop said, referencing the strait between Denmark and Skane.[1]

Sir Gordon dropped his napkin on the table. 'The Danes will not be so brave. Surely, they will sense the shift in power and grant Russia free passage, as they do for the Hanseats. Thus, will the Russian Bear be out of his cage. Is that not so, or does my meagre understanding thwart me.'

Dundee smiled. 'Your understanding is adequate; Denmark will not chain the straits.'

MacDonald was the only one to pay the food proper respect. His bowl was clean, as was the tablecloth beside him, and now he folded his napkin beside his place before folding his hands. 'All depending on *Lazarus*?' he asked.

'I believe so,' Dundee said. 'Men of good sense will always act to their best advantage, but the mind of Lazarus is a

---

[1] Skane was a Danish possession in southern Sweden. It was ceded to Stockholm in 1922. *N.W.*

mystery and if he has the tsar's ear, then Russia, also, is a mystery.'

'Quite extraordinary. Alas I fear you overestimate my position at court. I may eat at the same table as the tsar, but I very much doubt I shall see or overhear anything of interest. Really, you ought to consider persuading a servant or two: they overhear far more than they ever pretend.'

Sir Gordon had none of it. 'You are brother-in-law to the king. I suggest you have influence beyond what you claim.'

'I must correct you: the king is no longer my brother-in-law, not since the death of my dear sister. However,' MacDonald paused and glanced down the table in his direction. Far from being appalled by the company, he seemed amused by it. 'I *am* uncle to Prince Alexander and on good terms with Northumberland. Perhaps I have some influence. I hope so for my factor has charged me with persuading Lord Egan to renew the tariff on *barilla*.'

'Barilla? I am not familiar with it,' the bishop said.

Sir David signalled the servants to begin clearing the table. Dundee's bowl was still half full. It was a strange man who preferred speechifying to dinner, and it was he that assisted the bishop, describing *barilla* as Spanish soda ash.

'And the death of the kelp industry,' MacDonald said.

'And you seek protection for kelp?' the bishop asked.

'For the benefit of the people, yes,' MacDonald said, 'the collapse in demand has brought great hardship.'

'Anglia gains no advantage from artificially high prices,' Sir Gordon said. 'What benefits Skye will increase costs for industry and lead to raised prices all round. Protectionism is never the answer, as I am sure the Treasury will agree.'

'I will fail then.'

'I fear so,' Dundee said.

'I expected as much. However, I will do my best.' MacDonald paused and smiled warmly. 'If I may, I shall serve both our causes. I will keep an eye on the tsar's wizard, *and* I will leave my people exactly where they are. Skye breeds good fighting men, and it seems we may need them.'

'Ah, aha,' barked Sir Gordon, 'I believe he has us.'

'Lord Dundee, might we dispense with the globe, it is neither decorative nor can it be eaten,' Margaret suggested.

'Indeed, and I thank you for your tolerance, Lady Margaret.'

The globe returned to the drawing room and with its removal conversation soon turned to more familiar and familial affairs, the cost of labour and ambition of sons being chief among them, but Sir David remained intrigued by his cousin's explanation for travelling with a spaer. It had not rung true, though the company appeared convinced. It was difficult to believe anything said at his table might affect affairs of state, yet in a week's time cousin Kelso would indeed have the ear of the king, his ministers, and even foreign heads of government. His home might be falling into the sea and his carriages in bad repair, yet as dinner progressed, he had a renewed admiration for his cousin. The man had not conceded one inch to the Commissioners.

III

The gentlemen of the commission had retired for the night, citing an early start in the morning. Sir David rather thought his cousin might follow them to bed, but once the door had closed on Sir Gordon, *et al*, and he had let Gifford retire for the night, MacDonald thrust both legs to the drawing room fire and gasped a sigh of relief.

'I thought they would never go,' MacDonald raised his goblet to examine it. 'Continental?' he asked.

'French.'

'Very fine: *slàinte*, as they say.' He drained the glass.

'You will go native one day, Kel. But tell me truthfully,' he sat forward inquisitively, 'why are you taking your spaer?'

'I should have thought the answer obvious.' MacDonald smiled thinly. 'I wish to know who killed William.'

He spoke with such determination Sir David was taken aback.

'You assume a guilty party?'

'I presume a responsibility,' he said. 'Guilt is another matter.'

Sir David stood, removed two Grenadines from a silver and ebony box and offered one to his cousin.

'I will,' MacDonald said. 'Makes a change from a pipe.'

Sir David cut the cigars on a miniature guillotine. Like the vanitas, it appealed to his sense of the macabre. It also gave him opportunity to think.

'This morning's *Times* is respectful,' he said, 'though there is a deal of speculation.'

MacDonald rolled the cigar appreciatively. 'I have not seen today's edition. May I borrow it?'

'Take it with you. It has everyone from Princess Maria Isabel to the queen wishing him ill.'

Sir David plucked an ember from the fire to light the cigar. His cousin leant forward and did the same.

'Not Maribel,' MacDonald said. 'The girl's devoted to William. Was devoted, I should say. God knows what will become of her now.'

Sir David returned the ember to the fire and the tongs to the hearthstone.

'She might return to her family.'

'Perhaps; I dare say she would be happier there. Who else is being blamed?'

'More a case of who isn't. *Cui bono,* as they say.' Sir David paused to enjoy the cigar. With their fine sense of aesthetics, it was no surprise the Mohammedans made excellent smokes. Cigar in hand, he refilled his glass at the side table by the vanitas.

'Many would benefit from unrest in Anglia,' MacDonald mused, 'France, Russia as we discussed earlier, rebel Eirish.'

Sir David brought the decanter to the table and refilled MacDonald's glass. This act exposed the vanitas to the room, revealing a skull surrounded by objects of wealth and luxury.

'Do you have any allies at court?' he asked. 'I assume George will support you and your spaewife will be useful, even if she is inexperienced.'

MacDonald sat up. 'You remind me; I would like the loan of a drag for a few days, in exchange for my chariot?'

'Of course, but must I take the chariot in exchange? It is showing its age, Kel. What did I say to remind you?'

'Don't be sharp, David. You mentioned Eolhwynne. I have not told her of my plan, and you're right, allies would be useful. My carriage is too small for two in comfort, and I admit it is a little dreary. Also,' he hesitated as though remembering something, 'I believe Eolhwynne has some aversion to it. With your drag, I can bring her into my plans between here and Invermoriston. As for allies at court, I'm not sure who I can trust.'

'You spoke of Northumberland earlier,' Sir David said.

'Oh, I like the man,' MacDonald said. 'But he will do everything to protect the reputation of the Royal Court and I dare say he will not appreciate me meddling.'

'What of the king?' he asked. 'Reportedly, he is stricken with grief. Surely, he will be keen to know the truth.'

'Perhaps,' MacDonald rubbed his chin. 'What did *The Times* have to say?'

'Apparently, the king is in official mourning and Northumberland has taken over his royal duties.'

'The family is closing ranks,' MacDonald said. 'Maud always said she felt like an outsider at court. Besides, Edmund dotes on Queen Charlotte, and it's known she favours Prince Oswald, natural of course, but difficult in the circumstances. Stepmothers have an unenviable position in lore.'

'You need another outsider, like yourself,' Sir David said. 'Have you thought of the King's Huntsman?[1] I cannot recall his name.'

'Llewelyn Goodfellow,' MacDonald said. 'I have only met him twice.'

'Supposedly he was close to William and Alexander.'

'He struck me as a man who would give fair answer to a

---

[1] An historic appointment that lapsed in the 1930s. The King's Huntsman taught the king and his sons field and war craft. *N.W.*

fair question.' MacDonald glanced at the shuttered window, distracted by a cry outside. 'A rare thing at Winchester. What is that noise?'

Sir David had heard it too and stood to investigate. Lanterns in the courtyard showed two men scuffling with a third before dragging him away. A door slammed and darkness resumed.

'With luck, the servants will deal with him.' He closed the shutter. 'If not, I may be called away. But continue. You were speaking of your new spaewife. Why have you not told her of your quest?'

He returned to his chair.

'My *quest*?' MacDonald smiled. 'You make it sound like a novel by Tamburlaine MacGregor. Clara gave me something of his to read. Nonsense, of course, but passes the time. I have scarcely spoken to Eolhwynne since I appointed her at New Year. Clara and the child seemed more important, and I just let the girl get on with it. Clara saw more of her, and it was she persuaded me to take the girl. I'm glad she did.'

'Why so?'

'The Kyle ferry. She knew something wasn't right with it.'

'Not the accident?' he asked.

'Indeed, how did you know?'

'I had to provide pasturage for the cattle that couldn't cross.'

'No word of it had reached Duntulm,' MacDonald said. 'Loss of life, she said, admittedly only a few sheep—tell me, is it raining?'

'No, there is a deal of cloud.'

'She said we would get more rain. According to my coachman and manservant, both of whom have been with my family for twenty years, Eolhwynne is very well thought of at Duntulm by, so it seems, everyone but me. That should tell me something. I have been remiss and will correct it tomorrow on the way to Invermoriston.'

'But is she pretty?'

'Why do you ask?'

'Margaret was certain you would not have noticed.'

They were interrupted by a knock at the door. Sir David called and his gillie, Cuthbert MacEwan entered.

'Sir, sorra for troublin' ye at this hour. There's a fellow downstair protestin' to see ye.'

'What reason does he give?'

'He's no said,' the gillie replied. 'Gives his name as Adam Shaw o' Bearneas. Reckons he's shankit frae there the night, an' he look's it. He's worse fer drink.'

'Walked you say?' Sir David said. 'An impressive distance, especially for a drunkard.'

'Ay, sir, but if ye was t'see him, belike he'll be on his way. Otherwise, there'll be a deal o' trouble keeping him quiet.'

'What do you think, Kel?' Sir David asked.

'His cause must be pressing,' MacDonald said.

'Agreed. Very well. MacEwan, find me a warm coat and I'll come down. Where are you holding him?'

'The old Duty Room, sir.'

'Put him in the lock up afterwards. Provide him with a blanket, a candle, water and the necessaries.'

'Ay, Sir David.'

The servant brought him a coat. Buttoning it, he turned to MacDonald, saying, 'You needn't sit up. I may be delayed.'

'I am comfortable here. I shall wait,' came reply.

He followed the gillie downstairs. The air was damp from the sea loch and despite the coat, he was chilled. MacEwan lit his way to the old Duty Room where, until only ten years ago, servants had waited in the damp and cold before called to their duties. MacEwan pushed the door, and it gave with a harsh creak. A plank with rusting coat hooks and illegible nameplates ran around the room at shoulder height and an iron candelabrum hung from the ceiling. The hearth was bare except for twigs dropped by birds nesting on the chimney. A rush light on the wall and a lantern lit the room, the latter revealing a man slumped across the table and Sir David's grieve,[1] Shamus Caird, standing over him.

---

[1] Bailiff or overseer on a Scottish estate or farm. *N.W.*

Between the floor above and this room, they had slipped three centuries in time, or so he thought, and these men suited it far better than he did. In his drawing room clothes he was a peacock in a fowl yard.

Caird kicked the man's chair, and he sat up; his face was puce and round as a cabbage. Blood had dried across the chin and there was a dark bruise on the cheek. Seeing him, the eyebrows drew down like two dark clouds.

Sir David felt no friendship in the stare and kept his distance.

'You have something to say to me,' he said. 'I do not have all night.'

That was the flashpoint. The man's hand hit out, backed by bared teeth. Caird smashed the hand to the table and the man howled with anger. Levering open the fingers Caird pulled out a scrap of wood and tossed it into the hearth.

'Nae bannin', damn ye,' Caird muttered. 'Apology, sir. I didna check his pockets.'

'What was it?' Sir David asked.

'A cursestick,' Caird said without letting go of the man.

'Ye'd best tie him,' MacEwan said to Caird. 'Use yer belt if ye've naethin' else—best keep ye sicker, Sir David.'

'Thank you.'

Shamus Caird scowled, but loosened the cord about his waist and tied the man's wrists with it.

'You hail from Bearneas?' Sir David forced his voice to sound steady. 'Adam Shaw, correct?'

'*Seaghdh*,' the man growled. 'Ye'll ken o' Bearneas. No many o' us left there the noo. Just sheep, maistlins, an' fer ma sins I look after they bluidy sheep, Sir bluidy David!'

Caird's blow knocked Shaw and chair to the ground and the man's head thudded on the earth floor.

'No!' Sir David stepped up to the table, determined to show his authority. 'No violence against him. I will hear his case. MacEwan, help him up.'

Caird righted the chair and MacEwan dragged the man onto it. Sir David motioned the gillie to him.

'How bad is he?'

'Drouked tae the skin,' MacEwan said. 'Drink's kept him on, but if we're no carefu' we'll have a corp come morn.'

'No. Whatever ill he believes I've done him, I'll not compound it. Make sure he eats and get him dry clothes.

'Shaw,' Sir David addressed the drunk. 'There will be no more violence against you in my house. I do recall Bearneas. A few of the crofters left for Glasgow, most for the...'

'New Warld,' Shaw broke in. 'That's what Elspeth said.'

'She was your wife?'

'Sister,' Shaw corrected. 'My wife, God rest her bones, be five year gone this June. Elspeth took boat fer New Gloucester[1] wi' my god-brither, Brandr McNamara. He sent me this. Two days it's been burnin the heart o' me.'

Shaw took a folded scrap of paper from his shirt and dropped it on the table.

'Tek it. Show Sir *baa-baa* whit he's done tae us.'

Sir David had MacEwan bring him the letter. The writing was small, cramped onto the page, as though the writer had wished to diminish the words. They were clear enough for him to read by the lantern.

Adam, dear friend. We are both bereft...

Shaw's eyes seared into his. He stopped reading.

'Brandr took my sister, Elspeth,' Shaw said. 'An' Ailsa an' Megan, the two bairns. 'Gangin tae a better warld' she telled us, an' I'd my only son go wi' 'em for there's naethin' for him at Bearneas no more. Ye read it an' burn the damn thing. That's all I ask o' ye. "A better warld".' Shaw laughed bitterly. 'Maybe a priest would say it's where they've gone. Now get away frae me, get oot o' my sight.'

Shaw was dismissing him in his own house. It was the bravery of a man who has lost everything. He refolded the letter, wishing to crush it smaller and smaller.

---

[1] New Gloucester was the principal port of Christiania. It was renamed Marieville when Anglia ceded Christiania to the Republic of America in 1883. *N.W.*

'Very well. Tonight, you will sleep here. You will have hot food and a dry bed. Tomorrow being the Sabbath,' the words stuck in his throat for within his family the day was always called Sunday; Sabbath seemed to belong to an earlier time, 'you will have chance to pay your observances but will remain here. On Monday, a cart will return you to Bearneas. There you will gather all you can carry, and the cart will take you by any road you wish until you are clear of my lands. You will not return. Do I make myself clear?'

Shaw shrugged. 'There's naught for us here. Ye've seen t' that.'

'MacEwan, you have my instructions. Take him away. Caird, remain here.'

He stood aside as MacEwan got Shaw to his feet. The man had held his anger like a rod in his back all the way from Bearneas, but now drink and weariness had taken over and he could barely stand. MacEwan had to take Shaw by the waist as he helped him out the room.

Sir David waited until they were beyond earshot before addressing Caird.

'Thank you for saving me from the man's curse, but I'll not have violence in my house.'

'He ill-tongued you, sir!'

Sir David held his voice down. 'The man holds I sent his sister and his son to their deaths. God knows it is not true, but another man might have argued with a knife; an insult I can bear. Dismissed.'

Caird exited. Sir David took the lantern off the table and found the cursestick. It was a twig, flattened on one side and covered with knife marks. He did not believe in their power, but here, in this gloomy chamber, it set his spine tingling. He gathered a few sticks in the hearth, set light to them and watched the cursestick burn. Only when it had gone to ash did he extinguish the rushlight and leave.

His return to the drawing room woke his cousin from sleep. The man stared up at him in surprise.

'Good God. You're pale as a ghost.'

Sir David tore off his coat and flung it across the room before pouring a large whisky. The vanitas behind the drinks table now seemed in bad taste. Being drunk, being roaring drunk, was attractive. He took a mouthful and on returning to his chair passed Shaw's letter to MacDonald.

'Tell me if I want to read this. I have just met its receiver.'

MacDonald read silently, his face impassive.

'It is bad?' Sir David asked.

'I cannot imagine it worse.' MacDonald passed the letter back. 'I believe you ought to read it.'

Sir David rubbed his eyes and set the glass down. The letter felt like the sentence of a judge, and he had to hold it in both hands to read it. The only surprise was the manner of death. He had prepared himself for cholera, smallpox, typhus, even starvation. The truth was worse...

'An appetite for Scottish blood, isn't that what you said?'

He and MacDonald were now examining the globe.

'The Appalachia,' MacDonald said, tracing his finger along a mountain chain. 'This river, the *Ohio*?'

'The letter speaks of a great river, but does not name it; what do you suppose these are: *Miami, Illinois, Cherokee*?'

'Tribes,' MacDonald said. 'It calls them 'redskins'.'

Sir David spun the globe and the nations and seas blurred into one.

'He called me a murderer.'

'We disagree on the Clearances, but you have murdered no one,' MacDonald said. 'I do not know where the blame lies. They are savages, as the bishop says, but it is their name on the land, not Mackenzie, not MacDonald.'

'But you read what they did, even to his child.'

'They spared the girls, so it would seem.'

'To raise among them? Some saving.'

'My conscience is no easier than yours,' MacDonald returned to his chair, 'four men drowned near Raasay only last fall. I attended the burial for the two we found. The others were not seen again. The weather was poor when they set out, but a man must feed himself and his own and this life gives no pause for breath. Had I cleared the land and forced them onto ships they might still be alive.'

Sir David crumpled the letter and knelt by the hearth.

'What are you doing?' MacDonald asked.

'Burning it, as the man asked. I'll have your glass, cousin.'

'Here.'

He held the goblets side by side and watched the flames through the crystal before folding the letter in the bowl of one and setting the pair in the fire.

This room was one of the least changed since his childhood. French crystal sconces glittered in the lamplight and bookcases either side of the firebreast displayed the collected learning of his father and grandfather. The few pictures on show were equally intimate: a portrait of his father on his favourite horse, an engraving of the castle. The only grand painting was above the mantel: it showed the loch, the glen beyond, and the towering peaks of the Five Sisters. The artist had cunningly hidden within it an eagle, a leaping salmon, a stag and a lost lamb, all of which it had been his childhood pleasure to discover. It was only now he noticed there was one element the artist had omitted. In the entire scene there was not one man or habitation.[1]

    Matters coincidental?
    Though all men are by conscience
    Pricked, too rarely do they bleed
    And few attend the draught beneath their door.
Do not take your pleasure in the eyes of those you love, since there's no treasure in the reflected gaze. Only in the wider view is the heart's true measure: through the glass, not in the mirror.

    Editor's Remarks

The first draft continues from about the middle of the page with only a blank line

---

[1] MacGregor owned a number of such landscapes or 'mascarades' at Arbinger Abbey. *N.W.*

indicating the beginning of a new chapter and the date, in this case January 13, 1862. For the first two-thirds of the chapter the name of its central character is given as 'Sir?' until MacGregor went through several possible names in the margin before settling on Sir David Mackenzie. This name was then interpolated into the earlier part of the text.

MacGregor's journal records him attending Edenborough's Speculative Society on January 21 for a lantern show on the previous year's annular eclipse of the sun observed from New South Holland. This is described in admiring tones in his journal, along with a less pleasing visit to the offices of James Ludd who had completed drafting their design for the Madeleine Shrine at Arbinger. Their drawings have not survived, but a remark in his journal, "I requested a beacon and they have given me a monument" suggests something of his concern. In any event, once back at Arbinger, he wrote to James Ludd demanding alterations to their proposal. This letter has also not survived. Macgregor's return to Arbinger was timely, for Lady Helena's diary mentions heavy snowfall at the end of the month and Arbinger would be cut off for two weeks.

Turning to the text, there is considerable variation between the draft of this chapter and the published edition but, for once, the publishers are not wholly to blame. Their influence is mainly confined to the scene between Sir David and Adam Shaw, with the latter becoming a more malign and unsympathetic figure in the published version. We must recall Sir Sidney Beresford and John Lucas' sympathies aligned with Lord Dundee of the Emigration Commission, and both men regarded opposition to forced emigration as unpatriotic. Fortunately, MacGregor's popularity with King Charles and Scotland's First Minister, Lord Wells, licensed him to express an independent view, though it is clear this only went so far.

Neither Sir Sidney nor John Lucas appreciated that MacGregor invites the reader to side against the commissioners (at least, there is no indication they did so in the surviving correspondence), but it is certain they would have done so had they seen MacGregor's first draft. It appears MacGregor, having written the somewhat dour preceding chapters, namely Bheathain Somhairle's, My Lady of Remorse, and Lord MacDonald, relished the dining room scene and his first attempt is, one must admit, self-indulgent with the Bishop, Lord Dundee and Sir Gordon exhaustively justifying every wickedness practised during The Clearances.

Fortunately for your editor, MacGregor realised this heavy-handedness would not do and scratched out the offending dialogue and interlineated the more reasoned arguments seen here. Otherwise, the text of the first draft of this chapter largely matches the published first edition.

No natural physic
Chapter Four
Skye, morning: The troubles of BHEATHAIN SOMHAIRLE continue

No natural physic is
Man's when acquiring Grace
He is like the butterfly
Who endures pain to grow her pretty wings.
He has lost nothing: if anything, he has gained, yet it will be a time before he knows it.

1

A HAND AT his shoulder woke him. Bheathain flailed at it blindly.

'Bheathain, what is it?' Manus said. 'Eh! Bring us a light.'

Someone spoke but Bheathain could not name the voice.

'Have you no stones, man! The *coinneal*!'

Light blasted through his eyelids. Bheathain groaned and writhed away.

'What's wrong with his face?' a second voice asked.

What, indeed? Bheathain opened his eyes a glint, but the flame seared into his head, and he flinched away. The second man was Uilleam M'Illathain.

'You hear me, Bheathain?' Manus's bony fingers shook his shoulder.

He heard him, but the voice seemed ten yards away, not next to his head. Inside his head men were pounding rocks.

'His face, Manus. It's red-raw.'

His *nen* let go his shoulder and he curled into a ball. The men talked over him, like he was a sick beast.

'This is not natural,' M'Illathain said.

'You reckon it's the devil's work?' Manus answered, contemptuously.

'No; there's things in this world neither of God nor the devil, but if you let on to the wife I said that, there'll be devil to pay.'

Manus laughed. 'Your wife has your stones, then. *Dia*,

Bheathain, but you've always been a strange one.' His old *nen* was at his ear. 'We'll be calling on Doctor Ramsay. We want no trouble from you. As if you are not trouble enough.'

'Ramsay? What good is he for such like?' M'Illathain said. 'We ought cry on an outside-woman.'

'What outside-woman? Old Haelda's long time dead,' Manus countered. 'No. Doctor Ramsay's the man. Your old horse got wind enough to get us to Portree?'

'It has. But this is uncanny. Not doctor's business.'

'*Daingead!* Uilleam M'Illathain! It is no such thing. Bheathain's my charge and Doctor Ramsay'll see to him, y' hear.'

'Manus M'Dhòmhnuill, it is the Sabbath, and you'll keep a civil tongue. I should be gone to kirk, but I am here for the lad's sake. What've you got to pay the doctor? I see no silver in this house.'

'Not all silver shines. Besides, Dixon'll see to the expense.'

'The laird's man! And what is Bheathain to him?'

'He has his reasons. Don't ask more.'

'Well, fine for you to say.'

Bheathain let the men argue. He only wished they'd find another parish for it and leave him in peace. Instead, hands grabbed and rolled him on his back. Manus he might fight off but Uilleam M'Illathain was wily and tough-limbed. They stripped his nightshirt and had him helpless as a lamb for nipping. They'd have had more trouble getting him in shirt and breeches, save for the chill of the morning made him glad of clothes.

'We ought cover his face,' M'Illathain said. 'He'd scare a ghost.'

Manus tried to pull the scarf over him, but it was agony against his cheek.

'Hold still, lad,' Manus said. 'Can't—*mac an donas!* Damn you, Bheathain!'

Unable to bear it longer he had thrown his grandfather and ripped the scarf from his face. Manus cussed and kicked him in the back, but he barely felt the blow.

The board behind his bed had near split from the crack of the old man's skull, but it was his last defiance for both men set to with vigour. M'Illathain wrapped a jacket round his shoulders and together he and his *nen* dragged him out the house with his boot heels skyting across the stones. The cruel air struck him like a knife, and he stuffed his hands into the pockets of the jacket where his fingers met with the scrap of stone he'd rune-marked. He had a comfort.

M'Illathain hauled and Manus pushed until he was seated in the cart and pulled the bonnet down onto his head. Bheathain let the old man be, then reached up and set his bonnet as he wanted. Manus saw the stone in his fist.

'You can be rid of that.'

Wiry old fingers tried to work into his grip.

'What is it?' M'Illathain asked.

'Bit of stone,' Manus said. 'Fool scratched a rune on it.'

Bheathain snatched his hand back into his pocket.

'Is that all? Leave the lad with it. But Bheathain, listen. This is better than old magick.'

M'Illathain had a silver cross in his hand. 'Hold to Our Lord and he will hold to you.'

'Silver?' Manus asked.

'It is,' he said, 'and I want it back when he's mended. It reminds me of when there was good money in kelp.'

Bheathain closed his fist around the silver cross and M'Illathain prompted the horse. Together, they rolled toward the highway. The stone and cross gave comfort but were no recompense. The laird had stolen what was his, sure as if he'd reached from the carriage and rifled his pockets. But what was it he stole he could scarce imagine. He shut his eyes against the wind and let his thoughts roll until the very noise of them dulled him to sleep.

§

He woke to find M'Illathain leading the horse to water be-side a bridge. His back had stiffened, and he unbent a little.

'You've wakened,' Manus grumbled. 'An ill sight you be.'

He did not answer. The water swirling over the gravel whispered to him. Every drop from the crags, every pool, every waterfall sang to him. What was stolen from him had been here: had stood on this very plot.

'At least you're not bleeding. Queer thing, that mark of yours. But not magick, no, not magick or charm or sortilege. And you'll thank me for this, so you will. No damn outside-women for you, eh? Ramsay's the man, yes. You'll be well. Hey, lad, sit still!'

His old *nen* tried to catch his arm, but Bheathain was halfway off the seat. A quick thrust broke his grandfather's hold.

'Bheathain, damn *thu*!'

He slid down, but his legs failed on him, and he sprawled in the wet peat and gravel by the stream. The bit of stone jabbed into his hand, drawing blood, and he greeted with the pain and helplessness of it. For a moment he had felt the presence of what he had lost. It had passed by here, but now was gone.

M'Illathain dragged him onto his feet; 'Confound you, Bheathain, for trying a man's patience. You're no skin and bones to be heaving. Eh, still holding my silver cross, are you?'

He nodded but his words were blubber in his mouth.

'Lose it and you can crawl to Portree.'

He had lost something in a stream days before. His touchpiece, his lucky charm. He could not be trusted with things.

'Take it,' he gabbled through a mouthful of spit. 'I'm no good.'

'First I heard of it,' M'Illathain said, and pushed him onto the cart.

'Damn fool, so you are,' Manus said, his face sour as old milk.

M'Illathain led the horse by the bridle and backed them onto the road.

'The man is sick, Manus. You still reckon Ramsay's who he needs?'

'I do,' Manus said. 'And that's end of it.'

M'Illathain climbed up and they were on the move again, Bheathain closed his eyes. Caught between M'Illathain and Manus, he swayed with the slow movement of the cart until he rocked to sleep.

§

He did not wake until M'Illathain dropped the iron skid under the back wheel to retard their descent on the hill above Portree. The rattle of it pained his head.

'Quiet now,' Manus muttered and dug his fingers into Bheathain's arm.

'See he's decent,' M'Illathain said. 'Don't want to scare folk.'

Manus leant across and stared him in the eye before tugging his bonnet low across his face.

'We're almost there, lad. Hold still now.'

It was the first moment his old *nen* had sounded worried for him. He'd rather the old man cussing him. It was no comfort for folk to be concerned.

The road dropped toward the town. Shell-white houses gleamed through the rain and ships sheltered on the leaden waters of the bay. Bheathain tucked his head down and closed his eyes. He was cold and miserable and his hand ached where he had cut it on the bit of stone. Inside he felt hollow, like he'd not eaten for a day, only worse. He wondered if this was what dying felt like, if his mam had felt the same thing gnawing away at her insides until nothing was left.

The cart stopped and Manus got down and hammered at a door. Bheathain supposed this must be the doctor's house.

'*Cha bhi beud ort,*' M'Illathain said comfortingly.

This was how folk spoke to the dying. A dim memory of the muttered kindnesses bestowed on his sick mother swum in his thoughts. The laird had stolen from him and whatever it was the lack of it was the death of him. He muttered under his breath and glanced about.

The Royal Hotel was Portree's finest and not the kind of place he'd ever think of calling on but, for what reason he could not tell, it held his gaze. Meantime, a woman in black skirts and white apron stood at an open door talking to his grandfather. M'Illathain's eye was on them. Bheathain slid sideways along the seat and stumbled to the road. This time, his legs held.

'Bheathain! Damn *thu*! Manus!'

He flung himself toward the hotel, body reeling like in a gale. He fumbled at a door latch then crashed through the door. This was grand, his skin was on fire, and he was roaring. A hand reached behind him and grabbed his collar, but there was no stopping him, and he shoved the door back, bringing a howl of pain from his grandfather.

A second door led into a small room. Stones burned in a grate. Heads turned, mouths opened. Three men gathered round the fire.

'It's mine!' he bellowed and staggered into a chair back, pitching the occupant into the table where a pile of papers slid toward the fire. The third man leapt to save them.

'Damned fellow.' The man whose chair he collided with was on his feet. 'McNair! We are attacked!' The man tried to bar his way, but he pressed on. The farthest of the three was a large, red-haired man with full beard and whiskers, except it wasn't him he sought but the chair beneath him. The chair itself had stolen from him. He did not stop to think this strange but pressed on, intent on unseating the red-haired man and taking the chair.

'Mine!' Bheathain's voice was hoarse as a crow. 'You have what's mine!'

But the roaring in him was abating and a heavy blow on his back lessened his resolve. The next blow struck the nape of his neck, and he sank down, upsetting the table with his arm and bringing the rest of the papers onto his head. Many hands grappled him to the floor.

'We have nothing of yours, you scoundrel. McNair! Where is damned Mc—'

'What is the meaning of this?'

Bheathain bent sideways. A man at the bar had a pistol.

'I'll use this if called for.'

'It is not required, Mr McNair,' the red-haired man said. 'Murdoch, you see who the fellow is?'

'But what brings him here?'

The outer door opened and M'Illathain entered. Manus, holding a cloth to his face, followed.

'Sirs, oor pologies, lad's no hisself,' M'Illathain said to the assembled gentlemen.

'Do you see his face?'

'I do Murdoch, but let us hear them out,' the red-haired man said. 'Mr McNair, we do not require firearms. Murdoch, let the fellow up. Let's see what he thinks we have of his.'

Bheathain crawled forward. There were no more blows as he slumped into the chair and pressed his face against the leather. A bitter sob broke from his chest. It was gone.

'Mr Lockhart, you have saved your drawings?'

'For the most part. Do you know this buffoon?'

'We do,' the red-haired man said. 'After a fashion.'

'Apologies, Mr Lockhart,' Dixon said. 'It seems we must complete our business another time.'

'Perhaps somewhere less fraternised by madmen.'

'Indeed.'

The man bundled his papers and left.

'Forgie us, doctor,' M'Illathain said. 'Yurr hoosekeeper telt ye wur on business.'

'And so I was,' the red-haired man said. 'But the patient would not be kept waiting.'

'Sir, reckon we've naething fer yurr charges.' M'Illathain was wringing his bonnet in his hand as though were one of his own lying sick.

'Murdoch?' the red-haired man asked.

'The estate can be generous, in this case.'

'Tauld ye?' Manus said behind the rag covering his nose.

'This is a strange day,' M'Illathain answered.

'I, that is, we, would prefer word of this did not travel,' Dixon said.

The doctor tapped Bheathain on the shoulder. 'You're out of sorts, young man.'

'He's stole frae us,' he whispered.

'What is he saying?'

'He telt a'thing is stole frae him,' M'Illathain said.

'His sanity, it would seem,' Dixon said.

'It can be stolen from a man,' Dr Ramsay said. 'What's he holding?'

'A siller cross o' mine, fer luck.'

'Bheathain.' Dr Ramsay shook his shoulder. 'What was taken from you?'

He could not find the words. He liked the man and hoped not to be beaten again.

'Doctor, ye canna make sense o' him,' Manus said. 'A brainstorm it is.'

'No, I see it now; he has a cursemark,' the barkeep said.

'Yurr a fool, McNair! Doctor, be sae kind tae let him know thurr's nae sich a thing.'

'I cannot. His affliction is not and never was *natural* physic: You, what is your name?'

'Uilleam M'Illathain, sir.'

'Staffin, a kelp gatherer,' Dixon muttered.

'If you would aid me to get him to my surgery. I will do all I can for him. Manus MacDonald, do you require me also?'

'I shall mend.'

'Very well.'

M'Illathain took one of Bheathain's arms, Dr Ramsay the other. Bheathain clung to the chair.

'He winna lat gae.'

'It seems not,' the Doctor admitted. 'Murdoch, would you call at the surgery and ask Mrs Brodie for my black bag.'

'The laird has it,' Bheathain protested into the leather.

'The laird is not in the habit of stealing,' Dixon said as he left. You shall keep his good name out of this, young man.'

'Good God! Murdoch, I believe he is less crazed than he seems. You met the laird here yesterday, did you not?'

'I did. What of it?'

'And Bheathain took sick last evening, am I right?'

This was confirmed and Dixon left on his errand.

'Well, well,' Dr Ramsay said. 'And does any know if the laird passed through Brogaig?'

'He did so,' M'Illathain said.

All the talk was hurting Bheathain's head. What was taken from him was no longer here, but he was warm, and none were beating him. If they would only be quiet.

'And supposing Bheathain saw him also?'

'That I canna say,' M'Illathain said.

'What do you know of it, Manus MacDonald? You have a face like stone.'

'Damn! *Seadh*, so it is. He an' Tammas M'Neis saw the laird ride by. Och, but he's sick and that's all.'

'No, Manus MacDonald. I deal in natural physic, and I know its limits.'

'You're no say the laird stole frae the lad?' M'Illathain said.

'No, not wittingly, but he may have without being aware of it.'

'Och, ye speak in riddles, Doctor.'

'Perhaps. I will do what I can for him, but this needs spaecraft.'

'Reckon that new spaer's gone with the laird,' M'Illathain said. 'An' Haelda's langsyne dead, so Manus reckons.'

'She is, yes. But Ethelfeyrda, or Màiri as we must now call her, *is* with us. But Manus MacDonald, you knew that.'

'Will you not look at the wretch!'

The old man's shout startled Bheathain and he opened his eyes. Manus was in the centre of the room, one arm outstretched, and his face white as codflesh. 'See that!' Bheathain looked away as the arm pointed him out. 'D' ye reckon I can see that every day if I thocht... if I... och, tae the divvil with him!'

The door slammed.

'Should I gae efter him?' M'Illathain said.

'No, leave him be,' Dr Ramsay said.

Murdoch Dixon returned, asking, 'What's with his grandfather? He passed me with a face like thunder.'

'We strained his patience,' Dr Ramsay said. 'My bag if you will.'

Moments later the doctor thrust a glass at Bheathain's lips. It tasted bitter...

II

A full night passed in sleep, and he recalled nothing of the following day, of how he was brought from bed in Dr Ramsay's house and placed in a carriage, until a sharp motion of its springs wrought him from sleep.

'He's woken.'

He did not know the voice.

'He has, and not before time.'

Nor the second voice.

Bheathain sat upright and tried to loosen the thing around his face. A hand restrained him.

'Now, now. It is for your own good.'

Bheathain opened his eyes. The man restraining him sat opposite and a second man sat alongside him. The first man had red hair and small blue eyes.

'It is a bandage. I am sorry if it distresses you, but it is necessary.'

The man leant forward with a raised hand.

Bheathain flinched.

'You are safe here,' the man said. 'I am a doctor. You are my patient. Allow me.'

Bheathain held still and let the man touch his forehead.

'Feverish, still, and see how he perspires.'

'Indeed,' the second man said. 'The blanket protects your carriage leather as much as it warms him.'

There was something soft under his hand. A tartan rug. The corner of it draped over his shoulder and across his chest. He took the corner and pulled it across him. He had never been so ill. It was a novel feeling, like being drunk only no fun at all. His aches all had their own rhythm, but it was a job to tell one from another. Someone had bandaged his hand. He'd cut it on a bit of stone. He'd scratched a mark on it, the same as on his touchpiece. The touchpiece he lost...

'He sleeps,' the second man said.

'I believe so,' said the other.

He woke again when the men took him from the carriage. Being manhandled and brought to the waterside aggravated all his aches and strains but he had no strength to do anything but hang, like an empty skin, between them. Light shimmered off the surface of a loch and a third person joined them. A long green cloak covered his head. There was a boat at the side of a loch. Some dark memory reared up in Bheathain's thoughts and he kicked against the ground.

He wouldn't let death take him. This boat, the water, the robed figure...

'We must drag him in if needs be. He cannot step.'

Hands took his ankles and lowered him onto the thwart. The boat rocked and the cowled figure held his arm.

'Bheathain, easy now,' it said with a woman's voice. 'Hold steady now.'

He could not see her face, except for a fall of red hair from within the hood of her cloak.

The second man put down his cane and rowed them from shore. Bheathain watched the water drip from the oars and the ripples they made as they dipped into the loch. The red-headed man held him on the seat or he would have fallen. The man and woman talked the whole way across, but he could not follow what they said, except it was mostly about him. Landing on the far side of the loch, the two men carried him inside a house and laid him on a bed. The room was leesome enough with peat reek and other good smells. The woman put a pot on the fire and when it was warm, sat by the bed to bathe his face. There was something in the water, something sweet.

'Drink this,' she said. It was a foul brew, and he went to spit it out.

'No, drink it up.'

He drained it quickly and the woman gave him honey to take away the bitterness.

'You've grown since I saw you last,' she said. 'You'll sleep now.'

The bed was soft, and he needed no encouragement.

A second night passed, also unremembered, leaving him finally on the shore of wakefulness, sea-damp with sleep, sand in his eyes, tangle in his hair, salt-dry in his throat. The bed where he lay was not his own; it smelt and felt different, but pleasurably so, and the curtain dividing the bed from the room beyond had a pattern of flowers. Of greater comfort still was the smell. It was a deal better than anything he'd eaten in a long while—though his appetite was like to raise expectation in this regard—and it nudged his empty belly and watered his mouth.

This wasn't his bed, and it wasn't Manus by the cookpot.

His mind stirring, he stirred his body also but found the comfort of the bed concealed a hoard of bruises, each a reminder of his troubles. A man had thrashed him with a cane. His hand had cut open on a bit of stone. His other hand had held a silver cross.

Scenes tumbled in his head: a lost lamb, a stream and a white stag in the hills; but, save for the laird riding by, he remembered little of the following day and nothing of falling ill.

His mark was tender to the touch but no longer bleeding. His face was bare and under the blanket the rest of him was naked as an egg.

'So, Bheathain is awake,' the woman said. 'Reckon you'll be starved.'

'Ethelfeyrda?'

'You recall me then?' she said. 'I'm not Ethelfeyrda no more. Màiri is my name, or Miss Mulcahy, whichever.'

His memory was of a woman with long red hair leaning

down to hang the touchpiece about his neck. It was a good memory. He went to shift on the bed, but his bruises complained.

'What is the day? And where is this?' he asked.

'Two days after the Sabbath. Slept two days and nights, you did. Thank your friends this is not the Far Country, but only Haelda's Island on Long Loch. I am charged with seeing you right.'

'You gave me a strand of your hair for the touchpiece I had; I lost it.'

'I'll make you a new one.'

'I was ill. A man brought me here. I recall...'

He could not make sense of it and the words halted.

'Don't dwell on it now. You'll be sore and hungry. Two days you've not eaten a thing.'

He lay back and his head quietened.

'A fine bed you have,' he said.

'Glad you approve,' Màiri said. 'Not many I'd give it up for, but you'd greater need.'

He pushed his face against the blanket and breathed in. There was thyme and something else, orange water. The smell reminded him of his mother.

'I scratched a runemark on a stone,' he said. 'I had it on me. Can't say if it did me any good.'

'You're alive, still,' Màiri said.

He had slept in her bed, and she must have stripped the clothes off him. He should be full of shame, but he did not feel ashamed, not at all. Carefully, feeling every bruise in his back, he leant up and shifted the curtain, wondering if she matched the memory he had of her.

She had her back to him and the angle of light from the open door near-dazzled him. Her hair he thought paler, perhaps it had greyed a little, and she was smaller and slighter than he recalled. A cord around her waist held up an apron and a shawl trailed down her back to end in a vee between her hips. Her dress was dark green or black, he could not tell. The hem of it fell to her ankles and her feet were bare.

'Would you spy on me, Bheathain Somhairle?' she said without turning.

'I spy on those who spied on me,' he said. 'I was clothed when I came here.'

Màiri laughed. Her voice had a throaty sound like water pouring from a bottle.

'You're not the first man I seen without his clothes.'

She was bent over, preparing something.

'What are you doing?'

'Making up your pipe.'

'Bless,' he said, 'You found my baccy?'

'No, this is betony leaf. It'll do you good.'

He frowned. 'My *mathair* was always saying that; aught I didn't want to take was "good for me".'

The woman did not answer, and the pause became a silence.

'Màiri is a good Christian name,' he said.

'My mother hoped I'd follow Christ,' Màiri said, 'but if you get the gift you must bend with it. *Deny it, it will destroy you; untrained, it will destroy those you love*, so they say.'

'I thank you for the care you've given us, Màiri Mulcahy. Two nights I slept here?'

'No. First was at Dr Ramsay's,' Màiri said. 'For which I am thankful. You kept us awake with snoring.'

'I don't snore,' he protested.

'Och, so you do. I didn't mind so much.'

She untied her apron and folded it over a chair.

'Are you thirsty?'

He was and Màiri filled a pair of cups from a pitcher. As she neared him, he shifted over to give room for her to sit and pulled the blanket around him. Màiri handed him a cup and he sipped, then drank quickly. She laid the back of her hand across his forehead.

Her eyes were green. He had forgotten that, and madder root reddened her lips. A sprig of white heather secured the shawl across her bosom. He was torn between closing his eyes and staring at every inch of her. Enduring two days for this was not so bad. It was worth a great deal to be cared for.

'*Cus nas fhearr,*' she said and brushed back his hair as she removed her hand. 'You've a good strong face, Bheathain Somhairle.'

'So I've been told,' he lied. 'My mark's still there?'

'*Seadh,*' Màiri nodded. 'You'd hoped it gone?'

'I've always wanted it gone. Have you a looking-glass?'

She fetched a looking-glass. His cheek was swollen and flecked with dried matter where it had bled. The red stain was the same as it had always been. He returned the mirror, then stretched and grimaced.

'You'll be sore for a few days,' Màiri said. 'Murdoch Dixon gives his apologies.'

'I cannot find fault with him. It was I in the wrong.'

'None blame you.'

They would though. He was marked out, different. There was a time he fathomed either Mam knew little to tell or that he'd never wheedle it out of her. He had stopped chasing the truth of it years ago. The mark on his face would always be with him and he had best get on with it. And now this. Whatever this was.

'Did I hurt a' body? At the Royal, I mean.'

'No. Maybe a few bruises. No great harm done.'

'Ach, there is, though. Folk will talk.'

'You were ill,' Màiri said.

'Aye, so you say. They'll still talk. Always have.'

'What happened to your touchpiece?'

'I lost it stopping a lamb from drowning. I recall you hung it round my neck with your own hair.'

'I did. I shall make you another, keep you safe.'

'Then did losing it lead to all this?'

'Reckon so. I have what Dr Ramsay told me, and I heard you talking in your sleep. Can't say I know all of it. Whether you want to hear it is the thing.'

'I reckon this is the cause,' he turned his cheek to show her his mark. 'But go on.'

Màiri tucked her legs under her. The pile of her green

dress had worn smooth over her knees. He lay still, aware of her weight pressed against him through the blanket. Her eyes were on his face.

'A woman brought that on you. Most likely getting back at your mother or father for some wrong she held against them. It was a wicked thing to do.'

'Who was she?'

'I've no name for her. She's dead, that's all I can tell.'

'Dead?'

'*Seadh.* And being dead, and wishing she'd never harmed you, things can mend now.'

'Meaning I might be rid of it?'

For a moment he forgot how near Màiri sat to him and how green her eyes were and the way the light caught the soft hair on her forearm.

'It might be. Dr Ramsay said you spoke of the laird stealing from you.'

He forgot his aches and pains now.

'Aye. Reckon I did. But it was crazy talk.'

Màiri laughed. 'To any other it would be crazy, but not to me, or him. The laird did take from you.'

This had his attention.

'While living she could not change what she done, though it was her wish to. Now she's gone, what she made wants to unmake itself. It,' Màiri pointed at his mark, 'wants to be gone.'

'You speak as though it had a thought of its own,' he said.

'Aye, so it has. Reckon what the laird took from you is a *bòcan*, a wee ghostly thing sent to look for a' body it may bless. If it finds such a one, it will be gone from you.'

'Away with you. You mean another will bear it?'

He smacked the bed, making the frame of it shake. He wanted to be rid of his mark, but not hand it to another.

'Hush!' Màiri slapped him across the leg, like he was a child. 'It's not so at all. It won't blight another. It will be a blessing for them. Howsoever that will be, or when, I cannot tell.'

Bheathain sighed. 'Och then, soonest the better.'

Màiri laughed. 'No jumping at the looking glass each morning. It may take a time.'

'A *bòcan* wanting one to bless, eh?'

'*Seadh*. But a blessing for one is curse for another, and same around.'

Calluses ringed the soles of Màiri's feet but her ankles were smooth and pale as whalebone. He willed the hem of the dress to ride higher but then he thought of his own flesh and how a few inches of skin should rule the whole of it, like a king over his domain. One drop of poison in a cup of ale.

'I am grateful for telling me. I am thirsty, still.'

Màiri leant to refill his cup and the neckline of her dress fell, revealing the hollow between her breasts.

He could not but stare and his body answered the only way it knew.

'I'm flattered,' Màiri said.

He clutched the blanket to hide his shame. 'There's not many lassies will look at me.'

'Their loss,' Màiri said and slipped her hand about his. 'I washed your scarf, but I've no mind of your face.'

He held her hand, marvelling at how slender her fingers were. Only his mother had ever put her hand in his.

'I've need to go to Portree,' she said, 'There is tea and bread; eat what you want. Don't wander off this island. You're safe here.'

'Safe?' he asked. 'But I am mending, save for bruises.'

'Bheathain, I've a sense... I'm spaer no more, but stay *on* the island. I mean to call on Dr Ramsay and share my thoughts. Now, I have this for you.'

She presented him with his pipe stuffed with green leaf. He wrinkled his nose at the sharp stink.

'It's a purge,' Màiri said.

'I'm not an invalid,' he said. 'I mean to pay you back. Besides, I cannot lie here.'

'Then keep up the fire. You cannot do much for I have your shoes.'

'Why for?'

'They're falling apart,' Màiri said. 'I'll see to them.'

Most of the tackits had fallen out the soles but he did not think them so bad. He was not walking far in his stockings.

'I should read,' he said, wanting occupation. 'Have you a Bible?'

'Who has not a Bible?' Màiri's frown showed the lines in her face. It made her more interesting than the plump-faced girls his own age. Then she smiled, aware now of the intent in his gaze. He glanced away and his cheeks flushed.

'I didn't mean to stare. I'm not used to a woman so close.'

'Has no lass given you the eye?'

'They reckon a glance from me will bring a miscarry.'

'Then they are foolish girls. A mark like yours can do such a thing; but only if the heart wishes it, and yours is a good heart. If you're able enough, there is a task you might save us. This time I shall not spy on ye.'

Màiri fetched his clothes. They were clean and she had darned a hole in his breeches. The last woman to darn his clothes lay buried at Garafad.

>His wings are grown, but untried,
>The air is full of noises
>Mingled with a strange delight.
>The sound of women's work puts him at ease.
>*It is not my being hurts him so but the nature of what I am.*

>Editor's Remarks
>
>As before, a blank line marks the new chapter, with the initials, BS, and the date, January 24, 1862.
>
>According to Lady Helena's diary, the heavy snowfall at the end of January blocked the Edenborough Road and halted all local traffic. Fortunately, the estate was self-sufficient in most needs and the only significant loss was the mail deliveries. The isolation did not prevent arrival of a house-guest, a Mr Auburn

(or possibly Dyborn, Lady Helena's writing is unclear), on January 29. By Lady Helena's account, he was a friend or acquaintance of MacGregor, but as no one of either name appears in any of MacGregor's correspondence and his journal makes no mention of the visit, that cannot be correct. More probably, Mr Auburn had become stranded by the snow and took shelter with the MacGregors. Whoever he was, on the eleventh February the snow turned to rain, and he departed.

Now we must turn to the text. As the reader might guess, the nature of Bheathain's interest in Màiri Mulcahy is significantly less overt, albeit not entirely absent, in the published version. It is the first scene where MacGregor's declared intention to truthfully depict human emotion and physicality entered on the erotic and the reaction of Sir Sidney Beresford in particular was typical of the hypocritical morality of the mid-nineteenth century where prostitution flourished but any direct reference to sexual activity was unfit for print.

Aside from that scene, the text of the first draft closely matches that of the first edition, suggesting that MacGregor's sympathetic portrayal of Màiri Mulcahy did not trouble either Sir Sidney or John Lucas. Why that should be the case when MacGregor's portrayal of Eolhwynne in the next chapter proved the most contentious in volume one is intriguing, given that both Màiri Mulcahy and Eolhwynne practise magick. Naturally, your editor has some thoughts on the matter but to disclose them now would inevitably spoil much of the narrative in the following chapters. Suffice it to say there are many kinds of magick.

The servant of two masters
Chapter Five
Eilean Donan, eleven of night: The character of EOLHWYNNE, *with revelation of the nature and limitations of magick*

Sir David, to his credit, did not sleep easily that night, but I had no business with him and did not linger. The next morning, as he bade farewell to his cousin, I took my leave and passed to another.

A woman is inconstant:
The servant of two masters.
It is a law of nature.
Man is less fortunate: he serves but one.

I

GALGEARD, SIGEL'INGE'S PLUMP and aged cat had the freedom of the tower house at night and seemed content with that. Méirleach, though, needed to be let free for an hour a day or he grew fractious. That night, guided by a lad from Sir David's kitchen, Eolhwynne had carried the creature in his basket across the courtyard and through a gate in the wall. Beyond was a path and the shoreline of the loch, but having guided her thus far, the boy proved reluctant to leave. She was nearly a head taller, but pride told him *he* must look out for *her*. Patiently, she had insisted he go, asking only he left his lantern and the kitchen door unbarred so she may return when she wished. Even then, he had only left when bribed with a penny.

Once alone, she leant the lantern against a rock and untied the strap around Méirleach's basket. The marten scratched keenly at the wickerwork, but the moment the door opened he snaked up her arm and onto her shoulder, his claws piercing through her shawl, and chittering nervously. Here were unfamiliar noises and smells: the slither of waves, the tangy rot of the weed. These were not his familiar haunts, not the quiet walks behind the house at Duntulm.

'Safe,' she whispered. 'It is safe.'

Méirleach shook his head and sneezed, as if saying he

would be the judge of what was safe, but he did clamber down her arm and onto the rocks around her feet.

Seeking shelter from the wind, Eolhwynne left the basket by the gateway and followed the curve of the wall, using the lantern to light the ground under her feet. Emboldened, Méirleach nosed through the weed to the salt edge.

The air was chill. Stars and the rising moon threw more shadow than light. Folding the hem of her shawl beneath her, Eolhwynne sat and leant against the wall. A stone had fallen away, leaving a hollow where she placed the lantern.

She had not lodged with another spaer since leaving Iona, and never with one so much older, and more experienced. Like Méirleach, she was cautious in new surroundings, but could not complain of her welcome. Sigel'inge was cheerful company, though as she had attended Ynys Mannanan there was not the companionship of familiar memories and conversation had shifted from one thing to another.

She murmured a casting spell and threw a stone into the loch.

Why was she here? Lord MacDonald received news of his nephew's death three days ago and, within hours, the entire household knew he would be travelling south. She anticipated travelling with him, but when no word came, she understood her place was at Duntulm with Clara. She admitted to relief: barely settled at Duntulm she did not feel ready for such an adventure. Yet it hurt that her master did not think to ask her to scry for him, or ask her to grant him fortune, or any of the dozen things she might have done.

Then, when she had reconciled to being unneeded, he had called on her with instruction to pack for a passage and a two-week stay in Winchester at the Royal Court, speaking all the while with an air of distraction, as though his mind were full and she was only one of a hundred matters he must consider. Which perhaps she was.

Méirleach disturbed a crab. The fight was brief as his teeth made short work of the creature's claws and legs, but he could not crack its shell.

'Come,' she patted the ground beside her.

Méirleach brought her the crab and she slid her bronze knife under the shell and cracked it open, sensing the cold, silent life snuff out like a candle. The marten disappeared into the darkness to eat. The knife cleaned on the short grass she set to and stroked a whetstone along the blade with a sound rhythmic as a marsh bird. It was the most practical of her three tokens, and the most reliable. Her runes, carved from whalebone, were fine pieces, but she did not yet trust herself to read them accurately and the gold ring on her forefinger was no use at all, for it bore only her birth name and the month and year: March 1838. The day she did not know, nor did she set time aside to mark it. The edge of the whetstone left a deep groove in her hand. Square in section and long as her middle finger, it resembled an obelisk and the base was marked with 'stane', the rune of sacrifice.

A pounding at a door and a shout from the courtyard startled her. A moment later, Méirleach leapt into her lap, showering her with gravel, and in calming him she could not closely follow what was said or done in the courtyard behind the wall, except for three voices joined in argument followed by violence, stale as day-old bread and swiftly dealt. Light shone from a window in the tower house. Then a door slammed, bringing silence, and a shutter closed, leaving the tower in darkness.

The voice would not leave her. It had been angry and filled with hurt. Finding a pebble, she murmured a casting spell, threw it toward the loch, and listened for the splash. The man's anger left her, sinking with the stone: she wanted to freight a stone with her own fear and doubts, but her gift did not allow it...

§

Morning. Rows of swords and pikes decorated the walls of the hallway. Sigel'inge did not seem troubled by them, but Eolhwynne felt an unpleasant pricking, like pins and needles in her arms and legs and, making her excuses, exited into the courtyard where the morning sun made light of the shadows. The drag she had spent so much of yesterday in stood outside Sir David's coach house, but she could not see her master's servants about it. A second carriage stood alongside the drag but as it had Sir David's crest on the door, she supposed it nothing to do with their journey.

There was no sign of her master's carriage.

She had woken before dawn and lighting a candle had tried to foretell the day. Sigel'inge had spoken of the road through the pass to Invermoriston and Loch Ness; it was a good road, she said, well laid and sound. Eolhwynne was reassured but needed to be certain and to practise with her runes. She had wanted to exercise Fàidh also, but the runes were quarrelsome, giving no clear sign of good or ill, and by the time she reconciled herself to not knowing the course of the day, the sun was well into the sky and there was no time for the falcon. Until she knew her master's intentions, and especially what he required from her, she doubted anything would come clearly.

'My dear lady.'

Turning she found Sir David, her master's cousin, offering his hand to take hers, which she obliged.

His eyes were cloudy and shadowed: it seemed he had slept poorly, and though he smiled as he bent to kiss her hand, she knew he was troubled. Whether her impression was mere intuition or a deeper insight, she could not tell.

'Charmed, my dear,' Sir David said, repeating the smile, then he added in confidential tone: 'Be sure to guard my cousin well. He will need friends at Winchester.'

She did not know what to make of this, but before she could inquire, Lady Margaret joined them, saying, 'David, don't alarm the poor woman. Eolhwynne, your master is quite capable, but tell me...' she took her aside. 'Is Clara well? Or should I say, are both well?'

Lady Margaret led her away to be sure they were not overheard. Sir David and Lord MacDonald were busy talking with three other gentlemen visiting Sir David. One—they referred to him as 'Your Grace'—did not like her and had read a spiteful sermon in Sir David's chapel. A second, immensely fat and jolly-faced, insisted on kissing her hand and mauling it with his too-damp lips and beard, while the third, being in shape and mirth midway between the two, regarded her with mild curiosity. Sigel'inge lingered within the hallway and was ignored by all.

'It is not for me to say,' she answered Lady Margaret.

'I understand, but please, this once. Men are so unfeeling. I would visit, but,' she spread her hands. 'It is so difficult to find the time.'

'My mistress would welcome company,' Eolhwynne said. 'And I understand your fears.' She glanced up to see they were quite alone before breaking a confidence. 'All is well, both with my mistress and with the child she carries.'

Her eye caught Sir David frowning at his wife. Lady Margaret saw him also but dismissed his concern with a raised eyebrow and turned back to her with a weary sigh.

'Thank you. I do worry; I cannot help it. And I shall not betray your confidence.' She smiled. 'But of course, you will have been to Edenborough?'

Eolhwynne had not. She had seen no city larger than Derry.

'Heavens!' Lady Margaret said. 'Derry is scarce a city. And compared to Edenborough, well, Winchester is extra-ordinary! Everything, simply everything, is there.'

'For a price,' Sir David said, having rejoined his wife. 'My dear, what were you whispering about?'

As Sir David escorted his wife away, Sigel'inge came forward and took her by the elbow.

'Remember what I said of Lazarus,' she whispered. 'He is dangerous.' She quivered as she spoke his name. Sigel'inge was not being wholly honest, either with her or with herself. She might be afraid of Lazarus, but she desired him also. Male spaers were rare and mysterious.

'Graciana A'Guirre is wise,' Sigel'inge added, 'if you wish

to learn, she is the one. I do so envy you.' The woman squeezed her arm. Rumour had it spaewives and their familiars often grew to resemble one another. Sigel'inge's cat was plump and aged, and, provided there was a fire to warm herself, was content to be ignored. Likewise, Sir David rarely sought Sigel'inge's advice and Lady Margaret hardly spoke to her at all. Though Sigel'inge claimed not to mind, Eolhwynne felt sorry for her and hoped she would not share her fate. Graciana A'Guirre was the king's own spaewife. Born in the Basque lands and schooled in the Green Branch,[1] she had been in service over thirty years, a long time for a spaer. Of Lazarus, she knew only what Sigel'inge had told her.

'She's *not* gone!'

A girl of perhaps six with a fistful of crocus and snowdrops had run into the hallway. Lady Margaret held her as a maid rushed to join them.

'I'm sorry, ma'am. Hannah runs that quick.'

'Go away!' The girl shook her head so fiercely, the motion continued to her feet. The maid wrung her hands, looking nervously from the child to Lady Margaret.

'Now Hannah, this is not the time. Later perhaps.'

'But Mama, they are not for *you*. They are for *her!*'

Eolhwynne started, realising the girl was looking straight at her.

'Well,' Lady Margaret said. 'Perhaps you would like to give them to her.'

The girl needed no encouragement and ran out into the courtyard. Someone laughed and Lord MacDonald and Sir David stopped talking.

'I'm Hannah. What's your name?' Her face was bright as an apple and her yellow hair lay plaited down her back.

'Eolhwynne.'

The girl frowned.

---

[1] Also known as the Southern Tradition. The Northern Tradition was the White Branch and the Eastern Tradition the Red, or sometimes Black Branch. The Western Tradition, supposedly centred on Atlantis, was sometimes called the Root Tradition. *N.W.*

'Ale-win,' she repeated and knelt on one knee. 'Did you pick these, Hannah? They are very pretty. And you have such a pretty name too.'

Everyone was watching her, even the door attendants. The bishop scarce concealed his sneer. She was *exposed*. The pricking of the swords and pikes was preferable to this and secretly she touched the tip of her left thumb to the forefinger, making the sign of Thor, and the discomfort eased.

'For you.' Hannah thrust her hand out. Several of the stems had broken and the flowers hung in disarray.

Eolhwynne gathered them together.

'You ought to pick some for your mama.'

The girl shook her head: 'Mama picks her own flowers.'

The maid came and gathered the child to her. 'I'm sorra she bothered ye miss.'

'It was no trouble,' Eolhwynne said. She did not want the girl punished for her kindness. 'It was sweet of her.'

The maid curtsied and Hannah returned to stand with her mother. Eolhwynne saw Sir David exchange a word with Lord MacDonald. He had brought a sword to show him.

She turned away, relieved to no longer be the cause of attention. The flowers hung limp in her hand for Hannah had crushed the delicate stems. She would have cried over their brokenness, except for appearances and sight of a small window level with the cobblestones of the yard reminded her this was the second time in a few hours she had been close to tears.

§

Last night, as she returned to the kitchens after exercising Méirleach, she had been drawn to the window by the sense of sorrow in the room beyond. She had had to crouch to look within for the lintel was no higher than her knees. She had seen by the light of the single candle the cellar room beyond the iron bars, but not the cause of the sorrow.

She had turned to leave when a hand lunged through the bars and caught her ankle.

'That's enough. *Gun an còrr!*'

She scrambled free but lost the lantern and could not stop a hand snatching it up in a flurry of Gaelic and whisky breath. Méirleach chattered, anxious at the strange noise and sensing her fear. She did not hear what else the man said, except to recognise his was the voice she had heard earlier.

He was at the barred window. The lantern threw shadows across his face, but his gaze was hungry.

'I wish you no harm.' She crouched just out of his reach. 'But I must have the lantern.'

He refused to hand it over.

'*Tha mi 'cluiuntinn gu. Eireannach, than?*'

'My Gaelic is poor,' she said. 'Do you speak English?'

'Aye. A bonnie Eirish lassie, so you are. Why're ye keekin on us?'

'I was not prying,' she said. 'Return the lantern. It is not mine to lend.'

The man showed his face in the light. She gasped.

'I'm no sae bonny.' Blood had stained his jaw and cheekbone. One eye was closed by a bruise and his knuckles split open. 'If this be no yours, whose be it?'

'It's Sir David's,' she said.

'Him!' The man spat. 'Lanterns a plenty he has. Come hereawa.'

'I dare not.'

The man muttered something. Without thinking she leant forward to hear, and he tried to grab her arm.

'I can*not*,' she repeated. 'I cannot bear iron.'

'Iron? You're a spaer! By damn. Och, you're no that redhead he has. Who's your master?'

'MacDonald of Skye.'

He stank of drink and his breath laboured.

'I've naethin' agen him, though they're all belike. But this! This is Sir David's. Sir *bluidy* David.' He rattled the lantern, almost extinguishing the candle.

Then she spread thumb, fore and middle finger of her left hand to make the Tyr rune, the strongest protector. She did not fear his strength, she had only to keep her distance to be safe, but she sensed the deep pain under his anger.

'I wish to return the lantern.'

'An' I'm no minded tae give it ye. Sae what then?'

'I stay,' she said. 'I know you will return it soon enough.'

'Och, ye ken naethin.'

He withdrew the lantern behind the window bars. The room was a cell, scarce as long as he was tall with a pallet of straw and a water jug. The bottom of the window was only an inch above the courtyard paving.

Rain settled on the nape of her neck, and she tried not to feel the chill. Méirleach whimpered.

'Sir David put you here?'

'He did, and far more.'

'I may not leave you.'

'I care not if ye kep yer death of cold. Goodnight lassie.'

'I might trade for the lantern.'

'Ay,' the man said. 'If there were nae bars at yon window an' I was sober enough tae be a man, ye might well trade. But I'm tae drunk an' weary and they bars be there.'

'What I offer is not impeded,' she said.

'You give me drùidheachd, aye, is that what ye'll trade?'

'I do not call it that. I sense your pain. The drink makes you careless for now, but what when you're dry?'

'I shall drink when I am dry. The wife swore by spaers, but nae good did they do her.'

'Would she have you suffer like this?'

'Och, the wife cudna abide sufferin' in a' body. Shall there be no peace, woman?'

'You should be with your wife.'

'Ma wife? Damn ye! Ma wife be long dead and now ma son is dead wi' her. That bastard indoor saw to him.'

'Say on,' she whispered and made a second sign, that of Os, the mouth, to encourage the man to talk.

'He cleared Bearneas, sent the people awa' cross the sea. A New Warld, sae ma sister called it, an' a sent ma son wi her an' her gud man but seems the skraelings winna share their land. The laird has their blood on his hands, much as they damned savages.'

She eased her hand and his voice subsided. The rune had loosened his tongue.

'I might help you.'

'That Sigel'inge did naught fer the wife when she wis deen. Have ye nae bed tae gae tae? Nae warm bed?'

'It will keep,' she said. 'It will be a cold bed if I leave you without hope.'

'Will you then leave me in peace?'

'Gladly,' she said, 'if I also leave with the lantern.'

'I grant you are a trier.' He had stood on a stool to reach the window. 'What dae ye offer?'

'I can help you forget.'

'*Cha phòs!*' he jumped down. 'Lose mind o' ma boy! I canna, I winna. Gae, woman an' take your damn light.'

He put the lantern on the ledge between the bars. She did not take it.

'You will not forget him, but I know what it is to hate. It rots the spirit. What was his name?'

The only sound was the man's breathing and the patter of rain. She did not move and waited for the man to speak. Rain seeped under the neck of her dress.

''*S è* Conor,' he whispered. 'His name was *Conor*. He left fer the Americas wi ma sister. She's dead an' aw. Murdered by skraelings.'

He reappeared at the window.

'I mean no tae forget; *ach*, nor can a gae on. What maun I do?'

'Press forward, close as you can. I shall make a runemark on your head, but I must do it quickly and,' she swallowed nervously, 'you must not seize my hand.'

'Be these bars shall burn you. Ye've ma word. I shall recall Conor an' ma sister an' the good times?'

'And the bad,' she said. 'You will honour him and grieve but will not hate. I shall need the lantern to see.'

'Ye winna gae. 'Tis nae trick?'

'No trick.'

He pushed the lantern through the bars. The ground glittered with rain. She opened her purse and took out a pair of sixpences.

'A purge?' he asked.
'You know of it?'
'Heard of it; dinna ken it fer real.'

She put a coin on the back of her left hand and signed the five elements over it with her right.

'Ice for a fever, water for thirst, air to give life, and fire in the hearth, earth for our bread and rest for our dead.'

She put her hand out and asked him to take the first coin and swallow it.

'When you pass it, do not think to look for it. Turn your back and walk away.'

He stared at the sixpence a moment then tossed it down his mouth and swallowed hard.

'Take your hate and think of it as a snake; hold it as though its bite was death and lean your head on the bars.'

'Near as I can, lassie. Hewch, that iron's caud.'

She slipped the second coin into her palm and held it there with her thumb.

'You wish this?'
'Ay. Dee whit ye must.'

She let a drop of rain gather on her fingertip, then touched the man's forehead and drew the downstroke of Rathad, the rune of the road and the journey not yet taken. Her hand tingled, as though she had pushed it into snow. She trembled as she drew the loop of the rune and then the second downstroke. The numbness crept through the sinews of her wrist and into her arm. It was almost beyond her to keep her hand steady, and the finger outstretched. The words helped her, the familiarity of the incantation: ice, water, air, fire, earth, honouring the five. Her hand closed into a talon, with only the forefinger outstretched. It was closest to the iron. She began the second rune as the numbness flowed into her elbow. P'reth, the dice cup, the rune of chance and the rules of the game, she drew it over the first rune to bind them into one. Hate ruled this man and governed his road. Change the rules, and a new road opens.

With the last stroke made, she snatched away her arm and flung the coin into the darkness before clasping the arm across her chest. The numbness flared to her shoulder, as if a flame ate the flesh, then it ebbed and feeling returned with a thousand stabbing pains. She cried out and for a moment lost all time. When she came to, he was calling her.

'Lassie, shall I hammer the door? A' body shall come.'

'It's passing,' she whispered.

She had slumped against the wall beside the window and now slowly unbent her back and knees.

'I dinna ken it would be sae sore on ye.'

'All will be well.'

Méirleach, knowing better, scratched at his basket, wanting to protect her.

'You should sleep,' she said.

'In the morn I shall shit a sixpence an' ma troubles will be done.'

'Trust me, as I trusted you. Sleep is the great healer.'

'Ay,' he said, '*tha mi sgìth*.'

Eolhwynne knotted her shawl and used it as a sling to support her arm. Her hand trembled, but though she tried to close it into a fist, the forefinger refused to bend. The man needed no more persuading and settled on his bed. She collected the lantern and Méirleach's basket. She was cold and wet and exhausted, and her arm ached miserably, but she was proud also. She had saved a man tonight, saved him from despair, and for a spaer there was no higher purpose.

II

Overhearing the name of her master's son, her attention returned to the present.

'I was thinking of George,' Sir David was saying. 'A cadet's sword is a mean thing.'

Daylight revealed the cell beneath the window and the

man lying on a straw bed. A blanket covered all except his dark red hair and one grimy foot.

She took a crocus and a snowdrop, brightness of the sun, and the first flower after winter and threw them to the sleeping man.

'Eolhwynne?' Lord MacDonald was calling her.

'My Lord,' she curtsied, and the flowers bobbed in her hand.

'You will ride with me today. There is much I need to say.'

She looked away, thinking of his awful carriage.

'Is there some difficulty?' MacDonald asked.

'I mean no offence, sir. Only your carriage...'

'This is ours for now,' he pointed at the carriage with Sir David's arms upon the door. 'I have borrowed it from my cousin. I trust it will suit.'

It was large and handsome, with none of the dreadful aura of her master's black carriage.

'Forgive me,' she said awkwardly. 'I misunderstood you. My familiars?'

'They are inside already. They had no objection,' he said pointedly. 'We have much to discuss, Eolhwynne. It would be convenient to do so early.'

He returned to Sir David and Lady Margaret, leaving her alone. She walked around the carriage and found the door open. Méirleach's basket lay across the seat and Fàidh's cage stood beside the farther door. Neither was happy at another day of confinement, but it could not be helped. She touched the seat cushion, and it gave under her hand: *'Gaiety and children's laughter'*. There was nothing to fear and she took her seat and closed her eyes.

She must understand her master; learn to read his thoughts from a glance or a single word so she might aid and serve him. Perhaps today was the beginning of that journey. She hoped so. A closed book lay on the seat opposite her where her master would sit. Impulsively she took it up a moment and read the title, *Edwin & Morcar*, and the author, whom she had heard of but not read. She returned it to the seat. Sitting back, she closed her eyes a moment and allowed, or rather persuaded, her concerns to drift from her.

Presently, Lord MacDonald took his seat opposite her and McNeil closed the door.

'You are comfortable, I see. Good.' MacDonald lowered the droplight and glanced out. 'Hannah is waving. I believe you have made a friend.'

'She is very sweet.' Eolhwynne pretended to smell the flowers and held them up for Hannah to see. The girl waved.

'We must be going,' her master said. 'John, are we ready?'

'We are, sere.'

'Away then, no time to waste.' MacDonald rapped his cane against the door, drawing mock protest from Sir David.

'Cousin, be gentle! I require its safe return.'

MacDonald apologised with a wave but already the carriage was moving. Eolhwynne leant out the window to make her goodbyes, but her master pulled her back.

'Have care!'

She withdrew her head moments before they plunged through the narrow gatehouse.

'Thank you.'

'Perhaps it is better if we close this,' he said and raised the window, leaving a small gap for air.

'Hannah was a little robust with the flowers. They will stain your dress; allow me.' He spread a handkerchief on the seat, and she set the snowdrops and crocuses on it.

'I must apologise,' she said.

'Whatever for?' His surprise was genuine. 'You were charming, and no harm was done.'

'Her mother seemed unhappy.'

Her master laughed. He seemed changed this morning, as though he had received good news.

'She will not be for long. David will see to that. He may choose to flatter every woman he meets but he and Margaret are closer than they pretend. They are good for each other.'

He broke off and stared out of the window. They had joined the main road: on one side were mountains, on the other a sea loch. The far side of the loch was in deep shadow. She pulled the shawl close and wrapped her hand in its folds.

'The day is unfriendly,' MacDonald said, and this time shut the window wholly and sat rubbing his palms as he continued to speak: 'I have scarcely spoken to you since you arrived from Iona. We are still near strangers.'

'You had more pressing concerns, my Lord. I understood.'

'It is true, I have been preoccupied. I trust you are happy at Duntulm. I have heard no word to the contrary.'

'I am. Many have made me welcome there.'

'Many but not me. I regret I have all but ignored you.'

'I did not think you were ignoring me,' she lied.

'Then we need say no more on it. I must ask you about Kyleakin, you wished to…'

She began to apologise for the awful business in the chapel, but he dismissed her concern.

'The ferry interests me at present: you tried to raise your concern and I did not give you chance to speak. I am doing so now. What troubled you?'

It was so unexpected her thoughts whirled, like dandelion seeds. The sisters on Iona had taught her never to seek to understand a master's purpose or reason, only to listen and respond as he directed, yet even as she recalled everything she could about the boat and the men aboard it she could not but wonder what he sought.

'There was anger between Mr MacAuley and his son. No, that is inexact,' she corrected herself. 'The father was anxious, and his son was angry, with his father and with himself. They no longer trusted each other. I saw the boat had been repaired, but,' she recalled the new wood, pale against the salt-stained frames. Strong timber had a clear note to it, like a bell, but the new frames did not sound right, 'the repair was poor. I was uneasy.'

'You raised your concern with MacAuley?'

'It was not my place,' she said. 'Not without speaking to you first.'

MacDonald seemed pleased with her answers.

'Of course: your duty is to inform and advise me. Alasdair was most forthcoming. He is angry with his father because he is no longer trusted. His father is anxious his son may leave and go south. As for the boat, the repair *is* poor work and will need replacing. Does it agree with what you found?'

She nodded, covering her mouth with a hand. What had begun with surprise had ended in a smile.

'In the collision they lost two sheep,' he continued, 'not a tragedy, but "loss of life" there was.'

'I was over anxious,' she said and dropped her hand.

'Perhaps so,' he accepted, 'but you acted properly. I shall not ignore you again.'

With this he glanced sideways at the newspaper lying on the seat beside him. His smile faded and she understood he had not yet begun to speak of his true concern, the reason she travelled with him to Winchester.

'You have read the 'papers these last few days?'

'I have not,' she said, 'my concern is for you, for your wife and your household. Should I have done?'

'No, I would not expect it of you; but you understand why I am travelling to Winchester?'

'Of course: Prince William was your nephew.'

'Indeed, my nephew,' MacDonald tapped the 'paper. 'A young man, full of vigour, dead without apparent cause.'

He seeks an answer.

She had not sought an inknowing and pushed the thought aside, determined to listen only to his words.

'This,' he picked up *The Times* and shook it, 'is vile speculation and rumour, all printed between the lines, of course, but there nonetheless.'

'Sir,' she sat forward. 'May I speak openly?'

'Speak as you think fit. Only,' his eyes filled with anxiety, 'I believe I am obliged to my late sister to learn how he died.'

'But there must be others whose duty is yet stronger. I think of his father, people closer to him than you were.'

Her master grimaced as though he had bitten something unpalatable.

'William's father is not a strong man. He means well, but he is easily swayed. I fear he will be persuaded to accept whatever an "official" investigation reports.'

Scorn! She tasted it, bitter as the sloe. Powerful feelings often have a specific taste. Despite her intentions, her master's strength of feeling forced itself upon her.

'You believe Prince William's death was not an accident and the truth will be hidden,' she said, careful to speak only what she might reasonably assume from what he had said.

Her frowned. 'I did not mean to be so obtuse.'

'Your true feelings are plain. But I must advise caution.' Her heart was beating swiftly as she waited until she had his full attention. 'If evil was done to your nephew and you intend to expose it, it places you in danger.'

MacDonald folded the newspaper. She had risked displeasing him, but it must be said. Caught up in her master's affairs, she had forgotten the soreness of her hand.

'You must read this,' he said of the 'paper. 'Perhaps you can glean something from it I have missed.'

He slid the newspaper onto her seat and clasped his hands together, seemingly at a loss without something to hold. It was the act of a man seeking action; needing to grasp and affect and frustrated at delay. But it was also a mark of self-reliance, one hand closing on the other leaving no place for a third. It showed he preferred to rely on his own strengths rather than depend on others. She must prove her worth to him: he was defensive and aware of his frailties, but, like a moth, helplessly drawn to a light.

'Some will object to my meddling,' Lord MacDonald said. 'I even gain some satisfaction from the prospect...' he frowned. 'If I place myself in danger, then I put you in danger, also. I had not considered that.'

'Master, truly I did not think of myself, nor do I fear for you,' before he could object, she cupped a hand over his fists 'You act willingly, but I must think also of your wife and your son and daughter. I have a duty to them, also.'

She sat back, removing her hand from his. MacDonald

did not move or speak but remained staring at the back of his hand as though surprised by his own flesh.

'I do not understand. I have no daughter. I—Good God! I am to *have* a daughter!'

She closed her eyes. She had been so confident and proud, yet a slip of the tongue had thrown her.

'I am sorry, my Lord,' she whispered. 'I spoke incautiously. It is true; I know your wife bears a daughter.'[1]

She stared across the loch, unable to meet his eyes. Low tide had exposed a line of wooden stakes and fishing nets.

'Has Clara asked you the sex of the child?'

'No.' Still she did not turn to face him but sensed his gaze. There was surprise in his voice, joy also and self-reproach. 'She wishes for a girl, but she has not asked me.'

'I am not angry with you,' he said. 'And I admit I have allowed one obligation to overrule another. Has she a name for the child?'

'She has not spoken of it.'

'We have not discussed names; it seemed... presumptuous. I wondered if she had a name *in mind*.'

She smiled and wiped away her tears.

'You think too highly of a spaewife's abilities, my Lord. We cannot read minds.' She turned back to him but could not yet meet his eyes. 'I can hear hopes and regrets and fears in a voice and tell lies from truth, but what exists only in a person's thoughts is as hidden from me as any other.'

He took out a cloth to clean his glasses.

'The Kyle ferry, you saw the state of things between father and son; that I can understand. I also saw the repair to the boat, but you sensed something more, something amiss, and the same with my carriage. You said you did not wish to travel in it. Why?'

---

[1] In medieval times and earlier it was thought unlucky to seek any kind of foreknowledge concerning an unborn child. By MacGregor's day, it was merely thought improper and of course with the aid of medical technology the privacy of the unborn child is now wholly eroded. *N.W.*

'Things are not mute to me as they are to you. It is not the carriage but what you use it for.'

He smiled with the air of a man finding a coin. 'Burials, of course. The purpose taints it somehow. *The blade itself intends to violence.*'

'My Lord?'

'Homer,' he said. 'A sword gets a taste for killing. My chariot has a taste for death.'

'Not a taste; but when you ride in it you are preoccupied by death and any who see it knows there is a burial. Death casts a pall over it and I cannot bear it.'

'Perhaps Clara is sensitive also,' he said. 'She wishes I would get rid of it.'

He rubbed the ball of his thumb across his wedding ring as he spoke her name. She would not need to remind him of his obligations again.

'My wife understands my concern for William,' he said. 'I have not wholly abandoned her.' His manner had become formal. 'In truth, you travel with me at her suggestion. I had intended you to stay at Duntulm. She persuaded me and I am grateful to her. Make no mistake, I pray no one is to blame for William's death, but I must be certain of it.'

'I did not intend to question your resolve,' she said.

'I accept you only wish me to know the consequences of my actions.' He sighed. 'I am not used to sharing my troubles and I do not find it easy to admit that I cannot do this alone.'

'I did not think you alone. Your son will be with you.'

'True, but he is not part of my plans. I know my son; best for all he is not involved.'

There was no disrespect, but whether out of concern for George's safety or his temperament, she could not tell which, he did not trust his son. She thought it an error but now was not the time to challenge him.

'I understand,' she said. 'What do you know of your nephew's death?'

'I only know what is printed here,' he indicated *The Times*. 'It speaks of an intruder in the Royal Apartments. The queen found

William in her chambers but could do nothing for him. What the official explanation will be I cannot imagine.' He paused in thought. 'Can you tell with certainty if a man is speaking falsely?'

'Not with certainty,' she admitted. 'I cannot tell truth from untruth, but if he lies intentionally, I will know.'

'Good. I hoped it was so. There are two people I would have you give close attention. The Earl of Northumberland is one. *Edwin*,' he indicated the book beside him, 'was one of his predecessors. He wrote me of William's death; it seems he is acting as regent for the moment, a fact *The Times* has *not* published, thank God.'

She had a vision of an icy road: her master did not trust this man.

'He will put the interest of the crown above all. If there is anything unseemly about William's death, he will conceal it, from me and from anyone.'

'I must know more of this man,' she said. 'Do you have the letter you received from him?'

'Not with me,' he said.

'That is unfortunate; handwriting reveals character.'

'It was not in his hand; scribes take all correspondence at court. You have many skills,' he said. 'Iorpereth was my grandfather's spaewife; she described spaeing as similar to hindsight, except she knew the regrets of others, as well as her own.'

'It is true,' she agreed. 'It is also said that describing clearsight to one without is like describing a rainbow to one who cannot see.'[1]

He laughed easily at this, but his hands betrayed him for they had clasped together again. Like all men, he was wary of things he did not understand.

'But it might also be seeing what others do *not*,' she said.

He frowned and unclasped his hands. She waited for his response.

---

[1] According to Sister Ethelnyd of the Iona Fellowship of Grace, these insights strongly suggest MacGregor had personal contact with women blessed with the gift; most likely the booth-scryers of Edenborough's Old Town. *N.W.*

'You are testing yourself upon me. I approve. I believe I revealed something, but what it was escapes me. Please.'

'It is not great insight,' she said. 'You mentioned your grandfather and in the same breath spoke of regret. It suggests a connection. Regrets concerning the dead endure because we can never ask their forgiveness.'

The words echoed in her own life, but she pushed the memories aside. This was no time for selfishness.

'In his final years my grandfather asked me to clear the lands for sheep. He said I was young and had the vigour for it. I allowed him to believe I would follow his wishes and regret deceiving him.' MacDonald cleared his throat. 'You are very perceptive.'

'Thank you. I do my best with the skills I have.' She stroked the velvet seat covers. 'Your cousin clears his lands.'

'Perhaps if I had six children to worry for, I might put them above all others, as I think he does. I regret there is no clear right or wrong. Life on Skye is harsh for many and the estate makes a loss year on year. I do not know how long it can continue. My cousin would say I am not safeguarding the future, but I refuse to force men from their native land.'

She recalled the man she met last night. She was, in any event, oath-bound to inform her master whenever she employed her skills for another.

'Last night I spoke with a man held prisoner. He believes your cousin has done him a great wrong and wishes him ill.'

'I know of him, though he is no prisoner. How did you and he meet?'

'I was exercising Méirleach and saw him in a cell.'

'You helped him?'

'I believe so. Anger and bitterness would have destroyed him; I eased his suffering. My first duty is to you, my Lord, but you understand I have a duty to help all, when it is in my power.'

'I do know, and I approve wholeheartedly of what you did, as would my cousin. Do not think too harshly of him.'

'I believe Sir David is a good man,' she said, 'but fear his conscience speaks too softly.'

'It will speak louder after last night, at least for a time.' MacDonald laughed. 'In truth, there are times I wish my conscience quieter, but I am not made that way. I fear I was a very distant uncle to William and Alexander; perhaps I am trying to make amends.'

His hands lay open on his lap, palm uppermost as though receiving something.

'Your concern for one who is dead must not blind you to the living,' she said. 'Alexander will be greatly troubled by his brother's death.'

'Of course, and he is now heir, a burden and a great responsibility. My father died in Flanders fighting the French. Had he lived he would be sixty-three this year. I mourn him, yet I gained my inheritance a generation early, though Anglia is a rather greater inheritance than half of Skye and perhaps it is not such a good comparison. But I shall not forget my duty to the living, as you put it.'

'You spoke of the earl; who is the other I must be aware of?'

'The king's spaer, Graciana A'Guirre. What do you know of her?'

'I know her by reputation. She is of the Green Branch, and I know something of their practices. Although I studied the Northern Tradition, we learned how other traditions practise magick. I understand Lazarus, the tsar's holy man, will also be at Winchester.'

'Regrettably, yes, but I doubt he concerns us. Study A'Guirre for she may be the key.'

A'Guirre could also be a powerful and dangerous opponent to her master and to her also, but she kept her thoughts to herself. There was no need to alarm him without good cause.

Their journey had brought them to a small township. It was much dilapidated: several houses had lost their roofs and the bare walls were half-broken. Smoke drifted above the houses still with thatch, and just when she thought the place devoid of humanity, two small boys ran out to see them pass.

She caught a glimpse of their bare legs and hungry faces as they mutely watched the carriage by.

Their gaze was so hopeful, so lost in their own need, it took no effort for her to understand their position. The fleeting carriage with its gleaming horses had given them a glimpse of another world, a world without hunger or meagre fires. She had once lived in their world and only fortune—if the gift of Grace is good fortune—had lifted her from it: fortune, and the murder of her parents. Her master, sitting opposite her with forward view, saw a different landscape: that which was to come with familiar places and acquaintances resumed. She saw only what was receding into the past and journeyed into the unknown.

Méirleach woke and scratched himself and she wished she also had a wicker basket to curl into; some place she might call her own.

Her master was examining some papers filled with maps and calculations. The novel lay unattended beside him.

'*Edwin and Morcar*,' she said. 'You are not reading it?'

'No. Clara gave it me as we left. It is not my choice, though it is diverting. The *Edenborough Times* is more *useful*,' he said reproachfully.

'I understand. I shall read *The Times* tonight, my Lord. It will raise many questions and I do not wish to disturb you now.'

'Then by all means.' He passed it across. 'Might I recommend you start at the beginning.'

She took the book and felt the cover. The leather was unworn and the pages crisp. Few, if any, had read it. In truth, it had not occurred to her to begin at any other point in the story, for she sought the certainty of narrative and a refuge from chance and the unknowable. Certainty must be the chief pleasure of reading; knowing the ending, however improbable, was fixed upon the final page. The true story of the Earls Edwin and Morcar she knew:[1] Edwin's spaewife had been Igraine Swan-neck and though she was one of the most gifted spaers who ever lived, she had failed to save Edwin and his brother from their own ambitions, and so brought death into their lives and ruin on the kingdom.

Had Clara the subtlety to give her husband such a message? Had he the wit to understand it?

III

That evening at the Inn at Invermoriston, she was in a reflective mood as she tended the thirty-three pieces of bone with which she searched the future and hidden present. Holding each up to a candle flame, she studied them for the cracks and flaws which might sap or bend their strength. Near translucent, the bone seemed to glow from within, sharpening the dark line of the runestave and revealing shades of pearl and dove grey under the eyeglass.

The rune was Arbh: the ox, rune of stoic resistance, resilience and healing. A reminder success was born from endurance and not the ill use of others and, in this instance, a good spaewife always cared for her runes. Within reach on the couch were three almost complete rune-rows, her goatskin rune pouch, and a cedarwood box containing her beeswax: "Finest Quality Purified Bee—, McNeil's Household Supplies, O—" still legible on the card wrapper, and two polishing cloths.

All rune stones decay: stone chips, amber scratches, metals tarnish, wood splits, and even gold wears away. Bone is prone to cracks and splints and requires frequent care.

The couch was softer than Eolhwynne liked. Only

---

[1] In 1066, Edwin, Earl of Mercia, and Morcar, Earl of Northumbria, attempted to play off the rival claims of Harald Siggurdsson of Norway, William, Duke of Normandy and the Saxon, Harold Godwinsson, for Anglia's throne. Wishing to weaken the eventual claimant and ensure their own authority was undiminished, they succeeded too well, and a disunited Anglia fell to the Danish king, Sweyn Hardarcnut, at Lincoln in 1072. *N.W.*

spaewives favoured east-facing attic rooms and the couch was old and worn out, like the bed and everything else in the room. One corner was taken by a chimneybreast and a whole side truncated by the shelving roof, so it did not have the feeling of a room at all but rather something eked out of an awkward space unwanted by anyone else.[1]

A small window jutting from the angle of the roof overlooked a wooded hillside and secured within its reach on the wall outside was a sunboard. This she had swept of leaves and dead insects and found serviceable. Presently, when her runes were clean and polished, she would lay them out along the rack and secure them with the copper lattice. The brass dial once showing where the sun rose above the horizon had corroded away and the surrounding hills made it impossible to calculate with her tables. She must angle the sunboard eastward and hope her runes caught the sun the moment it broke the horizon.[2]

No sound reached her from below, but wind skittered over the slates and the drape covering the window shifted in a draught. A fire sulked in the grate and Fàidh's bell clinked. The bird was restless, impatient at another day's confinement. Méirleach shook himself and mewled irritably. He knew night had come and was impatient for freedom.

She sat with bare feet folded under her, kidskin slippers abandoned on the floor. Her few belongings scattered across the room, helped make it hers for the night and concealed

---

[1] In former times inns and lodging-houses maintained rooms specifically for spaewives travelling with their masters, but with the declining use of spaewives such rooms became less common and were often poorly kept. A reconstruction of such a room as it would have been in 1580, toward the end of the greatest popularity of spaewives, may be seen at the Geffrye Museum in Lunden. *N.W.*
[2] Science has confirmed the ancient and widespread belief that rune stones are only effective if frequently exposed to sunlight and linked it to the photoelectric effect whereby light—specifically ultraviolet light—modifies electrostatic fields; however, the exact process is not yet understood. *N.W.*

its drabness, if not its chill. Her nightdress lay upon the pillow, together with her journal in which she had pressed three of Hannah's snowdrops. Her father's watch—the hour was gone eleven—sat on the table. Over the fire mantel she had hung her stockings to dry, and on a brass hook beside the door, her walking cloak and drum waited with her staff.

Not hers was her master's copy of *The Times*. This she had read and made a list of questions to ask him in the morning.

Except for her stockings, she had not changed since dinner and mindful even a speck of wax will stain, she wore an apron to protect her dress. This was pale blue, cut square over the bosom with a lace tucker for modesty, and its short sleeves trimmed with dark blue crépe. It was her second-best dress, and she should have changed into something more suitable for polishing her runes—she would have to shortly in any case, she told herself—but its colour cheered the drabness of the room.

She set Arbh on the coverlet, completing the first line, and yawning with tiredness, fumbled as she drew a rune from the pouch.

It dropped on the floor.

'Ó *daor*,' she muttered, tiredness calling her old tongue.

It had not fallen beside the bed nor, and she shook them to be certain, had it fallen in her slippers. Reluctantly she slid to the floor with the colder air about her ankles. The rune stone had left a trail through the dust under the couch, and she reached for the stone without seeing the cobweb in her path. Its touch was like shaking death by the hand and grabbing the rune stone she leapt back onto the couch.

The rune was Loegr: rune of lake and ocean. Thirst slaker and flood maker; water marked all life's waypoints: birth, baptism, the loving act, childbirth, and finally death. Tomorrow, they set sail for Winchester. Had Loegr fallen by chance or was it speaking to her? It was impossible to know. After two days in the dark, her runes were too weak to resist the power of coincidence. She rubbed her hands free of the clinging webs, but her mood was broken. Now she saw the attic room as though for the first time: a worn couch, a cracked basin, the sputtering fire in the hearth and a candle losing against the shadows. She pulled her shawl about her.

The rune examined against the flame, she slowly waxed and polished it and then placed it between Fear and Yng, but her thoughts were elsewhere.

She had learned the qualities of materials suitable for rune-making on Iona, along with their care, and influences; jet would always scry darker than amber and beech more joyfully than holly. With others in her year she practised with tree runes of pale birch to darkest rosewood; shell runes of oyster, mussel, and scallop; runes of marble, onyx, opal, quartz (easily found but hard to work) amethyst, and slate; runes of common, alloyed, and noble metals; lightning glass,[1] which was rare and mercurial; amber, ivory, and bone. Each novice searching for the material best suited to her temperament and pocket, or, as was often the case, her father's pocket.

Most of the novices chose tree runes as they were the least costly. Except that it was rarely the wood of just any tree they sought, but that of a particular and treasured tree and for a month blocks of ash, elm, oak, holly, and yew came on the boat from Oban.

Only two novices chose other than wood, stone, or common metal for her runes. One was a girl whose wealthy father bought her a silver ingot. She was the other.

Remembering a yew close by her parents' grave on Derryveagh, Eolhwynne had begun to write a letter to Father Padraig, but before she could send it a great whale stranded on the shore below the Fellowship. As a child, Eolhwynne remembered the whales crossing the bay at Derryveagh, the great beasts surfacing like dreams into wakefulness before slipping away into the depths.

To her, whales were mysterious and beautiful.

---

[1] A type of stone found in deserts and thought to be caused by lightning fusing sand grains together. *N.W.*

But stranded on the beach, the dead whale poisoned the air with its corrupted flesh and the house-sisters decided to allow men onto the island to remove it. The men needed no persuasion for baleen and blubber had many uses, and soon only a dark stain and a scatter of bones remained which the birds soon picked clean, and the waves washed until they were pale as the sky. Eolhwynne would never send the letter to Father Padraig for her runes had come to her.

The runemaster helped her choose the best bone for carving. He was the only man on the island and the novices were in awe of him. Old enough to be her father, he was tall and black-haired and could turn his hands to any task. Whether or not he had clearsight, no one knew.

After three days he called her to his workshop to see his work.

'They are not silver trinkets,' he said. 'The whale-spirit lives in them.'

The last rune from the bag was Sigel: the power of light over darkness. It had lingered in the bag to admonish her.

'I have neglected you.'

Sigel was the rune of inspiration, but it was the last thing she felt as she waxed and polished. The smell of beeswax filled the air with drowsiness and the moment she put Sigel in its place, she slipped from the couch to open the window and lean out.

Wind soared through the oak and pinewoods behind the inn, and she longed to be under them, with earth under her feet. Leaving the window open, she laid her runes along the shelves in the sunboard and closed the panel to hold them in place. Not trusting the clasp on the frame, she looped a piece of cord through the lattice and secured it: it would be too awful to wake and find her runes scattered on the ground.

Méirleach called to remind her he was tired of his basket.

'Soon,' she whispered. 'Very soon.'

Fàidh flexed her wings, shaking the bell on her traces. She might rise early and fly the bird before breakfast but made no promises. Untying her apron, she folded it and put it away. A jug still held a little warm water, and she scrubbed her hands and soothed the chafed skin with orange paste.

Her dress would not do for walking. Unlacing it to the waist, she eased it down and laid it across the couch. Pearl buttons undid her lace tucker, and she laid it beside the frock and slipped out of her petticoat before using the close-stool, a poor thing with one leg so loose she must brace her foot against the floor lest she, it, and contents be thrown over.

Her waters were cloudy and pungent; she had drunk nothing between leaving the Mackenzie's and arriving at the inn and received an aching head for her foolishness. The wayside inn where they stopped to water the horses had supplied her master with small beer but had nothing for her, save stewed and undrinkable tea. Plain boiled water seemed beyond them, and she had gone without.

Thankfully, this inn provided drinkable tea.

Reduced to her bloomers, she shivered and rubbed her arms against the chill before pulling a plain green dress over her hips and buttoning it swiftly to the neck. She would have her shawl for warmth and her cloak in case of rain: the sleeve of her dress would get wet, but there was no avoiding that.

§

She borrowed a lantern from the inn, took the bridge across the river and found a path leading up, away from the road. The river would not do; she needed clear water and looked for a mountain stream. She held Méirleach under her arm. He wriggled, eager to be free, but it was not safe here. She waited until the woods had closed in and people were far behind before letting him free. Then she walked uphill, lantern in one hand, staff in the other. Méirleach, unsettled in an unfamiliar place, played around her feet but she shooed him away. She could not be distracted. There was work to do. She carried her drum across her back, an empty silver flask under the waistband of her dress, and the handkerchief given her for Hannah's flowers.

The moon had risen, and stars shone between the clouds. Under the trees it was all shadows and she moved in a pool of light through the darkness accompanied by the rattle of the cymbals in the frame of her drum. When the path grew steeper, she leant more on the staff or used it to test the rough ground. She had sat too long in her room at the inn. Walking warmed her legs and sent blood to her head and dragged air into her chest. She felt alive and able, if less than brave. Only her hand troubled her and she had to stop and clutch it in her shawl until the iron blains stopped aching.

Lord MacDonald had praised her, though she had done little to deserve it, and had at last confided in her. She had tried to talk to him again this evening, but he had retired early complaining of tiredness. Tomorrow, she hoped to share his carriage again. Once her master's son joined them at Inverness it would be harder to make time alone with him.

She had not yet met his son. There was a painting of him at Duntulm, but it showed him when still a boy. He must be her age now, if not a little older. A *daguerreotype*, recently taken, showed a tall, fair-haired young man wearing his uniform with pride, but gave away nothing of his character.

Perhaps she could speak to him without breaking her master's confidence and ask his help to dissuade him from any dangerous course.

She recalled her housemother on Iona: 'Eolh-wyn,' the woman spoke her rune-name distinctly: Eolh for how wary she was in her first weeks on Iona, like a wide-eyed fawn, they said, and Wyn for joy and happiness, 'Eolh-wyn, you must think less and feel more!'

She rubbed her hand. The housemother's advice was easier spoken than acted on. She did not trust her feelings for there was too much she did not know about herself, and about her master, and what they might face at Winchester, a place she knew so little of. Sigel'inge said Graciana A'Guirre was wise. If so, she would already know the cause of Prince William's death. But what if Graciana allied with the earl to conceal the truth?

Sometimes it was better not to imagine too much.

She walked a mile along the hillside without finding water. Sharp stones bruised her heels and twice she had caught her head on a branch. Roots looping from the ground caught her feet and the poor glow of the lantern left so many shadows it was a wonder she had not stumbled. She also could be reckless, she reminded herself, and other opportunities would come, though having come so far, she would not give up just yet.

Holding the drum out before her she turned to sense each direction, even the way she had come and tapped the skin with her fingers, letting the cymbals vibrate.

Silence answered and Méirleach joined her. The animal sensed her confusion, squeaking loudly and leaning upon her shin. The moon shone through the branches and close by a bright red light: Mars, the War-Bringer. She only knew the stars to navigate by, but the Southern and Eastern Traditions used them for augury, after the Greeks and Romans. Under northern, cloudier skies, runes found favour. Only one form of magick was common to all three traditions—animal familiars. Fàidh had let her down yesterday. Could she trust Méirleach? But trust needs time and opportunity and she and her familiars must learn to trust each other.

Closing her eyes, Eolhwynne let the marten's name form in her head: *Méirleach*.

Crouching, she held out her hand and the marten came.

'No play. Find water. Safe.'

The marten sneezed, showing his disgust. He did not understand everything she said, but he knew 'safe'.

Safe. Find water, Eolhwynne repeated in her thoughts. The marten ran a few yards and hesitated at the edge of the light before vanishing into the darkness beyond. She closed her eyes and let her senses follow those of the animal.

Ground, damp underfoot, mossy pillows, leaves big as plates, smells clear as light, the sweetness of a slug's boneless flesh, too irresistible for Méirleach to leave: Eolhwynne sensed it all, but there was an unfamiliar sensation, like a breeze on her face, as the marten felt his way with his whiskers.

Something murmured in the darkness. The marten leapt down a bank and under the looping tree roots. Wet gravel underfoot and the air full with the rush of water.

Eolhwynne gasped, almost breaking her link with the marten. It was as if she too had leapt into the stream.

The marten scrambled onto a rock and shook himself dry. Then she called him back to her and allowed herself a moment of pride before Méirleach playfully bit her thumb and rolled against her cloak.

'Enough, enough. Now show me. Show me.'

She followed him through the wood and with each step she saw as a woman what he had seen, even finding where he killed the slug. On reaching the stream she cupped her hands and drank till she had rid herself of its taste.

Méirleach splashed in the water. She called him back. He must not stray. Upstream, she found a pool beside a sloping bank and sat to remove her boots. She had never done this alone before. She rolled the words in her head, recalling them. She dipped her feet in the water and pressed them in the gravel bed. Méirleach whimpered. She pulled her shawl closer and unfolded her master's kerchief across her knees. When she was ready, she took a deep breath and holding the drum above the stream tapped it once to awaken the water.

'Lord, will you hear me? Lord of the woods and high places, of the still waters and silver stream, Smith of fire and ice, Horn of the wind, Berion, and Oberion, King of the Fair Folk, hear me...'

She had no more breath and leant her forehead on her knees. She was tired, exhausted even. There was so much to do. She closed her eyes and spoke again.

'Lord, I beg you to hear me; Lord of the woods and high places, of...'

She did not continue for He had come.

'Who calls me this night?'

'I, Eolhwynne.'

'A rune-wife. You chose these cold waters?'

'I do.'

'Why, Eolhwynne rune-wife?'[1]

'To ask your protection.'

'You have your own powers.'

'Not for I, for this. It is my master's.'

She placed the kerchief beside the stream. The water wetted it. She did not raise her head.

'Cunning rune-wife; if I protect this, I protect him also, for without your master this is nothing.'

'Yes.'

'Look at me, rune-wife. Do not fear.'

He stood upon the far bank. A slant of pale grey light fell behind him, limning his shoulders but leaving the rest in shadow. She could not see his face.

'Oberion?'

'It is one of my names. I answer to all.'

He came closer and the light followed. Something was moving above his head and she thought the trees bent as though to touch him, but it was his antlers brushing through their branches.

'Your offering tastes of salt. Are they, his tears?'

'Mine.'

'Shed for him?'

'For myself, and others.'

'This stream is well-watered. Your offering will fail in winter.'

'One passing of the moon is all I ask.'

'There is a round stone within. Reach for it.'

Through clear water, letting the current guide her, she found the stone. It did not come easily, and her sleeve unravelled.

'Tie your offering about it and set it as it was. One moon-month I grant Eolhwynne rune-wife.'

The stone was black and smooth. She tied the kerchief around it and set it back in the stream.

'Rune-wife, who is he walking beside you?'

---

[1] An old, perhaps ancient name for a spaewife. *N.W.*

'My familiar.'

'No, there is another walks with you.'

'I am alone.'

'Not so.'

'His name? Master, has he a name?'

'He is foul on the outside but fair within...'

The stream murmured the soft watery laugh any might hear. She wrung the sleeve of her dress dry and tied her shawl across her, then dried her numbed feet and buttoned her boots with shaking hands before asking the stream for water and filling her silver flask.

All the time Méirleach had not left her side.

'Home, now,' she said. 'Home.'

Her feet ached as blood returned to them. The inn was a mile distant through the dark woods and her room seemed like paradise. One moon-month; she dare not ask for more. She had to trust it would be enough.

IV

There was no warning, though she had woken with a nagging doubt over the events of the night before and perhaps that ought to have been enough. Again, her waters were cloudy and pungent and though she had slept well enough, her head was heavy. At breakfast, which for the first time in two days was pleasantly unhurried, she asked for a second pot of tea and drank most of it. The Inverness Road[1] was well-provided with inns and well made, Duff said. They would make the sailing from Inverness in good time. She was glad to hear this, but it had not lifted her mood.

What Duff had failed to mention, she now appreciated, was the loch. Her master said it continued almost to Inverness and the road being along its northern edge the

---

[1] Principal Highland roads were surveyed and laid to a high standard, though not primarily with consideration of commerce and communication. Parliament's chief concern was the rapid deployment of military forces to quell the uprisings to which, as late as the 1760s, the Highlands were frequently prone. *N.W.*

sunlight sparkling off its waters reached even into their carriage, lending a bright, gay scene quite different from yesterday's endless mountain and heather. An hour into the journey it had almost, if not entirely, removed her doubts until a cry from the roof brought them sharp again.

The cry, which she thought came from McNeil, riding with John Duff, was immediately followed by pressure in her back and the alarming sight of her master flying from his seat towards her. Duff was bringing them shuddering to a stop.

She held Fàidh's cage to prevent it falling and flung up an arm to protect herself. Luckily, her master saved himself by grasping the wooden frame of the door, but nothing could prevent his hat and papers, including *Edwin and Morcar*, taking brief flight and landing on Méirleach's basket. The poor creature shrieked and beset, not only by her own fear, but by the sudden contagion arising from her familiars, it was some moments before she realised they had turned around and were now speeding whence they had come.

MacDonald, pale-faced with alarm or anger, got himself upright and hauled down the window to call up to Duff.

'The blazes, John! What is this?'

'The drag, sir!' came reply. 'Look to the drag!'

She tried to soothe her familiars. Beneath the cover of her cage Fàidh flapped in alarm, then, sensing her near, settled on the perch. Little Sneak was less easily calmed and cried plaintively. Her journal had fallen from her lap and as she closed it, she noticed the last word had broken off into a pencil scratch. She could not recall what she had been writing. They were discussing Prince Alexander, now heir to the throne, though she had rather they talk of MacDonald's son who they were meeting at Inverness. Indeed, her master had reproached her and said she would meet him soon enough and form her own opinion, though that was not her concern at all.

Over the shaking of the carriage and thunder of horse's hooves a horse was screaming, and she knew her earlier doubts were manifest.

MacDonald's back filled the open window of the carriage

and his hands gripping the doorframe were white at the knuckles. It was his hand she touched to gain his attention and he brought his head inside to hear her.

'I must know,' she said, as much from a sense of guilt as any belief she could affect matters. There was always a price to pay for making charms and it seemed it was due.

MacDonald was reluctant, but she insisted and took his place. The drag had halted above the steep drop to the water's edge. All wheels remained upon the road, but the cabin tilted alarmingly toward the water. With a pang, she remembered some of her dearest possessions were aboard. If it fell the carriage would be dashed to pieces. One horse was down. The other stamped and reared, its motion shaking the carriage and its hooves catching its injured companion. A man, Neave, she thought, held its bridle but could not control it. Duff urged the horses faster.

Her own fears forgotten she splayed three fingers in the sign of the elk rune. It was all she could do for now. Then she saw a second man lying in the road.

'Iain!' she gasped.

'What do you see?' her master was close behind her.

She ducked back inside the carriage.

'Iain is hurt.'

'Damnation!'

MacDonald took her place at the window.

'You have my prayers and blessing, Mr Duff!'

'Thank you, Sir!'

MacDonald returned inside and flung the window up before turning to her.

'I pray the boy is not hurt. Go immediately to him, do all you can.' He opened his watch and glanced at it. 'I fancy the drag cannot be repaired in time. A curse on this day. You sensed nothing untoward this morning?' He was unable to hide the accusation in his tone.

'I sensed nothing ill,' she answered, truthfully enough.

His look was reproachful.

'Use whatever gifts God gave you, but I must make my

ship. The next sailing is not for three days.'

He dropped the window again and looked out. When he returned his expression was a little lighter.

'The boy lives, at least. Do as you see fit and brace yourself. I fancy we will stop as abruptly as before.'

Indeed, Duff dropped the brake shoe beneath the wheel and the carriage juddered to a halt. Duff leapt to the ground with McNeil close behind. MacDonald did not wait on any to open the door but reached out to the handle himself. It was no time for ceremony. She followed him, taking care to avoid the carriage's iron step. Their horses, unnerved by the screams of their fellow, whinnied and trembled.

Duff had gone immediately to his stricken son. MacDonald held the horses by the bridle to calm them.

'How is he, John?' he called.

'Living, sir.'

The screams of the injured horse were almost unbearable, but she did her best to shut it out and went to Iain. His face was grey, and he cradled one arm. His father crouched next to him.

'Lie steady, boy, till we see what's what.'

'I could not hold it, Da. I could not tell what happened. Reckon horse is done for.'

'Don't think of it. Eolhwynne, beg ye. Do all you can for him. Son, I am needed.'

Duff stood and began calling instructions to Neave and McNeil. She knelt beside the boy.

'A'm sorra, miss. It disna hurt.'

He was lying, but she did not call him on it. She rolled her shawl tight and rested it under the boy's head. His eyes were steady but as a precaution she ran her hand over his head. There was no bleeding or softness.

'Did you fall?' she asked.

'Nae, Miss. Gill–, meaning Mr Neave, helped us down. Banged my arm, I did. The car was possessed! I could not stop it. Thought we were off the road. I got the horses turned, but was too sharp, see. Meg lost her footing.'

The horse had a name, bringing its screams of pain into sharper relief.

From the way Iain held his arm, she supposed it broken. Otherwise, save for a cut on his cheek he seemed unharmed.

'Don't agitate yourself. I must see to your arm.'

The boy grimaced. 'It isnae good.'

She took his hand and squeezed.

'Can you feel that?'

'Aye, Miss.'

'It is not numb at all?'

'Nae.'

Something had broken on the drag. The farther front wheel was at a different angle to the nearer and the body had collapsed onto the axle. Duff acting swiftly cut the standing horse free and handed its bridle to Neave. Neave was limping. She would attend to him once she had seen to Iain. The injured horse lay on its side, breathing hard and its eyes wide open. One back leg kicked, trying to find purchase on the road. The other leg... she looked away.

'John, is there aught we can do for it?' her master asked.

'A kindness, sir. Nothing more.'

'He means to shoot Meg,' Iain muttered.

Blood oozed from the cut on his cheek and the boy flinched as she wiped it clean.

'It winna mark, will it, Miss? Dinna want a mark there.'

'A scratch. Emily will not care.'

Hearing the girl's name, Iain smiled, as she hoped he would. She could dull the pain of his arm, but first she must be certain of its cause. She made a kenning rune with her fingers and laid it on the boy's head. The connection was not as close as she had with her familiars, but it was enough and she sensed first the boy's impression of her, the softness of her shawl against his head and the scent of orange water. Beneath his pain there was something else: arousal. Swiftly she sensed through his body, anticipating a sudden change or a bar to progress, but there was none until she reached the arm. To her relief the sensation was immediate: a clean break like a flaw in a stone. The arm should heal.

'By damn, Miss, what was that?' His eyes were wide open. 'It was the weirdest thing.'

'You will mend,' she said. 'It is all you need know.'

The boy sighed. Beneath his bravery, he was afraid. There was no call for a one-armed coachman, and pretty Emily might not want a cripple for a husband.

She took the bronze knife from her belt, but Iain asked her to stop.

Duff and McNeil had wheeled the drag away from the road edge. Duff was loading a pistol.

'Sir,' he addressed MacDonald. 'I ask you to have care with the horses. We shall need them. Mr Neave, likewise. They may shy at the noise.'

The injured horse lay still. Duff leant down to whisper something, then shot it dead.

Her flesh pimpled as its life ended but immediately there was relief as the echo of pain faded.

'Poor Meg,' Iain whispered. 'She were steady.'

The gun smoke drifted away.

'I need you to let go your arm,' she said. Iain obliged and she slit the sleeve of his shirt from cuff to shoulder, as if gutting a fish.

Duff came over. She did her best to ignore the pistol he held.

'How is my boy?'

'His arm is broken but it will mend. Nothing worse.'

'That were a good shirt, lad. Tha ma will be after ye.'

'I can sew, also, Mr Duff.'

'Reckon ye can, lass, but ye'll be awa with the laird. But I jest and I thank ye.'

'Thank me later. His arm must be set. I need splints and something to tie them with.'

'Ye'll have it. Lad, the spring's shattered. Ye did well keeping it on the road. Miss, I reckon ye canna sense ought to do with iron.'

'I cannot.'

'Then you've no blame for not foretelling this. I checked the drag this morn and found naught wrong. Seems I did not look well enough. Hear that, lad?'

'Aye. Thanks, Da.'

'Now, fancy the laird's anxious for his ship. Best put his mind at rest. We shall sorely test his cousin's springs.'

Duff left them. She did not know what he intended, but his command was reassuring. Iain was smiling but still in pain. She made a kenning rune again and touched his arm. It was simple to find the path taken by the pain and she used her knife to make a single scratch across it.

'It will only last a few hours,' she warned.

'What did you do?'

'It is the ice rune. It will block the pain.'

'That was done well.' Lord MacDonald was standing behind her. She did not know how much he had seen or overheard.

'Iain, your father assures me we will be on our way presently. Ah, these must be for you.'

McNeil handed her two pieces of wood and the traces cut from the dead horse to bind Iain's arm.

'Finlay, you had best assist John. Eolhwynne, have you set an arm before?' He knelt beside her and Iain.

'I have not.'

'My service in the army sometimes has its uses. We need a field dressing, my lad.'

'There is no need, master.'

'Iain, your father does not want me in his way, and I cannot stand to do nothing. Allow me.'

She was pleased to see him work. Given a task, rather than his servants doing it for him, seemed to suit her master. His hands were assured, and she could not fault his work.

Iain sat up. A leather sling around his neck supported the broken arm and he had full use of the other.

'Thank ye, sir.'

'I thank you for not letting the drag go off the road. I grant as you were upon it you had some interest, but your father tells me it was well done.' MacDonald stood. His breeches were marked from the road, and he brushed them carelessly.

'Eolhwynne,' he said. 'I have seen Gillanders limping. I think he needs your ministrations. I shall stay with Iain.'

She found Neave fetching brushes and cloths.

'You're hurt,' she said.

'It will mend soon enough.'

'But you're in pain.'

'I ken ye wish to be of use, but my Sine wouldn't like it.'

Sine was Neave's wife and Lord MacDonald's cook.

'But she would not want you to suffer.'

'That's as may be.'

She could see him struggling between respectability and discomfort. 'Then at least rest it, for now,' she suggested.

'I canna. Look at the laird.' She understood now the purpose of the cloths and brushes. 'Excuse, miss. Work to attend.'

Neave hobbled to MacDonald. She, unwanted by any human, walked past the dead horse, and returned to the carriage.

'Sir, I cannot have you arrive as you are,' she overheard.

'You're hurt, man,' her master objected.

She did not hear the rest of the matter. Fàidh was wide awake and gloomy. Little Sneak fast asleep. Baggage piled high on the roof and on the back step. Duff's plan was simple. The drag could go no further, and Finlay McNeil would remain with it. They would transfer their possessions to Sir David's carriage. This would proceed to Inverness.

'Mr Duff, may I be of some use?' she asked.

He looked down from the carriage roof where he was busy with tying down.

'Nae, lass. Except if you take your seat. We shall be away presently.'

And they were within a further half hour, leaving the unfortunate McNeil with the broken-down drag.

'George will be anxious, but we shall be in time,' MacDonald said, and pocketed his watch.

Iain and her master sat opposite her. She now shared her

seat with Fàidh's cage and Little Sneak's basket. The floor where he had lain was now taken up by a trunk. For Lord MacDonald, the accident had been a chance act: regrettable, but not significant. The drag was repairable, and the boy's arm would mend. He would make his ship and be on his way. For the boy, it was a graver matter, but one he would recover from and again he blamed happenstance.

Both were wrong. Fortune was a balance and for every good a spaewife brings there is an unforeseen ill and from every ill she does comes something good: she could not create good or bad fortune but only guide them, like water in a channel to a place they were not meant to fall. Last night she had laid a protection on her master, knowing there would be a price but not how, or when, it would be due. The hurt to Iain and the horse seemed a harsh and hasty reckoning, but the fates could be cruel and impatient.

She stared out the window. Sometimes a spaewife must be alone with her thoughts, and this was such a time. The day had clouded, and the loch no longer sparkled.

Duff took the road slowly, protecting the overladen carriage. Two hours passed before MacDonald announced Inverness.

'It is grand, sir,' Iain said in awe.

She leant round to see the way ahead. Beyond fields, a river snaked through a valley and into a grey-stone city filled with spires—weathercocks gleaming—and beyond the river a castle on a hill. She had seen a city only once before with her own eyes and the sight of Inverness sent her back into the corner of her seat and away from the window.

That city was Derry: She was barely twelve, her parents were dead, and a stranger had come to take her away.

Six hours on the road from Derryveagh, four of them in the rain. The cart lurched along ruts deep with filthy water. Squeezed between Sister Gertyr and a large man with a white beard, she could barely move or breathe. At intervals, the man shuddered like a wet dog and sneezed, spraying her with damp.

The seating was back-to-back down the middle of the cart, so she had only to lift her head to see the sodden fields passing by. The sky had not changed all day, nor had her mood. Finding that if she slipped forward in the seat, she might rest her heels against the ever-turning wheel, she did her best to slow their progress until Sister Gertyr saw her.

—By all the mercies, lass, had you caught a foot in the spokes there'd be no saving you. Gertyr leant across and wiped her face with a dry cloth smelling of something sweet.

—You will like the island, Laoise. You have never been with your own kind.

Sister Gertyr did not know she did not want saving. Twice she had leapt from the cart, forcing the driver to give chase, but now Sister Gertyr had her roped like a cow.

—Cannot have you running off, Laoise; Derry's no place for a lass on her lonesome: not even one can do the likes of you. The rope was round her waist and as she breathed Sister Gertyr's knuckles dug into her back like stones.

But she was too afraid to run now. All morning there was only one road and home lay behind them. Running, or the thought of running, came easily. Now, with the twists and turns and the countless rain-drenched cobbled streets joining and dividing, she could not tell the way, and with father dead and mother gone and home with no roof to keep out the rain, she realised it was not Derryveagh—whose one-time friends, neighbours, uncles and aunts had given her up to this plump, smiling stranger with her bag of stones—she wanted, but something else, and she was grown enough to know she would not find the past on any familiar road.

Like its streets, the people of Derry had all the same look about them. Never had she seen so many gathered in one place and all walking with heads bowed against the rain, beneath hats and coats and bonnets and shawls, their faces grey, eyes flint, voices like barking dogs; and all hurrying with no time for any business but their own.

And amid the throng she would catch the familiar tilt of a head, a snatch of laughter, a voice raised to a child; and for an instant she would hear or see her mother, clear as a kirk bell, before the stranger turned or spoke and whatever she had seen or heard died like mist on a warm day. The man beside her shuddered and shook the bench with his sneeze.

She had seen her father die. She had his watch in her pocket. But of her mother, she had only their word and words were no good to her. Four lobster-backs had dragged mother inside and a fifth bolted the door from within. Her hands tied, she could not tend her father, or stop Mother's cries. She had stared and stared at the door, wishing it to open and her mother to stand there, arms open wide. A candle overturned, or so they told her. The door shuddered under the soldiers' fists as fire crackled, but it held firm, sealing all inside until the roof fell in with a splash of flame. Strands of reed broke free and drifted up.

People saw the fire, but they arrived slowly, knowing the soldiers had been and knowing what they might find. An old woman cared for her, but none could do anything for Father, except for the priest who spoke the rites. With the fire out, men searched the house. All they brought out was enough to fill a coffin and her mother's silver cross, blackened with smoke. Father's watch, they took from his pocket, still ticking. None had lived, they said; none could have lived. But what did they know? The house had two doors and the walls were only rubble-stone. In winter, you could feel the wind blow through. Mother was strong: even her voice was strong as the wind.

She had wanted to see in Mother's coffin, certain it was empty or only filled with stones, but they did not allow it, and in the chapelyard beneath an old yew, Father Padraig spoke his words and men filled the graves. She never learned where they buried the soldiers.

—Enough little'n; yer ma's with the Lord, peace now.

She did not believe them. Mother had run away to hide. She would come back when it was safe.

She stared at the crowd on Derry's streets, waiting for Mother to rush forward and claim her, and even on Iona, for a year she clung to the hope a boat would come for her, holding to the past, like a child refusing to part with its milk teeth. That day in Derry, she saw many who were like her mother: countrywomen drawn to the city, but still holding to the shawls and bonnets and aprons most familiar to them. But none exactly like her mother.

Iona introduced her to other, but far distant cities: Toledo, Byzantium, lost Atlantis, Babylon, home to Lilith the first spaewife, and Troy; each glorious painting showing what had been, or might have been, if only the builders had the artist's imagination, for these once great cities were the Seats of Wisdom from which the Four Traditions had emerged.

Inverness, from what she saw, was more like Derry than Byzantium or Atlantis, with narrow grey houses for golden temples, stepped gables instead of porticos filled with gods, and chasm-dark streets where there might be airy avenues and colonnades. Nor were the people so well dressed or so happy.

The corner of the carriage was not deep enough to hold her. Alone, she would have drawn down the blind but the eagerness on Iain's face could not be denied him. She would bear this.

'Are you unwell?'

Lord MacDonald was watching her.

'A little tired.' She forced a smile. 'Do I seem unhappy?'

'Withdrawn perhaps. What of you, young man? You seem affixed to the window.'

'Be it grand, sir,' Iain said. 'Makes Portree look like a—' the boy flushed and looked at the floor. 'I meant no shame on home, sir.'

'It is, indeed, very fine,' he agreed. 'Though not without fault; for instance, the castle is scarcely older than you. It is a perfect sham housing the Sheriff's courts and council chambers and built at great expense to the ratepayers.'[1]

'What was there afore, sir?'

'The last in a long line of real castles: Inverness commands the Highlands, Iain, and has been fought over by Scot against Scot, Scots against Danes and Scots against English.'

'My da's learning me of Prince Georgie and Queen Anne and all. Be something to see where things happened, though.'

Plainly, the boy thought Duntulm a place where things did not happen as he stared out, his head continually moving as though counting sheep.

'That's an awful many folk,' he said.

So many, yes. She closed her eyes a moment, shutting out the pinched, needy faces that appeared and vanished in the pane of glass. The compartment was stuffy, and she had lain awake for hours in the attic room at Invermoriston, listening to the wind and worrying about Winchester. Running her fingers over her rune pouch, she felt the pieces of bone clink and slide.

'Sir, what's to hold up the bridge? Be naught beneath it?'

Her master chuckled in reply: 'George is better at this than I. See the towers either end?'

'Ay, there's an archway through for the road.'

'The bridge is supported from the towers by a chain, see?'

'Ay, I do now, and it just hangs, like.'

'Exactly so.'

A tingle in her hand alerted her and rubbing the iron blains, she looked out to see massive iron links only yards from their carriage. From these cables supported the roadway. Either side of the road a pavement allowed people to cross, and they did so in throngs, indifferent to iron's effect. Shielded by the body of the carriage she was safe but were she to step outside she doubted she could reach the farther

---

[1] The sham castle still stands above the river, though its administrative purposes have long been superseded by modern offices on the opposite bank of the river. Today, the castle houses a military museum, with the rest converted to apartments whose prices are beyond the means of almost all whom it originally served. *N.W.*

side without fainting. The ache increased and she folded her arms to nurse the injured hand. If the soreness continued at Winchester, she would ask A'Guirre's advice. So much of the world now turned to iron and in Winchester she supposed a spaer could hardly avoid it. It also gave her cause to talk to A'Guirre and perhaps discover more of Prince William.

To her relief, the pain ceased at the far end of the bridge.

'Where are we to meet Master George?' She asked.

'He will be at the shipping agent waiting for us, if not already aboard. I fear he is newfangled; no doubt he shall find his way to the engine room.'[1]

'It's a steamship you're sailing by, sir?'

'Indeed, the *Dundalk* of the North Scotland Company,' MacDonald said.

The carriage jolted to a halt at the end of a press of carts, wagons and horse teams. The boy winced and felt his arm.

'It troubles you? Perhaps, Eolhwynne, I think you call it the ice rune?'

She shook her head sympathetically. 'In excess, the effect can be permanent.'

'Best not then, you'll be back at Duntulm soon enough and then you can be nursed to health. I am sure you will not go untended. Ah! The harbour.'

Lord MacDonald dropped the window and called up: 'Citadel Pier, John.'

The air had the tang of brine and smoke but mostly it carried noise. A smoking engine swung to life in a whirr of parts and lifted timber from a ship while an overseer in grey coat and black knee boots looked on. Displeased, he thrust papers at a messenger boy and ordered him away. The boy's feet were bare.

'Hanseatic Company,' MacDonald murmured. 'They have the monopoly in Baltic pine.'

---

[1] In its modern sense 'newfangled' describes a novel idea or object, but it was originally a description of those with a liking or interest in new things or persons. *N.W.*

She lodged her shoulder into the very corner of the carriage. *Newfangled*, her master had said. How cruel his son should care for that so injurious to her. Motes of dust and debris swirled into the carriage, carried, so it seemed, on the confusion of shouts and clattering machinery. Crates, bales, sacks, and timber swung overhead on iron hooks, or were barrowed, slid, and hoisted on men's backs, and despite each man's labours all seemed trapped under a canopy of chain and cable and ship's rigging like fish in a net.

They halted beside a small wooden office. A sign above the door read: STUART-KERR, AGENT FOR THE NORTH OF SCOTLAND STEAM SHIPPING CO. *For Invergordon and Edenborough, calling off for Banff, Cullen...*

'At last,' her master said. Duff opened the door.

'Thank you, John. Eolhwynne, we alight.'

Duff helped her out. Her master followed and spoke quickly to his driver and manservant. The business did not concern her, and she took a deep breath and steadied herself against the rear of the carriage. Here were no clanking engines, but she had no sense of being at ease. In the distance, another of the engines delved into a ship and brought out coal which it dropped onto a pile with a great mineral roar. Black dust settled on the water in an oily sheen.

She raised her shawl against the wind, but recalling who was meeting them, left her hair uncovered. She was not twelve years of age, nor was she an innocent in the world.

The ship was wooden, mercifully, and with masts and sail besides smokestack and paddle wheels. Perhaps they only made use of the engine when without fair wind. Regardless, her duty was as it had been with the little ferry at Kyleakin, and with a glance for dangers, she crossed the quay and laid a hand on its hull. The full heat of the sun was upon it, and it seemed alive, though as she let her gift see further she met the iron weight of the engines and boiler and had to let go.

'You! Back! Danger!'

A man stared at her. He stood beside a gangway, overseeing a line of porters. He waved her away and returned to his task. Neave and Duff were unloading their baggage: this too, would be overseen by the young man. He was small and slight, and though he wore a blue uniform with white braiding, was like a child in adult's clothing. He checked each item the porters brought aboard and gave an order. She could not place his voice, but he was no Scot or Englishman.

MacDonald was in conversation with John Duff.

'Have Emily look after him, John, she should keep him abed and ask Dr Ramsay to drop by. He will be attending Clara in any event, so it is no effort for him. Do not allow him to charge twice for—'

'Father! You are here.'

George MacDonald stood in the doorway of the shipping agent. She recognised him immediately, though he was taller than she expected. He had not seen or noticed her.

Lord MacDonald raised a hand, asking his son for silence as he counted banknotes into Duff's hand.

'It is more than needed, sir.'

'It must be more than *enough*. I fancy doctors here are dearer than at home. Best see the agent has all our baggage.'

'Thank you, sir. And thank you also, miss.'

MacDonald turned to his son. 'Now, George, have you been waiting long?'

'It was only my duty,' she replied to Duff. 'Be sure to say the break is clean and he received the Ice rune some three hours ago.'

'The ice rune,' Duff repeated. 'I'll so do.'

'Hours, Father. What delayed you?'

'An accident near Invermoriston. Iain's arm is broken, and we lost the drag, temporarily I hope. McNeil keeps it company.'

'Iain Duff? But how is he?'

'Eolhwynne might best answer.' MacDonald motioned her forward.

Now George noticed her, but before he could speak, she asked if Iain was his friend, though this was already apparent from his concern.

'We are almost brothers,' he said. 'For want of having brothers of our own... But, should we not be introduced?'

'Apologies.' MacDonald stepped in. 'Eolhwynne, this is my son, George Franklyn MacDonald. George, this is Eolhwynne. Ethelfeyrda left us at Christmas, you recall.

She curtsied.

'And you are travelling with us to Winchester?' he asked.

'I am.'

'Father, why did you not tell me?' The boy's smile was infectious.

'Because when I wrote I did not know myself,' Lord MacDonald said. 'I do not see how it changes anything.' He was gently teasing his son.

'Perhaps not,' George said. 'But I should like to have known.'

'And now you do. Your luggage is aboard?'

'It is.'

The officer shouted in his strange accent and waved his manifest at a porter heaving a tin trunk. He pointed back at the agent's office as he instructed the man and for a second his eyes met hers across the quay...

> Her grief, like the shipwrecked reef
> Lies hidden at high-water.
> Grace was met with tragedy
> And she has built her house upon its reef.

Of Eolhwynne I saw a quiet intent and clarity of purpose. All she need do is fear less. Knowing I could do nothing for her, I sought another.

Editor's Remarks

As before, the chapter division in the first draft is marked by a blank line and the date, here February 3, 1862. Arbinger remained snowed in and the MacGregors continued to play host to Mr Auburn. MacGregor's journal makes no mention of him, but Lady Helena found him a tiresome character with "ill table manners and an appetite twice what one expects." She marked his departure on the eleventh with an exclamation mark. The return of the Edenborough mail coach also brought a two week backlog of letters and periodicals, including a reply from James Ludd accepting MacGregor's criticism of the design for the Madeleine Shrine. He attached a number of sketches which seem to have met with MacGregor's approval and certainly reflected his request for a beacon, rather than a monument. The shrine, which would be completed in June 1863, bears a resemblance to a lighthouse crossed with a fairground helter-skelter and is unique.

Turning to the content of the first draft, this chapter is, frankly, a shambles. Much is crossed out and immediately rewritten and other parts are crossed out with new text interlineated with the old or carried onto the reverse of the page. Elsewhere, the sequence of the text is altered with arrows and marginalia indicating the corrections and scattered in the margins are tantalising annotations with query marks, exclamation points, or words such as "curtail", "emphasise" or "develop" which, one supposes, MacGregor acted upon in the fair copy. Unfortunately, lacking the fair copy your editor has been hopelessly adrift and in order to connect the various parts of MacGregor's text he was obliged to fall on improvisation far more than he wished. To compound the problem, not only has it been immensely difficult to produce a coherent text faithful to MacGregor's intentions, insofar as they can be determined, but this chapter is the longest in the volume!

The text of the first edition has, of course,

the benefit of coherence and editing, but here, alas, it has been of limited value for this chapter especially troubled MacGregor's publishers. We shall have more to say shortly, but for now we observe that MacGregor's apparent difficulty portraying the nature and practice of a spaewife militates against his possessing special insight or competence regarding magick.

In consequence, while your editor considers the text up to this point a good facsimile of MacGregor's intended text, he cannot make the same claim for this chapter. It is the best he could achieve with the materials at hand, but it must surely fall short.

Concerning variations, one almost recommends the reader sets this chapter alongside the previously published text and draw their own conclusions; however, that will not do. This chapter suffered savagely at the hands of Beresford & Lucas: the former disapproving of Eolhwynne's character, the latter disapproving of her practice. Thus, in the published text her mien is artificial and reserved while her magick has a sinister aspect, giving her an unsatisfactory and inconstant character. Suffice it to say no such issue appears in MacGregor's first draft where Eolhwynne's character and her practice are rendered harmoniously and sympathetically, albeit, as stated earlier, not always with the clarity your editor would like!

As noted, the thrust of Beresford & Lucas' objections to MacGregor's text—which, we must recall, was not the much revised first draft but the now lost fair copy—was two-fold: MacGregor's "shameless sporting of that which cannot be admitted" (the quote is taken from Sir Sidney's letter to MacGregor dated

Thursday, March 13, 1862), and its sympathetic portrayal of magick which—in the main—offended John Lucas who was a benefactor of the Alban Church. Thus, Eolhwynne's character and profession offended them both. She is a young and passionate woman—her interest in MacDonald's son is, perhaps not amorous but certainly flirtatious, as much as professional—and she is depicted as flesh and blood, to the point MacGregor has her pass water.

That scene in particular echoes a line in MacGregor's journal dated March 21, 1862:

> I must depict men and women, <u>in totus: corpus et animus, et anima</u>, body, spirit and soul as one, if I am to be true to their nature, whether that nature be God-given <u>or not</u>.

MacGregor's unique contribution—or a first for his age—was not appreciating the connection between body, spirit, and soul, but acknowledging it in fiction.

Nineteenth century literature was, to quote Louis S Robertson's *A Literary History of Alba vol. vii*, (Pembury Press, 1910), "full of maidens with tight waists and heaving bosoms who were seldom better than they ought to be," but no other reputable author of the time had acknowledged women possessed a body below the waist and above the ankle. Moreover, MacGregor's Eolhwynne is unusual for she is not a slave to her emotions but carries out her duties thoughtfully and professionally. Women who were sensual *and* intelligent challenged nineteenth century masculinity.

Eolhwynne's profession is, of course, the practice of magick and this pervades the chapter, beginning with her aid to Adam Shaw, through her relationship with familiars, then communing with Oberion and on to her nursing of Iain Duff. Indeed, MacGregor could be criticised for portraying so much of the spaewife's craft the chapter might be a manual of instruction! Moreover, Eolhwynne's magick is continually shown to be of good intent, even if the injury to young Iain is an unfortunate consequence, or balancing, of her charm to protect Lord MacDonald. This conflicted with the doctrines of the Alban Church which held magick to be intrinsically wicked and harmful to any who associated with it.

We have previously noted the damage done to Eolhwynne's character by, in the main, Sir Sidney Beresford, however, for John Lucas nothing less than the complete removal or severe reduction of offending scenes would do. Eolhwynne's meeting with Adam Shaw at Eilean Donan was sacrificed, there was no summoning of Oberion at Invermoriston (though she does make a votive offering of the handkerchief) and the tending of her runes, along with the analepsis to her childhood in Donegal, are reduced to a brief summary. Of all the characters in volume one, Eolhwynne suffered most at the hands of MacGregor's publishers and, though it is only to the best of his limited abilities, your editor is delighted to restore her to the reader.

Seemingly content, though its demands are many

Chapter Six

Portree, mid-morning: The character and circumstances of Màiri Mulcahy *interposed with* Bheathain Somhairle's *continuing circumstances*

In error I released a second shadow into the world. A poor, weak thing, it did not thrive and only Màiri Mulcahy bore it.

Feline is feminine Grace;
It purrs, seemingly content,
Though its demands are many,
Then leaves in the night without looking back.

I

Within living memory Portree had comprised one hotel, the island's lock-up, and a huddle of stone houses no better than any others on the isle. Even twenty years ago, when, as Ethelfeyrda, Màiri had entered the laird's service, the quay by which she landed—Portree's conduit for prosperity—was scarce a decade built and Beaumont Crescent, the first grand street in town, still less. But now the town boasted several good streets, a multitude of shops, two banks—both closed on Wednesdays—several inns, a church house each for three denominations of Protestant faith and a chapel for the Papists and was an altogether noble prospect for any visitor arriving by the Glasgow or Oban steamer. Furthermore, if matters were not all they seem; if behind each fine new house crowded three or four families and a good many windows were bereft of glass; we admit conditions in Portree were the envy of the rest of the island.

And yet, prosperity did not extend far beyond the environs of the harbour, and the upper reaches of Stormyhill by which Màiri entered Portree remained much it had always been; a scratch upon the earth serving the rough habitations below Kiltraglen. Typical of these habitations, Tearlach M'Leòid's flesher's shop had a thatched roof, earth floor and no windows. The open door told the owner was inside and through it the marbled flesh of a sheep carcass and the mute eyes of a half-dozen rabbits shone in the gloom, while beneath them, like an altar, lay the flesher's pinewood table. Against the bare walls several ill-matched dressers leaned and while there was no fire to warm the room a candle glimmered in its farthest corner.

M'Leòid's apron was a scrap of red canvas but the flesher made show of brushing it clean as he welcomed her. He had a pale, bloodless face, quite unlined but somewhat gaunt for twenty-five years and his clothes hung on him like sails on a windless day.

'Three-year-old,' M'Leòid answered her.

Màiri eyed the sheep. It was scrawny for a three-year-old.

'How long you had it hanging?' she asked.

'A sevennight. Be good yet.'

'Why've you not salted it?' Màiri asked, doubting it would be good for much longer without.

M'Leòid shook his head, his expression gloomy as the room he stood in. 'Died in yean. Took it only so it doesn't go to waste. What I can't get rid of will feed the dogs.'[1]

Having agreed on a price for the best end and the haunch Tearlach dropped the carcass onto his table and set to with his cleaver. She took a chair near the door and waited.

Voices, one a child's and the other a woman's, came from beyond a door at the rear of the shop. At first both were a mere chafe of sound below the thud of cleaver and bone-saw rasp, but at an instant the little one's voice shrieked, indignant, and as though forced by the mere quantity of sound the door flew open and outwith came a child of five or six years and indeterminable sex.

Seeing someone unexpected in the room halted the child and Màiri saw blue eyes, yellow hair, freckled skin and a

---

[1] The folk belief that it was unlucky to eat the meat of an ewe that died in lambing has proven to be correct for the diseases causing spontaneous abortion in sheep are easily transmitted to humans and have the same effect. *N.W.*

mouth round as an egg, before a shout from the back room impelled the child onward and out into the light of day.

The voice from the backroom faded into a cough. Newsprint crackled under the M'Leòid's hand, the ink defeated by blood, as he wrapped the joints. Silently an arm reached from the rearward gloom to close the opened door.

M'Leòid sighed as he returned the carcass to the hook. Turned to her, he wiped bloodied hands on the apron and asked what else she might want. Beside flesh and fowl, M'Leòid kept dry goods and household wares and Màiri bought a schilling of salt and a dozen tallow candles. The offer of coin, rather than adding to her account, brought a smile to his face and Màiri asked him of the child.

'Wee terror is that one,' M'Leòid said.

'Do you not worry about him?' she asked.

'She, miss,' M'Leòid corrected. 'Oh, you need not distress yourself. Where has she to run to?'

There was a deal of lonely moor where she might lose herself, Màiri thought, but M'Leòid seemed not to have considered this.

'What's her name?'

'*Brìde,*' M'Leòid said, 'after the saint. Though it be a misnaming, for no saint is she and you can ask the goodwife on that.' M'Leòid folded the receipt and gave it her. '*Chan fheagal dut.* Hunger will bring her home.'

She left and proceeded downhill toward the town. Presently the habitations of Stormyhill gave way to substantial houses of three storeys with mortared stonework and slate roofs. Sunlight glittered on the glass in the windows and the sickly stink of coal fires clung to the breeze. There were greater numbers of people, also, and though she was no longer the laird's spaewife, many had not broken the habit of seeking her help on an urgent matter of the heart or business or asking her to pass a message to the laird.

'Ethelfeyrda.' A man's voice, solicitous. 'Would ye help us now. There's this cow been right cussed of late. Could ye…'

'I cannot be of use. I am not a spaer now.'

'Ethelfeyrda, there's this no-good lad courting our Effie...'
'Ethelfeyrda, would you ask on the laird...'
'Ethel...'
'Ethelfeyrda, can you spare the time?'

The speaker was a woman, round faced and dark haired. She covered her head with a shawl patterned in red and green. Three wee girls from knee high to eight years crowded round her.

'I be with child,' the woman whispered, her eyes darting to the side, 'and seeing as we got the three lassies, we were wanting for a son...'

'I'm chancy[1] for you,' Màiri said, 'but you must be chancy with what you have. I am not Ethelfeyrda no more.'

'Are you so?' the woman asked.

'I am no more. My name is as I was born, Màiri Mulcahy.'

'I did not know. But has the laird another spaer the now?'

'He has; ask after Eolhwynne,' she said, thinking if Eolhwynne showed herself in town a few folk might pester her a deal less. The lass had hid herself at Duntulm: homesick, no doubt.

The woman shook her head in surprise. 'I'm no unhappy with what I have.' She gathered her girls about her skirts like a swan sheltering its cygnets. 'My good man is after a son, so he is. I hope for him it's no another lassie. Miss,' the woman smiled pleadingly, 'are you sure you cannot tell?'

'I cannot,' she said. 'The babe will be whatever it wishes to be.'

The woman sighed, the lines around her mouth resigned. The eldest of the girls tugged at her mother's sleeve.

'What is it, Christy?'

'Mammie; we don't mind another.'

'I know, pet. Miss, this new woman the laird's got, what did you say her name was?'

'Eolhwynne,' Màiri said. 'Send word to Duntulm. She is away with the laird for now but will return soon.'

---

[1] Chancy; happy. *N.W.*

'Thank you, Ethel... I recall, Miss Mulcahy. Come now wee uns, you're all my blessings, so you are.'

The woman crossed the street, herding her children before her. Màiri watched them a moment and tried not to feel sorry for herself. But for her gift, she might have children of her own, grown now and perhaps with children of their own she might pick up and put down as pleased her. A few times she had thought of giving it up for a man and settling with him—it was not unheard of for spaers to turn away from their gift—but it was never the right time and never the right man. Now the chance was gone: no more magick, and, save for a miracle, no bairns to grow and care for her in old age.

She turned away and kept on down the hill. No point dwelling on bygones. No point at all.

Between further solicitations and requests, all of which she directed toward Eolhwynne or Doctor Ramsay, as seemed fit, she called on a draper for cloth to make Bheathain a shirt to go with his shoes and purchased honey, blueing, soap, vinegar, a bag of oats, sugar—given her in a blue bag in the latest fashion—and a schilling of cheese and tin of matches. Of these, certain items she paid for direct while others she bought, as usual, on credit depending on whether she bought for Bheathain or for her own needs for she would only claim from Murdoch Dixon what was due her, though her next call might sorely tax his charity.

Gilleasbuig Rothach's workshop had a broad glazed window showing off a row of tidy brogues the like of which only those off the tour boats could afford. Inside, the light from the window fell across a bench strewn with tools for cutting, forming, and stitching leather. Rothach signalled toward a chair.

'Mind your feet, miss,' he said through the tackits gripped in his teeth. 'These days, if I drop one it stays dropped. Don't bend so good no more. Sit as you please. I shall be a moment.'

She took Rothach at his word and sat by the stove. The

air was thick with the smell of leather and wax. Lasts hung from the beams like giant bats. Besides the wholesome smells were the spirituous stink of polish and the reek of fish glue.

'Now, what can I do for you?' Rothach took the boot off the last and tossed it aside.

'I want your price on these.' Màiri held out Bheathain's shoes.

Rothach showed them to the window, then shrugged, saying they were fit only for the midden.

'I hoped you'd mend them,' Màiri complained.

'No use to it,' he said. 'Mending be near as much as new.'

She knew Rothach was honest but was unsure how generous Dixon would be.

'I can't go above twenty-five,' she said. 'This afternoon?'

Rothach nodded. 'I'll see what I can do, but it's a hard price. Come by in a while and I'll have something. Won't be fancy, mind.'

She left Rothach and made for the harbour where the air filled with brine, rotten seaweed, and filth swept off the town's streets by the rain. A banner strung across a warehouse frontage boasted *Highlands and Islands Emigration Committee, embarkation point* and beneath it a fiddler made noise from horsehair. His audience was a mill of bodies, trunks, baskets and dogcarts where animate commingled with inanimate. Braziers kept off the chill and a smaller party had gathered about a pile of burning driftwood above the shoreline. Their ship had moored at the far end of the quay where the water was deepest and here a third group of persons, more industrious than the first and second, provisioned it with fresh water, vittles, and livestock for its voyage. By noon tomorrow the quay would be a swarm of humanity but not until the hour before sailing would the ship's master let any aboard. Tonight, their only shelter was the lee of the warehouses, and whatever they had brought with them. Tomorrow they would take ship, dragging their children and worldly goods afore and behind them, and find some cranny aboard to be home for a month at sea.

Hunger brings the child home but drives the man away.

A bell above the door marked Màiri's arrival at Cameron's Apothecary; the noise interrupting the business of two well-dressed women at the counter. The elder of the two glanced her way and by her expression did not care for what she saw, and an indiscreet elbow invited her companion to share this opinion. The women's dress, modest in shewing no flesh below the neck and above the wrist yet not unconcerned with appearance, marked them as members of the Alban Church.

Not recognising the women, Màiri ignored their ill manners and gave both a polite nod and welcoming smile. Neither returned the pleasantry but instead turned back to the shopkeeper, one John Cameron whose ample frame principally occupied the space behind the counter with his son, Roderick, occupying the lesser part.

Màiri closed the door behind her. Most of the town still sought her aid, but a growing part of it now shunned her. The Alban Church was turning folk against the old ways, even here.

'Afternoon Miss Mulcahy,' Cameron called over the women's heads. 'Wait by. Be with you in a moment.'

Mindful of his customers, John Cameron spoke nothing but English in his shop.

The older of the two women; they were sisters, Màiri thought, the disparity in their ages being not enough to allow of parent and child yet their faces betraying kindred; was buying 'off catalogue' and she appreciated a catalogue sale would mean commission for John Cameron. Avoiding the eyeline of the two women, Màiri made show of looking for something on the shelves but in fact let her eyes be drawn to the proliferation of advertising extolling the virtue of soap, tinctures, cure-alls, polish, toilet water, tobacco, ale, sherry, brandy, tinware, china plate, linctuses, odourless lamp oil, and mothballs.

The shop was longer than it was wide, glazed at the front and with a door leading off at the back. Calico blinds printed with Cameron's name warded against the sun's damaging rays and a stove warmed the air. The yellow-painted shelves were clean, and each bore a little enamel tag so one might know where anything was, while behind the counter were racks of jars and a wooden cabinet.

As M'Leòid's shop on Stormyhill was typical of old Portree, so Cameron's Apothecary was typical of the new.

Cameron's son, Roderick, had open a dress catalogue over which the two women clucked and dallied, and with John Cameron supervising this was clearly an important moment in Roderick's education. Shame then he was failing to pay whole attention, for standing at the elder woman's elbow was a maid and it was plain as paper young Roderick was smitten. She wore a pale blue dress without stays, and a lace-trimmed bonnet.

'And these,' the elder woman asked, 'you can get also, at the same...?'

Roderick thumbed through the catalogue, his face pink and his voice wavering, as the wanted page escaped him. The fatherly hand on his shoulder slipped in disappointment and Màiri sensed the boy had lost his chance to shine.

'They can be had,' John Cameron said. 'But quality commands fair price, ma'am.'

Something in Roderick's expression must have betrayed his feelings for the lassie turned abruptly, rather than meet his eyes. But in the confines of the shop, it was too easy for her gaze to switch from one pair of eyes to another.

Yellow haired, a single strand visible below the close-fitting bonnet, and blue eyed, she was undeniably pretty, but in a china way. Her face too perfect, too symmetrical, and like china, one small chip, one sign of ageing would be irreparable. That is what Màiri saw. What the girl saw in Màiri was clear from the gasp and the flinging up of hands to cover her face.

'What is it, child?' her mistress said.

'A witch, ma'am. She spied on us.'

The woman glanced across the room, her look acidic.

'Nonsense, child. Ignore her.' But again, the woman refused to meet her eyes, and Màiri knew she also was afraid.

'Ladies, please,' Cameron senior asked. 'Miss Mulcahy, what is it you require?'

'Myrrh, oil of olive, peppercorns,' she said. 'I apologise if...'

'For potions,' the girl hissed.

'Medicines,' she said, with a mind to ask for "eye of toad".

'Miss Mulcahy, ladies, please no unpleasantness. Ladies, if you do not object, my lad will serve Miss Mulcahy?'

Whatever their true feelings, neither woman objected, though the girl hid herself behind her elders and could be heard muttering the catechism.

Reluctantly, Roderick dragged himself across to the part of the counter reserved for medicaments.

'You were interested in these...' Cameron senior drew the women's attention back to the catalogue.

At her instruction Roderick searched among the drawers in the cabinet and removed a small stoneware jar: myrrh loses its potency if exposed to light and air.

Some reckoned herbs and essences found nearest a sick man cured him best, but she knew whatever worked on a Frenchman or a Darkie worked much the same on a Scotsman. Assuming Bheathain *was* a Scotsman.

Roderick set the jar on the counter. 'Don't have much call for this, Ethel... Miss Mulcahy I mean.' His cheeks pinked.

'I would imagine not.'

The boy removed the stopper and frowned.

'Give it me,' she said, 'I'll soon tell ye if it's no use.'

The powdery lumps looked dried out, but the resin was potent still. She asked for three shillings' worth.

It was pricey stuff, and the boy took pains measuring it on the scales.

'A wee bit over makes no odds,' she said. This was not from her pocket. Murdo Dixon would pay.

The boy brushed the myrrh onto a page torn from an old book, folded it into a packet and sealed it with gum paper.

'And lavender oil?' he asked, glancing toward the women.

'Oil of olive,' she corrected.

Cameron senior had completed the order for the two women. Whether she had precipitated them to make up their minds or they had naturally arrived at a conclusion she could not tell.

'A good lad is our Roderick,' Cameron said. 'Has his father's eye for business. Glad to say.'

'He is a son to be proud of,' the elder woman said. 'He knows what he is born to and stays with it. Unlike the wretches at the quay who gamble on fate.'

Fate indeed; and no spaer to see them off. She would bless them, but without Grace it was only a token. With Eolhwynne away, she would ask Murdo Dixon to speak to Lord McLeod; he might lend his spaer. The emigrants were MacDonalds, but need must transcend clanship.

Roderick stumbled against the ladder as he lifted a bottle of oil.

'Careful, son.'

'My youngest is clumsy,' the woman simpered.

'Something troubles you,' Màiri whispered.

The boy frowned. 'I knows some gaen on that ship.'

'So do I,' She did not know this for certain, but it was likely true, 'your father needs you here. You can make your farewells later.'

'It'll be dark, and I'll not see their faces. How much was you wanting of the oil?'

'Smallest bottle ye have.'

The women's business finished, and John Cameron showed them to the door. Roderick glanced up, but by his face he had failed to see what he wished. Màiri wanted to tell him not to waste his time on the girl. She was damaged beyond repair, the crack deep within her pretty exterior. A man, even a man-child like Roderick, needed flesh and blood, not the chill of a would-be saint.

The bell rang as the door closed behind the women. Cameron remained just inside the entrance.

'Alban Kirk?' she asked.

'Ma customers' business isnae ma business, exceptin what they pays fer,' Cameron said, his English manner lapsing.

'Aye, fer sure they are,' Roderick answered. 'Seen the lassie outside the chapel.'

'Have ye now,' Cameron said. 'Mebbe ye'll moon at her there an' no here. Their numbers increaseth, as the Bible says.'

Cameron returned inside and cleared his throat as though he had tasted something unpalatable.

'Miss Mulcahy, I have served ye fer years now an' ye've always been good tae me, but times are changin' an' I must change wi them.'

'Da!' Roderick protested.

'I understand,' she interrupted. 'Ye neid tae keep folk happy an' it seems I make some unhappy. I should like tae send fer whit I need an' have a lad collect.'

'I didna mean ye be unwelcome here,' Cameron said. 'Only, should ye see customers in shop, might ye bide yer time till they're gone. I dinna like where the warld is gaen, but a shopkeeper has tae follow.'

'Peppercorns,' the boy said.

'Ye what?' Cameron asked.

'Miss Mulcahy was after peppercorns. Was it white or black, Miss?'

'Black, an ounce,' she said.

'Ye'll be wantin' credit,' Cameron reached for the account book.

'No, I'll be payin' now,' she said.

'Crivvens!' Cameron pretended to drop the book. 'Well, I'll let ye off sixpenn'orth. There's a good few in the Alban Kirk owe me half a year or more. Seems their Bible says naught of settling accounts. Ye'll be wantin' a receipt?'

'I do. An' did ye ken yer lad has friends leavin' on the ship? They wretches as that *fine* woman called them.'

'Has he now,' Cameron said, 'and whose fault be it?'

'None, Da. Only I hoped tae see them afore they're gone.

They have tae gae but it's nae fault o' theirs. They just want tae better theyselves, as did ye. "Better meet ma foes than beg frae ma friends," isnae that whit ye allus said?'

Cameron glanced toward the front of the shop and shook his head like a bull disturbed by a fly. The lad had pushed his father and she wasn't sure how he might shift. The light glowed yellow upon the calico blinds. Cameron placed his hands on the counter and looked up at his son as though seeing him for the first time in a long while.

'I did not know ye knew such folk as they.'

'Frae school, Da, I know three lads whit's leavin'. They're good lads, but what good is learnin' when the plough breaks on every stone.'

'Myrrh,' Cameron said.

'Three schillings' worth,' Roderick said, 'an' a wee bottle oil o' olive and a schilling of black peppercorn.'

Cameron wrote in his book.

'Belike, I'll no need yer help atween now and closing. But I'll not pay thee while you're gone.'

'I dinna care,' Roderick was halfway round the counter. 'Thank 'e Da, and thank 'e Ethel—, I mean Miss Mulcahy.'

'Wait on, lad,' Cameron cried. 'You're gaen empty-handed?'

Roderick came back and Cameron thrust a sherry bottle in his hands.

'Take this, frae Cameron and Son.'

Roderick raced to the door like his feet were dancing on embers. The bell jangled and the door closed, leaving her alone with Cameron.

'Ye were generous,' she said as she pocketed the receipt.

'It wasnae much, but it'll warm them. I'm sorry for the business afore.'

'Understand ye. World changes an' them what can maun change with it.' She examined her purse. She could not rely on Murdo Dixon for this last item; if she wanted to pretty herself it must be at her expense. She counted the pennies on the counter with a sigh for they were near the last.

'Macassar oil, *Belle du Soir*,' she said.

Cameron placed a slender bottle of red liquid on the counter. The gaudy label showed a woman with coiffured hair. She wanted spoiling; not often she had a young man come to stay and could she help if body and spirit sat at odds.

II

Màiri found scarce one well-fed body among the threescore gathered on the quay. Each man, woman, and child bore a ragged, weary look, as though the isle had worn them out of all strength before it thrust them into the sea's embrace. A few recognised her, creating a stir in the crowd and in her a touch of guilt, in part for her surety—a pension from the laird saw she did not want—but in the main because she was unworthy of the hope she sparked.

And what eyes held that spark; such life as remained in heart and limb seemed to find its nexus in their orbs. Even if in some it flickered like a candle, in others it burned with the intensity of a man who, in the act of falling, finds one handhold and clings to it. A common tale would have brought most to this departure: stony ground, dead beasts, sickly infants, winter hunger; their misfortune driven home by legend of fortunes made by those who had taken to the masted beasts. Account of any other manner of fortune got by emigrants rarely found them for the press owners knew what to print; leap the sea and life was made, so they were persuaded.

Eolhwynne, or another spaer, might for any in the crowd spy the shadow across their path and direct them away (if they would heed the warning) but such insights had left her, and she saw through the same dark glass as any in this crowd.

She carried a handful of charms written on scraps of linen and dangled them for any to grab. 'Tie it about you for safekeeping,' she said. Hands reached out and they went in moments. 'I shall have more on the morrow, fret not.'

The crowd swept about her and with the creel on her back she was in danger of being swamped. Another source of shame was the value of the goods in her creel; the fancies from Cameron's cost more than would feed some of these for a week. The image of the woman on the bottle of Macassar oil burned in her mind.

'Bless my babe, will you not.' A woman, face flushed, eyes bright with anguish, thrust a babe into her arms where it clung to her shawl. Its face was clay grey, like the fleshy undersides of a limpet startled from the rock and its eyes the sky-blue of the innocent. She wetted her finger with spit and marked its forehead with the dice cup and joyous rune.

Its mother had asked for a blessing. Others were not so gentle, grabbing at the hem of dress or sleeve and kissing it or wiping it on their forehead, as though she were an icon in a church.

They had no shelter, other than what they made, and for many it was only a stockade of what they had dragged or carried on their backs, and which now penned them like animals. Some had rigged an awn of canvas or tarcloth while others squatted in the open about a brazier. Behind them, set beneath the wooded slope of Fancy Hill, the merchants' warehouses shut them out with locked door and barred windows. Any of them might give all shelter for the night, but it seemed the rigour of the journey had already begun.

'Ruairidh Camaran! Anyone seen Ruairidh?' she asked, freeing herself from her creel and dropping it to the quay.

'Be here!' Ruairidh appeared with two lads in tow, having found his friends.

Màiri entrusted them with watching over her creel.

'When do you sail?' she asked.

'Afternoon the morrow,' one of the lads said.

'We be the first,' a voice cried. 'There be two hundred more a' coming.'

'I'll come back in the morning,' she said to all who could hear. 'Any wanting a blessing shall have one.'

'If you cannot bless us all, will you bless the ship, since its loss will be the death of us.'

'Ay,' she said, 'I will.'

One man stood a head taller than the rest and had a vigour about him missing from the many.

'Big man,' she said, 'them tar-britches will not treat kindly what I've to do. Will you come with us?'

Before the man could speak, hands were urging him forward, first among them his wife, a red-haired firebrand with an infant at her breast. 'Be at it, Dùghlas. Mind, he's a temper on him.'

'A warm head is called for,' Màiri said. 'Not running hot.'

'Might'n we all go?' a man called.

'Would you chance the night in clink!'

'There be food in clink!'

It was impossible for all to go. The captain would call out the law and have them arrested for disorder.

'One only,' Màiri said. 'Ye've a name, big man?'

'Dùghlas, Dùghlas M'Fhionghuin,' his wife snapped.

'Och, woman, I can speak for myself,' M'Fhionghuin said to a round of laughter.

'Come with us,' Màiri said. 'But don't look with any intent.'

'Aye,' M'Fhionghuin muttered as he came with her. 'Take them by surprise.'

'With luck,' she agreed. 'Mind me saying, you don't seem ill-fortuned as most.'

'Alice, the wife, she did not want to wait until we'd no choice. There's some...' M'Fhionghuin looked away as if ashamed to speak. 'Alice reckons they'll not live to see our landing. Got I a cousin in Quebeck City. He writes well of it. Alice reckons I, that is we, be meant for better things.'

'This temper of yours, reckon you can hold it?'

M'Fhionghuin grinned. 'I hold it with Alice, and there's many a man would not!'

The ship's figurehead showed Hector[1] naked, save for a shield, and hoary-faced. Like the ship he adorned, time had abused him.

---

[1] In Homer's Iliad, Hector is the eldest son of King Priam and the noblest of the Trojan heroes. *N.W.*

Men dangled in the spars and rigging. The stink of hot pitch scorched the air. Timbers sawn, caulking driven between planks, pitch spread, sails sewn. Aloft swung sacks of meal and potatoes, casks rumbled up the gangways and thumped onto the deck. Wooden hurdles penned a cow and three sheep, and chickens squabbled in wicker cages: milk, flesh and eggs for the journey. Like a great whale, the ship would take one last gulp before it ventured into the deep. One man loaded slabs of stone onto a barrow and wheeled them aboard. His pace was slower, more studied than the rest. The stones were blank, save for a single cross, and only waiting a name. Quebeck had rock aplenty, but Skye men would be remembered by the Old World, not the new.

By voice, half the sailors were English, the rest Quebeck French. Most were too engaged to notice them arrive, but one waved them away, shouting, *'Demain, soir! Allez, allez!'*

'Dè rud a tha ann?' M'Fhionghuin asked.

'Reckons we're after boarding,' she said. 'Walk on. Act foolish and likely they'll let us be.'

Below the figurehead, a diamond pattern showed through the layers of pitch protecting the timber. The ship had no more need of its curseyes—the natural enemies of a ship paid them no heed and even took offence—but they were still there in spirit. She also must make her mark on the timbers and with M'Fhionghuin on the landward side of her she pretended interest in the ship, gazing up at the masts and rigging and examining the hull. Cordage, thick as her wrist, climbed to foremast and bowsprit and the rusted arc of the anchor leant against the hull in a cradle of rope. Close to, the ship's timbers were ravaged, and streaks of rust bled from her fastenings. Though everything about *The Hector* had an immensity and strength, it was only a work of man, and it wore its age. With youthful impertinence, the painted smokestack thrust up through the rigging like an old woman fixing up her hair.

She was close enough now, abreast of the first mast. The ship's sides had curved out to meet the quay.

'Step between me and they,' she said. 'I'll be quick about it.'

'They're going to be a mite curious, miss. Cannot make out what they're saying.'

'You speak no English?'

'Scarce a word, miss.'

How would Dùghlas M'Fhionghuin fare with no English or French? God only knew, for Quebeckers spoke no Gael.

'It may be we'll need to hurry away once they see this,' she said.

'Reckon so, miss.'

Màiri leant against the ship's side. With her free hand she cut with the knife, leaving a score in the tar encrusted hull. She had to reach the wood, for tar would not hold a charm. She cut again, and this time found the oak.

'Any word, big man?'

'They've not seen, yet.'

Three cuts and she had made Wynn, the joyous rune. It was not big, no broader than her hand, but enough for any to see. The ship was moving as the tide sucked the water from around it and more of her weight fell on her outstretched arm. She glanced at the hawsers holding ship to shore. Grey water slopped between hull and quayside.

She hoped Hector was not offended as she cut the second rune: Loegr, the white-maned courser of the ocean. Before she could finish, a pebble cracked on the planking above her head and bounced away. They were seen.

'Miss, reckon they—'

'Wait on.' She dragged the knife one last time, making the slanting cut to finish the bindrune. Her weight was still over the water.

'Eh! *Sorcière!*' cried a man.

'They're not happy with us,' M'Fhionghuin said.

'Done, help us up. Don't stand on being a gentleman or I'll be swimming.'

M'Fhionghuin pulled her upright. Several sailors had downed tools and stood around them. One pointed at the rune marks and swore in French. Several had stones in their hands, others gripped makeshift weapons.

'*Sorcière, qu'est-ce que ça veut dire?*' The man wore a Breton cap and stripped jersey. A full beard hid his face.

'For good luck,' Màiri said. '*Pour bon voyage, oui?*'

They had not expected her to know French. Her tongue was rusty but lessons on Iona had not been wasted.

'You are witch?'

'I was the laird's spaewife. These people asked for my protection, as they wish for yours.'

'Spaewife is witch, no better than,' one cried, but several at the back dropped their stones and seemed satisfied.

'*Sans enchantement,*' the Breton shouted. '*Sans sortilege.*'

Several Frenchmen conferred and one spoke. '*Sorcière, nous,*' the man mimed holding a brush, '*peinture bateau.*'

'*N'importe,*' she said. '*Le fait.*'

Painting over the runes would have no effect on their power.

'*Sorcière, l'avenir nous le dira!*'

'I'll box his ears, he keeps on,' M'Fhionghuin said.

'Your wife will not thank me,' Màiri said. '*Na abair guth.* Let them argue among themselves.'

Màiri took M'Fhionghuin's elbow.

'Pray to your God,' Màiri said to the Breton. '*Dieu vous bénisse!*'

'Our God is a jealous God.'

The Breton spat at her feet and turned about.

'And good riddance,' M'Fhionghuin said.

'Come away now,' Màiri called. 'They'll not make a fight with all of you.'

She hauled M'Fhionghuin away. Behind them a single French voice shouted. Moments later a stone found the back of her leg and she stumbled.

M'Fhionghuin helped her up. 'Walk before me,' he said and so they returned to the crowd.

'Thank you, Màiri,' M'Fhionghuin's wife said. 'Have you to go?'

'I do,' she said. 'But I'll come again in the morn. Will men of the church be coming?'

'Ay, the lot of them,' M'Fhionghuin said. 'We'll see if we can keep them off each other's throat.'

Ruairidh Camaran had her creel and helped it onto her back.

'Be naught missing, miss, and none looked to gain by it.'

'Màiri?' It was the woman with the child. Her face was apologetic. 'I know you was right good to us, but see, we'd hoped to see a spaer afore we go.'

'Laird's spaer 's gone with him,' someone said.

'No matter,' she said. 'I take no offence; I know I am no spaer now. I shall see what may be done.'

'McLeod's got a spaer, but we be MacDonalds.'

'You are all men, women and children to God,' she said as she turned to leave them, 'and there are no clans in heaven.'

§

Once known as The Lump, a desire for civic improvement had provided the barren headland above the harbour with trees, a picturesque folly, woodland paths where ladies might walk without soiling their skirts, and a name to befit its new-found position. In summer Fancy Hill was the place for peregrinations and resort for hopeful young men and bashful young ladies, but on a cold day in April, Màiri, Rosie Quinlivan and the first cuckoo of the year had its shade and damp air to themselves. Rosie was looking good for seventy years. Her hair might be white as birch bark, but she did not move like an old woman and needed no stick to help her along. Màiri found her at the herb garden below the folly; a tower overlooking the harbour built to give employ to a few folk and keep them from the poorhouse.

'Mind if I join you?' Màiri asked.

'Company be fine,' Rosie said and sat up. 'Though you won't find much. Weather's knocked it back.'

Màiri dropped her creel to the ground and tried not to

hear her knees creaking. Old age might come early to her, following the pattern set by the change, or she might have decades of living to do. But such questions were best not asked when you've had a creel on your back all morning and stretching her arms over her head, she let the breeze wick the sweat off her back. Besides, she thought, Bheathain did not think she was old, and he was half her age, near enough…

'What you smiling at?' Rosie asked.

'Mightn't I have reason to smile?' Màiri rolled up her shawl for kneeling on.

'Lucky for some. Has he name?'

'Why should it be a he?'

'The smile you had, like a lass when she sees a laddie looking at her.'

Màiri shook her head, refusing to rise to the old woman. 'Betony's come on well,' she said. 'Better than mine.' The herb garden was open to all who needed it, but Rosie did most of the tending.

'Surprised aught grows on your wee island. Lonesome place it is.'

'Would you have me in Portree?' Màiri teased.

'I would not,' Rosie said. 'One auld spaer in the town will suffice. Och, you ought set up in Broadford, not that island.'

She ignored the suggestion: she was happy enough on Haelda's island for now. It was only five months since she left the laird's service, no time at all. Ten years on she might think differently. Rosie Quinlivan rented a cottage by the shore on the far side of Fancy Hill; a poor part of town, like Stormyhill it was little-changed in half a century. Rosie chose to live nearest those most in need of an old spaer's gifts and kneeling beside her, Màiri had an image of herself equidistant between Eolhwynne and the old woman, for she had once been the incomer and Rosie resigning from the laird's service.

Growing old would be a strange new journey.

Taking hold of a bunch of betony, she stripped off half a dozen of the youngest leaves and set them on a square of muslin.

'Heal all,' Rosie said, referring to betony by its herbal name. 'Have you none dried?'

'It's for a salve,' Màiri explained, 'feverfoul[1] too, if I can find some.'

'You might use burdock if you cannot,' Rosie suggested, 'but feverfoul, aye, there's a bit of it about. Have you seen much of the laird's new spaer?'

'Less than I thought to,' Màiri said. 'She has not dropped by to pick my thoughts.'

'Or to be sharing her own,' Rosie said. 'Och, she'll be worried though, fresh from schooling she is and dragged off to the big city.'

'Cannot see the laird troubling her much,' Màiri said. 'I scarce saw him last year. Clara, now, I saw a good deal, but he'd no need for us.'

'But take her he did,' Rosie said.

'Ay,' Màiri agreed, 'and I cannot understand it with Clara so near her time. The girl's place is with Clara. Reckon I'll be called on instead if he's not back soon.'

'He's dwelling on what befell the prince,' Rosie said. 'His sister, Lady Maud, meant a great deal to him. You wouldn't know it, but as children he and she were like two fingers on a glove.'

'That be why he has taken Eolhwynne, then?'

'Ay, reckon so,' Rosie said. 'Och, Màiri your face be all camel-like. Cheer up lass.'[2]

Màiri tossed the leaves down. 'It is not fair,' she complained, 'It is I should be going to Winchester; had I another six months of Grace, I would have been.'

'Lass, you must have known it was waning. How often have you scried this last year and found naught, or summoned a familiar and got no answer for it did not hear your call?'

'Times,' she admitted.

'So, you'd have gone off to Winchester with the laird and

---

[1] Also known as centaury or Centaurium erythraea. *N.W.*
[2] Camel-like. Sullen, unhappy, literally camel-faced. *N.W.*

been damn all use to him. When my time came, I knew right enough and I've never regretted the way I left his service.'

She had known, after a fashion, but she'd not believed what her body was telling her, not for a time. Rosie was right but it did not make her happy. At least one still had need of her.

'Do you recall ever making an amber touchpiece for a babe?' she asked, 'be twenty years ago.'

'Amber?' Rosie said. 'Why are you wanting to know?'

'The salve is fer the same lad; he lost such a touchpiece. I recall seeing him when he was a bairn, maybe four years old. Name of Bheathain, Bheathain Somhairle, the 'summer traveller'.'

'I know the name,' Rosie said. 'Is he sickened?'

'Ay, though he is mending. His grandfather brought him to Dr Ramsay, and he passed him to me.'

'And I'm just an auld hedge witch, and not wanted,' Rosie sniffed.

'Maybe Ramsay reckons I still have something of the gift,' Màiri said, 'He may be right.'

'It's a long time since I had any,' Rosie admitted. 'I mind something of the lad. Day or two back an old man was after a charm against such a fellow. He wouldn't give his name, or name of the lad—which helped me none at all, the damn fool—but reckon it was the grandda you spoke of. Well at his unease he was, he didn't *hauld wi magick,* sae he said, but was minded to keep canny and all. Save us, I near put a ban on the miserable old sod.'

'You did not?'

'Lass!' Rosie protested, 'as if it was in my power. I gave him something to keep him happy and sent him on his way.'

Màiri rolled up the betony leaves in the muslin and folded them away.

'For the mark on the lad's face?' Rosie asked.

'You recall him well. I've got him drinking betony tea.'

'Poor lad.' Rosie laughed. 'He'll not like it; they never do! Are you worried about him?'

'Ay,' Màiri said. 'He mends, as I was saying, but there's something not right in this. It isn't like Dixon to be fussed over a soul like Bheathain and he is paying for mine and Ramsay's care. Who is Bheathain Somhairle, truly now?'

'You never scried on him when you had the gift?'

'Once,' she admitted. 'There's a charm protecting him, which is strange enough. Did you put it on him?'

'Not I,' Rosie said quietly. 'Truly, do you fear for him?'

'Ay,' Màiri said.

'And did Ramsay say ought to you of the lad?'

'Only I am to see he's mended and tell him what the lad had sickened of. I shall be calling on him in the hour.'

'Meantime, the lad's biding with you?' Rosie asked.

'Ay, but for a few days. You've not given me answer.'

'Not for me to give, is it? Ramsay is a good man,' Rosie said. 'I know of the lad; he was a babe in swaddling when I saw him, and I know of the charm he has on him. Kicked like a horse but serves us both right for poking our noses where's not wanted. Call on the doctor and tell him your worries. This Bheathain is the one you're sweet on?'

Màiri blushed. 'What if I am? There's little harm in it.'

'Maybe not, but folk 'll tattle.'

'To be sure, but it's a long time since any man looked at me, I mean a man I didn't mind looking. But it's more than that,' she said. 'I can't be certain, but I reckon he has something of Grace about him.'

§

Doctor Ramsay's housekeeper, a stern-faced woman in starched blouse and with her hair done up in a bun, showed her into the doctor's room and asked if she wanted tea. Ramsay was away but expected back shortly. Màiri accepted the offer and sat by the hearth. The coal fire burned too hot for her and once the housekeeper had left, she stood to see the books shelved behind the desk. The lettering on the spines was obscure and hard to read, but the bulk seemed to be of medical purposes and gave little clue to the man. The exception was not in place, being marked by an empty slot and the canted volumes adjoining it. A copy of King James' *Demonologies* lay on the doctor's desk.

Màiri did not open it or look to see where the doctor had placed his bookmark. His path was natural physic and hers unnatural, but their paths were not wholly separate, and she guessed Bheathain's sickness had led the doctor to this particular book.

Hearing the housekeeper return, Màiri sat again by the fire.

'There's nothing else you're wanting?' the woman asked in English.

'No thank you. Excepting I'd like to rest my feet.'

'Of course.'

The housekeeper fetched a stool and left her propped up and sipping tea like an invalid. She had expected to convince Ramsay the boy suffered from a curse, but the *Demonologies* implied he was ahead of her. How much more he might know, or guess, she would find out. Presently, she stood and took a book from the shelf and pretended to take an interest in *The Escapades of a Perthshire Physician* to avoid all other thoughts.[1]

---

[1] MacGregor wrote a piece in the Summer 1857 issue of the Edenborough Review lampooning the fashion for 'reminiscences' from such worthies as curates, justices of the peace, and doctors. Though of great utility to future social historians and novelists, they were seldom of interest to ordinary readers and included such titles as *Reminiscences of a Highland Parish*, by Norman MacLeod, *A Memoir of the Christian Labours of Dr Nicholas Fortitude*, by His Nephew, *Sermons to the Natural Man*, by William Shedd, and *Recollections of Highland Custom as Observed by an Instrument of the Law*, by Thomas Quimby, JP. Of doctors, MacGregor wrote "[they] are in the main worthy men of great knowledge, charity, and expertise, but writing is seldom among their talents. Nevertheless, many take it upon themselves to set down their dealings with life, misfortune, death and childbirth among the ordinary people as

Presently the slam of a door announced Dr Ramsay, who, after a brief disclosure to the housekeeper, entered the study.

'Miss Mulcahy, afternoon. I had hoped to see you but was called away.' Ramsay removed his hat and coat and hung them on the door.

'Your housekeeper made me at home,' Màiri said.

'So I see. And did she place that book in your lap?' Ramsay sat behind his desk.

'No. This was of my own accord.'

She put the volume on the desk.

'I'd have thought this more useful,' Ramsay said of the *Demonologies*. 'Bheathain is recovering?'

'In a manner of speaking. His physical strength returns, and I know the source of his sickness.'

'I believe I know it also,' Ramsay said. 'But I should like to hear it from you.'

'He bears a curse,' Màiri said. 'His mark is the sign of it. Whoever laid it on him lived to regret it. I cannot tell who she was or why she acted as she did, nor can I tell why it alters now, but his curse wishes to end itself and I reckon it saw the laird's passing as its chance. It looks for one to bless.'

'My conclusion also,' Ramsay said. 'Though I scarce understand it. One it may "bless": is it *possible* it could find such a person?'

'It is probable, given enough time, but I fear I gave him too much hope in it.'

'You told him?' Ramsay was surprised. 'Is that wise?'

'Bheathain needs some explanation; he's not foolish, far from it.'

'Then I trust he'll keep it to himself. Folk will not suffer such talk, not here.'

'He knows,' Màiri said, determined to press the doctor for all he knew on the lad. 'It is not the first time I had

---

though they were some Roman chronicler tasked with recording Great Events. Perhaps historians may find some future use for these volumes, but the passing reader finds very little pleasure in a litany of boils, emetics, and broken limbs." *N.W.*

dealings with Bheathain. I know those who raised him were not his true parents.'

Ramsay gave her a sharp look. 'I understood you could not divine such things now.'

'It was years back. He broke the cord on his charm and his folks thought it worrying enough to call for me in the middle of the night. I knew something was amiss and scried on him. I learned he was born far away but before I could discover more, something struck back at me and near laid me out on the floor. There's a charm protects him.'

'You learned no more of his origin since?' Ramsay asked.

'No. Whatever it was warned me off.'

'That was sensible of you.' Ramsay frowned and she did not need any particular insight to see he was preoccupied.

'Tell me, has he spoken of a white stag?'

'No. Should he have?'

'He spoke of a white stag the night I kept him. He was not in sound mind, but it agitated him. There are no reports of such a creature anywhere on Skye.'

'It may be a harbinger,' she said. 'The sight of an unusual beast can prefigure a death.'

Ramsay nodded. 'Yet Bheathain is alive. Whatever it was, if he saw anything at all, it did not bring death. At least, it did not bring *his* death.' He rang a bell to summon the housekeeper. 'You have finished your business in town?'

'I have a pair of boots to collect.'

'For Bheathain?'

'Ay. What he has are falling apart. I'm after Mr Dixon paying for them, as he was generous enough to pay you for caring for Bheathain.'

'I do not insist on payment,' Ramsay said. 'But he refuses to let me give my services for nothing. I shall not say more.'

The housekeeper came to the door.

'Mrs Brodie, call for my carriage. Miss Mulcahy and I are leaving.'

'You'll not tell me what you know,' Màiri said, once the housekeeper had gone.

Ramsay hesitated, and then spoke to the point. 'It is not from choice. I am obliged to defer to Dixon. It is time others *should* know of Bheathain; he and I are not getting younger. But if he disagrees, I can say nothing, understand?'

'Well enough.'

'Later I shall have you dropped by Loch Fada. I take it Bheathain is safe there?'

'Safe?' Màiri sat up. 'Does any wish him harm?'

'Something in the *Demonologies* has set my mind to work.' Ramsay patted the book. 'It is possible he is in grave danger.'

'How so?'

'That is my dilemma. The danger comes from who he is; the very thing I cannot divulge.'

III

Left with time and his own devices, Bheathain found much of one and little of the other for such devices as he desired needed the presence of Màiri and she was absent. He stirred the fire and added peats from the basket but if he sat over long the chill nipped him and the ache in his belly increased. No surprise he ached, for he'd not eaten in two days and this morn filled it all at once. It minded him he was mending, but not yet himself.

He had no sheens but need not sit in bare feet and wiping the soles clean he found his stockings dry on a line. Màiri had washed them, and they smelled sweet. A crook hung over the fire, like at home, and he hung the kettle to boil. He would have tea and would wash. He might shave also but found no blade and hoped she would not mind.

The bed where she had slept was a heap of heather with a blanket across it. The heather was fresh, still with its green smell on it, but there was no other smell to the bed; nothing to mind him of Màiri, save the hollow where she'd lain. The heather was sparse and unforgiving. He would give her bed back for it was shameful to have her lying here while he was snug. After what was said that morn, he hoped none would be sleeping on the floor tonight for Màiri's bed was broad.

She'd left a Bible for him, but he was curious for her other books and stood at the dresser to read their titles. Some words he did not know and others he thought foreign, but seeing what she read was a little like seeing through her eyes. It was prying where he'd no business to pry, but he had purpose. He wanted to know of wandering spirits and if or when he might be rid of the mark on his face. He found a book at the end of a shelf. It had a yellow cover and the title *Natural Magick*. The pages opened exactly where he needed.

Wandering Spirit: of the air, see ZEPHYRS; *angels, see* GUARDIAN; *arts, see* MUSE; *augury of; banishment of...*

The type was small and hard to read. He did not bother beyond the first few words if he did not think it useful. There were a great many forms of wandering spirits, and it was curious such a thin book should have so much to say on them.

...ceaseless; celebrant; celestial; cemetery; chalice; chance; changeable nature of; charms against; cheese, see CHEESEMAKING; *children, effect upon; choleric effects of; Christ see* CHRIST; *clock, see* TEMPORAL SPIRITS; *chronic...*

...relating to curses; if a curse be made...

Several paragraphs followed, but he hesitated to read on. Had Màiri wanted to save him from the truth? What if there was no chance of ever being rid of it?

But he couldn't hold back; not now.

...a curse be made in haste or error and the one who laid it repent of the deed, then however great the repentance and notwithstanding the curse-maker's natural powers and learn'd skills be great, she may not undo what is done for the shattered vase may not be unbroken except by illusion and what is sought here is not pretence but return to what was before the curse was made. Yet, though the maker be powerless to undo her work, the curse itself is not so bound, and knowing its maker doth wish it never made, the curse suffers as a child doth suffer when spurned by its parent. Thus, seeking to bend to its maker's new will the curse releases into the world a WANDERING SPIRIT *to seek one for whom it may be a blessing. Once it finds such a one the curse*

atones in some measure for the suffering it brought into the life of the one who bore it...

The words made his head hurt. Many he barely understood, and the book had a way of stringing them together like an overburdened cart spilling its load.

Wandering Spirits of this nature may be commonplace, but their discovery is rare for a host is unaware of their presence, excepting they may suffer bouts of distraction and recollection as the spirit delves for some circumstance in the host's present or past wherein it may work a blessing. Thus far, the scribe writes only of what is known, yet much remains unknown concerning wandering spirits. To whit, how long may a wandering spirit dwell within a host, whether its nature be eternal or limited by the natural span of the curse bearer, whether a curse may release only one or many such spirits in succession and the manner in which the curse becomes a blessing remain mysteries. It remains troublesome, that while there are many apocryphal accounts of curses finding dissolution by means of wandering spirits, proven cases are rare.

WANDERING SPIRITS: *damaging effects thereof; besides the distraction and regression noted...*

He read on, but the words 'proven cases are rare' lingered. Had Màiri mislead him, or had he mislead himself?

He closed the book and returned it to the shelf and for a moment seeing it lined with its neighbours had the sense of a door opening onto another and much larger world. He took another book from the shelf, but once in his hand found it was a wooden frame about a drawing. It showed Màiri, though many years ago. She was naked with one arm across her bosom and a shift across her legs, but they were only tokens of modesty. Her nakedness, alone, troubled him, but there was something more, for even in a few lines the artist had captured something of her beyond appearance. Whoever he was, and Bheathain was certain it was a man's hand, he marked his name with the letter 'L'.

He replaced the drawing and wished he had not seen it.

Elsewhere on the dresser were curious brass bowls and jars with liquid inside. Bunches of herbs hung from the roof beams and on the coat stand beside the door hung a leather belt with strange markings. Some of all these things he understood, or rather, understanding hovered just out of reach, but the rest were a mystery, and it only increased his discomfort. This morning he and Màiri had seemed close; now it was as though he did not know her at all.

He turned to the door, to where sunlight made mockery of his worries and stepped into its embrace.

Opposite the house a wooden causeway a dozen yards long connected the island to the shore. From this side of the loch there was no need of a boat to reach the island, but all he could see was the empty moor and the line of a peat bank.

He was not to leave the island.

A rowan grew on its highest part and in its shadow was a grave. It was unmarked but he supposed it was old Haelda's. Below, on a patch of level ground, was something like the pit where the M'Illathains burnt kelp, but this was roofed with slabs. Màiri said it was a furnace to make a new charm for him and she'd speired him to fill the gaps between the stones with the mud exposed at the water's edge. He dug with bare hands at first, then from the little ben at the side of the house found a wooden spade and the work progressed.

It wasn't right to have the dead so near the living and for that, and any number of reasons, this was a strange place to set up home. Màiri must have her reasons, reasons also for the bits of bog oak, seashells, and sea-round pebbles scattered about, and the ram's skull leaning on the outside wall. At home the only inessential things brought in were notices for auctions of land and livestock, steamer timetables, and fliers from the Emigration Commission. Manus brought them in and pinned them to the dresser and doors or pasted them to the walls. The auctions had long gone, and he doubted Manus even attended them, nor did they have a use for the steamers or the tourists they brought to the island each summer. Nonetheless the notices mouldered on the walls until soot from the fire or mildew left them dark as slate. Manus took joy in the fliers of the

Emigration Commission and shipping companies, especially when they had a pretty drawing of the ship or the Promised Land they sailed to. These told of the grand life for a man sailing on the *Perseverance* or the *Janice Eileen* and the prospects awaiting him in the Americas or New Holland. When Manus brought one of these inside, he would stare at it as though thinking of taking the ten crowns, but always with a shake of the head he'd turn away. Bheathain brought nothing into a house save rain on his back and dirt on his sheens, but he liked how Màiri had made her place homely. It minded him what home had been when his mam was with him, though Mam would never have thought to have half what Màiri had and would reckon a ram's skull ungodly.

He could not tell if the difference was his, or Màiri's, but it made the distance between them greater.

He was near done and a thirst had grown on him, but before washing his hands in the loch, he marked her name and his in the mud plastered on her furnace. Then he returned indoors and made tea which he took outside to drink. Presently, the pot dry, he closed his eyes and dozed a little. It was good to have been useful but there was much else needed doing. The thatch was new but was a rushed job and not to his liking. Again, he thought this a strange place for Màiri to want to live, especially for one who'd spent so long at the big house. The wind had sent the shelduck and teal into the shelter of the reeds at the edge of the loch, but soon the air would fill with the scream of swifts, for the year was on the cusp between winter and summer.

It was a change, also, after so long hiding behind a scarf, to feel the air on his face and not worry if he was seen.

My Lady summoned me from wind and stone...

Beside the little ben was a peat stack. It was in good order, roofed with turf to keep off the rain, but it was not so big. The spade was not the only tool in the little ben, and he brought out a peat iron and a ripper for cutting the turf to get at the peat. Unused for years their edges had dulled but he found a whetstone in a pail and brought that and the tools outside and sat to sharpen them, dipping the whetstone in the pail and running it along the blade of the ripper.

It was long-handled, like a scythe, but with the blade in line with the handle and curved inward. The edge came bright, but the iron and water chilled his fingers and it wasn't long before the whetstone slipped from his hand. As he bent to pick it up, he sighted a man on the shore near the far end of the causeway. A hood covered his face, but by height and build he thought it Tammas M'Neis.

'*Haoidh! A-nall.*'

Bheathain beckoned him across, but the fellow did not move. Tammas would not have hesitated, and he recalled Màiri's warning and stood, holding the ripper before him.

'*Cò às a tha thu?*'

Again, no answer but the man turned away and presently he vanished into the expanse of moor.

Unease did not leave him and while he finished sharping the ripper and peat iron, he glanced up many times thinking he was spied on.

> There is wisdom in her lore;
> Beyond Grace, sage guidance draws,
> Once it is set in motion,
> Upon all nature's elemental laws.

Nature is the throne of magick.

Editor's Remarks

Once again, a blank line separates this chapter from the preceding material, with the name, "Màiri Mulcahy" against the left hand margin and the date, February 12, 1862.

Mr Auburn (or Dyborn) having departed Arbinger, life continued. On the 28 February James Ludd presented MacGregor with his proposal for the Madeleine Shrine which, after a tour of the intended location, MacGregor accepted. His journal entry for the day states,

"I believe Ludd has finally grasped my demands, which I confess are unusual, and if we can find a capable builder my dear Madeleine will have a shrine worthy of her."

As we shall see, finding a capable builder would not prove easy.

Turning to the text. This chapter survived the attentions of Messrs Beresford & Lucas rather better than the previous. Aside from the interpolated text of the book Bheathain finds, some of the details of Miss Mulcahy's wanderings around Portree—fewer of the citizens beseech her help and rather more shun her in the published text—and curtailment of the scene at the quayside, much here will be familiar.

Why, then, did Beresford & Lucas treat this chapter, and the character of Màiri Mulcahy leniently compared to Eolhwynne?

The straightforward answer is Màiri Mulcahy performs no acts of magick: that is, she does not draw on anything other than her craft skills. Further, the booth-scryer (the urban equivalent of the outside-woman) had been a stock character in Scottish poetry and prose for over a century so there was nothing remarkable in Màiri Mulcahy's character or position. In addition, while condemnation of booth-scryers by the Alban Church increased during the nineteenth century, Edenborough supported so many it appears, as with the city's brothels, public disapproval had little effect on private demand.

Dr Claude Crabtree in *The Wizard of the North* (King James University Press, 1930) proposed another explanation for Beresford & Lucas' apparent acceptance of MacGregor's depiction of Màiri Mulcahy. It draws on one of the witness statements gathered by MacGregor in *A History of Scottish Magick*. Your editor confesses he finds this by far MacGregor's most intractable work, but Dr Crabtree's evidence is compelling. Essentially, the appendix of *A History of Scottish Magick* includes some two hundred accounts from people claiming benefit from the practice of magick. Among them is one J. Lucas "whose leg was lately saved by the care of an old woman of the wynds after surgeon recommended amputation."

There is no further identification of J. Lucas in *A History of Scottish Magick*, but Dr Crabtree examined the Factory Inspector's records for Crosshaven Ironworks, presently housed in the Official Records Office and found an entry for November 24th 1861 stating, "proprietor John Lucas run down by railway waggon occasioning insensibility and breakage of the right leg."

There is, as Dr Crabtree concedes, no absolute proof the John Lucas struck by a loose waggon is the same J Lucas healed by a booth-scryer, but the correlation of date, name, and injury is persuasive. Had MacGregor known of Lucas' injury and recovery it would be entirely plausible for him to ask Lucas to contribute to *A History of Scottish Magick*. More curious is why John Lucas acceded to MacGregor's request. Perhaps he owed a debt of gratitude to whoever saved his leg which overrode his religious objections to booth-scryers.

Regarding *Natural Magick*, the text discovered by Bheathain, Sister Ethelnyd believes it is MacGregor's own invention (albeit the content conforms to accepted theories of magick) and not taken from a genuine book of magick. Invention or not, Beresford & Lucas required its removal from the published edition, and it appears here for the first time.

The bearing of the compass recalls home
Chapter Seven
At sea, near midnight: The character of PAAVO JUKOLA, *shewing the childhood act of cruelty that set him on his reckless path*

My Lady was not one for sea, woodland arbour was her harbour of resort, but if we are for the Unbridled Horse[1] *let us sail with one who knows the ropes of bow and stern, starboard and port, of compass, lead, and chart and course...*

    The man who lives for vengeance
    Always walks in his victim's shoes:
    Truly, he abhors himself.
    The bearing of the compass recalls home.

I

PAAVO JUKOLA KNEW the underside of his cabin mate's berth was only an arm's length above him but so intense was the darkness he could be staring at the heavens themselves.

Gabriel Stone's duties ended at midnight, and he might have enjoyed this rare moment's solitude, but the motion of the ship in a heavy sea quickly became wearisome and he swung his legs to the floor and lit the lamp by the washstand.

His hair was a tangle a sure sign he had slept badly—and there were rings under his eyes. A shave would improve matters and he poured water into the bowl and lathered his brush before allowing a drop of soap to fall into the bowl to stop the water slopping over the sides.[2]

---

[1] The Anglo-Saxon rune poem refers to Loegr, the rune of river, lake and ocean, as the 'horse that wears no bridle'. *N.W.*

[2] A brief passage in MacGregor's journal describes an experiment to verify this effect; however, Lady Helena's diary gives a more entertaining account. It appears he was too vigorous and over-turned the bowl, causing damage to the drawing room ceiling below his study. Thereafter, Lady Helena asked her husband to conduct his experiments in the garden. A wise precaution, for an experiment while writing *Works of the Master* resulted in him

The English had a poor opinion of his countrymen and not without reason. Too many Finns were illiterate farmboys given to melancholy and drink. He was proud to be a son of the byre, but he had learning and temperance. The middle watch began at midnight, but he would be shaved and respectable for the new day. His face soaped, he picked up the razor, only to hear a knock at the door.

'Mr Jacks? B' time, sir.' It was the peggy, the youngest watch hand.

He stared at the door. It must be a joke. He was never late for duty.

'Sir?' The knock came louder.

'Yes, yes. I am dressing,' he said, and reached for a cloth. The boy's footsteps went forward.

Unconvinced, he found his watch. It was no joke and swearing at his reflection, he washed his face and ran a comb through reluctant hair. He had lied to the boy. He was not dressing, not even close to it, and he hated the lie almost as much as the reason for it. At least he was sharing the watch with the mate. Better him than Captain Loveless. Whistling an old tune, he buttoned his shirt: *Tempus Adest Floridum*, the hymn leader called it.[1] It reminded him of church with Papa, Mama, brother Lauri, and digging thistles in springtime. Paavo Jukola is your name, he said silently to the reflection in the mirror. Not Papa Jacks, or whatever else they call you.

The door opened and Gabriel Stone came in.

'Still here, Papa?'

'I was too comfortable,' Jukola said.

The man squeezed by him. The cabin was small. Two bunks, two lockers and enough space for two men to stand without arguing.

'Leave the water; I'll have the use of it.' Stone sat and slid off his boots with a contented sigh.

---

breaking a finger and losing both eyebrows when he attempted to fire a cannon on a frozen millpond. cf. *A Writer's Life* by Professor Evelyn Bishop (Exeter Books, 1962) *N.W.*

[1] We know the tune as 'Good King Wenceslas.' *N.W.*

'Who is this, Lord MacDonald?' He knew Gabriel Stone would never turn down a gossip.

'Like any, he assumes you've only him tae think of. He's uncle tae William, the dead prince, ye ken?'

'And the woman with him, she is his wife?'

'Nae!' Stone laughed. 'She's a spaer.'

'A what?'

'Wise-woman. You have 'em? Like a witch.'

'Ah, like potions.'

Kaisa Heiskanen could fix horses, people as well. She was old and lived alone in the woods. Girls in trouble would go to her and come back pale but relieved. His father said Kaisa Heiskanen could curse a man with ill luck if he crossed her. Father Edelfeldt had been civil with her while she was alive but would not suffer her corpse near the church. The village buried her deep in the woods.

'Kind that'll treat what doctor winna,' Stone said as he sat to remove his boots.

'She is his servant, then?'

'Ay. Though his boy's tecken a fancy tae her.'

'Boy?'

'Lordship's son. Dazzle-eyed for her.'

A thin, whip-backed man without evil habits, Gabriel Stone was in several ways an excellent cabinmate. As chief-steward, he had intimate access to the passengers and was none too discreet about their affairs. Moreover, Stone had no interest in books, thus preserving Jukola's own affairs: after a childhood with only the Bible and the hymn leader's A-B-Cs, books had become his chief pleasure, and vice.

His collar straight and tunic buttoned, Jukola flung on his sea coat and checked its pocket for his spyglass.

'Can spaers tell a man's fortune?' he asked.

'So I hear. But only a fool wud want tae ken such a thing.'

Jukola left and climbed the companionway to the deck. Stopping outside the captain's cabin, he listened to the man snoring. Tynan Loveless was asleep to the world: an oaf whose chief pride was his appetite and the sharp wit he aimed at subordinates. Jukola owed Loveless the name 'Papa Jacks'.

All mariners are superstitious, but English sailors carry it farther than most. No mother of any man aboard the *Dundalk* would recognise the name he owned to: not Gabriel Stone's, not Tynan Loveless', and not his own.[1]

§

The wind was from the northeast, almost in their eye and their smoke blew across the afterdeck, leaving a bitter taste in the mouth. The distant light on the starboard quarter marked Kinnaird Head. Once beyond it, they could turn south and raise sail with a following wind. For now, with only foresail and mizzen set to hold the ship steady, all forward motion relied on their engine. The *Dundalk* was a glutton. Engineer Sam Johnson and his 'black squad' would be sweating tonight.

The mate and most of the watch were in the deckhouse under the bridge. Frank Farron, chief deckhand, was idly shuffling a pack of cards and Tod Martens was reading. The peggy was leaning over Marten's shoulder and he realised the Hollander was teaching the peggy his letters. Deckhand Clem Bowles was threading a needle to darn a sock.

'Papa Jacks, you had me worried,' Dewar said.

There was a murmur from the men. His lateness was noted.

'My apologies, it will not happen again,' he said.

'Imagine it will not,' Dewar said. 'I've never known you late afore. We will let it pass, this time. First watch is relieved, Mr Jacks. Mr Clarke has our helm; Howmore and Green are the lookouts. Any observations?'

'None,' he said.

---

[1] With increasing use of foreign labour in the merchant fleet the custom of 'sea-names' is less prevalent than it was, though it is still found in naval service. It was founded on a belief the sea could not claim those whose names it did not know. *N.W.*

'Good. Our course, Mr Jacks.'

Dewar led him into the adjoining chartroom. A lamp hung over the chart table where a pencil line showed their course from Inverness. He noted the abrupt change where the captain's florid style met Dewar's precise penmanship.

'Course, due east. Wind east-nor'-east, veering,' Dewar said. 'Heavy swell on the port bow. Cook reported few takers at dinner. Average speed, seven knots, last position taken eleven-forty made us here.' Dewar tapped the chart.

Most of their course had been plotted in daylight with shore marks—hills, church towers and headlands—to guide them. Night had come almost four hours ago, but despite only a handful of shore lights, and the log and lead to guide them, their pencilled course had not wavered.

'The Hansa ship, any sign of her?'

'A fool's errand; you really think we'll find her?'

'If I am honest, no; I cannot even recall her name,' he lied.

'Mind me, sir,' the peggy was at the door behind them, 'the *Schwarzer Keiler*. That is, the *Black Pig*.'

'Thank you, Billy, I am sure Mr Jacks knows German,' Dewar said smoothly.

Jukola flinched: 'I do not understand your meaning, sir?'

Dewar shrugged. 'They are your fellow Balts, Mr Jacks.'

'Of course; yes. I do have some German, though my Swedish is superior.'

'See, Billy: schooled is our Mr Jacks. And how is your Russky?'

Jukola snorted in disgust. 'Enough to show a man the door or make him beg for his life.'[1]

'Bravo!' Dewar laughed. 'Shame your barbs will not reach the tsar from here. What is it, Billy?'

'The men are wanting coffee.'

'Of course, make enough for all.' Dewar glanced at the chronometer and crossed to the starboard window.

---

[1] Finland was then a reluctant subject of Imperial Russia, hence Jukola's reaction to Dewar's comment. *N.W.*

'Orders, sir?' Jukola asked.

'I'd hoped to see Rattray by now,' Dewar said.

Rattray Light was the next after Kinnaird. Having two lights to starboard would give a reliable fix on their position.

'Our speed should be better than seven, even with this sea,' Jukola suggested.

'Read the log. Engineer reports bad coal. Full of clinker, so he says. Nevertheless, if we're not where we should be, we *must* know where we are. Bearings, Mr Jacks. I'll take the lead.'

'Sir?' He usually took the soundings and Dewar the more demanding compass work.

'Mister Jacks, you do want to work your way up to countermaster?'

'I do, yes.'

'Good. Take Bowles with you; he's the best of a poor lot.'

'Yes, sir.'

Dewar left and a moment later Jukola called Mr Bowles inside the chartroom.

'Bring the tri-legs, and this,' he said, handing him a lantern. 'Quarterdeck, Mr Bowles.'

The quarterdeck in the ship's stern was lively in a sea, but as far from the engine and boiler as could be had. Iron was the enemy of navigation and might sway the needle five degrees or more.

Jukola carried the bearing compass and followed Bowles aft. Both items were heavy, and they each assisted the other up the ladder to the quarterdeck. The tri-legs were solidly made in oak, walnut and brass, and provided a platform at working height onto which the compass case slotted. As a precaution, he had Bowles lash the apparatus down.

The lid removed on the compass case, he slackened two wing nuts projecting from vertical slots either side and drew the mechanism clear. This action disengaged a lock and the compass card immediately homed on magnetic north. Its perimeter showed degrees and the thirty-two points, while about the pivot were the sun and moon and the maker's name, *Le Graveran: La Rochelle* and the date, 1837. A gimbal below the compass card allowed it to maintain equilibrium, regardless of the ship's motion.

'Stand by, Mr Bowles.'

Pivoting on the compass glass was a device with two upright projections and a small mirror. This was the alidade and he aligned one of the projections approximately on the distant flash of the lighthouse.

'Mr Bowles, time is twelve twenty-three. The light, if you will.'

Bowles stood by with pencil and notebook as Jukola held the lantern above the compass and aligned the alidade exactly on the light—a difficult task as it rose and fell with the ship's motion—then read off the bearing in the mirror.

'South west, five degrees, Mr Bowles.'

'South west, five.'

He remained bent over the compass with his eye on his watch hand. Approaching a minute after the first reading, he realigned the sights and took a second reading.

'South east, two.'

'South east, two.'

They appeared to be going backwards.

A minute passed and he read again.

'South west, eight.'

'South west, eight, sir.'

'Good. Wait on, Mr Bowles.'

He returned the compass to its case and with Mr Bowles returned to the deckhouse. In the chartroom once more, Jukola averaged the readings and corrected from magnetic to true north then plotted a line from Kinnaird Head out into the firth. He was pleased Dewar remembered his ambition. Second Mate brought more responsibility and pay, and he would have charge of cargoes and mail. It also crossed his mind it would be wet in the bows tonight so this had been a doubly-fortunate exchange of duties.

The peggy knocked at the door with his coffee. He called the boy in and took the cup from him.

'You are not one for cards?'

'Tod Martens winna let us.' The boy filled the cup.

'Do you admire a man who wins at cards?' he asked.

'Reckon it's how he does it, Mr Jacks.'

A curious answer. The coffee was scalding hot and bitter. He admired the dedication of the English to a good brew.

'You think Mr Martens should let you play?'

'Och, nae sir, he's a guid man. He's teaching us tae read.'

'The Bible?'

'Ay.'

'There are easier books than the Bible,' he said.

'There's none a man should ken better, so Mr Martens says.'

'I would not argue with him.'

The door opened and Dewar came in. The man was soaked.

'Ay, I would,' he said, pointing at the coffee.

Billy poured another cup. Dewar drank and grimaced.

'Some for Burntwood and Hopkins, too,' Dewar said. 'Mr Jacks, twelve fathom, thirteen, thirteen and one half; mud and gravel. Where are we?'

He ran an eye along his pencilled line and matched Dewar's figures against charted depth.[1]

'Here, sir.' He marked a point on the line. It was two miles off their intended course, two miles nearer the shore.

'Reckon on seven knots and how long before we turn?'

Another calculation, distance over speed.

'Twenty-eight minutes, sir.'

'Good. Log it and relieve Green on the bridge. I'll see what's with our coal. Give me a chance to dry out.'

---

[1] Water depth was measured by a rope weighted with lead and marked in fathoms (six feet). The lead weight is hollow at the base and filled with grease which collects debris from the seabed. The depth and the material collected is compared with information on the chart and combined with a bearing to establish an approximate position. It is not as reliable as a bearing taken from two or more points, hence Dewar's desire to see Rattray Light. *N.W.*

Dewar left, leaving him to stow the compass and write up the log with their position, time, weather, and sea state.

One man had already dropped from the brag game. Farron did not cheat—at least there were no allegations against him—but he could make life hard for any man who won. No one wants to be clinging to a yardarm at the beck of a man owing you a week's wages.

'All's well, Mr Jacks?' Farron asked.

'It is. We shall want sail within the half hour.'

'Y' hear? Half an hour tae win back what ye've lost.'

'Or lose it all,' Martens answered him.

Farron glared at the man: 'Ye may have yer reward in Land-o-the-Leal,[1] Mr Martens. Ordinary sinners must take what we can when we can.'

'Any coffee left?' Jukola asked.

'Dregs, sir,' answered the peggy.

'No matter.' He held out the cup.

One hand for the rail and one for his coffee, he climbed to the bridge deck. Straddling the full width of the ship above the paddle sponsons and deckhouse it was open to the weather, save for a waist-high canvas dodger.

Helmsman Clarke had mastered the art of smoking a pipe upside down to protect it from the spray.

'How is she tonight?' Jukola shouted.

'Guid morning tae ye, Mr Jacks.' There was nothing ironic in Clarke's tone. With midnight gone, it was a new day. The man's feet were braced against a pair of wooden blocks either side of the wheel.

'No sae bad, sounds worse 'n it is. Would be glad o a wee bit sea room. Reckon Captain has us ouer near shore. He was efter keeping time, sir.'

'Do not worry, Mr Clarke. There are eight miles between the rocks and us. We are safe.'

Howmore, the portside lookout, greeted him with a grin.

---

[1] Land-o-the-Leal is one of many ancient names for the Land of the Blessed, or Heaven. *N.W.*

'Scared 'em awa',' the man swept a hand across the black water. 'Empty as a whore's promise.'

'We turn inside the half hour.'

''Bout time,' Howmore said. 'Christ, leuk oot!'

A rogue wave struck the port bow and the ship heeled violently. Jukola lost his footing, but Howmore steadied him. In a few seconds the bows plunged into the trough and an immense boom shook the ship, followed by a plume of spray across the foredeck.

'Big 'un,' Clarke said without drama. The blow had knocked the *Dundalk* three points south. Swinging the wheel, the man brought them back on course and felt the bowl of his pipe. 'Take more 'n that.'

'Any sign of the Hansa ship, Mr Howmore?'

'None whatsoever,' the man said.

'No harm looking.' Jukola drew his spyglass and scoped along the horizon, discovering nothing except the black sea and sky and no telling where they met.

'Empty, as you say.' Jukola crossed to the starboard side where a third man gazed into the night.

'Mr Green, anything to report?'

'Naething, sir. Mae's well be on'y ship on the sea.'

'Seems not likely,' Jukola said. 'You're relieved, get below.'

'Thank ye, sir.' Green turned and hurried down the ladder.

He took up the man's position and turned his eye from north through to east. In the long days of summer, the middle watch was his favourite, and especially in the hour of dawn when the infant sun he saw was already shining upon Kalkkinen's woods, warming its plough fields and silvering the shingles on the church roof. Abruptly he thought of Lönnrot's *Kanteletar* on the shelf in his cabin. Who else aboard this ship would ever sing its songs of harvest and sickness, grief and birth? Songs of land and love of a land; songs the Russians had forbidden in a book they had banned. It was the perfect place to hide his secret account of the *Dundalk*'s progress and passenger and cargo manifests along this dismal coast.

'Perhaps my barbs are longer than you think.' He doubted the ship had ever carried a greater personage than the king's brother-in-law. Otto of the Hansa would be pleased with him.

II

The steaming dung heap at Tyko Haanpää's farm gave the air a rich tang, and the crows basking in its warmth eyed him warily. He was nine and the first snow of the long Finnish winter had fallen overnight. His feet were cold and his cheeks red and he had grown dry in the throat from shouting. Minna, his father's old, sway-backed mare had broken down where the road climbed past Haanpää's Farm. She had managed this journey every other day Mama had sent him to the forest for kindling, but this day would be different.

The forest had been a strange, shrouded place. No birds sang and the only noise was the crunch of snow under his boots and the soft percussions as over-burdened branches shed their snow. Paavo had tied Minna to a tree and gone hurrying in among them, hauling out fallen wind-tangles and snow-broken branches of birch and pine. He had tied them in bundles and then to the long traces leading from Minna's collar and she was dragging them home. He held the harness and tried to walk her forward.

—Come on!

Minna took a pace then dropped her head and snuffled in the foot-deep snow. The forest was all streaks of black and grey, dark against white. Minna's hair was pale brown, the colour of forest mushrooms, and her once dark mane and tail flecked with grey. Clods of ice and snow clung to her fetlocks.

Paavo knew what to do from watching Papa: she had a stone caught in a hoof. If he had been watching he would know which foot gave her trouble, but he had been 'away in the forest', so Papa would have said.

He had forgotten to bring a pick and had only his knife. Papa would not want him using a knife to clean Minna's hooves, but he would be careful with it. Patting the horse on its side, he bent and pushed his shoulder against her ribs. Minna obligingly shifted her weight to one side and Paavo hoisted her near foreleg until he could hold the hoof between his knees. Minna let him scrape away with the knife until it was clean to the ridge of bone Papa called a frog, then he dropped the hoof and stood to catch his breath.

—Not that one Minna, he said as cheerfully as he could and clapped his hands, thinking he was doing well. Minna's ears turned to the sound and her long bony face swung round to watch him. Bending by her back leg, Paavo pushed his shoulder into her rump and the mare shifted, allowing him to lift the hoof off the ground. Again, he held it between his knees and scraped it clean. There was no stone, but the shoe was old; its once sharp ridges worn smooth. Paavo got the hoof clean, found nothing wrong and dropped it down. Minna shook herself and watched him as he sat beside the track. He was winded and hot and sweating; a bad thing on a cold day, so Mama said.

—I'll find it, Minna, so I will.

Paavo struggled to his feet. While he got his breath back, he checked the harness and traces, but everything was as Papa had shown him with each trace passing through the loops on the saddle pad to the collar and nothing twisted, broken, or binding. He even made sure the bundles of kindling were even both sides of the horse. Everything was exactly so.

Another shove with his shoulder and her off forefoot was between his knees. More digging and scraping. Still nothing. Three done, one to go, but it gave him a glow of satisfaction. Papa always said the last thing you tried always worked, but never the first. He leant into her and lifted the rear foot off the ground and cleaned away between the wall of the hoof and the frog, digging out the compacted snow and mud. This time, determined it must be the right hoof, he dug deeper until he poked the knife into the bone. Minna trembled and her weight shifted onto him. He leapt back as her hoof thudded to the ground.

—Minna! Paavo pummelled the snow. The horse snuffled

the ground and watched him from under her forelock.

He was less certain now; but as he sat on the bank, Paavo asked himself what Kaisa Heiskanen would do and recalled the last time he and Papa had called on the old woman.

He had gone with Papa on the ferry to Vääksy. Papa hoped to sell hams at the market, but off-duty soldiers had made trouble and good buyers were scarce. Papa had made half what he hoped and was in no hurry to tell Mama, so when he saw Leevi Pacius talking to Kaisa Heiskanen, he was happy to stop and talk and complain about Russian this and Russians that, which was mostly what Papa talked about. Russians, according to Papa, were to blame for everything from taxes and bad roads to a rain shower at haymaking time. While talking, Papa liked to take his hat off and hold it in his hands as if he were making a speech.

Leevi Pacius was a tall man with a habit of chewing on a bit of straw. Mama said Leevi was a fool and it was only chewing on a straw stopped his mouth hanging open. Papa liked Leevi. Leevi listened when he talked. Leevi Pacius had a gelding for Kaisa to look at; the horse was refusing its harness and he thought it might be witch-marked.

The old woman walked around the horse and prodded it with long fingers. She was small and hunched over at the shoulder. She wore a cowl over her head and the furthest thing forward on her was the tip of her nose. She was dressed like a fir tree, with layers of shawls and skirts, and she smelt funny, more like the forest than a person. Paavo thought she must be hot under so many layers for the day was warm.

—You got a horse, boy? Kaisa Heiskanen said. Remind me your name. I've no memory for names.

—Paavo, Paavo said. Papa lets me use a horse. She's called Minna. She's old.

The woman nodded her scrawny head and shifted him out the way as she came round the gelding.

—Old is not so bad, just not so good as young.

She was muttering under her breath, but whether to complain or recite a spell he could not tell.

—Four good pins on it, she said. So where be it, eh?

She had Leevi fetch a stool so she could stand to reach the horse's back. Papa was telling Leevi of all the troubles at Vääksy and the straw in Leevi's mouth had begun to twitch the way a horse's tail chases away flies.

—Now what's this? Kaisa said. This oughtn't be here, clear as day. Hmm. Boy! Where are you, boy?

—Here, Paavo said. He was stood not three feet away.

—Stand clear, y' hear me.

—Paavo, come here. Papa pulled him away.

—He's with me, Kaisa.

Leevi dropped his stalk on the ground and stepped on it.

—What've you found, Kaisa?

Mama was right. Leevi's mouth didn't close tight, and you could see his teeth between his lips.

—This! The old woman slapped the horse on the shoulder and though it wasn't a big slap, the horse shied as if given the whip.

Kaisa would've fallen off the stool if Leevi hadn't caught her.

—Thank you, young man, now bring the horse back and I'll show you why he hurts.

The horse was none too happy, but Leevi and Papa wrestled with it and brought it back to Kaisa who showed Leevi what troubled it.

—Damn, me. He's been cut. Leevi's mouth opened more than ever.

—More 'n once by feel of it, Kaisa said. Where's his collar?

—I'll fetch it, Leevi said.

The old woman patted his shoulder.

—Trouble isn't the horse, Kaisa whispered to Paavo and patted him on the head.

Leevi Pacius had the collar.

—Caused him no trouble before.

Kaisa slung the collar over her shoulder and pushed her bird-like fingers into the leather, tugging and pulling.

—Here somewhere, I reckon. Ah, there it is.

Kaisa grinned, showing a mouthful of stumps and swollen gums.

—Always harness him yourself, Leevi?

—Mostly, Leevi said. Of late Ulla's had care of him.

Ulla Pacius was Leevi's oldest daughter.

—Twelve, is she? Kaisa Heiskanen asked.

—Thirteen, just.

—Tall for her age, I recall, the old woman said.

—She is, Leevi said.

Papa had put his hat back on, but without it to hold his hands fidgeted. Sometimes, if Papa had nothing to do, he picked at the calluses on his hands until they were raw. Now, he half-turned and stared up the road toward home.

—But not tall enough, Leevi, not for a horse this big; she's dropped this, more than once, b' truth. Frame's broken, feel.

Leevi took the collar and squeezed the leather.

—By damn, he said. Blood on it too. I'll have words with my girl. She should have been cleaning his harness each time.

—Give Oskar a week to heal and get the collar fixed. Then have Ulla use a stool when she harnesses him. Girl's got to learn, but a teacher's got to teach. Now, where's the boy?

Kaisa Heiskanen grabbed Paavo's arm and he thought the fingers kneaded into him just as they had the horse's collar. Her other hand drew the cowl back and he saw her milk-white eyes. Kaisa Heiskanen was blind as a door.

—Remember, she said. Every step takes you by the right path or the wrong, but no matter how many wrong steps you make the right path is always alongside. Now, get on with you. Your Papa wants his tea.

§

Running his fingers through Minna's coat, Paavo found the hidden landscape of bones and sharp ridges. Sliding past the knee to the cannon and the fetlock, he mouthed the different names to guide him until he reached the hoof but found nothing amiss.

The rear leg had different parts. Again, he reached high as he could and worked down to the hard, bony hoof. Cuffing his wet nose, he ducked under the traces and tried the other leg. Minna swung her head round to watch him.

He found nothing and punched the snow with impatience. One leg remained. He blew on his hands. He looked for cuts, for swellings, for the tiniest protest from the old horse, but again felt nothing.

He slapped her on the ribs, the blow stinging his hand.

—Tell me, Minna, tell me!

Startled by his cry, the crows flew up and retreated to a distant field and Tyko Haanpää's wife looked out her door to see what the noise was. Paavo saw the crows but not Henriikka Haanpää.

Looking back, as he would do many times, Paavo Jukola saw the things he could have done. Halved the load and seen if Minna could pull, gone to the Haanpää's and asked for help, walked on to see if the horse would follow. But mights and shoulds and coulds haunt us. All he had, aged nine, was a stubborn bent and a sense he had missed something.

He bent and tried to lift Minna's foreleg. It would not shift. He tried again and the horse leant round and shoved him in the back. He fell, sprawling, in the road. Knuckles barked and bleeding, mouth open in rage, he ripped a switch from the bundle of wood and brought it down on her rump.

The horse jerked forward, eyes rolling and a scream in her throat. She had made a fool of him, there was nothing wrong with her except laziness. He swung again, relishing the slap of wood against flesh. The horse lurched, her hooves scrabbling in the snow. He ran after, driving her homeward like a pursuing demon; a trail of branches and pine needles and specks of blood littering in their wake.

What had Henriikka Haanpää thought, watching the boy torment his horse? Anger? Fear? Christian righteousness? Mama told him later she was only being neighbourly; what he had done was wicked and it was her duty to tell them. But it was hard to know why people did the things they did.

Home was in sight. The switch had broken, but he found threat was enough. If Minna slowed, he had only to raise his voice and she would jolt back to life. Sometimes he shouted and clapped his hands anyway, just to see her fear. Arriving back at the yard he leant against the stable door, his sides burning with cramp.

Minna whinnied and nudged an ice-filled pail. Paavo broke the ice on the trough and let her drink. He must take the harness and gear off to grease and store, but each time he tried, she shied away. He must walk her dry as well, but she dug her hooves in and fought him, eyes rolling in their sockets. Maddened, he untied what was left of the firewood and heaved the stable door open, Minna stumbled across the threshold and inside, colliding with the stalls in a clatter of timber and hooves and he slammed the door on her. He had firewood to cut for Mama; he didn't want to worry about a lazy horse.

Mama liked the wood cut short for the stove. It was easy work with the axe until he found a spruce branch too green and springy for chopping.

He needed the bowsaw. Father kept the blade oiled to stop it rusting and it lived on the wall in the house. He stamped his feet to shake the snow off and went in.

Mama was sitting by the stove and darning a dress.

—I didn't hear you, Paavo.

He shrugged.

—I need the saw, he said.

—I think Lauri had it. It will be dark soon; you can leave it for the morning. Mama yawned. Her eyes were round and dark rimmed in the candlelight.

Paavo smelled dinner and his tummy ached.

—Lauri's not here.

—He's at Father Edelfeldt's. He must have left the saw outside; you know how forgetful he is. He was out the back. Look for it there.

He found the saw abandoned halfway through a log. It was stuck and though he tried rocking it like Papa showed him, it stayed stuck. Breaking a sawblade was the worst thing he could imagine, and he let it be.

He swung the axe at the spruce. It bounced and slipped sideways. He tried again, holding it in both hands. The axe skidded toward his legs. His hands hurt from gripping and the cold hurt his throat. Seeing a pony and trap arrive, he stopped to catch his breath. It was Henriikka Haanpää in a black coat and bonnet. Mama welcomed her inside.

Suddenly the branch split and wrenching the axe free he brought it down with all his strength. This time the wood tore apart and he tossed the pieces on the pile. His back was wet with sweat and his hands bleeding, but he did not care.

A rag wiped over the axe blade, he hung it in the woodshed and gathering bundles of kindling together tied them with bark strips before taking them inside. Mama and Henriikka were at the table. Mama had the stove door open, and the heat was delicious. She had made tea and buttered slices of wheat bread for herself and Henriikka. Mama had even taken her apron off, but she had not fixed her hair up, not like Henriikka who never went anywhere without looking her best. Papa always said a wife must make an effort when there were guests, but as Henriikka hadn't taken her bonnet off perhaps she wasn't really a guest at all.

Paavo stared at the open jar of honey.

—Look at you! Mama said; Heavens, you're a sight!

Henriikka gave him a hard stare as he dropped the kindling by the stove. Bits of wood and spruce needles stuck to his jacket. He picked off a piece and dropped it in the basket but kept his filthy hands from Mama's view.

—Are you well, Paavo? Henriikka asked, yellow hair spilling from under her bonnet.

—Hungry, he said.

The wood basket was almost empty. He tossed the remaining logs onto the floor and tucked it under his arm.

—Henriikka saw you and Minna on the road, Mama said.

—Mmm, he said. I think she's getting lazy.

He ran for the door. Mama called after him.

—Paavo, be sure and brush your…

He did not hear the rest.

The short winter's day was ending, shadows creeping across the yard and filling the plough marks in the fields. Papa said you must plough in the fall, so the winter frosts loosened the clods. Papa said many things: when it snowed, he would complain, saying it would keep the ground too warm, and when it froze hard, he said it was difficult to drag timber from the forest. Papa said nothing was ever just right and you had to make the best of it.

He filled the wood basket. Papa would be home soon and Lauri also. Lauri had not finished his work and Paavo tried the bowsaw again. Tools had to come in at night for safekeeping. Holding it, he rocked the saw back and forth, but it only shifted the log on the sawhorse. Leaving it, he told himself he must let Papa know or tell Lauri himself.

Lauri was four years older and strong enough to haul the logs onto the sawhorse. There would have been a middle brother, but Simeoni died of croup in his first year. Lauri always had his head in the Bible and Papa complained that, 'even Jesus was a carpenter.'

But on Sundays after church when Lauri read the Bible at table Paavo had seen how Papa smiled with pride and Mama would butter Lauri's bread, while he would sit and scowl at Lauri, wondering what the trick was. Paavo was stuck on the a-b-c books in Mr Tammisto's class. The last page in the book had a drawing of a big red cockerel and Paavo longed for the day he could turn to that page and strut and crow just like it.

Paavo saw Henriikka leaving and after she had driven away, he dragged the basket to the house. Mama had put on her apron to scrub potatoes, but she dried her hands and helped him carry the basket indoors. Snow stuck to the underside fell on the floor and Mama swept it out before it could melt. Then she gave him a brush and made him stay outside until he was clean. Back inside he sat his boots by the stove and gave the brush to Mama.

—Paavo, is this blood? Show me your hands.

Paavo turned them over.

—They don't hurt, he lied.

—Oh *Paavo*. What shall I do with you?

Mama heated water on the stove and Paavo stood on a chair. Mama's fingers were soft and warm and slowly most of the grime came off, leaving raw and reddened skin.

—We have to do something with these, Mama said, patting his hands dry with a cloth.

Paavo bunched his fists and glared at her as she fetched a brown bottle.

—That's no good. Be brave, hold them out for me.

Reluctantly, Paavo uncurled his fingers and Mama tipped the bottle. He tensed as the liquid slid along the neck.

—I know it stings, Mama said, but it's for the best.

The alcohol dribbled onto the torn skin, and he stifled his cries.

Mama bandaged his hands and went back to peeling potatoes. When she had done, he would take the peelings out to the pigs. His hands stung from the alcohol, but it was not so bad.

A noise on the porch signalled the return of Lauri. Lauri was always quiet on his feet, while Papa would shout at the dogs and stomp about. When he came in, he was still wearing the clothes he had been sawing in, not clothes for being out so late, and his face was pinched with cold.

—Hello Mama, hello little brother. My, my, my.

Lauri rubbed his hands and drew a chair up to the stove.

—The saw's stuck, Paavo said.

—What, little brother?

—You left the saw. It's stuck in a log.

—Not now, Paavo, Mama said.

—But he *did*.

Mama shushed him and rested her hands on Lauri's shoulders.

Lauri reached up and held Mama's arms.

—I've spoken to Father Edelfeldt: I told him I want to

study for the priesthood. He has agreed to speak for me.

Mama drew her hands back.

—And the farm?

—The farm, yes, Lauri stared at the scrubbed tabletop. Father knows what sort of a farmer I'd make: a *forgetful* farmer; a *lazy* farmer; a *bad* farmer. Paavo knows it; I cannot even saw logs, can I, little brother?

—Enough, Mama said. Take these.

She gave Paavo the bowl of peelings and pushed him out the house.

§

They had three sows and once a year borrowed Haanpää's boar. Each summer the sty filled with grunting and squealing, and at the end of the fall the pig slitter came, and they had hams and bacon for the market in Vääksy. Paavo stood on a block of wood to toss the peelings over the wall and listened to the sows snuffle for them in the darkness.

The tramp of hooves told him Papa was home. Valko and the dogs were with him. Valko was a young horse and much too strong for Paavo. Papa used Valko for hauling timber to the lake. Papa liked to stay busy and in winter he worked for the sawmill.

The dogs jumped off the cart and bounded over, all barks and wagging tails.

—Paavo, that you?

—Hi, Papa, he said.

Mama came to greet Papa. They kissed and spoke quietly in the yard, then Mama went back indoors.

—Come, Paavo, help me with Valko, Papa said. Do the hold-backs for me.

Paavo tipped out the last of the peelings and left the bowl on the porch. The hold-backs were leather straps around Valko's hindquarters and stopped the cart banging into his legs, so Papa said. Valko was big and Paavo had to stretch to reach the buckles.

—I hear Henriikka Haanpää called by, Papa said.

—Mama gave her buttered wheat bread and honey.

—We must be neighbourly to those who've been good to us, Papa said.

Valko snorted and rubbed his head against Papa's chest.

—I know, Papa said. You're hungry. When Papa slapped the horse's neck, his hand made a noise like kneading dough.

The straps freed, Paavo unbuckled the trace from Valko's collar and gave it to Papa. Papa coiled it neatly around his elbow and gave it back to him.

—You know where it goes.

Paavo hung it in the tack room and came back to help with the cart. Together they lifted the shafts free of the saddle and pushed it under the lean-to.

—Get some wood today?

—Lots, Paavo said. But Minna is lazy. She wouldn't pull so I hit her.

Papa lit a candle and gave it him. It threw a pale, golden light over Valko. The horse had a dark coat, without any trace of grey.

He held the candle while Papa took off Valko's harness. Papa had big hands, but he never forced or strained the leather. Things lasted longer in Papa's hands, and he always got the best from everything.

—Take these, Papa said and laid Valko's reins and harness across his shoulders. Shouldn't have to hit a horse. Sure you didn't ask too much of her?

—No. The harness was hot and slippery with sweat.

—Put the candle down and take this for me. Papa eased the saddle pad off Valko's back. It was heavy and the holdbacks tangled round Paavo's legs.

—Put it on the rack and wipe it down. I can grease it later. Minna's in the stable, is she?

—Yes.

Paavo heaved the saddle pad over the rack and hung up the reins and harness.

—It's not like her to be lazy. Get the horse brush, will you?

Paavo fetched the brush and held Valko's bridle. Papa lifted the collar off the horse, but instead of taking it into the stable he hung it on Paavo's shoulders. It weighed more than he thought he could bear and bit into his neck.

—Papa?

—I want you to know what it feels like. Minna and Valko wear it all day long. You can bear it, just while I walk Valko and brush him down.

Paavo found a stool and sat in the tack room. If he rested the lower edge of the collar on the seat it eased the weight a little, but he could not stop it grinding against his neck.

—Papa, it hurts.

—A while longer, Papa called from the yard. This is life, Paavo. We all wear a collar, all of us. The harvest is bad and we go hungry, that is our collar. People are afraid to come to market and prices are down, that is our collar. And the tsar's taxes are a collar on every man's neck. Only a child is free, but you are getting older, so you must learn to bear the collar, like a true man, a true Finn.

Papa led Valko into the stall next to Minna. The older horse leant over the screen.

—Hello, old girl. Papa ran a hand down Minna's nose.

—Shame on you, Paavo. You didn't take her harness off. And where's her oats? There's only old hay?

Paavo thought his back would break and wondered if the collar was slicing his neck to the bone.

—I tried to take it off, he mumbled. She wouldn't let me. I forgot the oats.

He hadn't forgotten. He didn't think she deserved any.

—The collar hurts. Paavo wiped his eyes.

—It gets easier. Fetch water. Papa gave him the pails.

The pump was in the yard. If he wedged his elbows against the collar, it stopped it rubbing his neck as he walked. At the pump, he set the pail under the spout and leant on the handle. It needed two hands and now the collar bit into his neck with every movement. Water sluiced out, splashing into the pail and across his legs. It was icy cold, and the pump handle hurt his fingers. Papa was feeding the horses, fetching hay from the loft and scooping oats from the feed bin.

His knees were buckling as he brought the pails in. Laden down, he could not keep the collar from his neck and the leather pinched and gnawed at the flesh over the bone. Water spilt on his shoes. He set the pails down and Valko pushed him aside to get at the water and he fell back against the wooden stall. The collar was breaking him in two.

Minna snorted impatiently.

—I'll have something for you. Patience, old girl, Papa said. I'm hungry too. Stand up, Paavo. Help me with Minna; let's see how she is.

Papa felt Minna's teeth and rubbed a hand down her flanks.

—Poor old thing. See how thin she is. Just like Henriikka Haanpää, all skin and—'

The horse whinnied and shied away from Papa.

—Easy, easy, girl. What's this? Papa showed him a hand streaked with blood. Why, Paavo? What could she have done to deserve this?

He had no answer. Papa took off Minna's harness and saddle pad, laying each piece in the tack room until the old horse stood naked as a foal.

—She's not lazy, is she? Paavo whimpered.

—No. No, she's just old, Papa said. This isn't right. I hoped you'd understand and be kind to her...

Papa lifted the collar off him and hung it in the tack room. Paavo sat up. There was a deep groove across the back of his neck, but no blood. Papa leant against the division between the stable and the tack room.

—Go ask Mama for a turnip. Bring two turnips.

—Why?

—A treat for Minna; run along now.

Mama was sitting at the table, head in hands. Her cheeks were red and blotchy. She was by herself. Lauri had gone.

—Papa wants two turnips, he said.

—The storeroom, take them, Mama said.

Paavo took the best from the sack and ran out into the yard. Without the collar, his feet were light, and breath sang in his chest. The stars shone overhead, and the sunset had faded into purple.

Papa quartered the turnips and fed the pieces to Minna.

—Good, is it? Papa murmured. Here, you give her some, slowly now.

Paavo took a piece of turnip and held it out. The horse stretched for it.

—Say goodbye to her.

—Why, Papa?

—Everything has its time, and this is Minna's. She's worn out. It's not her fault. She stopped pulling, did she? By Haanpää's farm? That's where Henriikka saw you.

—She just stopped, Paavo said.

—The road is steep there. And her shoes are worn to nothing.

—What will you do, Papa?

—Take her into the woods. She'll understand.

Valko snorted and turned his head to Minna. It was as though the horses knew what was being said.

Paavo fed Minna another piece of turnip and, for once, Valko didn't complain and fight for his share.

—Couldn't she stay, Papa?

—Can't feed a beast I cannot work or sell at market. Little enough as there is. Besides, she'd be unhappy. She wants to work, always has. You think you could get used to wearing a collar, get to like it?

Paavo couldn't imagine it.

—You will, son. You will. We all find some trouble to bear.

III

Old Bear, Whitecap and Brown Berry standing at the crossroads in the hour before sunset. That is how Paavo saw them and even now he can see them no other way. But I, scratching in Paavo's skull for my redeeming act may stand any place I choose and so ask how might Lieutenant Gennadiy Zhulpa—Paavo's 'Old Bear'—of the Tsar's Imperial Lancers have seen the occasion of their fateful meeting two months after the death of the old horse with the land still in winter...?

—Damn this place, Kafelnikov said.

Captain Vasily Kafelnikov possessed the arrogance of minor gentry and had no field experience but this, Lieutenant Gennadiy Zhulpa thought, should have been obvious to him first thing this morning. He and his subaltern, Yuri Petrenko, had dressed for the journey in bearskin coats and hats but young Vasily Kafelnikov wore only a regulation greatcoat and a ridiculous white dress cap, which would not warm an ant. *Then*, Gennadiy Zhulpa now realised, his mood had been too forgiving, fortified by the good night's sleep he always enjoyed before a journey, and he had merely offered a mild rebuke, which Kafelnikov had not taken kindly to—the second warning, also not heeded—but *now,* having suffered the man for a full day, he was no longer inclined to be mild or forgiving. But out here it would be cold-blooded murder to abandon Kafelnikov, so he let the man ride with them. Left to himself the hapless captain would be dead inside two days. If the White Ravens did not murder him, the cold certainly would.[1]

Zhulpa glanced up from the military map. The sun through the mist dazzled his eyes. Dusk was an hour off.

—It is hard to damn a place when one does not know its name, he murmured. I see smoke: a village, perhaps.

The smoke formed a brownish haze perhaps three miles distant. Mist suggested a lake but as this country was half water it may or may not be one of the many lakes drawn on the map. He had seen the peasants burning the forest to clear new land but that was in spring, not the depths of winter. The smoke suggested a village.

---

[1] The White Ravens was a short-lived Finnish resistance movement opposed to Russian rule. They were brutally suppressed after a failed attempt on the life of the tsar in Helsinki in 1869. *N.W.*

—Is it *marked*? Kafelnikov's tone suggested the last thing he expected to find on an Imperial Army Map was a humble Finlander village: an opinion the mapmaker shared for he had drawn only the major towns, along with rivers, lakes and principal roads. The latter was the core of the difficulty: was this beneath their feet the same crossroads drawn on the map? If so, they must take the eastward road. If not, they must proceed north. They had come from the south, a fact plain by the hoof prints in the snow, and the westward path was beyond contention. North or east? In summer the matter might be easily decided, the road crossing theirs might clearly be no more than a farm track, but snow rendered the land mute and no matter how he screwed his eyes at the map, it would not answer.

Petrenko gazed about, his round Turkic face fixed in its eternal half-smile. Lieutenant Zhulpa guessed the man was considering which tree to build a shelter under. Raised in the Altai Mountains his dependable subaltern would have no difficulty spending the night in these woods, but he thought the idea deplorable, if only for hearing Kafelnikov complain all night.

—No, not marked on the map, Zhulpa replied to Kafelnikov. We may be two hour's ride from the post house or wander into nothingness.

The post house promised decent quarters, hot food, good company, and less chance of finding a Finlander's knife at your throat, but if they took the wrong path, they might find only miles of empty forest. Zhulpa glanced toward the smoke. He was certain it indicated a village, perhaps an inn. Even a farmer's cowshed was better than pressing on blindly.

—Damnation! We shall freeze where we stand. I say, this way. Kafelnikov indicated the eastbound road.

—On what evidence? Zhulpa asked, inclined, if he must make a choice, toward the northern road.

—None. A decision must be made, and I do not trust to tossing a coin.

Zhulpa suppressed a laugh.

—When faced with two unreasonable choices, consider a third, he said.
—And what might— wait! Kafelnikov stared along the eastbound track.
—What did you see? Zhulpa asked.
The track ran through the forest in a straight line: a white streak through the dark firs.
—A man, Kafelnikov said. He saw us and backed away, I am certain of it.
Zhulpa saw nothing but heard a dog bark.
—Convinced? Kafelnikov said.
—Every dog has a master, he agreed. Petrenko, fall in.
—We must not delay, Kafelnikov urged. He might escape into the woods.
—Perhaps, he pretended to agree. If I saw three Cavalrymen hurrying toward me, I might well do the same.
—Sir?
—I joke, man. Have you no humour? Naturally, had I only a dog for company I would stand my ground and be cut down like a hero of the empire.
—You jest in poor taste, sir.
—I am alive because of my poor taste. If you ever reach forty-seven you might agree with me.
—I shall not, I swear on my father's name. Ah, I see him now. Do you, sir?
He did. A boy and a dog were dragging a sledge up the bank alongside the road towards cover of the trees.
Kafelnikov's sabre slithered against its scabbard.
—Put it away, Zhulpa said.
Kafelnikov stared at him, his lips drawn back in a snarl.
—You would let him escape? The man spurred his horse and was away in a flurry of snow.
—Kafelnikov! He was talking to air. Mouth open in disgust, Zhulpa spurred his own horse and called for Petrenko to follow.
—Kafelnikov, it is only a child! Kafelnikov!
He had no hope of catching him; Kafelnikov was half his

age and two-thirds his weight, but for all his lightness, the fool had no rhythm on a horse and Zhulpa held the distance at forty yards.

—Halt! In the name of the tsar!

Kafelnikov was upon the child, but, arriving in haste, his horse skidded on the icy road and Zhulpa caught up before he regained control. The boy cowered against the bank, his eyes pools of fear and an arm restraining the dog. The sledge had stuck on a tree root. He doubted even a grown man could have hauled it up the bank and into the forest. The boy should have cut the traces to free the dog and abandoned the sledge: all it carried was firewood. Kafelnikov had scared the boy witless, just what he wished to avoid.

—Boy, is this the Sysmä road? Kafelnikov demanded.

—Sir? Petrenko's smile was broader than usual. The man shared the joke.

—I know, I know, Zhulpa said. Let's see how he does.

The boy did not answer or move a limb, but the dog was all hackles. Its eyes shifting from Kafelnikov to him and back again, as though deciding which was the greater threat. Zhulpa hoped it had no preference for bear skin. The boy had his arm around the dog's neck. Both were part way up the slope, on a level with or a little higher than Kafelnikov. The boy had found a hollow behind a boulder and sunk his backside into it as though wishing to disappear.

Zhulpa waited and let Kafelnikov make a fool of himself.

—*Sysmä?* Kafelnikov pointed down the road. The boy shook his head.

—Not Sysmä? Kafelnikov said.

The boy shook his head.

—The child is an idiot, Kafelnikov said.

Fear makes idiots of us all, as does bravery, he thought.

—The boy is terrified. Put away your sabre and stop shouting at him. Damned obvious he has no Russian. Zhulpa dismounted and passed his reins to Petrenko.

—They must teach it at school, Kafelnikov said. Our tongue is their tongue, we the conqueror, they…

Kafelnikov had jabbed his sabre at the boy, perhaps only for emphasis, but it was too much provocation for the dog. It lunged toward man and horse and, but for the restraint of the sledge, would have taken the latter by the throat. Kafelnikov drew his pistol but before he could aim, the sledge jerked free, and the dog leapt. The unfortunate horse reared back to escape the jaws but with no room to manoeuvre its hind legs found the ditch and it fell sideways, taking the rider with it. The pistol fired as Kafelnikov flung his arms up to save himself, then dropped from his hand as he fell. Instantly, the dog seized him by the leg and Kafelnikov thrashed about, trying to retrieve his sabre.

Ignoring the dog, Zhulpa stepped across Kafelnikov, put his boot on the blade to prevent its use and stood over him like a bear defending its cub. The dog backed off. Kafelnikov groaned in pain.

—Serves you right, damn fool.

The boy had not moved, save to dig his arse farther into the ground.

—Sir. Petrenko was calling him.

—Not now, old friend. Zhulpa took his hat off so the boy could see his face. He liked to think he did not look cruel, less the wicked stepfather, more a kindly uncle, though he grew his beard long to hide a few mementoes of battle.

—*Sinä poika.*

The boy stared at him, no doubt surprised at a Russian speaking Finlander. He would have liked to see the look on Kafelnikov's face but kept his eyes on the boy and the dog.

—Is this the Sysmä road? he asked in Finlander.

The boy shook his head. Zhulpa bent to retrieve the sabre and pistol. He stuffed the pistol under his belt and fought the temptation to sling the sabre into the forest. Boy and dog watched him intently.

—*Sysmä?* He pointed back down the way they came. This time the boy nodded.

—*Mainio, mainio. Kiitos paljon.*

Not many Finlanders got to hear a Russian say thank you.

Two hour ride and they would be at the post house.

—Sir! Kafelnikov called.

—Get up, man. Retrieve your damned horse. We leave, with or without you. You may freeze for all I care. The boy had scrambled down the bank to grab his dog.

—Sir, I beg, Kafelnikov was agitated. Look to your man.

He was inclined to ignore anything Kafelnikov said, but a glance at his subaltern said otherwise. Petrenko's reins dragged in the snow and his head was down.

—Petrenko?

No answer.

—The dog, Kafelnikov protested. I could not...

—I would the dog had taken your damned throat. As he spoke, he crossed to Petrenko. Something was gravely wrong. Kafelnikov continued to complain.

—My sword. Sir, I demand my sword and pistol.

—You are not fit to wear them. Petrenko, old friend, is it bad? He gathered the reins. The man was breathing and conscious and there was no blood at his mouth.

Petrenko indicated his midriff.

—Belly?

—Side. Not so bad, sir.

A belly shot would be fatal out here. The Turkic's luck might hold. In five years, the man had not taken a single wound of consequence. Some reckoned a *koldun* had blessed him, but Zhulpa had heard Petrenko deny this; the man was a good Christian. Kafelnikov was hobbling after his mount.

—Don't die on me. Can you ride to the post house?

Zhulpa sensed Petrenko wanting to say yes, but knew it was bravery over sense.

—No matter, old friend. Must be a village nearby.

The boy had not moved from the edge of the road.

—*Sinä,* he waved a hand at the boy. *Tohtori*? Need *Tohtori*.

—*Hän nukkua pois?* The boy asked.

—No die, Zhulpa answered the boy in Finlander. Him strong, no die. But need *Tohtori*.

—What did you tell him? Petrenko asked.

—You mighty warrior. Bullet like bee sting to you.
—Thank you, sir. Petrenko smiled. Big bee. Damn hurt.
Kafelnikov returned with his horse.
—Petrenko cannot ride alone so you will ride up with him. Give me your horse. We need to find the boy's village.
Kafelnikov, surliness gone, meekly handed him the reins.
—*Sinä, kylä?* Zhulpa pointed at the smoke.
The boy nodded, confirming there was a village.
—*Tohtori?*
The boy shrugged. He could not tell if he understood him or not: in any event, a doctor out here was unlikely.
—*Pitkälle?*
The boy shook his head. At least the village was close by.
Kafelnikov had hurt his arm and could not mount. Frankly, he hoped the arm broken, but for Petrenko's sake helped him into the saddle.
Kafelnikov mumbled an apology.
—Keep it. If you must grovel, grovel to Petrenko. He is less forgiving than I am.
He tied Kafelnikov's horse to his own.
—*Esittää*, he said and pointed toward the village.
The boy kicked his feet in the snow and ignored him.
—*Koto nyt, nyt!* Either the child led them, or they followed: either way, he must go home sometime. For emphasis he pointed the way with Kafelnikov's sabre.
The boy pulled the dog by its collar, then righted the sledge. Suddenly the dog turned and ran, with the boy straining to keep up.
—*Tasaisesti, peräti tasaisesti!* This is too fast!
The boy dug in his heels and the dog settled into a trot.
—*Mainio*, Zhulpa said. We get somewhere. He mounted and swung his horse round to follow the boy. The sabre was a damn nuisance without a sheath, but he could not bring himself to throw aside a serviceable weapon.
—Kafelnikov. Take this and sheath it. Do not draw it again in my presence. Petrenko, you can manage?
—He takes good care of me, sir. He has soft hands.

Zhulpa smiled. Petrenko had no greater insult for a man than 'soft hands'.

—Where do we go, sir?

Zhulpa realised Kafelnikov had absolutely no knowledge what was happening.

—Wherever he takes us, he said indicating the boy.

—But the post house? Kafelnikov asked.

—Two hours ride north. You are free to go. I shall not stop you.

—I shall remain with you, sir. I am now obliged.

Arrogant and a prig. But if they must spend the night here it was better to be three than two, especially when one of the two has a bullet in him.

At the crossroads the boy stopped and pointed north.

—Sysmä? Russky go Sysmä?

Zhulpa pointed west, into the dying sun.

—Boy go home. Russky follow boy.

§

It was dark now: the sky a rust-brown fading to black with only a pale, salmon-pink marking the sunset. The forest lay like a heavy blanket on either side. It would have sheltered Paavo. He still might slip Musti from the sledge and vanish into the darkness. He knew where to hide. So what if the Russian died. Wasn't his fault Whitecap shot him. None of this was his fault. Whitecap and Old Bear were talking but he couldn't understand them. They talked Russky to each other and only Old Bear talked to him. Whitecap's eyes were like flies crawling in the snow. He had tried to shoot Musti. He hated him and now he was leading them home. Then he saw Haanpää's Farm and knew the forest was behind them. He had decided without deciding for open fields lay on either side and there was no escape. He thought of the fireside. He thought of Mama and Papa.

§

—A hovel, Kafelnikov said as they dismounted in the yard where the boy had brought them. The place stinks.

—What did you expect: a palace? Zhulpa looked at the mean little house.

—Sir, I ask for the return of my pistol, else these peasants will see I am unarmed. We must show unity or seem weak.

Reluctantly, he accepted the man's point. The pistol was exactly what a wealthy man might buy his son; prettily decorated but no more effective than a standard model and with the same flaws. He took off his glove and turned the screw holding the flint until it loosened from its thread. The flint tossed aside, he thrust the screw in his pocket. The man would have spare flints but without the screw the pistol was useless.

—You will look the part, now act it, he said, handing back the weapon. And half the Imperial Army are peasants: Turkmen, Lapps, Kyrgyz, Finns, and Ukrainians; Petrenko is no better than a peasant, but I would not trade him for ten of you. If he dies, if he even comes close to dying—relief at finding shelter allowed his tongue to escape—I will have you sent back to your father like a beaten dog. Now, you will be civilised. This is their home, and we are guests.

It was too dark to see Kafelnikov's face. Perhaps it was unwise to write a threat upon a pane of glass—he was not rid of the man yet—but anger had boiled in him, and it was better released at this fool than at the boy, or worse, whoever the boy had brought them to.

§

His heart beating in anticipation of the beating Papa would give him, Paavo tied Musti to the porch rail and stamped the snow off his boots before letting himself in.

—Such a noise you make, Mama protested. She was sitting by the stove with her needlework. Paavo ran across the floor into her arms, knocking the sewing to the floor.

—Paavo! Mama protested.

—Soldiers, he hissed. We have to help them, or they'll shoot Musti!

Papa was sawing logs with Lauri. Mama called them in. The soldiers entered, Old Bear and Whitecap carrying the injured man between them. Papa came in with the bow saw. He glanced at the soldiers, then at Paavo, before hanging the saw above the door. Lauri stared at Old Bear.

Old Bear smiled and nodded at Papa and indicated a chair. Papa agreed and the two Russians sat the injured man down. Whitecap's hot little eyes batted about, taking in the room as Papa cautiously welcomed them. Old Bear said in broken Finlander what they needed, and Mama cleared the table. Whitecap and Old Bear lifted the injured man up and stretched him out. As Old Bear gently stripped off the man's coat, Paavo was reminded of the last time with Minna when he and Papa took her harness off in the stable.

There was a lot of blood under the coat. It had run down the man's leg nearly to his boot. Blood smeared across the table. Mama put the kettle on the stove. She hated mess on the table and always complained when Lauri spilt ink on it. Paavo wondered if blood stained worse than ink. Every time he ate off that table in the years to come, he would remember this moment.

—*Doktorr*, Old Bear said. He needs *Doktorr*. *Tohtori*, understand?

—There's Ola Svensson, Mama said.

—Vääksy's too far, Papa said.

—Anyone speak Russian? Old Bear asked, Roo-skeey?

—Father Edelfeldt speaks Russian, Lauri said.

—Roo-skeey? *Spa-see-bo*! Tell me, Old Bear said.

Lauri explained, showing Old Bear his Bible and shaping a roof with his hands.

—Here? Old Bear pointed at the ground.

—*Da*, Lauri said.

—Bring here, bring here!

—*Da*, Lauri made the sign of the cross and pointed at the wounded man.

—*Da! Da!* Christian. Bring here!
—Take your coat, Lauri, Mama called.
—*Da!* Lauri shrugged.
—Shush, now! Papa said.

Old Bear hurried Lauri out the door. Closing it the man looked round, a smile warming his lips.

—Progress, he said.

Whitecap was tall and stood awkwardly under the roof beams. Papa offered him a chair. The man snatched it and sat with his legs outstretched. Mama picked up her sewing, but the needle barely moved.

Old Bear squeezed Petrenko's shoulder and spoke in his ear. Then he finished removing the coat.

Papa sat next to Paavo on the bench.

—Are you hurt? he whispered. Did they threaten you?

—No, Papa. That one, he pointed at Whitecap, wanted to shoot Musti. Shot the other one instead.

Kafelnikov saw the finger and muttered something. Zhulpa waved him away.

—Where is Musti now? Papa asked.
—Outside.
—In the yard?
—Yes. They followed me home.

Papa nodded.

—Go on, best you see to the dogs.

He stood up.

—Eh, Paavo? Old Bear asked.
—My dog, he said.
—*Da*, Old Bear waved a hand at the door.
—Be quick, Papa whispered. Leave the wood for now and come straight back.

Musti was curled up against the cold. Paavo untied him and led the dog into the barn. Both dogs jumped and played as he stirred bran hash and the guts of a deer Papa had trapped in the forest. Valko whinnied. The horses outside made him nervous.

Slipping out, Paavo closed the door and leant against it.

The soldiers had left their horses tied up along the porch rail. No one had walked them or given them water. It wasn't their fault and feeling very grown-up, he filled a bucket at the pump and set it down. The horses were bigger than Valko, and their coats shone in the light from the window.

—I've given water to your horses, he said as he entered.

—You have a good son, Old Bear said to Papa. Whitecap muttered something.

They had brought a lantern to the table and stripped Petrenko to the waist. Mama had given them an old linen cloth to make bandages. Blood pulsed from a hole under his ribs. Paavo knew what bleeding looked like from watching the pig slitter at work. This didn't look so bad. He stepped closer. Petrenko's eyes were dark brown.

—Are you going to die? he asked.

—Paavo! Mama scolded.

—*Nyet*, the man whispered.

Two hands landed on his shoulders from behind and Old Bear steered him back to the bench beside Papa.

—He is too inquisitive; Old Bear ruffled his hair and returned to his friend.

—Maybe he will die, Papa whispered. Though I've seen worse, and men have lived. Paavo, his voice dropped. How many soldiers have you seen today?

—Three, Papa.

—These three and no others?

—Yes.

Whitecap was staring at them. He complained to Old Bear. Old Bear spoke harshly, and Whitecap was silent.

—Three only, and not comrades, Papa said.

Whitecap stretched his legs, letting his feet ride back and forth on his spurs. His boots came within a fraction of Mama's spinning wheel. Mama saw it but said nothing.

The kettle boiled. Old Bear cleared the wounded man's shirt and coat from the table and threw them at Whitecap with an instruction. Whitecap scowled, but picked the coat off the floor and began searching through it and holding it up to the light. Old Bear poured hot water in a bowl.

—What's he looking for? Paavo asked.

—The bullet hole, Papa said.

Mama put a pot on the stove and began stirring. It must be his supper. Kafelnikov sniffed and gave a look of disgust.

—Why?

—He wants to know if there's a piece missing from his shirt. Means it be inside, with the ball.

—Is that bad?

—It is for him.

Old Bear dropped the bandages in the bowl and steam coiled in the lamplight. Kafelnikov found the hole in the coat and poked a finger through. The leg stretched out again and this time just reached Mama's spinning wheel. Mama shot a glance at Papa.

—Lieutenant, we are offering you every civility, he said.

Old Bear glanced up and said something in Russian. Whitecap pulled his legs away and smirked. Then he tossed the coat aside and picked up the shirt. After a moment he spoke to Old Bear. Old Bear looked pleased.

—The tear matches, Papa said. He might live.

—Paavo. Mama passed him a bowl of broth with a lump of bread and a spoon. Eat up. Then bed.

His eyes widened.

—No protest, Papa said. It will be crowded when Lauri and Father Edelfeldt get here.

He ate slowly until Papa warned him off it. Despite his earlier look of disgust, Whitecap watched hungrily as he downed the broth. The bowl cleaned with bread, he handed it to Mama, and she gave him a cup of water from the kettle.

—Bed now, Mama said, taking him by the hand. She had lit a candle as she always did.

—Stay quiet, Papa whispered. We help them and they'll go.

His bed was in a recess behind the stove and shielded from the room by a curtain. The stove kept it warm, and the curtain stopped the draught. Kafelnikov grinned, showing pointed teeth, and drew his leg back to let him pass.

—*Te Paavo!* Zhulpa was smiling. *Proshanye peryed snom.*
Mama entered with him and closed the curtain.
—What did he say?
—Nothing. She pulled his breeches and stockings off.
—Will he die?
—I don't think so. Ola Svensson will see to him.
Mama pulled his shirt over his head. He stifled a yawn.
—Poor boy, you've had a long day.
—Don't they have their own doctors? he asked.
—Yes, but in Heinola with the battalion. It's too far.
—What's battalion?
—Lots of soldiers together; a whole army.
He climbed into his nightshirt and slid under the covers.
—Prayers, Paavo, Mama admonished. Especially tonight.
He knelt beside his pillow: the words came swift.
—God save Papa and Mama, and Musti, and Halli, and Lauri and Valko.
He ran out of breath and yawned.
—And you, Paavo.
—And me, he murmured. Amen.
He slid down and Mama pulled the covers round him.
—Go to sleep. Papa and Father Edelfeldt will see to everything.
—Mama, should I pray for the soldiers?
Mama hesitated.
—Let them pray for themselves. The Lord can decide.
She kissed him, took the candle and slipped out. He heard her footsteps cross the room.

The curtain let through a little light and he stared at the shadowy underside of Lauri's bed. If Old Bear or Whitecap spoke, he listened to the temper of their voices and if they were silent, he listened harder. Papa said little but Mama was busy fetching and tending. Boots on the porch told him Lauri was back. Father Edelfeldt and Kaisa Heiskanen were with him.

Old Bear spoke to Father Edelfeldt in Russian. Whitecap kept interrupting noisily and Old Bear shouted him down.

Father Edelfeldt repeated in Finlander for Mama and Papa, and he heard 'Vääksy' several times over. There were familiar noises of pan scraping and spoon stirring and other noises as well: Whitecap's spurs on the floor; then Kaisa Heiskanen's strange mutterings.

Someone walked heavily across the room.

—Petrenko. Old Bear's voice was weary. How are you old friend?

There was a movement near the curtain and Lauri joined him, holding his Bible and a candle. Paavo sat up.

—What's happening? he asked.

—You should be asleep, little brother.

Lauri closed the curtain.

—Well, I'm not! he hissed.

—Clearly: It's not certain if they'll send for Ola Svensson or take their man to Vääksy. That old witch is here as well. God knows what she will do to him. They're deciding if he's strong enough. If not, he'll stay here.

—Here!

—Or at the church, Lauri said. Papa isn't happy, but what can we do? The Lieutenant has given him a few roubles; he can tell we haven't much. He seems—

—But what about the other one? Paavo hissed.

—Oh, him? Lauri wriggled out of his breeches. He just scowls at everyone. He and the Lieutenant were riding to the post house on the Sysmä Road, that's how they met. I don't think the Lieutenant thinks much of him.

Lauri pulled his nightshirt on and knelt on the floor to pray.

Paavo sat up. —He shot the other one. He—

—Ssh! Lauri bowed his head and clasped the little black Bible to his chest. Paavo could barely wait for him to finish whispering.

—He wanted to shoot Musti, but he missed.

—So you said, Lauri yawned. Why would he want to do that?

—Musti was barking. It made him angry.

Lauri climbed to his bed. Well perhaps he's just a bad sort. The Lieutenant, though, is rather fine, don't you think?

The bedboards creaked as Lauri settled.

—He's going to Kajaani, they're recruiting a militia. He told me they're looking for good men to fight for the Duke against the Turks. There was a dreamy tone to his brother's voice.

Paavo sat up:

—You said you want to be a pastor, like Father Edelfeldt.

—I know, Paavo. Lauri flattened his pillow and lay down. Some days I think I just want to be anything but a farmer. Go to sleep.

From beyond the curtain was a low murmur of voices. Papa whispering to Father Edelfeldt: Old Bear talking to the wounded man. Pipe smoke drifted through the curtain, mingling with the smell of broth and damp clothes. He blinked heavily, trying to stay awake. Sometimes he wasn't sure if he had slept and missed something, or if he had only dreamt what he thought he remembered. The front door opened and closed many times, and he felt the cold draught under the curtain. Then, without fuss, footsteps tramped down the porch, and the horses and Father Edelfeldt's cart clattered from the yard. The door closed behind them, and Papa and Mama sat talking for a long time but Paavo could not hear what was said.

Days later Paavo heard the wounded man and Old Bear got to Vääksy by dog sledge across the lake. Father Edelfeldt and Kaisa Heiskanen went with them. Whitecap got a room for the night at the lodging house used by the sawmill workers. Father Edelfeldt told Lauri, and Lauri told Paavo, that the wounded man would live. He was brown because he came from the Altai Mountains far to the south. Mr Tammisto found them for him in a schoolbook.

Old Bear waited a few days in Vääksy, and then rode north alone, intending to cross the frozen lake to reach Kajaani. Come spring, the warming water melted channels under the ice, leaving traps big enough to swallow a horse and rider, so the ice fishermen said. That was one account of it. Another story said the White Ravens got him. Either way, Old Bear was never seen again.

Lauri vanished one night after breaking into Papa's chest for the papers he needed to enlist. He left a note on the table—still stained with Russian blood, despite Mama's scrubbing—along with the prayer book Father Edelfeldt had given him. The small, black-bound Bible, he took with him. The militia, the note said, would give him means, discipline, and purpose. He would write often and send money at Christmas. They were not to worry for him.

Mama cried. Papa was silent. Father Edelfeldt could not understand it and refused to take the prayer book back. In December a letter came and money with it. Lauri was in Turku. The militia suited him, so he claimed. He wrote again the next year and the year after. Then Lauri was posted to Russia and there were no more letters at Christmas or any other time. At night, Paavo would lie awake. Mama's eyes had no more tears. Papa didn't care for things the way he once did. Sometimes he even broke them.

§

Paavo woke early the morning after Old Bear had gone. Lauri was snoring softly. Motionless he listened to his heart and the creaks of the house. Apart from Lauri he could hear Papa's snores also and the wind down the stovepipe. There was nothing wrong in any of it, but he swung his feet to the floor and dressed silently. He slid round the curtain and crept to the cold stove for his boots. A grey light pricked the shutters. No one stirred as he slid his boots on and left.

He ran across the yard, eased the stable door and slipped inside. The dogs growled.

—It's me, he whispered, and a cold nose pressed his hand. Musti rolled onto his back, legs waving. Something squeezed in Paavo's chest, and he buried his face in the dog's furry throat. Halli joined in and knocked him into the straw, then both dogs were licking him, and he laughed.

Sneezing from the dust, Paavo sat up and felt all over Musti for any hurt from the day before. Finding nothing, he lay back, exhausted and happy. Something hard pressed against his arm and he pushed the hayfork away. Musti lay across his shins and kept him warm.

The noise, when it came, was sharp as a dropped coin. He sat up, his hand curling round the hayfork, found a crack in the door and peered out. A shadow fell.

He backed away with the hayfork. The door shook and a man entered. Paavo saw the white of the cap, the raised sabre, the sneering grin, and with all his weight behind it thrust the hayfork into the man's chest.

IV

Midday at the Caledonian Shipping Company office and Paavo Jukola waited in line behind Sam Johnson. That morning in earshot of the entire crew, Captain Loveless had rebuked the engineer over the 'bad coal', insisting he was too liberal with it, and 'no fire will burn if you choke it with generosity.' The glow of anger lingered on Johnson's neck and Jukola had not sought conversation with the man.

The pay office was a large, sparsely-furnished room divided by a partition. Company notices faded either side of a brass-cased clock and the solitary window let in a grey light. They had been waiting some time and temper had found voice more than once before the pay hatch opened.

'Peace, gentlemen, please,' a reedy voice said from the grilled opening.

'Peace when we're paid,' a nameless voice answered.

Ink-stained fingers took the first mate's papers and pushed out the ledger. Dewar signed and counted his wages before moving on. The line stepped up.

Jukola squeezed his brow, feeling a throbbing ache under the skin. He must be back two hours before sailing. Plenty of time between then and now, he told himself. The agent had taken off the Edenborough mail and a few passengers boarded for Inverness. Several more had signed in their luggage but remained ashore for now. There would be a few late arrivals, there always were, but nothing he could not deal with in an hour.

He followed Johnson and reaching the hatch found a small, coffin-faced man with spectacles and a prominent gold tooth. The company seemed to employ an endless number of clerks and too few good seamen.

The man checked his papers: 'Papa Jacks?'

'I am.'

'A Finn? Lang ways frae home.'

'So I am told.'

The clerk pushed the ledger toward him. He signed and received his packet, rifling through it in sight of the clerk. It matched the payslip, and he passed down the far side of the partition and out. The daylight dazzled as he paused to slide the envelope inside his serge blue jacket. A man looks differently at life with money on him, even if he is about to give most of it away. Smoothing the jacket over his hips, he filled his lungs and caught a homely, farmyard stink along with coal smoke and brine.

An excise cutter lay alongside the Custom House. Two men hung over its rails, suspended on ropes. One, probably an apprentice, blacked its topsides while the other picked out the curse-eye in the bow with white paint. The Scots considered it bad luck to show a ship's eyes in port, but he supposed it allowed when a ship needed repair. The excisemen ran handy little boats and it was surprising the *Schwarzer Keiler* had evaded them.

Shading his eyes, he picked out a ship at the Hansa wharf beyond the Custom Quay: the *Swan of Visby* offloading a deck cargo of fir. Visby was midway between Sweden and Finland, and he fought the familiar urge to sign, even as a peggy, aboard any ship sailing toward home.

Christian Bodie, the second engineer, passed him.

'Gaen nae where, Papa Jacks?'

'No, somewhere,' he said and turning upstream recalled

sailors' superstition no longer applied and mouthed his true name: Paavo Jukola.

In the reach beyond King's Bridge, he found the source of the familiar smell, a flat-bottomed wherry and a row of muck carts waiting to up-tip into its hold. A crowd passing down the street brought him close to the carts and as he passed a curd of manure slipped over a tailboard and spattered his shoe. Cursing he stepped back to scrape the filth on the wheel. The carter glanced over, saw a sailor's uniform and turned away without interest. At the rear of a cab stand, he found a driver watering his horse and asked for loan of his pail.

'Whit gaes in flows out,' the man said. 'Sailor artow?'

He bit his lip. The company did not allow men ashore out of uniform, leaving them prey to every hawker and villain, and a foreigner in a blue serge jacket and walking by a dock could only be a sailor. The man was after something.

'Onny nae need tae gae up line if ye're efter a cab. Old Town, is it?'

He sluiced the shoe clean. The man broke a cabbies' rule: the next hire belonged to the man at the far end of the stand. What else might he break?

'Canongate,' he answered.

'Oh, sae y' ken your way round?'

'The fare?' he asked.

'Hard tae say this time o day,' the driver sucked his cheek. 'We may discuss it when we're there, if it's a' the same.'

When you have the city bailiff on your side, Jukola thought and deciding to play the greenhorn, he thickened his accent.

'Only normal three schilling I paying.'

'Three schilling!' The man laughed.

'It is normal, yes? Perhaps I ask man at front whose fare you steal.'

'You could try but, hang on—'

He stepped back quickly. 'Thank you for the loan of your pail,' he said as formally as he could.

'Aye,' the man snatched the pail off him. 'Get awa' wi' ye.'

He walked on. The leading cab was clean, and its horse well turned out. The driver swung the door, and he dropped a coin in the outstretched hand.

'Tron Kirk, Old Town.'

Slamming the door, he dropped the glass down and sat back, marvelling at the incessant movement and noise along the streets.

Cities—any large grouping of people and commerce—puzzled him. He had grown up with the simple rhythms of plough and scythe: the turning of stones from the fields (not mere pebbles but boulders springing from the earth like coffins in a graveyard) and the drawing of wood from the forest and water from the pump. Courses easily plotted on a chart, regular as the salmon run and reliable as the herring shoals of older times.

This raising had not prepared him for the chaos and cries of cities, which most resembled, if they resembled anything familiar at all, the flocks of crow, rook and jackdaw at sowing and harvest time.

Sliding off his wet shoe he reflected how a simple farming rhythm could reach into the city. Hay for the horse, horse for manure, manure for the field where grew the hay. The farmer made a profit on the hay, the city fed its horses, and the muckrakers cleaned the streets and sold on to the farmer. As trade went, it had a pleasing harmony.

Smallholdings and the parks of great houses separated Leith from Edenborough, albeit by only a few minutes, and each time he travelled it—he had lost count how many times—the city had grasped another patch of green. At Kalkkinen men lifted stones from the fields; here men laid them down, building great manufactories and houses, tight-as-teeth, for the workers.

Old Town lay above this, its sawtooth roofs sharp along the ridge. In the west, like the prow of a ship, the bluff-walled castle squatted on a crag, and the poop matching it was the mound of Arthur's Seat, as Herr Danneberg called it. Men walked their girls across it on summer days and peasants gathered its heather to sell on the streets. Below the ridge, a gridwork of airy tenements and handsome streets were spreading toward the sea but Herr Danneberg complained this 'New Town' sucked the life from Edenborough's ancient heart, causing the visible decay of buildings and people.

The day was pleasant, and Paavo struggled to hold his eyes open in the warm sun, only waking when the cab pitched up in High Street. Having set down he paused at a newsstand for a copy of the *Edenborough Times*, then joined the jostle of elbows, shoulders and broadcloth coats making haste, not allowing the shops and market stalls to beckon him inside. A sedan chair passed him, carried by a pair of tight-jawed men in green livery. A small dog, no doubt harbouring some grievance, darted from a doorway and chased the sedan before making purchase on the carrier's stocking. The man flicked out a leg without impeding the sedan's progress and the dog swaggered back to its vantage. A few yards on and the sedan stopped beside a tall stone edifice. A pair of wooden legs dropped down to support the chair and the leading carrier opened the door. Broadcloth and hats surged around the sedan as the occupant emerged rear-first, like a moth from its cocoon and the movement of the crowd impelled him on until his elbow made smart contact with the man's back.

'The devil!'

The man's face was quite round and highly coloured, resembling an apple. Wig powder dusted the air.

'Damn you, sir. Have a care!'

Jukola stepped back, making a slight bow to convey his apologies. The man had not looked before stepping into his path, but he was not about to protest.

'Rude of you, sir. Frightfully rude. Knocking a man from his feet.' The fellow had remained quite upright. 'Who knows what—, I say—, scoundrel, stop!'

Paavo had backed into the crowd, letting it sweep him away and bent to hide his distinctive yellow hair. The man's voice faded and was gone.

What was there beside his hate?
Overwhelming desire for life
And other contentment.
Hate takes its bearing from a wrecker's light.
I found nothing in Paavo Jukola to bless; not then and not ever.

Editor's Remarks

Once again, a blank line and the date, either March 2 or 5, the number is illegible—indicates the start of a new chapter. Initially, MacGregor did not know the name of the character and in the first draft he is referred to as "the Finn". Later, once he had settled on Paavo Jukola, MacGregor edited his text and replaced this with the initials P.J. or, more usually, J.

According to his journal MacGregor was now spending eight or ten hours a day at his writing desk and working six days a week. The exception was Sunday which he had always scrupulously preserved and after the service at Arbinger Church he would, weather permitting, walk the bounds of the estate or venture into the Moorfoot Hills accompanied by Jock Strange. Those Sundays when the weather did not allow outdoor activities he retreated to his library.

Thus, the weeks went by as the first volume of *This Iron Race* progressed.

Compared to the previous two chapters, this chapter was little altered between first draft and the published text; moreover, what changes there are appear to have been of MacGregor's volition, rather than forced on him by his publishers. Chiefly, they numbered several alterations and refinements in the description of Finland and the Finnish language while a few concern the characters of

Lieutenant Zhulpa and Vasily Kafelnikov.

The former, one presumes, reflects information MacGregor gathered on his research while the latter demonstrates the difficulty of working from a first draft, rather than the fair copy of the finished manuscript.

Comparing the published text with the first draft the portrayal of Lieutenant Zhulpa is noticeably more sympathetic and, as neither Sir Sidney Beresford nor John Lucas ever objected to MacGregor's portrayal of Russia and Russians elsewhere in the text, we can safely say this change was of MacGregor's own volition. Two questions now arise; the first is why did MacGregor make this change? The second cuts to the heart of our enterprise: if MacGregor was prone to making significant changes between his first draft and fair copy then to what extent can your editor create a finished text that does justice to MacGregor's intentions?

The first question has a two-fold, though relatively straightforward, explanation. The simplest explanation is the softer portrayal of Zhulpa makes Lauri's decision to join the Russian army more plausible. In the first draft Zhulpa is commanding and authoritative, and while he does not share Kafelnikov's contempt for Paavo's family, it is clear Zhulpa merely uses them for his own end. Nor does he seem to have much regard for the wounded Petrenko, who is merely an inconvenience delaying his journey north. In the published text, Zhulpa becomes, if not compassionate toward Paavo, at least aware that kind words get results where authority cannot and his relationship with Petrenko is fatherly. Thus, he becomes an officer a young man like Lauri could willingly follow into battle. A more complex answer is that MacGregor resisted making his characters dichotomous, preferring to add shade and nuance wherever possible. Vasily Kafelnikov remains, essentially, a bad lot, but Zhulpa becomes an altogether more complex and conflicted character. It would appear the trio of Lieutenant Zhulpa, Vasily Kafelnikov, and Yuri Petrenko conforms to the Rule of Three (see Appendix 2, page lxviii) and perhaps MacGregor attempted to depict the totality of Russian sovereignty in Finland through the three characters.

The differing portrayal of Lieutenant Zhulpa in the first draft and published text suggests, worryingly for your editor, that it is dangerous to assume all alterations between first draft and printed text were at the behest of Beresford & Lucas. Plainly, MacGregor was also making changes of his own volition, adding considerably to the difficulty of re-creating the text he intended. Your editor has referred to the absent fair copy of the text MacGregor originally offered to his publisher and must do so again for its absence makes our task much more difficult.

Both the Finnish setting described in this chapter and the depiction of Russian soldiery were departures from anything MacGregor had previously written. Fortunately, Leith was a major destination for Baltic timber, furs, amber and salt fish, and there were many Finns in the ships' crews. As for the Russians, they made poor soldiers and were universally hated by the Poles and other Baltic races. Most likely MacGregor had contacts within the Muscovy

Company whose ships sailed around the North Cape into Murmansk.

In any event, any alterations between the first draft and published text that add to MacGregor's descriptions are included in the revised text on the assumption they were freely made by MacGregor. Contrarily, your editor has favoured instances where the first draft is saltier than the published version as those changes were more likely to have been forced on MacGregor by his publishers.

His ink discovered me beneath a stone
Digression
Edenborough: THE AUTHOR begs leave to shew the character of Sir Sidney Beresford & describe the conception of this tale

>None are master of their muse,
>Although many of my
>Association have drowned it
>In sorrow, then in drink, at last in blood.
>
>*'Muse' is but the artist's word for Grace.*

SIR SIDNEY HAD lost the yellow-headed man in the crowd and made silent oath raining misfortune on all men of low stature from Napoleon Buonoparte to Genghis Khan, whose likeness he had never seen but was persuaded was short, like many of his race. He had the distinct impression this fellow was a German, the mumbled apology as they collided forming his evidence, but it certainly pleased him to think no Scotsman had caused mischief to his person. The carriers of the sedan chair fussed over him, brushing down his coat and such, and Sir Sidney was torn between pleasure at the attention and irritation at the distraction, being hopeful yet of seeing his abuser in the crowd.

'Ach, he's awa', sir,' the carrier said, ''Tis your dignity he bruised. Nae injury done.'

'No injury!' Sir Sidney broadsided. 'Why, a man cannot step on his own pavement without being charged down. Well,' he glowered at the carrier. 'What is owed?'

'A schilling, sir.'

The knight of the realm dipped his hand into a purse and took out a silver coin.

'Had you stopped the ruffian you'd have had two. Good day.'

And with that, Sir Sidney entered the premises and climbed the stairs to the first floor where a secretary, thin and pale of face, leapt to his feet; this jack-in-the-box antic sending his chair screeching back on the floor and setting Sir Sidney's teeth on edge.

'Afternoon, sir, ye have a visitor.'

'He has a name? You do not admit men to my office without a name.'

'MacGregor, sir. You were expecting him.'

'I am?'

The reader should understand that Sir Sidney is suffering a form of amnesia chiefly found in the hours following a generous lunch and is not naturally forgetful.

'His name is in the book for three o'clock,' the secretary said with the mildest reproach.

'The damn fellow!' Sir Sidney protested. 'A gentleman is never *punctual*.'

And so, Sir Sidney Beresford passed through the walnut-panelled door of his office and found a tall, good-humoured man leaning at the window.

'You failed to catch him,' the man said.

'Devil d'you mean?'

'Your *assailant*. He is proceeding toward Canongate, unapprehended.'

'Much as I regret it,' Sir Sidney said with a show of rubbing the small of his back. 'Devil are you?'

'In good health,' the author replied. 'And good heart. These are very satisfactory.' A bundle of loose-bound pages lay on Sir Sidney's desk. 'The proofs for 'Lays of Brigadoon',' MacGregor explained on noting Sir Sidney was not entirely himself. 'You were expecting them.'

'So I was. But it is a *slim* volume, very slim,' the publisher said, mindful of those readers who purchase literature like tobacco: which is to say, by its weight.

'Brevity is the soul of poetry,' the author answered.

'Perhaps so, but most will hope for more substantial repast. You are *indeed* well, I take it?'

It would be tedious to relate every fragment of discourse between author and publisher. Suffice to say, by this polite inquiry Sir Sidney intended the author to understand his real question concerned whether, and to what purpose he was writing, since to a publisher this is the sole barometer of an author's health. To it, the author protested the reader may not wish for any writing at all, so much of their time had he already taken up with inconsequential fancies. Answering, Sir Sidney upbraided the author for being overly severe upon himself, and, more pertinently, upon the reader and his own good offices; for did not the author, by implication, insult the reader's good taste by dismissing what had given them pleasure and cast doubt upon the reputation of its publisher?

Naturally, the author recanted at once, appreciating a mantle of modesty cast upon his shoulders must necessarily o'ershade all who associated, both professionally and in private, with such works of his as are thought fit to print, and which, though he permits himself no great opinion of his talent, he is nevertheless in the habit of ensuring are no worse than they need be. Thereupon, as one whose livelihood is the printing of works in the hope they may sell, the publisher returned to his question.

The author replied he had a fellow in mind who might carry a tale. A man born among the highest in the land yet deprived of his birthright by disfigurement and raised by the poorest of the poor. Yet this proving the making of him, he ends twice the man as those whose mistreatment he bore.

Having briefly described the conversation thus far, the author shall permit dialogue to return.

'And where is this set?' the publisher asked.

'Here,' the author said truthfully, 'and upon the island of Skye, for this fellow is a man of Skye, although the tale begins and ends in Winchester.'

'*Man of Skye,*' the publisher ventured, 'That would be the title, I think.'

'I have a title,' the author begged to differ. 'I shall call it *Curseborn*'.

'*Curseborn!?*[1] Is there magick in this?'

---

[1] MacGregor would abandon this title and by June 1862 was using *This Iron Race* in correspondence with his publishers. *N.W.*

'Indeed, for good and ill there is magick.'[1]

The publisher delivered the author a hard stare. 'Above all,' he said firmly, 'write nothing that will distress the ladies.'

'My good wife shall be the judge of what may or may not distress a lady.'

'But there will be battles?' the publisher asked, mindful of his balance sheet.

'And murder too,' the author said.

'Battle between whom?'

'Between those who seek to take and those who seek to hold to what is theirs,' the author replied.

'And this *Man of Skye* is your hero, I take it.'

'He is not.'

'The villain then?'

'He is a good man,' the author admitted, 'but neither hero nor villain, for I have done with such artificialities.'

'But, sir! The reader shall expect a fellow they can cheer and another they may condemn.'

'Then they must look elsewhere, for I will have neither. That is today's?' The author referred to an edition of *The Times* tucked under Sir Sidney's commodious arm.

'Indeed, I have read all I saw fit to read,' he said and gave up the paper to the author who instantly opened its pages.

'You will recall the *Lachesis*,' the author bent his finger to a report on page five confined between an advertisement for gentlemen's snuff and complaint of depressed cattle prices in Fife.

The publisher adjusted his spectacles: '"with all hands,"' he read, adding, as though it were a mere footnote, 'A tragedy, though not uncommon among emigrant ships.'

'That such losses are unexceptional is a crime,' the author

---

[1] MacGregor shared his interest in magick only with close friends, notably Cecil Balanchine and Sir Charles Palliser, and with a few sympathetic members of the Edenborough Speculative Society. His publishers, Sir Sidney Beresford and John Lucas, were not among either number. *N.W.*

said, 'but not, I should argue, a tragedy. Lost with all hands, *indeed*. Yet among those unfortunates you would have found men of good heart and men who held nothing but ill will toward their fellows, men who died bravely and men who trembled in fear, men who died holding the Bible and others who clung to their purse. Men, women and children of all character, but among them no heroes and no villains, for heroes endure or else die heroically in saving others, while villains must perish alone.'

'Such is life,' the publisher declared; 'but the reader shall expect you to describe the world as it *ought* to be.'

'No longer!' For emphasis the author smote the air, as though dealing with a troublesome fly. 'I have tired of heroes and villains, I shall write only of *players* making the best of their luck, whether their cards be good or bad. I will describe reality, Sir Sidney, not *dreams*.'

'I may not dissuade you?' the publisher asked.

'I sincerely doubt it.'

'Then write as you must,' he said grudgingly, 'only beware that in avoiding dreams, you do not induce mere slumber.'

And with this parting witticism the publisher gathered the emended proofs and stepped out the door to pass them to his secretary for forwarding to the printer, whereupon your author, briefly alone and mindful of forgetting what he had spontaneously conjured, noted all that had passed between himself and Sir Sidney upon the back of a convenient laundry bill to provide evidence of his intentions for future reference and thence, having bade farewell to Sir Sidney, returned to his lodgings in thoughtful frame of mind, as yet trapped in squid-dark clouds of his own making, being puzzled as to who might have laid this curse and why, and moreover, if the man be innocent how all could be made right, for despite his intention to uphold reality, the author had no intention of disregarding the unacknowledged contract between writer and reader whereby if the former is to satisfy the latter in all regards, he must remember the very essence of a tale; that wrongs must, howsoever it be done and howsoever long a time passes, at the end of all else be righted!

If upon his homeward journey the author had, by one small degree, begun to comprehend the magnitude of his task, verily upon arriving home from Edenborough he should at once have written his publisher advising he had condemned the scheme as out of all proportion to his abilities.

That he did not, lies with his tale but slowly revealing itself, like Salome through her veils, or as a landscape through clearing mist, which puts him in mind of the great French balloonist, Dedalus Le Pilote, who claimed the perfect weather for a nervous flier is dense cloud, wherein he cannot see the vault of sky above nor the abyss below, but is seemingly entirely free from awful sights!

In any event, having reached his desk with only a little of his tale clear, the author gazed sometime from his window before sketching a bleak and rainswept hillside and a humble shepherd and his flock.

But enough, for I fear continuance must exhaust the dear reader's patience.

> Think you MacGregor made me?
> Well, consider me amused
> (all bear straw upon their back);[1]
> His ink discovered me beneath a stone.

Spare me the arrogance of writers who presume to be God!

Editor's Remarks

The 'Digression' did not form part of the manuscript rejected by Beresford & Lucas. The first page is dated June 6, 1864, and marked "Interjection" and the Pages then inserted

---

[1] MacGregor referred to writing as akin to mucking out the Augean Stables in an article in the Edenborough Review, Issue ix, 1854. *N.W.*

between chapters seven and eight. However, correspondence between MacGregor and the publishers proves he argued for its inclusion in the first edition. Sir Sidney, not unsurprisingly given his portrayal in the scene, objected, while John Lucas, perhaps amused at MacGregor's lampooning of his business partner, agreed an authorial note explaining why so many characters vie for the reader's attention was necessary and best done in a form the reader might easily digest. For once, your editor agrees with John Lucas and the text is included in the new edition.

The sound of women's work puts him at ease
Chapter Eight
Portree House, afternoon: MÀIRI MULCAHY learns of
BHEATHAIN'S SOMHAIRLE'S origins
(Paavo Jukola's narrative resumes presently)

Poverty makes land-fellows
Brave the unbridled courser
That treats oak with such contempt,
Trading one cold, grey rock, for another.
The Western Seaboard claimed near all aboard: they live.

I

PORTREE HOUSE LAY a half mile out of town and even allowing for collecting the shoes it was not a quarter hour before Màiri and Dr Ramsay arrived outside its stuccoed porch. Built at the height of the kelp trade, it was a two-storeyed, slate-roofed building of severe, if well-proportioned appearance and provided home and offices for the estate's factor. Modern and convenient for the town and the steamers, Lord MacDonald had admitted in private that, but for tradition, he would happily exchange Duntulm for Portree House.

The housekeeper introduced them into the estate office. Mr Dixon sat behind a desk in one corner and his secretary, a young man with the complexion of tallow, sat at the farther end. Between them a window, glazed with more glass than might be found in a whole township of crofters' dwellings, looked over the drive and a small courtyard.

The clerk barely glanced up as they came in. Mr Dixon was more effusive.

'Come, come,' he indicated two chairs near the fire. 'A pot of tea, Mrs Smith, and shortbreads. You'll both take tea?'

'Tea would be very welcome,' Ramsay said. 'But we are in some urgency.'

The window was shut, and a coal fire made the room over-warm. Màiri took off her shawl and folded it over her arms. She resisted the urge to speak plainly, suspecting the doctor knew better how to handle Mr Dixon.

'There is trouble at the quay?' Dixon asked. 'The emigrant ship is, I assume, the purpose of the visit.'

'You are mistaken,' Ramsay said. 'Our concern is for one man only.'

'Ah.' Dixon glanced at the secretary and then at her.

'And your part in this?'

'I do not wholly know,' she admitted. 'Dr Ramsay insisted we call on you. Bheathain has—'

'Please!' Dixon interjected. 'One moment. Alasdair?' The secretary sat up. 'You have written to Mr Lockhart?'

'It is ready for the postboy, sir.'

'Cannot wait. Deliver it by hand and wait for Lockhart's reply. Then proceed to the harbour and ask for the superintendent, he may have arrived by now.'

'He had not two hours ago,' Màiri said.

'It sails tomorrow afternoon,' Dixon said, gloomily. 'How many were there?'

'Three score. They think they're abandoned. They had me bless the ship, but they sorely need a spaer.'

'I wrote to both churches,' Dixon said. 'I only hope they attend; they detest each other so.[1] You may go, Alasdair.'

The lad took his coat from the stand and exited.

'And a spaer?' she repeated.

'With respect,' Ramsay said, 'this is not what calls us here.'

Before he could continue, Mrs Smith entered with tea and cake.

It might not be Ramsay's main business, but it was not without significance and she continued to speak of the ship.

'Eolhwynne's travelled with the laird, but what of McLeod's spaer?'

'I wrote to him,' Dixon said. 'He is in Glasgow. His spaer is at Dunvegan but I have not communicated with her.'

---

[1] As stated previously the Alban Church and Free Church were estranged. *N.W.*

'Then I shall,' Màiri said. 'Unlike you, I am no longer beholden to the MacDonald's. There's clan business and there's common humanity.'

Dixon drew out a sheet of paper and thrust it towards her. 'Then write what you will. I promise a runner will have it at Dunvegan by this evening. I am not heartless.'

'Thank you.'

She wrote a plea no spaer could refuse. Dr Ramsay harrumphed, believing the matter a distraction, but did not intervene. Dixon sealed her message and addressed it.

'Mrs Smith. See this into the hand of a runner. I am not to be disturbed for one half hour.'

The housekeeper left but Dixon waited until footsteps had gone from the stairs before asking Ramsay to speak.

'To return to our reason for troubling you.' Ramsay shot a glance at her, which she ignored. 'I believe Miss Mulcahy should be made aware of certain facts.'

'Then I must disagree,' Dixon said. 'Miss Mulcahy, is Bheathain recovered?'

'He is, and I know what ailed him.'

'You do? Then I am sure we can prevent a reoccurrence.'

'It is not so simple. I cannot protect him if I do not understand his condition.'

'But you have cured him,' Dixon protested.

'Murdoch, old friend,' Ramsay said. 'I believe we must defer to Miss Mulcahy. From the little I understand of magick, Bheathain is in danger because of *who* he is. Perhaps if Miss Mulcahy were to tell you what she has comprehended we might take matters from there.'

'Very well.'

She repeated what she knew of wandering spirits and how Bheathain might be freed of his curse. Dixon's face grew sombre.

'Bodily, he is out of danger?' he asked.

'He is safe on the island where I left him. Beyond that, I cannot say. I do not know what you know.'

'Which raises the heart of the matter,' Ramsay said.

'Between us we would know the sum of our parts. If there is danger to Bheathain it arises from who he is and recent events therewith.' Dixon raised a warning hand, but Ramsay continued regardless. 'Frankly, no disrespect Miss Mulcahy, I should prefer to be speaking with Eolhwynne; a spaer at the height of her powers would be a boon at this moment, but matters cannot wait her return.'

'I could not allow it,' Dixon said. 'Eolhwynne is oath-bound to tell MacDonald. If, or rather, when Bheathain returns to Staffin, what manner of danger awaits him?'

Dixon's eyes flickered between them like those of a cornered beast.

'In extremis,' Ramsay said, 'spiritual possession, madness, and death.'

Dixon shook his head in disbelief.

'It is so,' Màiri said. 'Now listen the both of ye: if it's your grand secret that Bheathain's the laird's son, then I have guessed as much. Enough with this foot-shuffling.'

Ramsay muttered, if only it were so simple, but before she had time to absorb this, he had turned to Dixon.

'There is another pressing reason to confide in Miss Mulcahy. Neither of us is young and we must eventually pass on what we know. She served the laird for the better part of twenty years and is worthy of our trust. In the circumstances, I believe the time is now.'

If Bheathain were not the laird's son, then she was wholly perplexed, but Ramsay's exhortation at last put Dixon on his feet and she hoped an answer was forthcoming.

'Though I do not thank you for recalling my mortality, your point is a fair one. Very well.'

Dixon was some moments removing a plain wooden box from the safe and setting it on the desk to unlock it. It contained a rolled parchment tied with ribbon.

'This is a codicil to the last will and testament of the present laird's grandfather. Miss Mulcahy, you may read it.'

The codicil required the estate to provide Bheathain with a living and to prevent him ever leaving the island by any means short of injury. There followed a clause swearing the signatories to secrecy; these were Mr Dixon, Dr Ramsay, and John Duff, the laird's coachman.

'The laird has not signed this?'

'He does not know of its existence and there has been no call to inform him,' Dixon said. 'You'll understand, soon enough.'

She used Dixon's pen and added her name beneath Duff's.

'It does not say who Bheathain is,' she said, returning the parchment.

'For that we are indebted to Lady Maud,' Dixon said.

'She is Bheathain's *natural* mother,' Ramsay added.

Màiri realised the implication. 'And his father?'

'King Edmund. There was no infidelity. Bheathain is, was, William's alike twin,' Ramsay continued. 'Whether he is the first born or not, we do not know. Lady Maud would not tell. You recall her visit some fifteen years ago.'

She did.

'She called on me and asked of a boy of five years with a mark on his face. I knew of such a child and directed her to him, though without knowing her interest.'

Dixon took up the story. 'Subsequently, Lady Maud asked me to arrange for Bheathain to be brought here, in secret, to this very room. Her feelings for him were obvious and I think it was a relief to own to his existence. Subsequently, she brought Doctor Ramsay and I into her confidence. She had seen famine on the island and feared it happening again.'

'And if you knew who he was, he would be spared the worst of it,' Màiri said.

'Is that so wrong?' Dixon asked. 'Lady Maud wished to protect her child. She sorely wished he might be nearer Winchester. Fate is unkind.'

'Were he born now, matters might be different,' Ramsay said. 'People have less regard for magick, in Anglia, at least.'

Dixon disagreed. 'They believe in it less; but the scandal would be terrible. Kings, even the brothers of kings, must be without blemish, and with William passed over Bheathain

Somhairle is *now*, if he was not before, heir to the crowns of Scotland and Anglia.'

It was merely a figure of speech, but it jolted her up in her seat.

'But William *cannot* pass over. Not while Bheathain lives!'

'What?' Dixon stared at her. 'What riddle is this? William is dead!'

Ramsay shook his head and glanced regretfully towards her. He understood matters.

'Aye, Prince William is dead,' she said to Dixon. 'But his spirit cannot pass over. The bond between alike twins is stronger than death; I tell you, the prince's spirit resides in this world still. Doctor, this is what you feared, is it not?'

Ramsay admitted it was.

'This is absurd, both of you. How can Bheathain be in danger from William?'

'I cannot put it more plainly,' she said. 'William's soul will have come for him, but William's *spirit* cannot pass over while his twin lives. Bheathain ties him to this world.'

'But if William's soul attacks Bheathain, as it may do, and kills Bheathain, which it may do, then William's spirit is free,' Ramsay said. 'That is why Bheathain is in grave danger.'

Dixon blenched but would not accept.

'There is another possibility,' Ramsay continued. 'If he is the stronger, he might take possession of William's spirit. However, that would also bring consequences. Miss Mulcahy, would you agree that Bheathain's sufferings are akin to those acquiring the gift of Grace?'

'He does not know it yet,' she said, 'but while he lay sleeping, he spoke—'

'To Prince William?' Ramsay interrupted.

'No. It was another. But Bheathain has the gift or is growing into it. I see the sense of it now. William is caught between this world and the next, making a channel for Bheathain. Doctor, this ought to have been foreseen when you first had news of William's death!'

'I did foresee it,' Ramsay said. 'But I did not put faith in what I read until Bheathain's sickness convinced me.'

'I could never have foreseen this,' Dixon protested. 'I can barely accept it now.'

'But you must,' Ramsay insisted. 'You are his guardian.'

Dixon shot Ramsay the glance of one given good advice he does not wish to hear.

'Can you sense how powerful his gift might be?' Ramsay asked her.

Màiri sighed. They wished for an answer, but how to describe such powers to them? There was only one man she might liken to Bheathain.

'If he achieves Grace through William, then he shall at least be the equal of any spaer; but the nature of his curse may increase that. By what degree I cannot say. The only male spaer I can compare him to is Lazarus.'

Both men stared at her. They had had her at a disadvantage; now it was her moment.

'But he will need guidance,' she insisted. 'The Iona Fellowship or anywhere willing to take him.'

'What is the old saying?' Ramsay said. 'Ignored, magick will send a fellow mad; untrained, it will bring misfortune on his friends?'

'The codicil does not permit Bheathain to leave Skye,' Dixon said.

'Yet our promise to Lady Maud was always to safeguard Bheathain,' Ramsay murmured. 'Should not our word to a queen take precedence?'

She could not stand and watch them argue. She must trust Ramsay's good sense won Dixon over.

'I must settle these,' she said and handed Dixon her receipts. 'I am grateful for your confidence, but now I know who Bheathain is, I wish I had not left him.' She paused. 'What are your immediate plans for him?'

'Plans? Why, none,' Dixon said.

'But if Bheathain is in danger from William's ghost?' Ramsay asked.

'Just so,' she said. 'He cannot hide forever on my island. I can make a charm to protect him, but the danger remains.'

'Then we must also pray,' Ramsay said. 'I will encourage the thought of sending him to Iona, if they will have him.'

Without examining her receipts, Dixon opened a cash box, removed several banknotes and handed them to her.

'Do not spoil him. You understand Bheathain can never know his birthright. I... rather, we will consider what can be done for him.'

II

It was an hour from sunset when he heard Màiri at the door. He stood as she came in and wrapped his arms around her.

'Ach, you big lummock. Let go of me,' she complained.

He could smell the sweat on her back where the creel had lain. The last of the sun beamed through the door and reddened her hair. Perhaps she wasn't unfavourable after all or maybe she was only tired and glad to be home. Bheathain saw it the way he wished to.

'I was misslie,' he said,[1] his tongue slipping between English and Gaelic. 'I did what ye wanted.'

'Thank you. Kettle hot?'

'Will be,' he said and helped take off her creel.

'Make tea,' Màiri said. 'Make it the way I likes, not that stew you drink. Have you drunk the betony?'

'I have.'

'And all was well here?'

'Well enough. Spent time thinking of you.'

Màiri sighed. 'You're a sweet boy; I'll have to find ways to keep you busy. Can't have you idling. I got these for you.'

She handed him a parcel done up in paper and twine.

'I must owe you for them.'

'It's not me you owe; I can't say more.'

'A gift they are?'

'Aye. But you're not to pry on his name.'

It would not be his old *nen*, of that he was certain.

---

[1] To be lonely owing to the absence of another. *N.W.*

M'Illathain, then, though why he should gift him new sheens he had no knowing. The M'Illathains were not so poor, but not so well-off to be giving charity. It must be Tòrmod; the old goat had a bit stashed away, so folk said.

Whoever had paid, they were a fine pair of sheens. The kettle set over the fire to boil he sat himself down beside it.

'So, while I have been in Portree getting and fetching and tending the poor devils taking ship for the New World, what have you done? You stayed on this wee isle, like I said?'

'Aye, I did not move from it.' He paused, recalling the visitor. 'There was a' body called by.'

Màiri glanced up sharply. 'Did you get a look at them?'

'No, not to know them. Have you a fancy man calling?'

'Chance would be a fine thing. Did he not give a name?'

'No.'

'And he did not try to come on the island?'

'No,' he said firmly. 'First, I thought was Tam M'Neis for it is he I knock with more than any other. This fellow came to the end of the causeway an' nae further, then he went off over the ways. Do you ken such a man?'

'People call, but no, I haven't seen a man of that mien.' She hesitated, then turned away to attend the creel she'd carried. He had no answer to who bought him new sheens and no answer to the stranger who called. He rubbed his hands together and showed them to the fire. Then he picked up one of his new shoes and held it, softly running his thumb over the iron tackits. He shivered.

'You're healing?'

'My back is sore, yet,' he said and decided to speak of the book and the mysterious picture.

'I took to reading,' he said. 'There's nae book in our house, save The Lord's. I was curious, but dinna mean to pry.'

Màiri stood and ran a hand along the books until she laid hand on the one he'd been reading. He must have left it misplaced.

'Reckon you be lifting my spirits over high.' His voice broke as he finished speaking.

'There are many books, and none say the same,' she said reproachfully. 'You must be patient.'

'Seems I been all my life reckoning on things being better, one day being well, and the years went by. My old *nen* cannot be long for the world and what then?' He was shaking now. The last three days were catching up on him.

'Bheathain?'

'Ach. I had overlong to dwell the day.' He ground the heel of his hand against his cheek. His mark was tender and the pain sharp. He wiped away a tear, feeling shamed to cry in front of Màiri.

She came over and pushed a hand through his hair.

'All will be well,' she said.

'Màiri, I know you're no spaer. You canna foretell.'

'True, but trust me. You're not wholly out of danger. Tonight, I'll make a charm for you, but what will truly keep you safe, God willing,' she crouched bringing her face to his, 'is the strength within you. Nurture it, and it will serve you.'

'It is so much so quick. I can scarce catch my breath.'

'Has so much changed?'

He could not answer and while he was silent and brooding, Màiri kissed him on the brow.

'I've a fire to set. I'll be awake most of the night making this charm. Bring the tea out when it's done.'

Màiri left and he cuffed away the last of his tears and sat listening to the kettle. He did not feel any great strength within him, far from it; his back ached and his face was raw. But something had changed, and he doubted it was for the better. He made tea and took it out to her. She had fire in the hearth, and it had begun to roar. Only the western sky remained bright with the evening star poised above the Storr. The glow of the fire made her seem younger, closer to his age. He sat to watch, liking the certainty of how she did things, working without fuss or waste.

'How long does it need?' he asked.

'Two, three hours,' she said. 'Hungry?'

'Ay. Sorely.'

'Then mind the fire. Feed it slowly while I get us a bite.'

He fed lumps of charcoal into the fire, spreading them evenly. He could not look directly into the flame without his eyes smarting. The heat and roaring were all-consuming.

Presently, Màiri brought him herrings fried in butter and they sat eating them. The bones set aside he wiped his plate clean with bread. It was better than anything he'd eaten in a while but might be appetite telling him so.

'Dr Ramsay reckoned ye spoke of a white stag.'

He stopped chewing to think.

'When I lost my touchpiece it was. At first, I couldn't tell if it was real or a trick of the light.'

The thought that he had talked of it while out of his wits troubled him. He had recall of seeing it another time but could not recall how or when and thought it was imaginings.

'You've not seen it since?'

'What of it?'

'Those with the gift of Grace can see what makes no sense in the ordinary way of things. I can't scry no more, but I know magick. For every ill it does, there's a good beside. Some woman laid a curse on you, but I reckon there's a blessing close by.'

'A blessing? I should like to know where, I sore would.'

'Dr Ramsay said he's never known you to take ill.'

'What would he know of it. There's few can afford to get sick. It is true, though. There's mornings I dinna want to shift a leg, but any sickness going passes me by. Maybe my face scares it off.' He tried to laugh.

'Maybe so,' Màiri said without humour.

'But it's nonsense, Màiri. You don't know what it is like to be marked out your whole life. I would be like any man.'

'I know too well,' she said. 'I received the gift of Grace when I was thirteen and my life has been set apart ever since. This day, many came to me for help that I can no longer give, and the laird depended on us for near twenty years. But my life was not their life, and all knew it, understand?'

He did not. At least, he did not understand how it applied to him.

'There is something inside of you, something growing. Embrace it. Don't fight it.'

She leant against him, and his arm slipped around her. Her eyes shone. The fire roared, echoing the noise in his blood. Màiri's lips parted and without asking if it was to speak or sigh or breathe, he kissed her.

III

Copper was a poor man's ward, but amber was not to be had on the island, save for a bauble in St Mary's in Portree and they might notice should it vanish of a sudden. Copper would do; most of the power lay in the runestave. Untying a linen bag, she poured lumps of powdery green stone into a bowl and began working it with her pestle. Crystals glinting in the firelight echoed the stars above.

Once she had filched and begged copper from the boatwrights at Portree till one, tiring of her nagging, told of a seam in the hills and offered to take her. A dark-haired, dark-looking man a few years older than she, he chose the hottest of days for a walk and made the way harder and longer than it need be. Each time she had paused for breath he wiped sweat from his brow, pointed ahead and beckoned her on until beside a lochan high in the hills he pointed at a distant crag and said they might cool off before making for it. She had been young, but not as innocent as he hoped, and while he swam in the cool brown water, she sat on a rock and waited, ignoring the itch of sweat and the midges and ignoring him also, for stripped of his shirt he was a fine looking man for all his deviousness. Though the man did not get what he sought, nonetheless, he had led her to the seam and copper won from the rock holds a charm better than scraps from a boatyard.

The change had crept up on her, like the shadows of late afternoon. For half a year, she had puzzled over her runes, unable to make sense of the answers. Even when her menses grew irregular, she would not accept it was the change. It was not till she sent to the cat one time and got no reply that she realised she had been calling it by name for three months, unaware the link between her and her familiars had broken. The cat came and went as he chose now, his way of seeing the world closed to her. Her rook had stayed a few months, then flown and not returned. She thought she had seen it about the loch, but it no more came to her hand.

She could not scry; no portents came to her; and no insights, save those any woman might have; but she had not forgotten how to make a charm, a potion or a poultice and she had seen Bheathain right. He was abed now, though she doubted the man in him slept. There was an urgency there and it roared loud as the furnace and burned as bright. She had forty years and neither mirror nor her bones said otherwise, but he reminded her how it was to be young and desired and if he desired her only because none his own age saw beyond the mark on him, then so be it. She did not fear him; she only feared her own desires, but if regret is to be met along either path then pick the sweeter. He would be well soon and would go home. Though God knew she feared for him and would miss him.

Still, she would have some dignity.

Kneeling, she stared into the centre of the furnace, gauging the heat from the brightness and colour. Sweat ran into her eyes, but she wished for a few coals from Murdo Dixon's fire, for peat did not burn half as hot as coal. She pumped the bellows to force air into the heart of the fire and as she worked, she recalled first meeting Bheathain.

§

It was night and the boy should be abed. Instead, he was wide awake, his eyes intense above the scarf covering his face. He wore an amber touchpiece, but its cord had broken. The touchpiece bore the elk rune: a powerful protection.

—Ask why he wears this, she told Mr Duff. Mr Duff spoke to the woman.

—He has the Devil's Hand. It protects him. Duff said.

The woman spoke no English and she did not yet understand their Gaelic well enough. Duff would speak for her. It was he brought her from Duntulm out into the wilds.

The father spoke up, his words angry and slurred. He sat in the far corner of the room, his face in the shadows. As she came in, she had smelt drink on him.

—What did he say? she asked.

—*He* says it's to protect *them* from the boy.

The woman gave her husband a look. It was hard to tell its message in the gloom, but he was silent after.

—When did he lose the cord? she asked.

—This morn I found the bead in his bed, the woman said.

—And the cord, it must have been there? Duff spoke for her. The woman answered.

—No sign of it. She thinks he'd been halding it. Can ye make another? Duff said.

—If I take the bead now, I can return it in the morning.

Duff spoke but the woman shook her head fiercely and she did not need a translation.

—Tell her dawn is best.

Duff spoke but the husband interrupted, and she heard the name of Iorpereth, her predecessor with the laird.

—They insist it be done now, Duff said. Please help them. He says Iorpereth used her own hair—'

The husband interrupted Duff, pointed at her and rattled off a few words. Erse shared enough with Gaelic for her to recognise the words 'sun' and 'day' and she turned to Duff for explanation.

—He said ye've had sun on your hair all day, why be dawn so special?

His words stung her. Pride was a sin, and she was proud of her hair.[1] Even in her home the woman wore a headscarf.

---

[1] The instruction of spaewives shared with Christianity an emphasis on the corrupting influence of the Seven Sins, characterised as lust, covetousness, envy, pride, anger, gluttony, and sloth. Unlike Christianity, which took a purely moral view, spaewifery

—Tell them I'll do it. Ask if they've a stick of wood.

They had and she burnt the end of it and scratched a circle on the floor with the char. Inside this she laid a double-circle of rune stones, one inside the other, to make a protected space. She put the bead at the centre and reached with her knife to the back of her scalp for a twist of hair.

—I've tae braid it, she said, and began working the hairs together. Not a one spoke.

She had heard of the Devil's Hand but never seen it. The malison was not made against the child but on its mother or father, though she doubted either of those before her were his natural parent. The mother loved him, yes, but there was a distance between them. Belike she could not bear a child and this unwanted thing was the best she could have. A glance about the room showed nothing of worth and under his anger the man seemed weak and cowed. Such men were prone to drink and lashing out, but the boy was unbruised, and his wife also. Without knowing why, she realised the man feared the boy. If need for a child, any child, had persuaded the woman, what had persuaded the husband?

The boy pushed in front of his mother. She tried to hold him, but he shrugged off her hands. The scarf was ill fitting and hung to his knees.

—Let him come, she said. Duff spoke and the boy came nearer to watch intently as the hairs became one strand that she fed through the bead and tied to make a loop.

Before offering it back, she secretly made a kenning rune with her left hand, wanting to discover more about the boy and who had left the malison on him. There was resistance, as though she were pressing into wet clay. She tried harder and something struck back, rocking her onto her heels. Someone had protected the child, but she had confirmed these were not his natural parent for there was a cleft

---

stressed the damaging effect a spaer's personal desires had on her ability to interpret the signs around her. cf. *The White Branch: a history of the Northern Tradition* by Hugo Grynn (Faculty of the Higher Realities, Mannin University Press, Peel, I.O.M, 1957). *N.W.*

between this house and his birth. Hiding the effects of the blow, she laid the bead and cord across her hand to give to the mother, but she refused it and spoke to John Duff.

Why did this fall to you? she wondered. Duff was years younger than the parents but seemed to have a hold over them.

—She wants you to put it on him, he said.

—Then tell her I must see his mark.

He spoke and the woman glanced at her fearfully.

—Insist, she said.

The coachman raised his voice and the woman suddenly turned and left the room. Her husband swore, flung her an evil look and followed, slamming the door.

—What of you? she asked Duff.

—I'll sit behind him. Must you see it?

—I must. It'll not harm me, if that's what worries you. I must know if their fear has cause.

—I can vouch for his mark, Duff said.

—You've seen it?

—Ay, when he was a babe.

Duff had known the boy all his life.

She smiled for the boy's benefit, but it was impossible to read the expression under the scarf and after the warning, she was not tempted to pry. She trusted the little Gaelic she had learned would be enough.

—What's your name? she asked.

—Bheathain, the boy said.

—How old are you?

The boy looked to the door his parents had taken.

—When is your birthday? she asked.

The boy did not understand.

—He is four, near five, Duff said. Reckon they do not mark his birthday.

—Where's he from?

—Ye seen his parents, Duff said.

It was a lie and she let Duff see she knew it. He shrugged.

—Canna tell ye, he said. Sworn on 't.

—No matter, Bheathain, can I see your face?
—With this? The boy pointed to his cheek.
—Yes. I won't mind.

Holding the boy against her, she slipped the knot and the scarf fell into her hand.

The mark was a red slash from cheekbone to jaw, as though a whip had struck him, and seemed to mark out whoever the boy looked on. It would be an ill-gift on a grown man, but terrible on a child.

—Is it sore? she asked.

The boy shook his head.

—It's hot sometimes.

She held up the scarf.

—I must put it back, she said.

—Want keeking-glass. The boy pointed to the dresser.

—Let me hang your touchpiece and I'll carry you.

She slipped the cord of hair around his neck and carried him to the dresser. The boy bent forward and gazed into the glass before burying his face in her shoulder.

Who protected him, she could not guess, but she knew these were not his true parents and though he might hold to the bead of amber, the real power lay elsewhere...

§

Sweat pouring from her face and neck, she levered the stones from the mouth of the furnace. The heart of the fire was a bright orange-red. The heat dried her eyes and caught in her throat as she trapped the crucible in the tongs. Shifting away from the fire, she put it on a slab of stone and released it. The ruby-red glow pulsed in the cooling wind. In a few hours she would break it open for the copper and at dawn heat it again to cast the charm.

The furnace had burned an image on her eyes and vivid yellows and greens flashed in the darkness.

'Cold.'

Something had called to her. She had not sensed anything

in six months, but there it was. And close by, within the circle of firelight.

'Who's there?'

Nothing spoke, but a faint answer came from within.

'Cold, alone.'

It had unnerved her, but she recognised it now. It was a messenger, like the one Bheathain passed to the laird, only too weak to pass from her to another. There was only one thing to do and closing her eyes she reached inside herself.

'I see ye,' she said. 'Be safe now.'

> The failing spark seeks oneness
> With far greater fires amid
> The pale moon's nightly empire.
> Shadow, before your magick dies, depart.

It would be cruel to let you linger.

Bheathain lay in Màiri's bed. Same as last night he was naked beneath the covers, but now he was delightfully aware. He had not drawn the curtain across the bed and could see the whole of the room in the glow of the fire. His back still ached but he did not care. He would wait. He would not sleep...

'Bheathain?' Màiri came in and closed the door.

'Here,' he said.

'Thought you'd be sleeping.' Màiri sat beside him on the bed. 'I must be away early.'

'I know.'

She took off her shawl and laid it over a chair back. He reached out to touch her, hoping she would not push him away.

She rested against his hand.

'There are conditions,' she said, without turning her head. 'No pawing at me, now.'

'I won't,' he said without moving his hand.

She unbuttoned her dress and slipped it to her hips. Her shift was smooth and warm as skin.

'And you'll not snore or keep me from sleep, you hear?'

'I hear.'

He could scarcely speak. His heart would keep her awake if he did not quieten it.

'Draw the curtain; I'll not be stared at.'

He lay in the darkness, then moved aside to make space as Màiri slipped beside him. She was naked as he was.

'Hold me,' she said. 'Prove you can do that and want nothing more.'

She turned to lie against him, her face against his shoulder. Her breath caressed his skin, and her smell filled his senses. He did not kiss her and willed himself to be still and lie patient.

'Màiri?'

'Shush, now.'

He would not be shushed: 'Was wondering where that spirit of mine may be.'

'Many miles from here, or no distance at all,' she said. 'Hold me, Bheathain. Make me warm.'

Editor's Remarks

As stated earlier, the previous 'chapter' is an interpolation and in the first draft chapter eight follows directly from Paavo Jukola's chapter: indeed, the identical penmanship and shade of ink (penmanship varies depending on the wear of the nib and the shade of ink often differed from bottle to bottle) suggests there was minimal delay, if any, between MacGregor ending one chapter and commencing the next. As is MacGregor's habit, the text begins with a blank line and the chief character's name. The page is dated March 19, 1862.

On the 27 March MacGregor received a quote for construction of the Madeleine Shrine from Angus Douglas of Galashiels, some twelve miles from Arbinger. The price asked was 1,300 Crowns but with a rider stating this only covered "the masonry of the tower with all ironwork to be charged at cost." The masonry was an eighty-foot tower, reminiscent of a lighthouse, while the ironwork was an external staircase and balcony. MacGregor did not accept the bid and commented in his journal that if Douglas could not put a price on the complete work, it was because he did not know how to build it.

What Lady Helena thought of its curious design or of MacGregor's determination to build a shrine to his first wife, she did not record in her diary.

Turning to the text. As with Màiri Mulcahy's previous scenes, the majority of this chapter escaped lightly from his publishers. However, no one will be surprised that the final scene where Bheathain and Màiri share a bed did not appear in the published version.

This sanitising was precisely what MacGregor wished to dispense with. Sexual immorality was denounced at the pulpit and roused the press into a frenzy and was permissible in respectable literature only by suggestion and provided the characters were punished for their behaviour. Yet prostitution was rife in Edenborough and a gentleman could provide a house and allowance for his mistress without scandal! As MacGregor wrote in a letter to Sir Charles Palliser dated June 5, 1862, "what should be intimate must be described as though observed from a telescope on the far side of the world." (King James University. Palliser Collection: box *ii*, 1862)

No good son trades his ploughshare for a keel
Chapter Nine
Edenborough: Herr Danneberg of the Hanseatic Company offers PAAVO JUKOLA an opportunity

    Judas quits morality
    And sins upon his father
    With Hanseatic silver.
    No good son trades his ploughshare for a keel.
All those with a cause will find a man to lead them. That is their good fortune and our regret.

JUKOLA HAD NEARED the end of High Street when three children surrounded him.

'See the sights, mister, tour o' En'bro'. Best places tae gae.'

Their leader was a fuzz-chinned lad of uncertain age and in his and the other children's faces, Jukola recognised the same needy hunger he had once known. In a kind-hearted moment he had taken such a tour but found nothing worth seeing twice over and, as time was short, he answered in Finlander and pretended to know no English. The lad gave him a cold look and leant forward, revealing a crown of scabs erupting through his sparse hair, to hawk sputum on the toe of Jukola's shoe before stepping smartly away from any fist.

'Ye reckoned on I canna read, ye cunner,' he sneered. 'Be *The Times* ye haulden an' if ye can read English ye can speak it.' The lad shepherded his companions down an alley.

Known as "wynds", these alleyways riddled Old Town. More like chasms in the earth than things made by man, Jukola had only ventured among them once and sworn never again. Piss-puddled and stinking of every foul thing, he had found his way almost barred by debris of material, animal and humankind: collapsed and part-collapsed walls; all manner of creature with four legs and two (and three by misadventure), including milch cows and horses where no grass grew, loitering dogs and squealing swine, all living cheek by jowl with a human contingent of loafers, idlers, knife sharpeners, pudding-faced drunkards and painted whores, and above all this filth, flying from jetties, open windows, and ropes bridging the narrow sky, more canvas than carried by the loftiest barkentine. White linens, shifts, tartan shawls, shirts and flannel petticoats, all drawn in the air as though the good women of the wynds, despairing of their lot, had hoisted sail in an effort to be gone. An effort only foiled by the wind's refusal to taint itself on these noisome depths.

Swallowing his pride, he scraped the sputum on the kerb and folded the newspaper under his arm. He did not wish to cheat the children, and he could spare a sixpence. Their mamas and papas had fires to keep and how else might they do it with no forest to cut. But it was too late to put things right; the three had gone, vanishing like rats into the dreaded wynds.

He was in Canongate now. The road had narrowed, and the buildings grown more decrepit. Glancing up at the Tolbooth clock took his eye from the pavement and he narrowly avoided collision with a fishmonger's cart. Seeing his delay, an old woman stepped from a doorway and blocked his path.

'Buy a bit o' luck sailor.'

Sprays of heather were pinned to a wickerwork tray propped on her bosom. Teeth, like gravestones, jutted from her face and one eye was milk-white: she was no poster for the efficacy of her charms, but the children had stung his conscience and he lifted his purse.

'Thank ye sere. Wantin' white or dark?'

'The white, if is same price?'

'A furriner,' she said, appraising. 'Be three pennies an' I'll pin it fer ye?'

'I have it,' he said, wishing to keep her distant. And taking the stem he dropped a sixpence in her shrivelled paw.

'Safe voyage,' she said.

He pushed the stem through a buttonhole and walked on. The Tolbooth clock chimed the quarter hour behind him and the Hansahal lay beyond. Herr Danneberg said it was three hundred years old, but parts seemed built on even older ruins. The highest floors leant over the street, climbing like a forest tree among its equally tall and ramshackle neighbours.

Ignoring the main entrance, Jukola turned down Grimmer Street, and climbed to a small, nondescript door.[1]

It was unlocked and inside he surprised a workman descending a ladder with a painting clutched under one arm. Lit by a pair of lancet windows either side of the door the yellow limewash of the entry had long ago darkened and the painting had left a rectangle of original colour on the wall. A second rectangle revealed where the bow-fronted specimen case resting on the table had hung. Glancing inside, having never seen it properly when it was hanging, Jukola found three decrepit herring spilling scales and fins on the floor of the case. Much of the Hansa's early wealth came from the Baltic fisheries. Ignoring the workman, he crossed to the desk and rang the bell. The sharp sound diminished into silence.

The workman glanced at the painting and leant it against the table with a shrug. Age had enveloped the artist's work in a brown twilight.

'Methinks,' he said, wiping his hands on a rag. 'None'll come. Gae straight up if I were ye. Furriner an' a sailor?'

'Finlander, and a sailor, yes.'

'So ye ma' have no heard.'

'Heard what?'

'Hansards are gaen, an' good riddance, t' 'em.'

'But why?' Jukola leant forward, feeling the papers in his jacket chafe against his chest.

'Laddie,' the man waved his cloth, 'I ken naught o business, but I ken a wall wants pointing, or a rotten window

---

[1] Unlike the rest of MacGregor's description of Edenborough, which has been accurate in both geography and character, no alley of this name has ever existed off Canongate or in any other part of the city. Presumably it is MacGregor's own invention and may be a fanciful corruption of grimoire. *N.W.*

frame. See this,' he showed Jukola the rusted stump of a nail in the wall, 'haulden up yon case o' fishes. No silver, that's why they're gangin.'

'But Herr Danneberg?'

'Oh ay, he's here. Best gae an' find him, eh?'

Hurrying up the stairs, Jukola noticed a Delft vase missing from a windowsill and dust spinning where a tapestry had hung. Much had vanished from Danneberg's chamber, also. A moth-eaten beaver, forever chewing a willow stem, and a codfish of monstrous size were absent, along with the walrus-tooth carrack and the cabinet of pewter drinking cups.

'I do not accept it is missing, Alberic. I do not.'

Otto von Danneberg was staring at his apprentice. Danneberg had brown hair and a broad face flushed with blood. Mutton chop whiskers reached to his jaw and a small, always neatly trimmed beard crowned a double chin. His waistcoat and breeches were green twill and a matching coat hung over a chair. The apprentice knelt at the foot of a pinewood dresser.

Hearing him at the door, Danneberg hesitated before greeting him with a smile.

'Mr Jukola, we were expecting you.' The man opened his watch. 'Indeed, normally I might suggest you are a little late, but *today*...' Danneberg shrugged his broad shoulders. 'I may be here all evening. Any luck, Alberic?'

The boy sat up. He was fair-headed, with a long Roman face.

'No, sir.'

'Keep trying. It's here somewhere.'

The window was open onto Canongate and street noise drifted through. Sheaves of paper smouldered in the hearth but the array of penholders, inkstands and sand-shakers, and the carriage clock remained on Danneberg's desk.

'But why?' Jukola asked, and as he gestured round the room his copy of *The Times* slipped to the floor.

Danneberg bent to retrieve it.

'Please, we have enough to do,' he said reproachfully. 'This will answer your questions.' He waved the newspaper and returned it with a heavy wink. 'Though not entirely truthfully.'

He had no idea what the man meant. The upheaval appalled him.

'Sit, Mr Jukola.'

Danneberg pushed a chair over and as he sat Jukola took the envelope from his jacket. The German saw it.

'The *Swan of Visby* sails for Turku tomorrow: Roubles, as usual?'

'Two hundred and thirty crowns,' he said and drew out banknotes to that value.

'Bad month, eh?' Danneberg took the money.

'The weather,' Jukola complained. 'Days lost at sea. My share is down.'

'It happens. Two hundred and thirty; I think we can forgo the charges, for old times' sake. A bill of exchange, Alberic, dear boy—no, not those, idiot. Mr Jukola is not dealing in thousands!'

The boy passed Danneberg a blank document. The man dashed out the instruction and handed it to Jukola with an automatic finger indicating where he should sign.

'Good.' Danneberg gave him a receipt. 'Now, I suggest a toast to the last days of the Edenborough Hansa.'

He took a bottle of Madeira from a cabinet and poured two generous glasses.

'Least I can do for an old friend.'

The man slid a glass across the desk. Jukola drank it in one, finding it sweet and cloying. Raising a brow, Danneberg refilled it.

'As for me, retirement in Bremen. Alberic, dear boy, where is it you're off to?'

'Cologne, sir, as I have said.'

'So, you have, though I thank you not to remind me of what you have or have not said.' He smiled warmly at the apprentice.

'Cologne, yes: excellent cathedral there, finer than any in Anglia. As for this,' he indicated the room. 'The valuables will go to Hamburg or Lübeck. The rest...' Pausing, Danneberg sipped the wine. 'What can I say? I would offer you an heirloom, but is unwise, eh? Your employer would be unhappy to discover you sold their secrets to a rival.'

'I didn't sell them,' he protested.

Danneberg held up his glass in apology. 'Let us not quarrel. I accept you gave them freely. Our arrangement sending monies to your father, albeit in such small amounts our commission barely covers the cost, is unimportant. Alberic?'

The boy was deep in the cupboard under the dresser.

'Sorry, sir, no.'

'Try harder. We have mislaid one of our charters, Mr Jukola: a most particular document which we require to formally close the Hall.'

'Close it?' he asked.

'Don't worry, my boy. All in there.' Danneberg pointed at *The Times*. 'Edenborough has always been on the periphery of our affairs and cannot be supported longer.'

'Then you have no use for these?' Jukola took the copies of the manifests from his jacket.

Danneberg laughed. 'Until we rescind our charters we remain, theoretically, in competition with the North of Scotland Company.' He took Jukola's manifests and dropped them on the desk. 'However, do not think the Hansa has no more use for its friends or abandons them lightly.'

Danneberg opened a silver box, removed a card and spun it between his fingers while giving him a careful glance.

'Tell me, Paavo... I may after all this time call you Paavo?'

He nodded. The wine had left a sickly aftertaste.

'You assist us because you hate the Russians?'

'You opposed them in Crimea. My enemy's enemy is my friend,' Jukola said.

'Quite, quite. Noble words,' Danneberg replied.

Alberic was moving bundles of paperwork from the cupboard and piling them beside Danneberg's desk.

'But not strictly correct,' he continued. '*Emperor Leopold* fought the Russians; the *Hansa* fought no one.'

'But you sent the Emperor ships?'

Danneberg laid the card face down on his desk.

'The Hansa's business is trade, as it is for all shipping companies. To maximise our trade, and increase profits, it is vital no one restricts our affairs. As Holy Roman Emperor, Leopold could make our lives difficult, so we gave him a few ships. However, the late tsar might also have made our lives difficult, so they were only a few ships and not our best. Frankly, the Hansa would be as happy to carry Russia's goods through the Black Sea as we are the Baltic.'

Jukola glanced at the copies he had just given Danneberg.

'Why do you tell me this now?'

Danneberg raised the card to his lips and studied him.

'I am about to retire, Paavo. I have my house in Bremen and a garden by the river where I will cultivate roses: English roses, of which I have grown exceedingly fond. My housekeeper tells me they grow best for a man of clear conscience, which mine, I confess, is not. However, I do not wish to darken it further. I like you, Paavo Jukola, and I hope you have grown fond of me...'

A pigeon had settled on the window ledge. A large cob, it looked warily into the room and, satisfied of no immediate danger, began strutting and calling loudly for a mate.

Danneberg offered Jukola the card. 'If you wish to be of further use to us, speak to this man.'

Jukola read, *Herr Friedrich Diesler*. The card bore the Hansa seal and an address.

'The Steelyard in Winchester?'

'Where else? You will need this also.' Danneberg gave him an envelope sealed with wax. 'It is a letter of commendation. Do not open it. Show it to Herr Diesler.' Danneberg tapped the name on the card. 'He and no other must see this.'

It was a curious reward. The Steelyard was immense. Only Bergen and Antwerp surpassed it outside the Empire. Sensing its danger should a crewman find it aboard the

Dundalk, he slid the card and letter deep inside his jacket.

'It must be your decision,' Danneberg said. 'The Hansa requires intelligent and diligent men. Herr Diesler...' the man pursed his mouth. 'He requires other qualities also; you must decide if you have them—'

'Aha!' The apprentice flourished a rolled parchment.

'You are certain?' Danneberg asked.

'It has the Bergen seal. I think it must be.'

Herr Danneberg received it and unravelled it towards the windowlight. The pigeon flew off.

'Bergen, as you say. *Twenty-third August 1648.* The missing date?'

'Sir, it is.'

'Excellent. What the Devil was it doing there? Well, we may go.'

As Danneberg stood up his chair rolled into Alberic's carefully piled paperwork. The boy tried but failed to stop it sprawling across the floor. Danneberg viewed the mess.

'Foolish. Most foolish. Perhaps, Alberic, you need stay, make the place presentable. Eight of the evening, no later, and remember to secure the window and door when you leave. I have business in town this afternoon. Mr Jukola is leaving also, if it is acceptable to him?'

He stood and leant on Danneberg's desk.

'The last time,' he said, glancing round the room. This was his battleground, his war against the tsar and all his minions, all his Vasily Kafelnikovs. He did not want to remember it like this: stripped, destroyed, ruined.

'Indeed, the last time,' Danneberg said. 'Of course, the building is rotten; stonework's falling apart and the wood is rotten. Thankfully,' he clapped Jukola on the shoulder, 'it is no longer our concern. This way, my friend, the entrance hall retains a little nobility.'

Danneberg led him down the main staircase, a far grander affair than that he ascended by. Its furnishings remained intact and the faces of Hanseatic Aldermen, dead and long dead, gazed from the walls.

The stairs led to a broad hall lit by mullioned windows and an elaborate fanlight of stained glass over the door. Suits of armour with halberds and white plumes guarded the door. The unswept hearth was the only sign of neglect.

'See this?' Danneberg indicated a scroll carved in the alabaster mantelshelf. 'It is the first charter between the Hansa and Scotland, signed by King James III. See the date?' It read 1474. 'Almost four hundred years there's been a Hansa Hall in Edenborough. Accountants have no sense of history.'

Danneberg fitted a key in the door.

'Consider what I said. For the right man, Herr Diesler is a generous paymaster. No more 'bad months', eh? Best I say no more.'

Danneberg swung the door open, and dust blew in on a welcome breeze. Paavo stepped out. Danneberg followed and locked the door behind them.

'And so goodbye, Paavo Jukola, I wish you well.'

'Thank you.' He took the offered hand and shook it limply. 'Bremen?'

'To grow roses, yes; each to our separate ways.'

Danneberg broke his grip and stepped to the pavement.

'Mine is this.' He pointed toward Holyrood and left without formality. Certain he would never see him again, Jukola kept Danneberg in sight until losing him in the multitude.

'Goodbye,' he said to the door and, aware it must appear foolish, ran his hand over the carved doorjamb. Then he dropped to the pavement and retraced his steps. Tron Kirk stood high and proud against a pearl-white sky and a line of cabs waited in its shadow.

But there was no hurry. It was hours before he need return to his ship. He had not eaten since six and his throat was dry.

'Mind the way!' A man pushing a handcart brushed by, 'Oysters, sixpence a dozen,' chalked on the side. Up ahead the three children were watching him. The oldest turned away without meeting his gaze.

'Hey,' he called after them.

The lad backed toward an alley.

'No!' He pulled out his purse and waved it. The lad hesitated but held his ground, pushing the others behind him.

'A tour noo?' The boy called. 'Best be catchin' yer ship.'

'No, no tour. The finest drinking house and these are yours.'

He took out three crown. 'Yours, if you take me.'

The children looked at the coins as if they were sugar, their lips parting hungrily. The older lad was wary but would suffer a revolt if he refused three crown.

He rattled the coins.

'Nae funny business.'

'I offer none but take none.'

'We likes to hear that; this way, hide the purse. Some's no decent like us.'

The children led him down a wynd, past a derelict stable and into a small yard. At the precise point where a shaft of sunlight cut between the roofs lay a small house built of timber and striped cloth of vermillion and blue. No bigger than a chicken hut, it leant back against the wall, as though borrowing it for shelter. On entering the yard, he thought the curtain across the doorway rippled, as though a hand disturbed it.

One of the children picked up a stone. It missed the house and clattered on the wall behind.

'Bluidy witch. This way.'

He followed, ducking through a passage overhung with beams and jutting floors. The half-rotten beam ends were carved with leering faces. At passage end, a black door darkened the gloom. It had lettering carved in the frame, but the light was too poor to read.

The children left him, calling out as they ran.

He doubted this was *the best*, but no matter. He went in, mindful of noise in the room above, and lay ten schilling on the bar.

'Throwing it around?' the barkeep said.

'A good day,' he said. 'One beer.'

There were shouts and heavy footsteps circling above. Puzzled, he looked up at the beams.

'Boxing: even fight,' the barkeep said. 'Free if you bet on the winner.'

He shook his head and drank thirstily. Overhead the feet circled the boards, pounding like summer thunder. He drained the glass and took another…

…Rolling from the passage into the yard, he saw the sun had dipped, the rays of light only just reaching the little house. The curtain twitched and he moved closer. A hand held the cloth and a face watched from the darkness.

Inside, he sat on a stool and ringed fingers lit a candle. The flame revealed a woman. A scarf covered her hair and a veil half her face. Her eyelids were darkened with paint or stain. He was disappointed. It was how a whore would pretty herself and he wondered what lay behind the veil. He could not tell her age, but her hands were smooth and plump.

A table separated them, its brass top engraved with the moon and planets and other signs. The candle gave off a scent. For a moment, it was elusive, shifting between warm meadow and sun-baked herbs before settling on pine resin.

'The cards, is it?' A tarot pack sat on the table. A card with a naked man and woman entwined lay uppermost. 'Or is it palms.' The woman spread a hand out, cupping it, as though weighing something.

He shook his head, recalled what Gabriel Stone had said. 'Runes.'

'The Elder Way?' She reached to a drawer beneath the table, fetched out a cloth bag and reached in. He heard the stones turning over each other. Drawing the hand out, she scattered nine runes across the table.

A sharp breath disturbed the candle.

§

Tron Kirk was calling two as he emerged from the wynd. His head throbbed and he could not get the stink of the scryer's candle from his throat.

Stumbling across the road, he hailed a cab.

The driver looked down with a wordless sneer.

'Docks?'

'Customs House,' he said.

'Get in, keep the window doon.'

The lurch as they moved off set his stomach churning and a tremendous fart shook his bowels. At least his stink drove out the scryer's. He loosened his jacket and patted his belly contentedly. For now, his purse was light but Herr Danneberg had given him the means to fill it. The scryer confirmed that, if nothing else.

Yards short of The Shore, his insides rebelled and leaning forward he groaned and vomited on the cab floor.

'Damn you!' The cabbie pulled up. 'Too early in day fer this malarkey.' The man dragged him out. 'Fucking mess. Five schilling. Three fer ride, two tae wash oot.'

He fumbled the coins and the cab drove off. Stumbling on the cobbles, he sprawled, drawing blood from his lip. If he was to kill a man, pray God it was not himself.

He sat up, feeling his teeth. All were firm.

'Papa?' It was Frank Farron. 'Bluidy hell, whit a state.'

Farron helped him up and gripped his arm like a vice.

'This way; God help ye when ye're sober.'

His stomach rebelled again. Stumbling against a saddlers' window he heard the glass crack. Behind it was harness and tack. He mumbled Minna's name as tears filled his cheeks.

'Lassie, was she?' Farron said. 'Too langsyne for sorry now. Come on. Hey, sir, a hand there if ye would.'

'Jakov, no!' A woman's voice, protesting in German. A moment later, a second arm took him on the far side.

'Sarah, one must help our fellows.'

Who were these people? The man had a smart coat. It would be a shame to get it filthy. He could not see his face.

'He is a Finn,' the man said. 'Like us, a victim of the tsar…'

He did not hear the rest. Blood pounded in his head. If he had strength, he would not bear Loveless one more day.

'What is your ship?' the stranger asked.

'The *Dundalk*,' Farron said. 'Bound f' Inverness. You've a cautch?'

'A grip?'

'Ye've hauld o' him?' Farron asked.

'I have.'

The two men marched him toward King's Bridge. The wherry had not finished loading but the painters had gone from the excise cutter.

'I hope it was worth it,' Farron muttered. 'God knows ye'll suffer.'

'Sarah, you should not see this.' The stranger was shouting back over his shoulder. The man's wife must be following them. He craned his neck to see. She was small in height and thin as a heron, reminding him of Henriikka Haanpää.

'And do not fret so,' her husband called. 'Think of Winchester, all the pretty dresses to see. In four days, all will be well.'

Jukola laughed and turned back to the pavement. The skinny bitch would need more than a pretty dress to lift a man's prick. But Winchester, now there was a thought. He straightened up and stared Farron in the eye.

'I go,' Jukola said.

'We all bluidy gae,' Farron replied.

'No,' he said forcefully. 'Tell Loveless, I go. Collect what is mine. Go.'

'Leave like this an' ye'll get nae letters,' Farron warned. 'Ye winna get anither ship without guid report.'

'Loveless fuck him, I have report I need.'

'Sarah, go! You must not hear this.'

Jukola leered at the woman and let his feet drag on the cobbles.

'Papa, be civil,' Farron warned.

'He is a Finn, what can one say,' the German said in English.

'A Finn, yes!' Jukola crowed.

'Sarah, return to the lodging house. I shall return shortly.'

'Jakov, why must you do this? He is not grateful. And I *hate* that room. I shall take tea. In a *café*, on my own!'

'Go. Obey me! Here!' The man threw the woman a key. It landed on the cobbles. Hearing the noise, Jukola glanced back, and as she stooped to gather there entered into his heart a moment of pity.

> He looks back and calls her name,
> And in his lightning crisis,
> Reeled in insobriety,
> The snow revealed the falseness of his trail.

As with the spaer, hurt and sorrow were his foundation and his wife: to meddle there was to meddle with his life. What's long past cannot be unmade and once again I sought another.

Editor's Remarks

The chapter begins in MacGregor's usual habit with a blank line and the addition of the chief character's name, written as PJ, in the margin. There is no date, but it was probably begun in late March or early April 1862.

MacGregor had received a second quote for construction of the Madeleine Shrine, this from a Niall Coldacre of Dunbar. Coldacre priced the job at two thousand crowns and impressed MacGregor with a reference from the Scottish Maritime Board for whom he had built the North Berwick light. MacGregor's immediate acceptance of the offer suggests price was less important than confidence in the builder. Coldacre gave May 1 for beginning construction.

Turning to *This Iron Race*, MacGregor's continuing deliberations regarding the conflict of expression and likely publication are shown again in his journal entry for April 4.

> The writer is free to resort to all manner of circumlocution to describe matters of the flesh provided the reader need not necessarily understand that which he plainly intends the reader to understand. Or, to put matters another way; provided his words can be taken to mean something entirely innocent, no matter how unlikely that may be, a writer can suggest all manner of things to sow the seed in the reader's mind. The peril therein is the writer cannot set limits on what flourishes in the reader's imagination! How much simpler it would be if he may write plainly of such matters so the reader, any reader, comprehends perfectly his intention. But I am advised plain speaking is disapproved of less it besmirch those innocents who cannot apprehend the writer's subtle code.

It is difficult to know how to read the statement. Is it a declaration of intent? Is it a note of encouragement? One would also like to know who said that plain speaking is disapproved of. Regardless, he had little to fear with this chapter for apart from the removal of a handful of obscenities from the dialogue, the text was almost unaltered between first draft and published edition, and what few changes there are seem to have been MacGregor tidying his text.

This is curious because the portrayal of Scotland's greatest city is hardly flattering and, as Member of Parliament for Edenborough South, Sir Sidney might have been assumed to object. Having said that, Edenborough was the subject of a good deal of unflattering poetry by MacGregor's contemporaries, in particular Fergus Crean and Malcolm Mallinson, and missives from the Edenborough Review also condemned the unsanitary wynds so perhaps MacGregor's criticisms were not especially notable.

A currency of little worth
Chapter Ten
Haelda's Island, Skye: BHEATHAIN SOMHAIRLE'S *circumstances are about to change*

Though hope uplifts in poor times
It falls careless as the sun
And being freely given
Becomes a currency of little worth.

I

DESPITE MÀIRI'S WARNING Bheathain had, first thing that morning, glanced in the mirror. His mark mocked his hopes, though the heat and rawness had gone, and he washed his face. Somewhere in the world a wee spirit was looking for one to bless and when it found such, his mark would be gone. He prodded his cheek and wondered what he might look like without it. Much like any other, he hoped, though the copper touchpiece around his neck reminded him he would never be quite the same as another. His mark would be there, whether it reddened his flesh or not, for it was as much within as without.

Màiri had left early for Portree and would be gone most of the day. An emigrant ship was sailing, and she was to bless the folk leaving.

'New France,' she said when he asked where it was taking them.

He thought there would soon be as many Skye men in the New World as there were in the Old. He'd heard tales there were forests big as Scotland and trees two hundred feet tall. A man might have fuel for his fire for a quarter the effort it took his cousin on Skye. But what use was it if it burned not in the hearth, he held dearest but somewhere he'd been cast like tangle on the shore.

Màiri had asked him to cut peat and shown him an old peat bank. It had grassed over and there would be a deal of digging before he got at the peat. He thought it too early in the year: better to wait a month so the peats dried and could be stacked. Chance was rain would break up the peats before they dried. He'd said as much, but Màiri had scolded him, saying he was fit to walk, and she would not have him lingering like a draught by the fire.

'If your back gives you trouble, rub this on it,' Màiri said, handing him a jar of salve.

Thinking about Màiri made him confused. The woman had more sides to her than a grain of sand. Some he liked, some he liked so much it made him sweat, others he liked less and some only confused him. He took out his thoughts with the ripper and soon the peat bank had a clean edge to it. This he thought worth stopping and making a brew for and it was near an hour before he was back at the peat bank and sharpening Màiri's peat iron. It was old and he thought if she paid sixpence for it, she was robbed. The rivets fixing the blade to the handle were loose and he'd need to be light footed or risk it breaking. He would tell her it needed fixing. She might know about herbs and charms, but he doubted she had ever cut peat.

Digging from the top of the bank he made one cut, then a second to free a slice of grass and moss. This he tossed aside and setting the blade neatly alongside the first cut, drove down to take a second cut. The top layers were no use. They burned badly and made an ashy fire. Once he'd cleared the moss, he went back and cut again, now into the good peat and laid them beside the trench, taking care none broke.

It was warm in the sun and for the first time since fall, he stripped to his shirt. Even then, the sweat ran off him and twice he'd to stop and beat off the black flies that swarmed out of the sky, then vanished on the wind.

After a time, he began to enjoy the rhythm of digging and imagined him and Màiri sat by the fire of an evening or heating a tub of water earned with his own sweat. The feeling left him warm inside, not lustful, just warm, like he had felt when he was small and Mama held him. Manus might cook his champ, but he and Mama had belonged together. Now he belonged here with Màiri.

Far side of the loch was the Portree road and above it the Storr, where the land fell in a line of crags and pinnacles like giant steps. Among them a finger of rock prodding the sky. In summer, trip coaches or walkers came out from Portree to gaze at the Old Man. A few climbed into the crags and stood at about it but none had assailed it. In Portree they sold graven pictures of the Old Man or the Quiraing, to the tour boat crowds and a few folk brought easel and brush and dodged the summer showers. They thought it a wonder to be stared at and painted but to Bheathain the rocks were there if the weather was grand, not there if the weather was bad, and in no way of use to man or beast.

A corncrake called from the reeds beside the loch.

Digging finished, he washed the tools in the loch and greased them. Màiri would not be back for a time yet and he could not drink tea all afternoon, so he made a pipe of betony leaf and went wandering.

Out beyond the peat bank he met a track and followed it north. It ended at an abandoned house where he found a well. The water tasted good and from there he turned eastward to the cliffs overlooking the strait and Raasay. Gulls and kittiwakes clustered on the cliffs or hung on the wind. He did not feel up to climbing down to rob the nests and let them be, but they did not take kindly to him and swooped within feet of his head as he watched the ocean prowl about the rocks below. A pair of luggers made the most of the wind but there was no sign of the emigrant ship.

As he returned, Bheathain saw a man on horseback approaching and presently recognised Dr Ramsay.

'Good day to you,' Ramsay said without dismounting. 'You're much improved.'

Ramsay spoke in English and Bheathain replied likewise.

'Be less bad than I was,' he said. 'Màiri done good by me. Thankfu' for a' ye did. Taud I wasnae a good patient.'

Ramsay laughed. 'A man bears no guilt for what he cannot help. Màiri has told me what ailed you. It is, as I thought, *no natural physic*. Bheathain, would you show me your face.'

'Fer certain? Yer no troubled by it?'

Ramsay dismounted and claimed he had seen worse. Bheathain obliged and the doctor examined him.

'It has not altered in extent or colour?'

'Reckon not, sir.'

'Good. I hear Màiri has spoken of a *wandering spirit*; I trust you are not giving it too much hope?'

Bheathain frowned. The doctor knew more than he spoke.

'She said I wasnae.'

'Good. Trust to Divine Will. You would be a changed man without your mark. Very changed.'

The doctor spoke without meeting his gaze and there was something in his manner belike a good neighbour calling on the dying. The doctor was hiding something and though the thought only lasted a moment it was long enough for the man to mount his horse before giving his deliberation.

'Tomorrow, you return to your grandfather in Brogaig.'

It was blunt as the iron spade he'd held, but he could not accept he had heard the doctor right.

'He is your only kin,' Ramsay said. 'I cannot say he welcomes you, but for the time being, it cannot be helped. You are in my prayers. Good day, Bheathain.'

II

'It is settled,' Màiri said.

'And I have no say?'

Her eyes did not meet his.

'I know what you would say.'

'I thought you couldn't scry anymore.'

'Any would know. It is my grief I put thought in your head.'

'You grieve for last night?'

'I should not have welcomed you to my bed.'

'You wanted us well enough.' He put his hands on her shoulders. She did not resist; nor did she acquiesce. 'You reckon I have something of the gift. Maybe I do, for I know this is not your choosing.'

'I can't keep you here.'

He slipped his hands to the blades of her shoulders, bringing her nearer. Again, she neither protested nor welcomed him.

'Folk will talk; is that it?'

'They'd call me a scarlet woman; you would be the fool I had bewitched.'

'Behang't, Màiri, you have bewitched me.'

It surprised him to think ill of her. It brought to mind his father's drunken rages and the bruises hidden by his mother's skirts.

'I was weak last night. Can you forgive me?'

'I'd forgive you murder, but this is not what you want.'

'What would I say to Dr Ramsay? You're well and there's no cause to keep you here.'

'And there's naught for me at Brogaig, save my old *nen* and he can't stand me. I don't care what Ramsay thinks and nor do you.'

'Do you care what any thinks?'

'I've cared all my life!' He jabbed his cheek. 'If any knows what it is to be ill-tongued, it is I.'

'Then will you care what they think of me? I am old enough to be your mother. There are times I think you see me as her.'

Her words struck bone and he took a moment to reply.

'She's long-time dead.'

'But I'm the age of her. Bheathain, there's times you make me feel girlish again, and I would have more of it.' She smiled, deepening the lines on her face. 'Other times, I see a son thankful to his mother, and that grieves me. The world would mock me, and I would not care, but I'll not be bedwife *and* mother to you.'

'You are not my mother, or she you.'

He wanted to speak with his heart but could not. In Màiri's company his childhood seemed very near. No other woman beside these two had ever cared for him.

'Be kind and make us tea,' she said. 'Grand lot of peats you cut. You can scarce wonder Dr Ramsay thinks you're mended.'

'My back is well enough,' he said and hooked the kettle on the fire. 'It is not what sickens.'

'You do love me so do not pretend it.'

'One night does not make love,' he admitted. 'But I might love you, and you me.'

She was silent and the kettle had begun to warm before she admitted it was so.

'Truly?' he asked.

'I admit to speaking as I must and not as I wish.'

'You would not be here alone?'

'I thought to follow old Haelda.'

'But you are not old; and there's many would agree with me. You could pick any man.'

'Any man?' She slipped inside his arms and leant her head on his shoulder. 'Thank you. I shall take that.'

'Ay, Tòrmod M'Neis said as much. And there is me. So, two I know of.'

'Tòrmod always had a soft spot for me. There were others when I was younger.'

'It does not surprise me. You never wanted to marry?'

'I had my vow to the laird. I could not keep it and marry.'

'He would not give you leave?'

'I did not ask. I was made different. I could not marry or have weans and keep the gift. It is cruel, but there it is.'

'And now?'

'I am past child bearing.'

'Not what I meant. You may marry?'

'I may, yes.'

'Then I would be he.'

He buried his face in her hair and breathed deep. Her scent was strong. She had something on her hair that made it cling to his face.

'You don't know what you are wishing for. When you are in your prime, I will be lame, black veined, cold limbed, white haired.'

'And I will care for you. I shall not leave. I cared for my mam when she was sick. I know what it calls for.'

Màiri pushed away from him.

'The duty you owed her you do not owe me.'

'If I were your husband—'

'A husband gangs with his friends and comes home drunk and chases the lassies.'

'Ay, and beats his wife until she sickens.' He met her gaze with anger: a spark of his father kindling in him. 'Then he puts her corp out in the byre. Is he the man you would have?'

'No. Your father did that?'

'I was too young to stand against him.'

'I did not know it was so bad.'

'Ma let few know. My old *nen* knows. It was he found her corp. It is his shame he did not save her from the brute.'

'You would save me, as you could not save your mother.'

'I do not reckon so. I do not hold you as I held her.'

Her face softened into a smile of acceptance, and he folded her in his arms again.

'Bull-headed you are.'

'Tomorrow, I will not shame you by being dragged from here or bleating like a lamb taken from the ewe.'

'Or a son from his mother,' Màiri said. 'I said you could be free of your mark one day.'

'You reckoned I should not set much hope on it.'

'But if you *were* free of it.' Her cheek rested against his, her lips almost touching his own. 'If lassies half my age were glancy at you, lassies who might bear a child, would you stay then?'

He did not answer. Not because he did not know his heart, but because he could not see the future. Màiri did not push him for an answer and when her arms slid from his back, he let her stand.

'I'll sleep there, the night,' he said of the bed of heather in the corner of the room.

He made tea, taking care to brew it to her taste and not let it steep. Then he made up the fire, seeing in his mind's eye the stack of peats he'd dug that day. He need not spare on peats; he sensed there would always be more than enough.

The bright fire reminded him of the copper touchpiece around his neck. Màiri set the cookpot to boil.

'The amber bead I lost; was it you gave it me?'

'You had it when I first saw you. You were no more than four.'

'I was not born with it.'

'Maybe the fairies give it,' she said.

'Don't hold with the wee folk.'

'They're real enough. If you have the gift, they'll find you.'

'If not fairies, then who give it me?'

'I don't know. What I made you will do in its place.'

He brought her tea and set it beside her. His eye was drawn to the glint of the glass bottles on the shelf and bunches of herbs hung from the roof beams. The glass bottles ended in a line of books.

'Yesterday, when I looked through your books, I found this wee drawing of you. I did not mean to pry, but who was he?'

'You think it was a he? Are you jealous?'

'No... a little,' he admitted. 'It was a good likeness of you.'

'His name is Lazarus.'

'The Mad Monk?'

'He is neither monk nor mad.'

'But he's a wicked man.'

'He is not, even if his master was. It was the wedding of King Edmund and Queen Charlotte. I was flattered he paid attention to me.'

'Flattered you out of your clothes.'

Màiri laughed. It was not the reaction he wanted.

'You're jealous of a man I have not seen in a dozen years.'

'And why should I not be. It was not decent.'

'It is not hanging on the wall.'

He sat and put his feet out to the fire. Màiri had her back turned. She was busy with supper.

'You were lovers?'

'Lazarus never loved anyone. But I was flattered.'

She had answered his curiosity. He did not think less of her but did wonder about Lazarus.

'You reckon I will be like him?'

'No. You have the gift, but the gift does not make a man who he is.'

'What if I don't want it?'

'Few want it, Bheathain. I did not. Lazarus did not. It is the gift few can refuse.'

'I refuse it.'

'It will hurt you if you fight it and there's another reason to accept. I tried to help your mother in her last illness. I know I could not have saved her, but I would have made her life easier.'

'My da would not let you in the house.'

'You remember?'

'He could not bear magick. He could scarce stand me. You say I should accept this gift for the help of others?'

'It is one reason, yes. You visit your mother?'

'Aye. I mind the grave and sit and talk.'

'Would you tell her of me?'

'Of you?'

'Yes: tell her of this lonely Eirish woman on a rock. Tell her you want this woman as wife and ask her blessing. When you know her answer, I'll be here.'

> Daunted in desire, yet faithful,
> He bows to his love's wishes
> (as all men who love ought do)
> Nothing shall be the same from this day forth.

The End of Book One

Editor's Remarks

There is a small but significant difference between the first draft of the concluding chapter of volume one and all the preceding chapters. Here is the usual blank line and the date, in this instance April 10, 1862, alongside Bheathain's name, but additionally there is the word "homeward". It is the only chapter in the first draft to begin with any kind of title beyond the date and name of the principal character but what MacGregor might have meant by "homeward" is unclear as it was not the chapter title he eventually chose. Perhaps "homeward", and this is little more than a guess, alludes to Bheathain's progress at this point or perhaps MacGregor is noting a suitable division between the first and second volumes of *This Iron Race*. In any event, this is the final chapter of volume one and Bheathain is about to return to Brogaig.

There is little to report of MacGregor's private life at this point. On the eleventh he attended a concert in Edenborough with Sir Charles Palliser and his wife—the venue was most likely St. Cecilia's Hall on Cowgate, but the concert programme has not survived—and returned to Arbinger the following day, a Saturday. On the Sunday Jock Strange was unwell, Lady MacGregor's diary suggests he had been drinking the night before, and MacGregor went for his usual walk alone. Some four miles from Arbinger he was caught in a downpour and though he returned safely he succumbed to a chill and spent the following day resting.

Turning back to the text. Other than the removal of sexual references, the text of this chapter was little altered between MacGregor's first draft and the published first edition of 1864. This is especially so in the first part of the chapter where the only alterations assist with the flow and phrasing of certain sentences without altering their meaning. These changes, presumably made of MacGregor's own volition, appear in the new edition. Missing from the published text was any direct reference to Bheathain and Màiri having shared a bed and any suggestion her relations with Lazarus were sexual. Readers of the 1864 text would perhaps have inferred both but MacGregor was attempting to write directly of such matters, without the need for codes and obfuscation.

MacGregor is of course subtle when it suited him, but he also wished to speak plainly to his readers and in this edition, he is at last able to do so.

'O' concluded
The Red Lion, Avebury

'Now, the second act, as it were. As I was about to say, the Reserved Manuscript Depository at King James University is little known outside academic circles. Access is strictly by written appointment, and one must sign a waiver absolving them of liability. Only then will Solomon Drake ask you to sign the visitors' book. It is an old book, dating to the eighteen-eighties and it would be enlightening to discover the names of the good, the bad, and the mad who have signed it, but Mr Drake would never permit it. Well, *almost* never: he did once make an exception for me. The legalities dealt with, Mr Drake takes a large iron key and escorts you through a small iron door into a windowless chamber. Once it was lit solely by candlelight, but early last century gas was installed, and this still serves today. No mains or battery-powered equipment is allowed inside. On entering, your attention is drawn to the iron cage in the centre of the room and the reading desk and chair within. A man may stand in that cage and touch any two of its five sides at once. The bars are about a hand's width apart and the base is cast iron. I advise thermal socks.'

Tried to lighten the moment there but not even a flicker of a smile from O. Assume I don't need to tell him magick cannot abide iron and its alloys. Editors lead frightfully dull lives, and as the depository is the nearest I get to anything perilous I like to play it up a bit.

'All said,' I continue, 'it is an appalling room, and many give up at this point. Assuming your nerve holds, you sit at the reading desk within the cage and wait while Mr Drake retrieves the requested texts from the strongroom. These he brings in copper-lined boxes and puts on the reading desk. Do not attempt to touch them.

'Then comes a little speech. The reader must not open the boxes until Mr Drake has exited and locked the door of the cage. Cotton gloves must be worn at all times when handling the books. When your hour is finished you must return the manuscripts to the boxes exactly as you found them—this will be checked—and dispose of the gloves in the waste bin. Believing you are overawed by this litany, Mr Drake attempts to reassure you by smiling. You are not reassured. Lastly, Mr Drake tugs at a rope suspended from the ceiling and you hear a bell ring in the distance. This, he assures you, will bring someone to release you from the cage.

'Now, I dare say you think this is to prevent theft, yes?'

O shrugs. I have no idea if this is in reply to my question or mere indifference. There's something odd on the ceiling above his head. Wonder if it's a spider's web catching in the light. Damned if I can see it properly and I can hardly stare at it. Desperate for a glass of water. Pork scratching's stuck in a tooth.

'Well, you are partly correct,' I tell him. 'I have been in that ghastly room three times and each I think more unpleasant than the last.

'But, back to Van Zelden. Several months after the encounter in New Amsterdam, I was reading a monograph by Organ Morgan in the King James University reading room when I noticed Van Zelden at the enquiry desk. Of course, I knew immediately what he was doing, so I hid my head behind Organ Morgan. When Mr Drake told Van Zelden he needed an appointment for the depository I thought there would be a scene; but no, he was all smiles at the desk and only the slight twitch of his head as he walked away betrayed his impatience. He has a nervous tic, have you noticed? It's only apparent when he thinks no one is looking.

'Excuse me one moment. Feeling a bit warm.'

If I don't loosen my tie, I'll gasp. Sip of whisky to ease the pipes.

'When I returned Organ Morgan to the desk I asked after Van Zelden and said I knew of his interest in MacGregor.

'Ah, indeed? Drake replied. That would explain why the gentleman asked if we held anything on magick, theosophy, and hermeneutics from MacGregor's library. I thought it unusual he should know exactly where we might keep such works.

'Of course, most embarrassing. Drake knew I'd spilled the beans, as it were. For obvious reasons the library doesn't advertise the works it holds in the Reserved Manuscript Depository. I enquired if Van Zelden had mentioned me at all. Drake raised an eyebrow in reply and asked if I wanted him to mention my name when Van Zelden returned.

'That was the very last thing I wanted. Instead, I asked Drake if he thought Van Zelden would return.

'Oh yes, he said. He'll be back. They always do.'

Really, I have to get a drink. I'm gasping. Pork scratchings have done for me.

'Sorry, you'll have to excuse me a moment. Glass of water.'

Jonathan is round at the other bar. Bunch of lads in the back room. All leathers and beards. No doubt the owners of the motorbikes outside. Red Lion draws a rough crowd at times. I try to catch Jonathan's eye.

'One moment, Nevil. Serving these gentlemen.'

I glance back at O and catch him staring at the fire. He's dressed entirely in black. Hadn't noticed that before.

'Right, Nevil, what can I get you?'

'Just a glass of tonic water. Bit dry from all this talking.'

'Quiet sort, your friend?'

'Oh, you noticed that as well. Hardly heard a blasted word he said, frankly. Still, keep our voices down. Don't want him overhearing.'

'No. We wouldn't want that.'

He gives me a wink and I give him a coin for the tonic water. I take a sip and it instantly hits the spot and I rejoin O.

'Where were we?' I ask.

O turns to face me. He has the most extraordinarily long face and frightfully dark eyes. Reminds me of an African mask I once saw. Still, mustn't let it bother me. H&D surely know what they're doing.

'Van Zelden, that's where,' found my place again. 'I can only give you my version of events, but I think you'll find

I'm perfectly reliable. I seldom pay attention to show business, but, knowing Van Zelden's interest in MacGregor I caught one of his television shows. Most disturbing. I have no sympathy for the dark arts, but, if one's expertise is Scottish literature one cannot help learning something about magick. Van Zelden's talent for psychic manipulation and divination was beyond rational explanation. He had acquired, as he put it to me in New Amsterdam, the *real thing*. It brought applause from his audience and, as I later discovered, condemnation from the Roman Catholic and Lutheran Churches. Quite right too. Whatever Van Zelden had sought in MacGregor's books, it was obvious he had found *something*. I wrote to him immediately, warning of the danger he was in, but he never replied. Then, last year, Van Zelden announced in *The Times* that he was the first practising seer in public view in over a century and the heir to Sir Tamburlaine Bryce MacGregor!'

I sit back expecting some sort of reaction from O, but it's the same enigmatic stare.

'Anyway, you can imagine what I thought of that. I had given Van Zelden what he wanted, and now he accused MacGregor, to whom I had given half a lifetime of study, of witchcraft.'

I'm getting quite cross recalling all this. Slow down and take a sip of tonic water. Don't get flustered.

'Frankly, I was furious. I learned of Van Zelden's claim a few days earlier when *The Times* contacted me in my capacity as secretary of the Sir Tamburlaine Bryce MacGregor Society. I refuted everything and cited the evidence of MacGregor's journals and twenty years of research. The reporter seemed sympathetic to my argument, but it was a charade. The published article ignored everything I said. No offence,' I leant forward. 'But in my experience journalists prefer a good story to good facts. One or two scholars dismissed Van Zelden's claims, but the majority had no opinion and a few even agreed with him.

'Obviously, I had to do something. So, I proposed a new

edition of *This Iron Race* to counter Van Zelden's lies, and Hare and Drum agreed. Which brings us here.'

Not that he's taken a blind bit of notice of where we are, and he's still not touched his pint. Still, not my coin so why let it bother me. On with the story.

'I don't know how much of this you know, so forgive me if I go over old ground. MacGregor's publisher rejected his first manuscript. Sir Sidney Beresford even threatened to burn it if MacGregor didn't remove it from their premises. I confess, I had always regarded Sir Sydney as a typical pietist—public virtue private vice, that sort of thing—but having read MacGregor's first draft, I believe he had a real fear of prosecution. Under Scottish Common Law, it was an offence to print, publish, or otherwise disseminate material liable to cause public disorder. Of course, the real objection was against politicking and religious dissent, but it included offences against public decency, and I am certain MacGregor's text would have fallen foul of the law.'

O raises an eyebrow so at least he's paying attention.

'It may surprise you, but MacGregor's original text is quite different from the familiar version. The sexual content, though unexceptional by modern standards, would alone have condemned it, and the Alban Church would have denounced the explicit practice of magick. Even had Sir Sidney and John Lucas accepted the first volume of *This Iron Race*, the Lords Advocates would not.'

He nods, which I take as agreement. There *is* something on the ceiling. Saw it move just then. Of course, could be a reflection from outside. Passing car or a chap walking by the window.

'Now, in my view, the new edition is a much better work than the familiar version; it is richer, more truthful about human emotion, and the merging of the supernatural and spiritual with the natural world is more satisfying, even for one, such as I, who disapproves of magick. In other words, what improves it today are the very attributes that condemned it in MacGregor's time.

Of course, this leaves us with a puzzle: why would anyone write a text knowing it cannot be published? Especially if one is newly married and has a growing family to support, as was MacGregor. I cannot imagine Beresford & Lucas' reaction came as a surprise to him, and for all his protestations of wishing to write with a new naturalism, he must have known it could not be published, which, when you think about it, rather militates against any notion the book had some hidden magickal purpose, don't you think?'

O shrugs. Better say again. Damned important point.

'A book only has power if it is read,' I tell him. 'Without the application of the reader's consciousness it's quite impotent. Why then would MacGregor produce a text no one would read?'

O looks doubtful.

'Of course, I mean *hardly* anyone. Sir Sidney and John Lucas must have read enough to reject it and MacGregor's wife read it in full, along with a few of his close friends, Sir Charles Palliser among them. Possibly King Charles as well, though one cannot be certain on that. And of course, the original text has been unseen for the last one hundred and fifty years!'

O leans forward and taps the cover of the new edition. I accept his point.

'Indeed, with this new edition he is *finally* getting what he wanted. Or rather, I believe this edition is as close as we shall ever get to it. I accept if it has some hidden purpose regarding magick, then I am not the one to see it. But nor am I inclined to fancy what is not there.

'I cannot say this edition is definitive. Were the university to give Zelden access to MacGregor's text he might interpret them differently, though whether he has the necessary skills is another matter. It is one thing to make an uncertain text read as you wish it to read; quite another to understand what the writer intended.'

As I say that I am painfully aware of the many times I had to trust to my own judgement on the matter.

MacGregor's text was at times impenetrable. One got the gist without knowing the precise phrasing intended. Another sip of water.

'Even so, I cannot condemn Van Zelden. In fact, I admire his abilities, even if I cannot approve how he uses them.'

Doing one's best not to sound bitter. Known too many old duffers always moaning about the latest new poet or novelist who catches the moment and outsells them by thousands. They forget they were once the darling of their publisher's eye. Though I'm not sure I was ever anyone's darling. Except for Edith. I was hers, for a year or two at the beginning. Another whisky would be welcome. Tonic water soothes the throat but does nothing for a man's spirits. Still, better not.

'Returning to the text. MacGregor knew the published text was inferior to the original, but he had hopes it would be published unexpurgated in his lifetime. Of course, that wasn't to be, and he died in 1872.'

He was only a few years older than I am. There's a sobering thought.

'Lady MacGregor offered them for publication in 1905, a year after L H Durrants' *Wives and Lovers*. No British publisher replied but there was interest from the French. Félicien Alberix wanted to translate and publish them in Paris—French literature had been progressive ever since the failed prosecution of Flaubert's *Madame Bovary*—but Lady MacGregor's death in 1907 put an end to that hope and MacGregor's literary effects were donated to King James University where they should have been perfectly safe.

Unfortunately, by the time public taste in Anglia was ready for an unexpurgated *This Iron Race*, MacGregor was out of fashion and the fair copies had gone missing in mysterious circumstances.'

O sympathises.

I have my suspicions but best keep quiet about them. There are rumours of an unpleasant mishap during the Zeppelin War when the library was short of staff. An under-librarian misfiled a reserved manuscript on the main shelves and apparently several dozen texts vanished into thin air before they realised the error. My hunch is the fair copies for *This Iron Race* were among them. There's a certain irony if they were gobbled up by a bit of misplaced magick.

The other possibility is theft, but nothing has been proven.

'Collectively, the lost fair copies for *This Iron Race* have become the Holy Grail for anyone fascinated by MacGregor's legacy. Though as Van Zelden's purchasing power rather dwarfs mine, I would prefer they remain lost than have them fall into his hands. I suspect he thinks they're in the Reserved Manuscript Depository, but I'm certain MacGregor would not have written something hazardous to his reader!'

O cracks a smile. Least I'm not boring him. I take a sip of tonic water.

'Now, as I saw it, my task was to restore MacGregor's original text but without the fair copies I turned detective, examining MacGregor's journals, correspondence with his publisher, even his source materials, where they are known; hence my three visits to the Reserved Manuscript Depository. I immersed myself in his creative world and became as much amanuensis as editor. Though of course I would never claim MacGregor was guiding me and, unlike Van Zelden, I never attempted to communicate with his ghost! It was an *entirely* academic and scholarly process.

'Where MacGregor's intentions were not obvious and I had to make a creative choice, I took care to leave a note explaining my decision. Alas, Hare & Drum decided that was too intrusive and cut them. Not a decision I approve of. In any event, I hope this is the book MacGregor intended it to be. Others can judge whether I succeeded.'

'Now, why did I choose to restore *This Iron Race*? A good question, no?'

It would be if he asked it. Rum sort of interview where one chap does all the talking.

'The text rejected by Beresford and Lucas gained an unwonted reputation as a panegyric for magick, which is what Van Zelden picked up on. Supposedly, it's filled with formulae for summoning demons, angels, and ghosts! Well, I promise you I haven't seen any. It is simply a novel and, in my estimation, a damn good one. I hope the new edition proves popular and in due course the rest of the series will follow.'

He seems content. Hard to tell with that face. Assume I'll have a chance to look at the proofs.

'Van Zelden has put me to a great deal of trouble, but truly I pity him. Mr Drake has shown me the visitors' book for the Reserved Manuscript Depository. I said the precautions are to prevent theft, but the danger is to the reader, not the books. Van Zelden made seventeen visits in eight months. Believe me, no one could do that and remain untouched by what is in those books. He is, I'm afraid, past saving. But what I may save is MacGregor's reputation as Scotland's greatest writer, and to do so I must reclaim him from Hendryk van Zelden.

'Now. I believe that concludes matters. Are we agreed?'

He nods.

'Excellent. Would you like your book signed? Of course: what name shall I give?'

At last!

'May I borrow your pen? Thank you. *For O'Brien. Kind regards, Nevil W.*'

Hendryk van Zelden
Manhattan

'A right of reply, I like it. But listen, I don't need to protect my reputation from Nevil Warbrook, oké. Good. This is the thirty-fifth floor of the Adirondack Building. See most of the city from here. Come to the window; this might interest you.

'The street with the trolley line. Come up from the intersection. Those brownstones on the right. One in the middle is the Koningin Hotel.

'Oh, I wouldn't say it *began* there. It began when I was ten or eleven. But, sure, it was a stepping stone.

'I guess you don't know so much about me, but I give much the same story on chat shows. There's nothing new here. Like I said, I was ten, maybe eleven. I figure it's no different for guys, magickally speaking. If it wants you, it'll call around the time your balls drop and girls get interesting. Hormones trigger something in the parahippocampal gyrus. And you need a dead twin.

'Don't know about you, but I try not to think about it. If I ever figure out how it all works, I'd worry about losing it. Anyway, it starts with crazy dreams and seeing things that aren't there. Sometimes I got lost in places I knew really well. One time I was three hours late getting home from school because every street seemed to turn back on itself. My dad whacked my ass when I got home. I didn't tell him what had really happening.

'We were a church-going family. The Dutch have a reputation as liberal dopeheads, but that's only in the city and really only in Amsterdam. Out in the provinces it's pretty strait-laced. Had I told my parents about the dreams and getting lost I'd have got a visit from the priest and the bell, book, and candle treatment. That wasn't the first or last time I got my ass whacked. Guess I can identify with Captain Wolfe; my life could have gone the same way. But at fifteen I ran away from home and kept running till I landed at a commune in the Ardennes Forest. They had a cunning man, and he took care of me for a couple of years, then he got me a place at the Heidelberg Fellowship.

'That should have set me up, but there's no trade in magick. It was dying in MacGregor's time and now the fellowships only teach you how to control the gift, not how to act on it. Such a waste.

'So, after a couple of years at Heidelberg I got into stage magic. I was good at it. Great at it. Hell, I got rich and famous, but it wasn't me. Then, bored on a flight one time, I picked up MacGregor's *Willoughby Chaste* and it was like, wow! This dead guy knew what I was feeling.

'So, I read everything he wrote and then I started on everything written about him. I knew enough about magick to know he was drawing on it in some way, either directly, or he had a source. Sure, maybe one of the booth-scryers helped with some of it, but his knowledge had depth and that couldn't have come from an old fortune-teller. Trust me.

'Then Crabtree's book told me about MacGregor's library but when I checked with King James University none of the books I needed were in the catalogue. Where were they?

'So, Warbrook is secretary of the MacGregor Society. I mailed him, politely. No reply. I mailed again, still no reply. That pissed me off. Anyone can give a denial, but to ignore someone? So, I mailed again, but a little less polite. That got an answer, of sorts: he denied MacGregor had anything to do with magick, denied the existence of the books and said if I mailed again, he'd report me for harassment.

'So, when I read he was signing books over here I went for the direct approach. Sure, I lied to him. I'd read pretty much everything by MacGregor, even his history of The Merchant Adventurers Company. I played dumb to appeal to his vanity. But hey, he lied to you. Sure, the Koningin was the first place we met but he knew who I was. He was economical with the truth. That's his job, dammit. An editor shapes the text to tell whatever story he wants, even if he's not conscious of it.

'I'm not proud of what I did, embarrassing him like that, but he told me what I needed to know.

'What do you reckon of him?

'Doesn't surprise me, he enjoys a drink. Reckon it doesn't like him so much. Oh, yeah, that business at the King James Library. I saw him trying to hide behind a book. But ask him this: if he's worried for my sanity, why didn't he warn me off the Reserved Manuscript Depository?

'Seventeen times? Wow. Do I sound crazy? Oké, depends what you mean by crazy. It's no big deal, but I've been bipolar since I was fifteen. Guess it's the 'celebrity' illness. We use the 'highs' to conquer the audience and hide during the lows. Some use coke; others are born with a buzz. I was the latter.

'Being thought a little crazy is no bad thing in my line, but, yeah, I thought of suing him for libel. I didn't because even though Warbrook's useless he's helped put MacGregor out there again. If I bankrupt him, and he is not a wealthy man, there'll be no more new volumes of *This Iron Race*. He's the wrong man to do it, but he's the one making it happen, and I guess a big part of me is envious as hell.

'Anyway, he knows what he's doing at a *technical* level, but he has no sympathy with the text. I'm quoted in the *New Amsterdam Post*. Let's see: *We cannot blame the editor if Nevil Warbrook's restoration of Sir Tamburlaine's great work ultimately disappoints. One does not send a blind man to count the stars.* That's taken out of context, by the way, but Warbrook is out of his depth.

'A mixed metaphor. Guess I'll never be a writer. Lucky for me, we shape reality, not its retelling. Or to be exact, we shape perception. But perception is reality for most people and maybe we all need a little illusion. I try to challenge what people think. The motivation isn't the fame and money.

'Sure, this is a great penthouse, but it's rented. I've got a month-long run at *Le Moulin* on L'Avenue Cinquième. It's not like I live here.

'Unlike Warbrook I really do have sympathy with the

text, but I'm no editor and I don't have the time and patience to wade through four different versions of the same line and figure out which was closest to MacGregor's intent. And no, I'm not summoning his ghost. That was a joke. Even if I could, why would he play ball? I think the dead have better things to do. Besides, in volume two MacGregor warns about calling on the dead. So, yeah, Warbrook isn't the right man, but neither am I.

'He's still working off MacGregor's first drafts? Hasn't found the fair copies?

'Figures. Has anyone scried for them? I'd say it's more than likely someone has tried; whether it can be done is another matter.

'You serious? Warbrook and I work together? Have to be one hell of a rapprochement. Besides, I'm touring for the next six months and it's not like I can make time. No, really, I can't. That thing Jung said: *magick does not exist, unless we make it so*; get it? It's all in the mind. Stonehenge never moved, trust me.

'Oké, well I'm happy you were impressed. Been great talking but I got to be elsewhere. Let me have your card.

'Thanks. "*O'Brien.*" Is that Eirish?

'Apologies. I didn't recognise the accent. You know the King James University?

'Really? So, all three of us are in Drake's book. You stay in touch, Mr O'Brien. I'll show you out.

Appendix 1
The critical reception of volume one, as recorded in the collections of King James University

Stretching the definition of the word, one might describe the critical reception to volume one as 'mixed', but in truth most reviews were negative and where it was not negative response was muted. Most critics took pains to distinguish between the work, which they did not like, and MacGregor who still commanded respect as the author of *Edmund Pevensie* and remained a favourite of the king. However, a number speculated whether MacGregor had been lastingly deranged by his grief for Lady Madeleine and if it would be preferable for his long silence to continue. Hardly any thought to consider the first volume of *This Iron Race* in the light of 'Lays of Brigadoon', MacGregor's first published work following the death of Lady Madeleine. Grantley Borset of *The Daily Sketch* was one of the few to do so:

> Some three years ago when I reviewed 'Lays of Brigadoon' I wrote that despite its superficial charm there lurked within the township of Brigadoon a baleful presence quite at odds with Christian piety. When word of this new work, a novel, came to our notice one hoped the charm would remain and the world of magick exposed in Brigadoon would return to the ancient fastness where it belongs. Alas, with publication of the first volume of *This Iron Race* what was charm is now grimness and despair and magick is loosed upon the present in all its antique awfulness.

Borset's complaint lay against MacGregor's intentions, rather than his execution, and he was not the only one to charge MacGregor with writing something improper. *The Disseminator*, the monthly journal of The Society for the Dissemination of Useful Knowledge was especially damning:

> We cannot recommend the book in any degree. Though it undoubtedly contains a great deal of knowledge, it is of an archaic and unuseful nature, except when it touches on the practical aspects of highland living. Even then, the portrayal of the supernatural is bound to perturb all but the least sensate reader. We had hoped with publication of this novel the author of *Edmund Pevensie* would be returned to us, but alas, it is yet further evidence of his unsettled sensibilities.

Gilbert Morrell of *The Highland Home Companion,* a weekly magazine published in Elgin, was more charitable:

> Many in rural districts mourn the loss of the old ways and perhaps it is they for whom Sir Tamburlaine writes in this curious lament for bygone times. However, we must observe that those who mourn the old ways are oftentimes the poorest and least literate of people and we cannot think it altogether wise to write a novel for those who cannot or will not read.

Which might appear unenthusiastic but did address problem that those most attuned to the old ways—and most likely to feel their abandonment—were among the most impoverished and neglected portion of the populace. Alas, Mr Morrell appears to have missed MacGregor's intention of bringing their plight to the notice of those able to address their condition.

The *Alban Church Recorder* was never likely to approve the work, but even so, its review was unusually hostile:

> We do not commend this work. It is not the product of a Christian mind and nor should any Christian stain their conscience by reading

it. That its author was recently feted in all of
Alba is neither here nor there and rather than
read his book we advise prayer for his soul.

The Engineer, a periodical devoted, as the name suggests, to mechanical and civil engineering, did not usually review novels but made an exception for the first volume of *This Iron Race*:

> As the late Earl of Rochester discovered when his foxhounds strayed into the path of the Dover Express, progress shall not be obstructed by traditional pursuits. Where the good earl wished only to pursue his fox, Sir Tamburlaine MacGregor's novel aspires to something more particular, viz, the retention of the Old Ways of sibyls and soothsayers to whom the railway is, if by other means, as inimical as it proved to the earl and his hounds.
>
> Progress is, as the student of history well knows, inevitable, and 'praise to it' say us and all who wish for the improvement of mankind. Sir Tamburlaine, however, cautions otherwise and writes: "[for] iron—and you cannot have steam without it—is the ancient enemy of magick and even as the rail burrows our hills and leaps our valleys, we must consider the ill effect its irons have upon those granted with what the French call clairvoyance, [and] the Scots call clearsight."
>
> The ill effect is undeniable but, in your reviewer's opinion, it is a necessary price for the betterment of national prosperity and no different in kind from the temporary upset to age-long custom occasioned by the drainage of the fens and enclosure of common lands which deprived a few of their livelihood but brought the populace greater quantity of produce at

lower cost.

    Perhaps Sir Tamburlaine's work will find an audience among the nostalgists, but one cannot see a work so backward-looking faring well in these times. One only hopes Sir Tamburlaine's loss will be less severe than that which befell the Earl of Rochester who, it will be recalled, paid with his head.

The incident described occurred on November 21 in 1858 when the earl attempted to hold up the express near Ashford to allow his hounds to flush out a fox. The earl was decapitated and two of his companions died of their injuries, while four horses and some sixteen hounds perished or had to be destroyed. The fox, it was reported, escaped.

The unusual delay between announcement of the novel in the *Edenborough Review* and its publication had led to a good deal of curiosity and rumours of disagreement between MacGregor and his publisher had piqued the interest of an anonymous correspondent to *The Speculator*, the quarterly journal of the Edenborough Speculative Society.

Under the nom de plume of 'Vesuvius' he wrote:

> If this strange, misshapen work is what Beresford & Lucas has seen fit to print the reader may wonder at the peculiarity of the manuscript they spurned. She may allow for some misshaping to occur during the rewriting of the text—which is the cause of the delay in publication—but not that Sir Tamburlaine, who is, or perhaps we must say 'was', among the most prolific and competent and lauded writers of our time, should submit a text so deficient in his publisher's estimation. None of what left the work unpublishable concerns MacGregor's craft, for he remains a fine writer whose ear for a well-turned phrase and ability

> to draw recognisable characters is undimmed. Rather, we very much fear the fault lies in the content which would have brought attention from the Lords Advocates and scandal upon author and publisher.
>
> We shall draw a veil over MacGregor's purpose in writing a work so improper he surely knew it could not see publication by any reputable publishing house, and regret that while removing the scandalous material the patient died on the surgeon's table.

Some of the phrasing may suggest 'Vesuvius' had read or was at least familiar with the work prior to MacGregor's revisions but I suspect he was attempting to curry favour with the reader by alluding to knowledge he was not privy to. The only copies of the original text in existence at the time were MacGregor's first draft and the fair copy seen by his publishers. The publishers were most unlikely to have shown MacGregor's text to anyone—if you recall, Sir Sidney demanded its removal from their offices—and I cannot think it likely MacGregor would have lent either text to a critic. The identity of 'Vesuvius' is unknown, but MacGregor had shown the work to a number of close friends, which included members of the Edenborough Speculative Society.

None of MacGregor's previous works had received such damning reviews and the effect on sales, particularly to the circulating libraries, was soon felt. MacGregor responded by dashing off a number of essays and articles which were published as *Rough Harbour: Observations of Highland Life* on October 30, 1864. This received favourable reviews and went some way to allaying his publisher's concerns and adding to his income. Then in early 1865 Beresford & Lucas brought out a new edition of *Edmund Pevensie* which sold well, followed in 1866 by *The Saxon Trilogy* to mark the eight-hundredth anniversary of the ascension of King Harold II.

With MacGregor's finances reasonably secure, Beresford

& Lucas published volumes two and three to complete *Acts of the Servant* in 1865 and January 1866, while MacGregor composed *Works of the Master*, which would become the fourth book of *This Iron Race*.

Appendix 2
Commentaries on the text

Front Matter
Epigrams
Hesiod was a Greek farmer and poet active between 750 and 650 B.C. and this line comes from his most famous work, *Works and Days*. This is chiefly a tract on agricultural practice but it was also a critique on Greek society and the line refers to Hesiod's contemporaries, who he believed were depraved and corrupt, while conceding, "even these shall have some good mingled with their evils" (Hesiod, *Works And Days*, translated by Hugh G. Evelyn-White, 1914). Preceding the line Hesiod described earlier races of men passing through ages of gold, silver, bronze (or brazen), and of heroes, each being less noble than the former. MacGregor appropriates Hesiod to comment on the Industrial Revolution and its evil effects on the use and prestige of magick.

Leonardo da Vinci needs no introduction from me. The line comes from *Treatise on Painting*, originally published in Italian in 1651. This was not translated into English until 1956 (A P McMahon, Pub. Biblioteca Apostolica Vaticana) and it is likely, though by no means certain, that MacGregor took the line from a German edition by Archelaus Winter, (Pub. Munich, 1834) and provided his own translation. The meaning of the line is ambiguous. It may refer to the relationship between an artist and his assistant, for not all artists of da Vinci's time, and since, were wholly responsible for every brushstroke but would employ lesser artists to add the backgrounds and secondary figures once they had completed the main subject of the work. Alternatively, and I owe this interpretation to Dr Claude Crabtree's *The Wizard of the North* (King James University Press, 1930), master and servant may be one and the same for what we are master of we also serve.

The chief concern of this novel is magick
This line comes from a much longer piece by MacGregor which appeared in the Edenborough Review shortly before publication of volume one. Intended as a *mise en scène* to set the context for the reader, MacGregor later decided *This Iron Race* should stand on its own, save for this single, self-explanatory line.

Prologue the First

The candlesnatcher

With the obsolescence of the candle as an everyday object, 'candlesnatcher' has lately dropped from usage. Essentially, it is a lost spirit, or revenant, suspended between this world and the next, although there are numerous accounts of faerie sprites pretending to be revenants in order to make mischief, such as Peggy Pickwick whose theft of a candle is blamed for the Great Fire of Lunden.

The Catholic Church long maintained that the primary cause of suspension of the human spirit is a failure to baptise children, citing the childlike behaviour of Candlesnatchers as proof; however, this is contradicted by the works of Pliny the Elder and Aristotle which describe similar phenomena long before the advent of Christianity. Today, most authorities agree the cause of spiritual 'suspension' remains unknown.

Although uncanny, candlesnatchers are harmless and are usually discouraged with an unkind word or, on the rare occasion they prove persistent, with a show of iron or steel whose magnetic properties are anathema to all forms of magick. The majority are ephemeral, although folklore suggests those with a permanent home near water can survive for many decades, albeit a number of these may be the elemental spirits which habitually frequent watercourses. Despite this partiality for water, candlesnatchers are, like all magickal phenomena, unable to cross *running* water owing to the etheric field created by the current.

Much of this is necessary to understand the candlesnatcher's purpose in MacGregor's narrative. The most obvious is it immediately introduces the supernatural, for, as MacGregor informed us, "The chief concern of this novel is magick."

The less obvious purpose is to illustrate an aspect of Captain Wolfe's character. A candlesnatcher is an interstitial phenomenon and trapped in a permanent state of unbelonging, as is Captain Wolfe whose clearsight prevents him being the son his father wished and the heroic officer he wishes to be. In essence, Captain Wolfe's reaction to the candlesnatcher mirrors the loathing in which he holds himself.

A dark and foggy night

MacGregor is borrowing a device from the meteorological school of Gothic novel popular in the eighteenth and early nineteenth century. Popularised (and mocked) as 'dark and stormies', these sensationalist novels sought to terrorise the reader with howling gales, blizzards, tempestuous seas, vertiginous heights, and icy wastes, all acting in opposition to a lonely traveller (or sometimes a body of mariners or travellers) at the mercy of the elements. Essentially, dark and stormies were the novelist's response to the poet's expression of the sublime but where the poet sought to create a sense of metaphysical wonder the purpose of 'dark and stormies' was more commercial in aim: put simply, excitation of the reader's fears sold books.

In 'dark and stormies' the external scene often mirrors the inner nature of the character, and this is the aspect of the genre MacGregor draws on. Captain Wolfe has turned away from his true vocation (the embrace of his gift) but in the fog, missing the familiar landmarks of duty and position (signified by the tower), he encounters the candlesnatcher, then hears the death cry of Prince William's spirit, and ultimately reveals his secret to Queen Charlotte and tacitly acknowledges it to Colonel Howe. It is an extraordinary run of misfortune and the close of the chapter suggests fate has not finished with Captain Wolfe.

The Tower & the 'old men'
The Tower is, from Captain Wolfe's perspective, everything he is not. The "cold certainty" of its stonework represents endurance, tradition, and material reality, contrasted with his transient moods, transgressive nature, and fluxal sensitivities. Yet his perspective is false for the faux-medieval facade of the Tower of Winchester was an attempt to erase Anglia's six hundred years under Danish rule by creating a past that never existed.

Wolfe's reliance on his material surroundings is emphasised several times in the chapter. First when he reaches out to the wall of St Alfred's Chapel, again when he beats his hand against the parapet to focus his thoughts, and lastly when he navigates from the wall to the royal apartments by way of the drainage channel and its sump. Each time he resorts to the tower's physicality rather than drawing on his innate abilities. Only when he relinquishes control and allows the "North Star" to guide him, is he able to provide true service to those he is committed to protect.

The "old men" of the tower are equally what Wolfe is not and cannot be. In this chapter, Warder Thomas and Warder Jones are foremost of the "old men". Comfortable in his skin and proud of his accomplishments, Warder Thomas's loose remark concerning sewage in the river brings out the martinet in Wolfe and Warder Jones's (admittedly serious) lapse of duty leads Wolfe to issue a charge against him. In effect, Wolfe's zealousness is a reaction to his inability to impose discipline on himself, illustrated by his 'reading' the writing woven through A'Guirre's "guardian".

Iron & steel
After magick, the second theme MacGregor introduces in the first prologue is the danger of iron to those with clearsight. His main concern was the use of iron and steel in industry, but here we see it in a military capacity: specifically at sword-point.

Sensitivity to iron and steel varies considerably among those with Grace, both from person to person and Individually. MacGregor references this when Wolfe rests his hand on the door strapping of the guard post on St Catherine's Tower. Research has shown an individual's sensitivity to iron is proportionate to their awareness of psychic activity, much in the way we most feel the cold when unwell.

We will discuss the scientific theory for the effect iron has on the gifted in a text note for chapter five. For the moment, simply note that MacGregor has introduced two of his major themes.

"Cursed to hear things no man ought"
Captain Wolfe's admission invites us to question what it is he heard. Warder Jones hears nothing and nor, apparently, do the King's Men guarding the royal apartments, and ultimately the queen's reaction to Wolfe's claim to have heard a cry from the tower walls tells us there was no *audible* cry, at which point Wolfe admits he is "cursed to hear things no man ought."

In popular belief, men, women and children cry for their mother at the point of death; this is especially so when it comes unannounced or is preceded by terror and the individual is unable to make their peace with death. Experimentation has shown that animals release a spike of auric energy at the moment of death and spectral analysis of its wave form reveals a (perhaps superficial) resemblance to audible sound and it is assumed this spike is what psychics can detect.

Professor Dyson Higgins of Dublin University controversially proposed some years ago that this release of auric energy is a signal directed at the geotemporal point where a person was born and thereby (as Professor Higgins clumsily phrases it), "became individuated from the mother's energy nexus". However, cosmologists argue the Higgins' Proposal cannot be reconciled with Universal Expansion (the universe is literally bigger at both the macro and micro level at a person's death than it was at their birth), and it is not widely supported. Many paraphysicists, most notably Vitas Salazar and Oliver Søndergaard, contend the release of auric energy is a trans-dimensional signal to summon the person's soul from the Far Country (where all souls are said to dwell) so it may guide the deceased's spirit to the land of the dead.

My thanks to the paraphysicist Professor Hans Frum of Israel College, Oxford, for his kind assistance with compiling the above.

Chapter One

The lamb

Apart from providing useful activity for MacGregor's hero (he would have objected to describing Bheathain thus, but it is useful shorthand for the principal character) the lost lamb is a metaphor for Bheathain's circumstances, as revealed in an authorial aside:

> Only an amber touchpiece around his neck, his tobacco and tinderbox, along with the strand of hemp and the iron for the tackits in the soles of his worn-out shoes came from off-island.
>
> And half of himself, though he did not know it.

Thus, we know what Bheathain does not: he is not wholly a native of the island. What his true origin might be is hinted at in the scene with Tammas M'Neis, but the key point is Bheathain is not who he supposes himself to be.

'Orphaned Heroes' appear in many mythologies from the Greek, Theseus, to Romulus and Remus of Rome, and in the Hebrew account of Moses. Often, the Orphaned Hero is not truly orphaned but is lost or abandoned or disinherited or banished by his or (rarely) her parents.

In Arthurian legend Arthur is sired by Uther Pendragon on Igraine, the widow of King Mark of Cornwall, their liaison having been arranged by Merlin. As part of Merlin's bargain with Uther, the newborn Arthur is taken away and raised in ignorance of his birthright. Years pass: Uther grows old, and Arthur grows into a young man. Then, all changes: Uther dies, and Arthur enters Camelot, proves his inheritance by drawing the sword from the stone, and is revealed by Merlin as the son of Uther.

Arthur is the orphaned hero with a happy ending. Much less happy is the tale of Oedipus, son of King Laius and Queen Jocasta of Thebes. Learning of a prophecy that his son will grow up to kill him, Laius binds the newborn Oedipus hand and foot and abandons him on a mountain to die. He is discovered by shepherds and eventually adopted by King Polybus and Queen Merope of Corinth who raise him as their own. However, fate cannot be thwarted and learning of the prophecy and fearing he is to kill his father, who he believes is King Polybus, Oedipus leaves Corinth for Thebes. There he kills King Laius in combat and to compound matters marries his widowed mother.

We must thank Hugo Ouellet of *L'Académie de les Contes des Fées en Français* for bringing your editor's attention to what may be the strangest variant of the orphaned hero motif: the medieval French tale, Knight of the Swan, later adapted for the opera 'Lohengrin' by Richard Wagner. In Knight of the Swan a lord discovers a swan maiden or fairy in an enchanted forest and marries her. She bears him six sons and a daughter, each born with a golden chain about their neck, but her wicked mother-in-law steals the children away and replaces them with dogs. The lord blames his wife for their disappearance and punishes her, at which point the boys' chains fall away and they are transformed into swans. Eventually, their sister, who alone retained human form, exposes the mother-in-law, the swan maiden is redeemed, and the boys return to human form, save one whose chain was melted down. Trapped in swan-form, he draws the boat of the Swan Knight tasked with rescuing damsels in distress.

Lying in the mysterious zone between myth and fiction are fairy tales where the orphaned, abandoned, and lost, appear more frequently than their parented fellows, reflecting a time when bereavement from plague, famine, and violent death was commonplace. Among the famous names are Cinderella, Rapunzel, Hansel and Gretel, and Snow White, each respectively orphaned, stolen, abandoned, and sentenced to death by a wicked stepmother. Curiously, fairy tales ignore stepfathers who are surely just as numerous and potentially malevolent.

By MacGregor's time the orphaned hero was a popular literary trope from romantic poetry like 'Little Orphan Nell' by Gilbert Worthy to the penny dreadfuls sold by newsstands at railway stations. Among the latter is one of your editor's favourites, Caroline Ramsden's *Miss Wetherby Expects*. In summary: Jane Wetherby grows up believing her parents are the Reverend and Mrs Wetherby in the Suffolk village of Little Grebe. On her twenty-first, when she comes of age, she learns Mrs Wetherby is in fact her nurse and her real mother, Ophelia, the Reverend's first wife, is locked up in the belfry where she has been confined ever since the birth of the bastard consequence of her affair with Spurge, the undergardener. This child, named Peter Anmery and raised in Owen Grubb's brutal orphanage, is now apprenticed to the pharmacist in Great Grebe where Jane buys her father's indigestion powders. On meeting, Peter and Jane are instantly smitten, believing each is the other's soulmate and wholly unaware they are half-siblings. A secret courtship follows until Peter promises to call on Jane's father to ask her hand in marriage. At the novel's climax, Spurge, still in love with Ophelia and returned from the Antipodes where he has made his fortune in sheep farming, discovers Ophelia's fate and returns to Little Grebe to rescue her. Alas, she has been driven mad by the ringing of the church bells and attacks Spurge, overturning a lantern and setting fire to the belfry at the very moment Peter Anmery, who is of course unaware he is their son, calls on the rectory. Hearing the cries from the church tower, he braves the flames to rescue Spurge but on attempting to save Ophelia, she clasps him to her breast as the belfry floor gives way. She dies instantly while Peter Anmary lives long enough to learn Spurge is his father and Ophelia his mother and his beloved Jane his half-sister, before perishing from the effects of the fall and, one always imagines, excessive plot revelations.

Spurge then confronts the Reverend Wetherby who confesses all. Jane is distraught at their deception and at the death of her beloved Peter and makes a speech which so impresses Spurge he offers her the fortune he had intended sharing with Ophelia and his son. Freed of her deceiving father and stepmother, Jane founds the Little Grebe School for Lost Children and opens a Haberdashers shop for her own employment.

Miss Wetherby Expects always has your editor laughing uproariously at all the wrong moments and you will be relieved to know MacGregor's plot bears no resemblance to it, though it demonstrates MacGregor's readers would have been familiar with the motif of the orphaned hero.

Gaelic
I should like to thank Dr Domnhall Iain MacDomnhallach of Oxford University for his observations on MacGregor's use of Gaelic and assistance transcribing the text.

MacGregor had employed Gaelic in a few of his earlier novels, but never so extensively as in the first volume of *This Iron Race*. When Sir Sidney Beresford objected, arguing it would discourage readers, MacGregor replied with this observation:

> Gaelic is the natural language of a Skyeman, yet you need not fear I expect knowledge of the Gaelic tongue to appreciate the work. On occasion when there is need for full comprehension of the dialogue, I shall present it in a form more helpful to ordinary understanding. In this scene, however, there is no such need for Bheathain is saying nothing of weight or consequence, but mere words of advice addressed to himself, and encouragement addressed to the lamb. Accordingly, I allow him to speak in his native language without translation. If the reader regards it as a dumb show, or a French mime, they will have understood sufficient for the narrative.

Thus, while none of the Gaelic dialogue is essential to understanding MacGregor's narrative, it serves to embed the story in its location. This explanation satisfied Sir Sidney but out of concern for the modern reader this edition includes explanatory notes where appropriate.

Castration complex
As noted previously, the published text omits all references to the castration of lambs. Although not a major loss, it removed an

explicit reference to the motif of the maimed hero/heroine, albeit, we are primarily concerned with psychological, rather than physical, maiming. However, to explore the motif further would bring premature revelations unwelcome to any unfamiliar with the text; therefore, we will return to the maimed hero later.

MacGregor referred to the castration of lambs in a letter to his friend, Charles Palliser, written during his stay on the Isle of Skye in the fall of 1861. Though intended to amuse, it reveals something of MacGregor's creative process as he draws out deeper meanings from the everyday:

> We are lately prone to seeing in nature all that is good and moral and in man all that is unfit and immoral, as though nature was the true work of God and man, having strayed from Eden, is corrupted. We cite the habit of a male lamb left to its own devices and 'intact', which is to say with the 'devices' it was born with, of attempting to mate with its mother even before she has weaned it as proving man corrupts all he touches (for man has long meddled in the breeding of sheep) and not as proof of nature's limitations as a moral guide. The canny farmer, not wishing the lamb to breed with its mam—offspring thus made are invariably weak and sickly—while wanting it to drink of mother's milk for as long as possible so it may grow plump, nips, or castrates those males he does not intend to breed from. Whether lambs thus treated bleat at a higher pitch than their intact brethren, as do the Italian castrati, I leave for the musically minded to discover.

King James University. Palliser Archive: box vi, 1861.

Bheathain's world

The majority of chapter one presents us with Bheathain's Ordinary World prior to any initiatory event. It is true the loss of his touchpiece, and the appearance of the white stag prepare the reader for the chapter's remarkable conclusion, but the lost lamb, The Staffin, and Bheathain's relationship with Tammas and his grandfather shows his life before it changes. We do not yet know what manner of change it will be, but we understand Bheathain's character and circumstances, and those from whom he will draw his allies, mentors, and enemies.

While the text references the supernatural throughout, the depiction of Skye and its people is naturalistic. Life along much of Scotland's north west seaboard after the collapse of the kelp trade was as harsh and disagreeable as anything experienced in the tenements of Glasgow but offered considerably fewer trades and opportunities whereby a man might improve himself.

For much of the eighteenth and early nineteenth centuries the English-speaking lowlanders who dominated parliament in Holyrood regarded the Scottish Gaels as an insurrectionist threat. However, according to Hamlet Mountstone's *A Long History of The Gael*, (Dunsany, 1898) the threat was always exaggerated and would be eliminated, "not by prohibition of custom and the Gaelic language, but by the gentrification of the once-mighty chieftains and the maggoting of land previously held in common by the black-faced sheep." (ibid.) Conditions for the Scottish Gaels only became a matter of public and ecclesiastic concern during the famines of the 1840s; however, while this brought charity it did not change policy, which continued to focus on depopulating the Highlands.

Quite rightly, many critics of *This Iron Race* have devoted much time to analysing MacGregor's epigraph, stating "The chief concern of this novel is magick: its place and purpose in the modern world." However, all focus on MacGregor's 'magick' and ignore his portrayal of "the modern world" as it existed in the 1860s. This is a sad omission, for it is a remarkably honest depiction. This is not the 'och aye the noo', oat-caked, kilted and sporranned, bonny Scotland popularised by W F Shakeshaft in *The Highlands For Me*, (Samuel Merryman, 1842) or even as portrayed in several of MacGregor's early *Romance* novels, but rather life as it was lived in some of the harshest lands in the Britannic Isles.

Such conditions are, blessedly, no more but their flavour is preserved at the Museum of Island Life, at Kilmuir on the Isle of Skye.

Representation of the human soul
The claim that the soul exists outside the body and manifests (though not exclusively) at the point of death is, of course, at odds with the teachings of the Abrahamic religions. However, belief in an external soul appears to have been widespread in ancient times and there are many references in folklore to a person's soul being placed in safekeeping external to the body. The same belief in an external soul also appears, albeit in fragments, in the teaching of certain Far-Eastern faiths, but by far the largest body of evidence for an external soul comes from accounts of near-death experiences.

Common to almost all such experiences, a person's soul appears in animal form to escort the spirit to the afterlife. Or rather, in the case of near-death experiences, to deny them passage because it is not yet their time. Only rarely, usually to herald great change or conflict, does the soul manifest outside of a near-death experience.

Bheathain's soul appears as a stag. It is a common animal in the Scottish Highlands, but that is not the case with all soul forms and parapsychologists have spent much effort theorising why certain animals occur much more frequently than others and why some are rarely, if ever found.

The more harebrained parapsychologists (the pun cannot be resisted) such as Dr Lennart Östberg of Stockholm University, have argued for an astrological connection, but while many soul forms appear among the constellations, notably the antelope, whale, goat, bear and lion, many do not, and a great number of the constellations are not named after animals at all. Moreover, as detractors of Dr Östberg's theory point out, astrology is a subjective discipline, and one cannot attempt to lever together two non-rational beliefs in order to create something more than the sum of their parts.

The Slovakian parapsychologist and ardent feminist, Professor Zukana Molnár, is much more reliable. She has drawn on the fossil record to show a correlation between the fauna of the late Palaeolithic and Mesolithic periods and typical soul forms. This, Professor Molnár argues, explains why domesticated animals, such as the dog, never occur as soul forms and why extinct animals, like the mammoth, do. She then proposes that this is evidence of a race memory dating from the earliest development of mankind's spiritual beliefs (universally assumed to be animist in nature) and connected to the Jungian concepts of Symbolism and Archetypes.

This is far too complex to elaborate further, but it is sufficient for the reader to understand that a northern European is as likely to have the soul form of a mammoth as a weasel, whereas a native Latin-American might have the soul form of a macaw or giant sloth.

Professor Molnár's *The Perception of the Ancients* (Príroda, Bratislava, 2009) examines the depiction of human-animal hybrids, such as mermen, centaurs, minotaurs, and sphinxes, in the literature of the ancient world and concludes they are allegories of our dualistic nature, being half human and half beast, rather than descriptions of actual species. The acceptance of the dual nature of humans was, she argues, common to all beliefs until the advent of agriculture when we began to think of ourselves as distinct from all other species and concomitant with this distinction humans could only acknowledge their innate animal desires as sinful.

This, Professor Molnár argues, is the true nature of The Fall described in the Book of Genesis and she claims in *Sexual Awakening: Freeing the Beast Within* (Príroda, Bratislava, 2014) that the denial of our animal nature is the cause of almost every modern psychosis. The book created a scandal among parapsychologists and when the mainstream media picked up on the story, they portrayed her as a sexual degenerate with the morals of an alley cat.

Your editor, when an undergraduate at Israel College, Oxford, perhaps unwisely at the end of an evening in the Lamb and Flag, had his soul 'read' by a female student of whom he was somewhat enamoured and, after much hand waving, she pronounced his soul was a toad. Having babbled something about her confusing the Amphibia and perhaps he might be a frog—alluding to the fairy tale—she pronounced him, which is to say, me, too ugly to be a frog. The humiliations we suffer for love and its pretenders.

Although outside the remit of his task, your editor directs the interested reader to a piece in the winter 2012 issue of *The Silver Trowel* (Prisma Press, Woking) discussing the differing interpretations by archaeologists and archaeoparapsychologists of the prehistoric cave paintings at Altamira in Spain and Lascaux in France and, increasingly, all animal representation in prehistoric art. Do such scenes illustrate, as archaeologists argue, hunting rituals? Or, as proposed by archaeoparapsychologists, the ascension of the human spirit accompanied by the soul? The article in *The Silver Trowel* makes no definitive answer but provides an overview of the evidence.

In Scottish folklore and that from Wales, Cornwall, Eireland, Mannin, and Basse-Bretagne, accounts of the soul guiding the deceased's spirit to the afterlife are widespread. In most tales, the soul travels by "green lanes", or pathways to an afterlife named variously in Celtic lore as the Hesperides, Tir Na Og, Land O' Leel, or the Summer Country. Often the green lane is described as sunlight reflected on the sea, in others it is a green ray seen at sunset, in yet more it is a shooting star or the aurora borealis.

Speaking as a practising Christian, your editor suggests the precise whereabouts and form taken by our soul is less important than listening to its demands, rather than demanding its tolerance of our indulgences. One only regrets not understanding this many years ago when one might have proved a more constant father to one's son.

Prologue the Second
Geography or psychogeography?
St Catherine's Hill lies on the edge of chalk downland overlooking the city of Winchester and makes, as your editor can vouch, a pleasant afternoon's stroll. However, at no point in or about its summit can one stand above a sheer drop and consider suicide.

MacGregor's description does not fit the facts, but it is not a careless error. He visited Winchester several times, often accompanying King Charles in his capacity as Master of The King's Revels and if he had not climbed St Catherine's Hill, he could not have avoided seeing it as it dominates the vicinity of the Tower.

Why then is MacGregor describing a landscape that is not there?

Dr Claude Crabtree in *The Wizard of the North* (King James University Press, 1930) argued the description accords equally well with the edge of a quarry as a natural cliff. Chalk, he points out, is quarried to make lime mortar and the growing city of Winchester would have need of lime mortar. However, as no quarry has ever existed on St Catherine's Hill and MacGregor never refers to a quarry on St Catherine's Hill, Dr Crabtree is mistaken.

The answer lies in the young woman at the centre of the scene. All we see comes through her: we see what she perceives and, while no physical cliff exists, in psychological terms it does. Therefore, MacGregor has her shape the landscape to her desire. In effect, it is an extreme version of what we all do when our mood, be it happy or low, shapes how we view the scene about us. Our eyes give us vision, but we perceive with our thoughts and thereby see what we wish to see.

Magickal texts

The book MacGregor describes appears typical of the many cheap (though no less effective in the wrong hands) magickal texts, or grimoires, printed in the early nineteenth century. Such books were never openly displayed for sale and most reputable booksellers refused to stock them, but often a market or travelling fair would have a herbalist or soothsayer with a side-line in esoteric literature.

A discerning collector of magickal texts, MacGregor owned a pair of thirteenth century copies of the Seventh and Eighth Books of Moses, a Greek ANOTHEM, (the, so-called, 'Prologue to the Book of Genesis' now regarded as a ninth century forgery) papyri fragments in Samaritan and Aramaic and an early sixteenth century collection of *Volkskunde* (a precursor to folklore) thought to have been transcribed by a young Martin Luther during his years at Erfurt University.

It was while researching such texts your editor became acquainted with 'the cage' in the Reserved Manuscript Depository at King James University.

As previously stated, possession of books of magick no more proves a man practises the dark arts than a subscription to *Ornithology Magazine* proves a man wishes to fly. MacGregor took research very seriously but while his library contained far more works on agricultural practice than books of magick, no one has ever suggested he was a farmer.

Sturm und Drang

> *Wenn eine andere Generation den Menschen aus unsern empfindsamen Schriften restituieren sollte, so werden sie glauben es sei ein Herz mit Testikeln gewesen. Ein Herz mit einem Hodensack*

Thus wrote Georg Christoph Lichtenberg, the German physicist and satirist, of Sturm und Drang in 1776-1779 (Schriften und Briefe, pub. Zweitausendeins 1968–72).

Lichtenberg is critical, even dismissive of Sturm und Drang, but as he unwittingly provides a near perfect description of Bheathain Somhairle's character it deserves quoting in translation:

> If another and later species comes to reconstruct the human being from

> the evidence of our sentimental writings, they will conclude it to have been a heart with testicles.

Sturm und Drang—the meaning is storm and stress—was primarily a literary movement originating in 1770s Germany. Though it existed for only a dozen years until its abandonment by Goethe and Schiller, Sturm und Drang shattered the rationalism imposed by enlightenment thinking and heralded an era of literature that emphasised human emotion and individual perception and promoted anti-aristocratism and the natural world. Weimar Classicism, which succeeded Sturm und Drang, sought to merge this emotionalism with the best of enlightenment rationalism, but in its initial form Sturm und Drang provoked the reader's emotions rather than their intellect using shock, terror, and the erotic to create a visceral connection between reader and text. In essence, it was an early attempt to achieve in literature what two centuries later came naturally to cinema.

In a social context, Sturm und Drang was part of a growing recognition of the primacy of the individual after the collapse of medieval feudalism and rise, albeit in limited form, of the democratic principle. Although primarily a literary movement, it influenced several pre-Romantic artists including Caspar Wolf and Henry Fuseli. It also had a limited effect on a number of notable composers, including Haydn, Carl Philip Emmanuel Bach, and Mozart.

As we have seen, the first volume of *This Iron Race* has much in common with the Sturm und Drang movement. The focus on individual perception is almost unwavering; characters are ruled at least as much by their emotions as by rationality; and nature, in the guise of fog, Bheathain's rainswept hillside, and the sunset on St Catherine's Hill is not a mere backcloth but accentuates or influences the action. The evidence is clear; under the influence of Goethe and Schiller's early works, MacGregor believed Sturm und Drang was a means of being truthful to the human condition while not offending public taste. Alas, he was only half correct.

For our purposes, any story where the principal motivation is revenge or hatred can be classed as Sturm und Drang because such responses are particular to the individual. Stories where the motivation is power or wealth are not because such motivations are shared by many, even if not all act on them. Thus, the Second

Prologue is a clear expression of Sturm und Drang: motivated by revenge, the unnamed character acts while her rational mind is suspended and though she will regret her actions her "act was irredeemable as murder."

Repeatedly we have seen characters acting in haste; first Captain Wolfe's irrational behaviour, then Bheathain Somhairle's impulsiveness, and now the unnamed 'Lady of Remorse'. Other characters in later volumes of *This Iron Race* will also reveal their irrationality and impulsiveness, but we must leave them to their time and place rather than bring premature revelations.

This brings us to another aspect of Sturm und Drang expressed in *This Iron Race*: the focus on individual perception. We experience the novel through the eyes and other senses of the characters and are privy only to their unique perspective. For example: in chapter one we only see the view of Staffin Bay and its environs at the moment Bheathain observes it. The bay was there all the time, as was the sea beyond and the mountain above, but until Bheathain glanced homeward he had been preoccupied and taken no notice of his wider surroundings.

There are various literary terms to describe this focus on a character's perceptions, but in effect we only see, hear, taste, touch and feel (both physically and emotionally) what the characters experience when they experience it with little mediation or comment from the author. The character stands, or falls, without the author passing judgement upon them, albeit the Curse, the unseen narrator, often does pass comment.

The third aspect of Sturm und Drang is its exaltation of nature, and this chapter shows it exceptionally well in the description of the sunset over the city. We also saw it in the previous chapter when Bheathain stood upon the hillside and again when he gathered seaweed.

Both Bheathain and the unnamed character of the second prologue are isolated in a landscape over which they have no sway. Indeed, Bheathain cannot even stay warm and dry! In contrast, Enlightenment art and literature portrayed man in command of a benign nature. Nature that was not biddable or benign, exemplified by The Alps crossed by northern Europeans embarking on the Grand Tour of Italy, excited terror and loathing and many travellers over the high passes drew down the blinds on their carriage windows to avoid the fearsome sights.

It took a paradigm shift before we appreciated that mountains possessed a beauty inextricably linked to the terror they instilled: a beauty we would call exhilarating. In short, provided any real danger was controlled, we enjoyed being afraid and Sturm und Drang exploited this pleasurable fear.

Understanding the connection between Sturm und Drang and *This Iron Race* reveals MacGregor's desire to give free expression to human emotion was not *sui generis* but part of a wider movement freeing itself from the rationalism imposed by the enlightenment. Alas for MacGregor, those in the vanguard of an artistic or literary movement rarely prosper in their lifetimes.

Chapter Two

Character transition

The chronological disruption at the beginning of the chapter draws attention to the moment the perspective moves from Bheathain to Lord MacDonald. This change coincides with his awareness of 'a curious smell, half sweet and half rank that did not belong and for a moment he had the sense he was in two places at once'. Once this sensation passes, Bheathain carries on as though nothing has happened which, from the reader's perspective, is the case until the beginning of chapter two proves otherwise.

Bheathain's sense of being in two places at once suggests this is not a conventional narrative shift enabling the author to continue the story from another character's viewpoint. Rather, an undescribed element embedded within the story is at work. This is an unusual device in fiction and because it recurs throughout *This Iron Race* MacGregor ensures we take notice the first instance it happens. Having done so, he uses an analepsis to show the comforts and family duties Lord MacDonald leaves behind at Duntulm, before returning to his journey.

MacDonald's world

MacGregor's journal gives us a detailed account of his brief tour of the Isle of Skye in August 1861 and while it is not clear how much the island inspired *This Iron Race,* his notes proved invaluable when he began writing at Christmas the same year.

Duntulm, Lord MacDonald's home, is largely MacGregor's invention, or rather a reconstruction, the MacDonalds having abandoned their ancestral home in the 1700s. By 1861 the greater part had collapsed into the sea and MacGregor's description is taken from a few engravings dating from the 1780s when the house was largely intact and Lord MacLeod's residence at Dunvegan.

Drawn by the remarkable rock formations of the Quiraing, MacGregor made Staffin Bay the principal setting for Bheathain Somhairle's portion of the tale. This had the happy effect of making Bheathain a tenant of Lord MacDonald rather than his host, Lord MacLeod; however, he then requires Lord MacDonald to take an unlikely route from Duntulm to Portree in order to bring the two characters together.

By 1861 a Parliamentary Road ran south from Dunvegan to Portree and extended north along the Trotternish Peninsula far enough to give MacGregor sight of the remains of Duntulm Castle. It would have provided Lord MacDonald with a safe and reasonably fast route to Portree but taken him away from Staffin and Bheathain Somhairle. The eastern side of the peninsula was much less accessible, being served only by a drover's track unsuitable for carriages. MacGregor's solution was to imagine a road where none existed.

This discrepancy between MacGregor's narrative and reality is not like that described in the previous chapter and, despite informing Sir Sidney Beresford he would depict "reality, not dreams", MacGregor indulged in considerable invention when it suited his narrative. This has led some to interpret MacGregor's variations from known historical or geographical fact as part of a wider and coherent purpose. Your editor recalls a particularly surreal meeting last year with the self-styled Madam Sosostris (née Merci Belvedere) at the Carrillion Hotel in Lunden and as it serves rather well to illustrate the sort of nonsense the serious scholar of MacGregor's work has to contend with it is worth relating.

Unsure what to expect, having no prior knowledge other than her name and the place and date of our meeting, your editor was a little startled when Madame Sosostris proved to be a vibrantly dressed black woman of statuesque build. She was a decidedly exotic flower among the beige tones of the Carrillion's luncheon room and unfortunately, sensing his surprise, Madame Sosostris quite leapt to the wrong conclusion—a curious thing for any clairvoyant—and our meeting got off to a bad start from which it never recovered. Editors are naturally retiring folk, preferring to remain in the shadow of the one we edit and what with my short stature, tweed jacket and brown brogues your editor felt like a mouse at the mercy of a very large cat.

In Madam Sosostris's opinion MacGregor's description of the Isle of Skye is inspired by the lines and ridges of the human hand—*quelle surprise* she practises chiromancy—and her 'reading' of Skye's landscape, as described in the first volume of *This Iron Race*, reveals the ultimate fate of Bheathain and Lord MacDonald and several other characters. Her scheme is, of course, utter nonsense but her manner was certainly persuasive (in the sense artillery *persuades*) and no doubt she will provide encouragement (as if he needs it) for Hendryk van Zelden. Having argued MacGregor's description of Skye accords perfectly well with any *map* of the island, she replied with "the map is not the territory" and claimed MacGregor's Skye is a psychogeographic construct inspired (literally) by his own hand. One responded (a little heatedly and to the irritation of our waiter) by drawing a map of Skye upon a napkin, at which point Madam Sosostris placed her hand upon his and said in a loud voice dripping with honey: *denial ain't just a river in Egypt*, which caught the attention of the entire room.

Such was the shock to his system your editor spent the rest of the afternoon in the sanctuary of the Britannic Museum and then in the Golden Compasses on Great Russell Street. He did not arrive home in Avebury until the small hours of the following morning.

Parallels between Lord MacDonald & MacGregor

The parallels between the fictional life MacGregor created for Lord MacDonald and recent events in his own life cannot be overlooked. Certainly, MacGregor was very aware of them and writing in the fall 1865 edition of the Edenborough Review he was at pains to report that while he and Lord MacDonald had much in common the fictional character was "the better man".

To sum up the key similarities:

Both men are recently married to second wives after a period of widowhood.

Clara MacDonald is expecting a child, as, at the time of writing, was Lady MacGregor.

The duties of both men take them away from their wives: Lord MacDonald to Winchester to attend a funeral, MacGregor to his writing desk to earn a living.

There is one other parallel which MacGregor confessed to in his journals but to include it here would be premature. We shall refer to it in due course.

Against this there are numerous dissimilarities:

MacDonald has a son from his first wife. MacGregor's son died in the same tragedy as his wife.

MacDonald's new wife is young and inexperienced. Lady Helena was a widow in her middle-thirties when she married MacGregor.

MacDonald's separation from his wife is total, but of short duration. MacGregor's separation from Lady MacGregor was partial (both shared the same household) but arguably permanent since he continued working until his death.

In *The Wizard of the North* (King James University Press, 1930), Dr Crabtree notes the parallels between MacGregor and MacDonald fall well short of proving MacGregor made him his simulacrum. Notably, outside the marital and domestic arena their circumstances and obligations are quite different. However, the tone of Dr Crabtree's argument is questionable. In particular, his opinion, "for the female of the species a good marriage is the main event of life while for the male it is always an accessory," is dated and, as proved by his reaction to the death of Lady Madeleine, did not accord with MacGregor's views on marriage. Sadly, it probably reflects Dr Crabtree's unconventional marriage to the actress and socialite Liberty Pearl, as revealed in her autobiography *Shadows on the Sky*, (Partridge Press, 1956), though as his ex-wife would tell you your editor is no expert on marital relations.

MacGregor on Skye, August 1861

MacGregor landed at Dunvegan aboard the *Caledonia* on August 3, 1861. With him were Lady Helena, his manservant, Jock Strange, and an unnamed maid for Lady Helena. They intended to spend a week with Lord MacLeod at Dunvegan before travelling on to Portree and thence to Lord MacDonald's estate on the Sleat Peninsula in the south west of Skye. From there a decision would be made (presumably based on the weather) to sail west to the Outer Islands or return to the mainland via Kylerhea. However, events back in Edenborough waylaid their plans.

MacGregor was not a horseman; indeed, so far as we know he never rode a horse or made any attempt to learn. This was highly unusual in an age when the horse was the principal means of transport and a particular handicap in the north of Scotland where railways were few and most roads were unsuitable for carriages. We must also bear in mind polio had left him permanently lame in his left leg and walking any distance or on rough terrain would have severely strained him.

Despite his infirmity, he saw as much of Skye as he was able and as he travelled, he made notes and sketches in his journal which would later form the world of Bheathain Somhairle and Lord MacDonald. In particular he made extensive notes on the Staffin district, including the inn and the curious rock formations of the Quiraing, so he must have had some means of access. It is possible he hired a driver with a cart capable of taking the drover's track (a carriage with its narrow wheels would have been impractical) but it is conceivable he was carried in a sedan chair. In any event, while the story of Bheathain Somhairle did not arrive until some months after his return to Arbinger, we can see in MacGregor's journal the first seeds of his story.

After a week with Lord MacLeod the party travelled south to stay at the Royal Hotel in Portree, remaining there for four days. From Portree he took a carriage south via Broadford to view the ferry at Kyleakin, though he did not cross the strait, and a short boat trip to the neighbouring island of Raasay. Of this excursion, he noted "catch seals here," and heavily underlined the phrase, suggesting he was already thinking of how this might fit into a narrative.

On the morning MacGregor and party were preparing to leave Portree for Sleat, a telegram from Edenborough brought news his father was gravely ill. Plans were immediately changed, and they left hurriedly for Kyleakin, stayed overnight in Lochalsh and then travelled to Edenborough via Invermoriston and the Great Glen, thus taking much the same route as Lord MacDonald. MacGregor would not return to Skye until 1866, two years after publication of the first volume of *This Iron Race*, and accompanied only by Jock Strange, Lady Helena having a young family to care for.

Spaewifery & the kirk

MacGregor accurately describes contemporary attitudes of 1860s Scotland toward magick and, if anything, understates the church's hostility toward spaewives and their craft. The tradition of clan chiefs keeping a spaewife, together with certain magickal practices, (particularly keeping familiars) was subject to no less than four parliamentary bills at Holyrood between 1847 and 1882. Each was an attempt to limit or proscribe the practice of magick and each received unanimous support from the Scottish Bishops sitting in the Upper House.

The church's hostility to familiars hinged on the false claim that such unions constituted intercourse between man (or rather woman since all spaers in Scotland and Anglia were female) and beast and were a form of bestiality. Revisionist historians argue politics more than spiritual concerns drove the church's hostility to spaewives, but from the many sermons on the subject, it is obvious that familiars aroused strong opinions among church ministers and laity, even if the justification for their hostility was false. In any event, whatever their true motive, the church eventually won at the pulpit what it failed to achieve in parliament and in 1889 Lord MacNeil of Barra became the last clan chief to appoint a spaer.

The Free Church, represented by Father Dobie, was notably less intolerant of spaewifery than the Alban Church but even so, MacGregor's Father Dobie is a portrayal of what he saw as the very best kind of churchman contrasting with the Bishop of Stirling who he introduces in the next chapter.

Chapter Three
Congested Districts & the Clearances

Initially simply a description for land carrying a larger population than it was able to support, congested districts were given legal definition in the 1843 Congested Districts Act. The act brought considerable advantages to the owner of an estate deemed "congested". Low interest government loans paid for 'improvements' such as sheep pasture and fishing stations, and the common laws of tenancy were set aside, legalising forcible evictions.

The two great waves of Clearances were the late 1780s through to the onset of the Napoleonic Wars in 1803 and again with the collapse of the kelp industry after the peace of 1832 with a peak during the famines of the late 1840s. The first wave of emigration was locally organised with individual landlords pressing their tenants to leave, and in some cases enforcing evictions with local militias, while parliament in Edenborough—in which, it must be remembered, many landlords sat as members—turned a blind eye.

The principal destination for people in the first wave was Glasgow and the northern cities of Anglia with less than a third going overseas, mainly to Quebeck and Van Diemen's Land. The second wave of Clearances saw far greater numbers affected and was pressed at government level with many forced evictions and often violent confrontations, creating lasting damage to relations between the Highland Scots and their English-speaking governors in Edenborough.

The highland economy had, by the 1840s, shifted to sheep farming and most attempts to employ tenants in fishing or weaving had failed, leaving an excess of underemployed and usually poverty-stricken crofters. However, the greater pressure to depopulate the highlands came from parliament in Holyrood which, under pressure from Anglia, was determined to support colonial ambitions in the Americas where encroachment by the French and Spanish on tribal lands to the west of Anglia's colony threatened to block its future expansion. This focus on territory in the Americas led a number of commentators to draw parallels between the outlawed trade in African slaves and the transportation of Highland Scots and the Eirish, a great many of whom perished from disease or shipwreck.

One of those who compared the traffic in highlanders to that of African slaves was the Reverend James Vimy (1794–1865), a churchman and tireless campaigner for highland rights who, in an edition of the Glasgow Post in June 1858, claimed the Congested Districts Act, "licensed barbarities not seen since the Vikings." Most modern historians, such as Fulton Montmorency in *The Scottish Burden* (Barbary Books, 1987), are more temperate in their criticism, accepting the clearances were often badly managed and had a high cost in human misery, but arguing that failure to relieve the excess population would have brought decades of starvation.

The Commission Men & the Rule of Three

The function of the Emigration Commission is largely presented by the three characters. Essentially, the majority of landowners welcomed their inspections as the commissioners could award funds from the public purse for improvements to land and industries, such as fishing, while justifying, in the landlord's opinion, the clearance of land for sheep. A landowner in the good books of an Emigration Commission could believe he ran a well-ordered estate even as he sent his tenants overseas. Naturally, the tenants took the opposite view of Commission Men, and it was not unknown for their progress to be sabotaged. The most notorious incident came in 1850 when a mob of evicted Campbells ambushed three Emigration Commissioners in Glencoe, overturning their carriage and bludgeoning two of them to death. The third commissioner escaped on horseback, along with the coachmen, and was later able to identify five of the ringleaders who were tried and hanged at Inveraray Castle, alongside a coachman who had colluded with the attackers. Another two-dozen Campbells were found guilty of obstructing the king's highway and deported to Van Diemen's Land.

The rule of three refers to MacGregor's fondness for using a trio of characters to create a strong dynamic. An example in the First Prologue is the scene between Captain Wolfe and Warders Pengallow and Thomas which quickly established Wolfe's character and his relationship with the men under him and the same can be said of the scene in chapter one between Bheathain Somhairle, his grandfather and Tòrmod M'Neis at the Staffin Inn. In those examples the three characters take centre stage, whereas the Commission Men act within a larger group. Their function in this scene is to bring the wider world, as seen by the privileged, into the domesticity of Sir David's dining room and thereby prefigure the later scene between Sir David and Adam Shaw which shows the world through the eyes of the dispossessed.

Some critics have argued these repeated groups of three (we shall find many other examples) are a veiled reference to the three branches of magick, while others maintain it is based on the concept of soul, spirit and body. A few have even suggested it draws on a proto-Freudian triumvirate of ego, superego, and id, and it is true these trios often contain a mediator, or ego figure, such as Tòrmod in chapter one who intervenes between Bheathain and his grandfather, and in this chapter Lord Dundee censures the intemperate bishop.

In my opinion, this over-complicates matters. There is no need to see some allegorical purpose for three characters, rather than two or four, when narrative purpose answer perfectly well. Two characters in a scene, as in life, are more likely to adopt polarised positions without either expecting the other to alter their view, leading to stasis. Three characters allow more possibilities where one can act as mediator between opposing views, two may take a common position against a third, or two opposing arguments can sway a neutral party. Thus, three characters offer greater complexity and the possibility of change or development in character and therefore narrative.

A negative effect of the 'rule of three' in literature is individual characters can appear too stylised, resulting in a loss of nuance and humanity, as is the case with MacGregor's Bishop of Stirling. As stated previously, MacGregor substantially rewrote the bishop's dialogue to make him less of a mouthpiece for the clearances and more of a human being, but he is still too obviously the villain of the piece. A further criticism is the focus on the bishop largely exculpates Lord Dundee and Sir Gordon when both are equally culpable while expressing their opinions less harshly. Arguably, greater subtlety could be had in the discussion but only, in my view, by increasing the number of characters so a range of views might be expressed. This would raise two problems: firstly, Commission Men only ever surveyed in parties of two or three; secondly, a large number of characters risks too many discordant voices and the loss of the central idea.

In this instance, as the focus is on Sir David and, to a lesser extent on Lord MacDonald, the lack of depth in the bishop's portrayal is tolerable because he functions primarily as a prompt for Sir David's thoughts and conscience rather than as a character in his own right.

From chieftain to landlord—the decline of Scotland's ruling families

This is much too short a space to give more than an outline of the immense changes in Scottish society by which the honourable clan chieftain became an absentee landlord blinded by fine living and preferring sheep to the loyalty of his clansmen.

According to Humphrey Lytton's *A Modern History of Scotland* (Carnegie Books, 1974) the rot set in with the Union of Crowns under Queen Anne in 1702. Henceforth the crown ruled from Anglia with Holyrood Palace reduced to an occasional residence when the monarch had business in Scotland. With the monarch gone south, those chieftains wishing to keep influence with the crown followed and found in Anglia a completely different society where a people's obligations to the ruling class were many and those of the ruling class to their subjects few and rarely enforced. In Scotland a clan chieftain was historically obligated to provide employment to his clansmen because they served as his private soldiery and defended his territory from aggressors. Thus, less employment meant fewer men he could call on when his lands were threatened by neighbouring chieftains. In Anglia there was no tradition of clans, and a *national* army took men from the general populace while the poor depended on parish charity. Furthermore, the Gaelic-speaking chieftains found their country ways unpopular in Anglia and soon abandoned much of their cultural identity to fit in with the gentry, further distancing them from their native peoples. Lastly, but by no means least, good living—or at least being respectable members of the gentry—cost a great deal more in Anglia than in Scotland which put an immense strain on their estate's finances, resulting in rent increases and, eventually, clearance of the population to make way for sheep farming. Thus, according to Lytton:

> All but a handful of the great Scottish families became strangers in their own lands and their people reduced to hardscrabble until the ships took them away and the glens stood empty, save for the woolly maggot.

Chapter Four
Outside-women

An 'outside-woman' was any woman who offered her skills with herblore and charms to her neighbours in exchange for food or a few coins. By custom, such women often dwelt away from towns and settlements, but the popular image of 'outside-women' living under hawthorn bushes or in hollowed out hayricks is false and derives partly from a misunderstanding of the name and partly from propaganda by the church. 'Outside' in this context simply means outside the town or at the edge of the parish boundary.

The more familiar English expression for such women is hedge witch, but today's fashion is for Latin or Greek names and outside-women have become reflexologists, astromancers, homeopathists, aromatherapists, and herbalists, to name but a few. One can only assume an outside-woman's knowledge was too broad and we now favour specialism.

Historically, many spaewives following 'the change' or menopause, to use the medical term, subsisted as outside-women, practising magick reliant on craft and knowledge, rather than innate ability. According to Bryce MacGregor's *A History of Scottish Magick* (published posthumously in France, 1899 as *L'Histoire de Écossais Magie*) Edenborough's booth-scryers were an urban variety of outside-women for whom fortune-telling for city folk gave a better living than offering herblore to the rural poor.

While spaewives had the protection of their master, outside-women were vulnerable to assault and far worse. This was greatly exacerbated by propaganda from the Alban Church, and many were murdered by those they sought to serve and others thrown out of their parish and forced into begging. This was especially true in the south and east of Scotland which was dominated by the Alban Church, while the Highlands and Islands where the Free Church was prevalent saw little persecution of outside-women and they survived in rural districts until the middle of the last century and the advent of state-funded medical care.

Acquiring Grace
The alert reader will have noted that from taking to his bed after the visitation from his soul to his awakening in Màiri Mulcahy's bed some sixty hours elapse during which Bheathain is either unconscious or delirious. This should not be a surprise.

Acquiring the gift of clearsight, or Grace, is a traumatic process akin, so it is claimed, to the transformation of a humble grub into a damselfly, with the proviso that unlike the metamorphosis of the damselfly, which is organised, and predictable, psychic transformations differ widely. As in the Zygoptera, a period of torpor or quiescence is essential and Dr Diane Fanshawe claims (Psychic Insight Magazine, August 2011), the allusion to the metamorphosis of the larva into the adult insect is closer than one might suppose for acoustic imaging of the brains of people acquiring clearsight reveals the breakdown of neural connections and their reconstruction. Essentially, this is a form of self-inflicted brain injury and can, if interrupted or unfinished, lead to a permanent catatonic state, insanity and even death. As the neuroscientist Charles Sherrington memorably wrote:

> ...the brain is weaving anew its
> tapestry of meaning and though
> each—the before and after—was and
> shall be perfect upon completion,
> the execution risks the unravelling of
> loose threads.

Your editor is no expert, but allowing learning is itself a form of mental rewiring, one imagines Charles Sherrington is stating in his own terms the advice given Bheathain by Màiri Mulcahy:

"Deny it, it will destroy you; left untrained it will destroy those you care for."

One can argue—indeed, we should say it has been argued—that Bheathain has hardly been quiescent: indeed, he will continue to resist at every turn. Unlike the damselfly, one who acquires clearsight does not emerge from the chrysalis able to fly on instinct alone. Bheathain's transformation is incomplete and, like a child learning to walk, he lacks self-control. He has many further boundaries to cross and challenges to meet and MacGregor intends to show us this journey.

Your editor wishes to thank Eileen Provender of Belshade College, Oxford for her assistance with the above.

Chapter Five

Spaewifery

Igraine Swan-neck in *Edwin and Morcar* was MacGregor's only previous attempt to portray the standpoint of a spaewife. It was, by his account, a failure:

> E&M is done, and the fair copy sent this morning. No doubt B&L will be happy, but it is not satisfactory. Igraine eluded me and without her the story is compromised. I could capture the appearance of magick but never its texture.
>
> *MacGregor's journal, August 4, 1843.*

The texture of magick is, according to Sister Ethelnyd, only experienced by practitioners, whereas all can experience its effect. MacGregor's journal does not give a complete explanation for his failure, but it appears he thought one could describe the practice of magick by extrapolating from the creative processes of painters, composers, sculptors, and poets, the latter of which he understood perfectly. His failure in *Edwin & Morcar* found its way into Eolhwynne's remark that, "describing clearsight to one without is like describing a rainbow to one who cannot see."

Having restored MacGregor's portrayal of Eolhwynne it is clear she is a far more complete character than Igraine Swan-neck, and must ask what had changed in the interim to allow for the improvement.

Much can be ascribed to experience: *Edwin & Morcar* was MacGregor's fifth novel while this, the first of his *This Iron Race* series, was his twenty-fourth; however, the principal reason is the different role played by magick in *Edwin & Morcar* and in *Acts of the Servant*. In the former, magick has a secondary role while the focus is on the power struggle between the title characters and Edward the Confessor and Harold Godwinsson, whereas in *Acts of the Servant* and its sequels magick and the supernatural are at the forefront. Aware of his previous failure and knowing a repeat would undermine all his intentions, MacGregor studied magick in great depth and many of the magickal texts in his library at Arbinger date from the time of writing *This Iron Race*.

Particularly useful—the margins of his copy are full of notes—was Celestine's *Die Mondblutbibel*, (The Moonblood Bible) an account of the life of a Spaewife at the court of an unnamed German nobleman in the years 1510–1540. Genuine accounts by spaewives are very rare due to the code of confidentiality between spaewife and master, hence 'Celestine' is a pseudonym; but it has been dated to 1546, only three years after the expulsion of all practitioners of magick from the Holy Roman Empire and is believed to have been written either out of revenge or financial necessity. In any event, though written some three centuries prior to *This Iron Race*, the rarity of such texts made it essential reading. In addition, MacGregor acquired transcripts from inquisitors at the so-called witch trials preceding the expulsions from the Holy Roman Empire and while they are of doubtful veracity (inquisitors were prone to exaggeration and some of the information was gained by torture) much of their content verifies Celestine's account.

However, texts have their limitations, and none would enable MacGregor to describe the exact experiences of a spaer practising their craft. For that, we must assume MacGregor consulted the booth-scryers operating in the backstreets of Edenborough. Among the booth-scryers were many ex-spaewives who had lost their gift at the menopause and now eked out a living selling potions and fortune-telling. No doubt, some would have been willing to give or sell MacGregor their first-hand knowledge, though we accept this is supposition for he did not record any such meetings and though he had opportunity on his many visits to Edenborough, we cannot say with certainty MacGregor met with any booth-scryers.

Sister Ethelnyd and other practitioners of magick claim it would be impossible for MacGregor to describe accurately the receiving of a kenning, or to have such insight into the relationship between a spaer and her familiar without intimate knowledge of magick, but this misunderstands the nature of fiction. One does not need to be a man to write from the perspective of a man and similarly one does not need intimate knowledge of magick to describe its effects and practice. In your editor's opinion, those who claim MacGregor could not have described magick without direct experience of it underestimate his powers of imagination. In addition, it is clear he found this chapter exceptionally difficult to write. For example, the scene where Eolhwynne summons Oberion appears in three different versions before MacGregor settled on a fourth and final version and much of Eolhwynne's dialogue with Adam Shaw exists as lines interlineated with an earlier version. In short, the difficulty MacGregor had depicting a character blessed with clearsight vindicates your editor's belief he himself had no such gift.

Iron & steel, continued

> Perhaps dear reader, you have had cause to plunge your hand in an icy torrent or the misfortune to lift a pot from the stove without first wrapping the handle in a cloth. Indeed, I have done both and can vouch the pain is no light matter; however, I have not frozen my arm in ice or seized a blacksmith's work from the forge in my bare hand, yet they are more alike to the pain iron causes a spaer.
>
> MacGregor writing in A History of Scottish Magick (Paris, 1899).

Iron and steel have long been known to be harmful to those with clearsight, but according to Mikhail Orlovsky's study of Russian magick in *Darkness Bound* (Zenit, 1989) it was not until research during the Russian pogroms of the 1920s that the effect was understood. In short, the magnetic field generated by iron and its alloys interferes with a spaer's ability to project and receive psychic radiation (also known as auras).

The Russian research proved magnetic and electromagnetic

fields can cause acute pain, brain damage, and eventually death, while even low-level fields disrupt a spaer's abilities. From this, it was deduced clearsight is a form of sensitivity to the electromagnetic auras generated by all living creatures. According to Orlovsky much of the research conducted during the pogroms is tainted by the dreadful suffering and deaths of its victims.

Today in our more enlightened times, lead and lead-impregnated plastics shield high voltage electrical equipment and cabling to protect those with gift of Grace from the effects of electromagnetic radiation; however, they must still beware iron and steel.

Oberion
The name appears in several earlier novels by MacGregor including, *There and Back Again*, *Camberwick*, and throughout his *Arthurian Cycle* where Oberion is a father-figure to Merlin. The name has no known antecedents in Scottish folklore but appears in several medieval accounts, including a number of French *chanson de geste*, or 'song of heroic deeds' where the name is variously given as Oberon, Oberyon, Huon or Auberon. In the handful of medieval English texts where Oberion appears he is merely a familiar spirit summoned by an incantation to do a person's will, whereas the *chanson de gest* honours him as *Le Roi de Féerie*, or 'King of the Faeries.' It is the latter role he takes in *This Iron Race*.

A king of the faeries appears under various names in the folklore and legends of Wales, Germany and Scandinavia, but is absent from that of Scotland. In Wales he is Gwyn ap Nudd, king of the *Tylwyth Teg* or 'fair folk'. 'Ap' is a patronymic indicating Gwyn is the son of Nudd and Nudd may be cognate with the Irish god Nuada, or perhaps both Nuada and Nudd derive from Nodens, the horned god of the pre-Roman inhabitants of the Britannic Isles.

Mythologists have proposed that the deities and beliefs of an invaded and subjugated people are invariably subsumed into or supplanted by those of the invader. The Romans and Romano-British, for example, were willing to accommodate Brythonic deities, such as Sabrina of the River Severn, into their temples, whereas the Anglo-Saxons imposed their Germanic deities onto Anglia and pushed the old Brythonic gods aside. Thus, a deity once worshipped by humans might find himself demoted to king of

Faerieland. The Christianisation of the Britannic Isles eventually displaced all the old gods and, with no pantheon in a monotheistic faith to accommodate them, all were condemned to haunt the hills, woods and byways alongside the faerie folk.

In Germanic mythology the king of the faeries is Alberich, ruler (rihhi in Old High German) of the Elben, or elves, with the elven folk being cognate with the faeries, or *Beann Sidhe* of Scottish legend and folklore. Alberich is often portrayed as a malignant dwarf, in which guise he is guardian of the Nibelungs' treasure in the *Nibelungenlied*, or 'Song of the Nibelungs', the epic medieval poem later made famous by Wagner's opera. Whether Alberich ruler of the elves and Alberich the treasure hoarder have been conflated, or whether Alberich's character has been blackened and diminished by later Christian writers is uncertain.

In Norse mythology Alberich is cognate with the god Freyr, whose name is more accurately given as Yngvi-Freyr; Freyr being an honorific title rather than a given name. Uncommonly, although ruler of the Álfar or elves, Yngvi-Freyr was not elf-born, but son of the sea god, Njörðr (Njord). All the realms in Norse mythology are under the rule of the gods, or Vanir, and Njord shows this by giving Ingvi-Freyr dominion of Álfheimr (elf-home) as a teething present. Unlike the dwarvish Alberich, Yngvi-Freyr is a handsome warrior who had numerous lovers, including his twin sister, Freyja. He is associated with fair weather and virility, and sometimes depicted with an erect phallus.

Njord and the Celtic Nodens are associated with the sea and fishing, and it is suggested both are embodied in the Fisher King, the wounded ruler of a waste land who appears in Arthurian legend (see "Maimed Heroes", page lxxxv). The Fisher King's wound is a euphemism for castration—the wasting of his realm being a direct consequence—and there may be an echo of this in Yngvi-Freyr who gave up his magic sword for marriage to the beautiful Gerthr, and so perished at Ragnarok.

In Scottish legend and folklore, and to a lesser extent in Eireland (Scotland and Eireland share much of their Gaelic heritage) no single name appears in the role of king of the faeries. This may reflect the powerful and divisive clan systems which dominated both countries until the medieval period and prevented either from uniting under one individual. To put it another way, Scots and Eirish culture no more acknowledged an individual having dominion over the faeries than they acknowledged an individual having dominion over Scotland or Eireland.

MacGregor describes Oberion as having horns like a stag and a similar antlered god appears on the Gundestrup Cauldron discovered in Denmark in 1891. The figure is believed to be the Celtic god Cernunnos and one can hear in the name a distant echo of the Irish gods already mentioned. Other horned gods under various names and guises are found worldwide. Many are styled after bulls—the Minotaur may be regarded as a fallen god—or sometimes goats and often the entire head takes the animal form. It should be noted there is no clear distinction between faith and mythology, other than the latter is more studied than practised and vice versa.

In Christian iconography the Antichrist is often depicted with horns, and this has led to an unfortunate conflation between Satanists and those who revere the old horned gods. Your editor has himself engaged in heated discussion with fellow Christians on this exact point, especially at midsummer eve when Avebury becomes a magnet for Wicca folk. It may well be that early-Christian missionaries deliberately conflated the old gods with the enemy of Christ in their efforts to convert our pagan ancestors, but Herne, Oberion and Cernunnos, along with the other members of the pre-Christian pantheons, are not at all like Satan in nature. He, alas, is a quite distinct entity.

The branches of magick

Your editor thanks Sister Ethelnyd of the Iona Fellowship of Grace for her assistance with the following.

Practitioners of all three surviving branches of magick appear in *This Iron Race* and this is only a quick guide to the various characteristics and practices of each as they apply to the narrative. All three branches have suffered a marked decline in the last one hundred and fifty years (especially the Red Branch which is all but extinct) and despite the resurgence of interest in the study and practice of magick in the last few decades many of the techniques and customs described in *This Iron Race* are no longer current.

The White Branch or Northern Tradition is primarily represented by Eolhwynne. Its practitioners are called spaewives or rune-wives (archaic) and are exclusively female. It practiced runic divination and charm making, weather-reading, familiars, and herblore, and it forbade using magick for aggressive purposes or for self-interest. Geographically, it extends south and west from Scandinavia (excluding Finland), through the Holy Roman Empire and the Low Countries, and across Northern France to Eireland and Greater Britain. Schools are known as Fellowships of Grace (in France, Écoles des Etudes Esotériques) and the principal ones were Iona (Scotland), Peel (IOM), Lindisfarne (Anglia) Mont Dragon (Brittany), Hills of Tara (Eireland), Aalborg (Denmark), Teutoburger Wald and Heidelberg (Germany), Carcassonne (France), and Uppsala (Sweden). Only Iona and Mont Dragon remain active.

In the Red (or sometimes Black) Branch or Eastern Tradition practitioners were variously called starets, shamans or kolduny and were always male. Its practices included self-flagellation; onanism; coitus with male and female partners, either singly or in groups; alternate heating and cooling of the body (sauna); animal sacrifice; capnomancy (smoke-reading), and cartomancy. Unusually, the Red Branch discouraged the use of familiars but starets could co-opt animals as and when required. Geographically the Red Branch extends north and east from the shores of the Black Sea through parts of the Ottoman Empire and into Austria and Hungary and thence across Bohemia, Finland, and western Russia. Unlike the White and Green Branches, novices were traditionally apprenticed to an older practitioner rather than being schooled alongside their peers; however, limited reforms by Peter the Great established Akadimías at St Petersburg and Kiev, in modern-day Ukraine, and at Riga in Estonia. Lazarus is the sole representative of the Red Branch featured in *This Iron Race*.

Graciana Zabala A'Guirre represents the Green Branch or Southern Tradition in which practitioners are called oracles or sibyls and are exclusively female. Their practices include astromancy, capnomancy and pyromancy, familiars, and the evil eye. Dedication to the master is at the centre of the Green Branch and ethical issues are secondary. Geographically it extends north of the Mediterranean from the Iberian Peninsula to the Levant. Its schools are Villa Sophia, and the principal establishments were at Zaragoza, Montserrat and Gran Canaria (Spain), Gernika (Pays Vasco), Marseilles (France), Gozo (Malta), Lesbos (Greece), and Venice and Ravenna (Italy). Only Lesbos remains active.

Said to have originated on the islands of Atlantis and Thule, the Root Branch or Western Tradition has been extinct for three millennia. The only historical references come from Plato and the

Greek explorer Pytheas. According to Plato its practitioners were called prophets and might be male or female and practices included divination by observing the flight of birds, cartomancy, aeromancy or cloud-gazing, oneiromancy, astromancy, and the casting of seashells. However, Plato's account is considered unreliable, and this may be an incomplete or erroneous list. Pytheas also refers to scatomancy and animal sacrifice but as his account, titled *On the Ocean*, only survives as a few references in other classical texts and he was more concerned with astronomy and agricultural practices than magick, it may be unreliable. As the name suggests, the Root Branch is considered the origin of the three surviving branches of magick and at various times each has claimed to be the most faithful to the form of magick practised on Atlantis and Thule.

In modern times the historical existence of both islands has been largely disproved, leading to speculation that the true origin of the branches of magick lies further west. In the late eighteenth and early nineteenth centuries, Christian missionaries among the Inuit and other First Nation Americans noted (even as they attempted to discourage its practice) that their ritual magick resembled that of Plato's Atlanteans, leading to speculation that First Nation Americans were their descendants. For a few decades of the mid-nineteenth century this became a popular theory among Neoplatonic scholars and Gramareans and MacGregor elaborated on it in *Devices and Executions*, the final volume of *This Iron Race*, although it is unlikely he ever gave it much credibility. Recent ethnographic studies of First Nation Americans have shown their magick derives from the Laplander and far-northern inhabitants of Siberia whose practices are so different from any of the three surviving Traditions they must be regarded as a wholly distinct form of magick.

Plato's text gives us the name of only one school on Atlantis, but scholars have disagreed on the translation from Ancient Greek with most referring to it as "House of the Blessed" while others regard "Electium" as closer to Plato's meaning. At one time Tara in Eireland claimed it was founded by the brothers Autochthon and Azaes who had fled the destruction of Atlantis, however this is dismissed by all reliable scholars.

The balance

The balance in magick is much like the balance in a fiscal economy: it is not possible for everyone to be satisfied without the entire apparatus ceasing to function. Incentive, crudely expressed as necessity and avarice, is essential for an economy to function for without it nothing is made, and nothing is bought and society collapses. Magick, like the economy, requires suffering and those who experiment with the voodoo economics of socialism and the forcible redistribution of wealth are as misguided as a practitioner of magick who tries to bring good luck to all.

As Howard Cobbler, the philosopher of applied economics, put it in his 1976 lecture, 'Unfair State: the Socialist Ruin':

> Fortune and misfortune are the two faces of the coin we are given: there is no middle ground, no coin of mere contentment.

Indeed, it is probable if such a coin were ever minted, we would despise it, for it is human nature to strive against each other. A point recognised by Otto von Bismarck who is alleged to have said prior to the onset of the 1870 Franco-Prussian War:

> We may be free, and we may be brothers; but, unlike the French, by God we are not equal and do not wish to be.

To add injury to insult, Bismarck then said the French were hypocrites for championing *égalité* while being no more equal or desiring of equality than any other nation.

Prussia's crushing of France led directly to the unification of German speaking territories in 1872 under Prussian leadership so whether or not Bismarck's assessment of France was correct, he certainly knew how to win a war.

It is plain there is no *equitable* balance in human affairs or in nature where survival goes to the fittest, and nor is there equity in the world of magick. Instead, we must see the balance in magick as a battle between opposites, as described by Eolhwynne:

> Fortune was a balance and for every good a spaewife brings there was an unforeseen ill and from every ill she does comes something good: she

> could not create good fortune but
> only guide it, like water in a channel.

The unpredictability of the balance is the chief limiter on the usefulness and application of magick, especially so in the Northern Tradition with its emphasis on ethics.

Runes

> Runes in the hands of one with clear-sight are effective for divination and protection from wickedness, though the exact mechanism defies explanation. However, their effectiveness when used by a layperson or an ex-spaer is much less certain. Naturally, if success in an endeavour were guaranteed by scratching a rune, we would find them everywhere and misfortune nowhere.
>
> In truth, no amount of runic inscribing shall ward off *all* misfortune, any more than do four-leaf clovers, crossed fingers, and prayer, and yet it is human nature to do all of these. Perhaps we might best understand the runes in a negative sense: misfortune may not be denied entry into our lives, yet failing to take precautions shall invite it.
>
> MacGregor, *A History of Scottish Magick (Paris, 1899)*.

Remarkably, despite decades of research the exact mechanism defies explanation even today.

The runes are an ancient form of alphabet originally from Dark Age Scandinavia, though some claim they are far older and derive from Egyptian hieroglyphs. In Norse mythology the runes were given to Odin in exchange for the blinding of an eye and while they served as an alphabet—there are a many stones inscribed with runes scattered across Scandinavia and even a few in Anglia and Scotland—they have always been associated with magick: indeed, the word rune derives from rūn, meaning 'secret'.

According to Reginald James's *The Rune Cast* (Argent Books, 1987) the runic alphabet is called a futhark in Scandinavia and a futhorc elsewhere and is named after its first six letters, just as our alphabet is named after its first two letters, alpha and beta. There are several variations across Scandinavia, Germany, and the Britannic Islands ranging from sixteen letters in the earliest form to thirty-three in the Northumbrian and Ionian runes. In all variations the runes are drawn with straight lines for easier carving in wood or stone and each is associated with a human desire or action, or a natural object. Thus Feyr (the F of futhorc) means wealth in the form of livestock or gold, Rathad refers to riding or journeying, while Eolh is the stag (the elk in the Scandinavian futhorcs) and symbolises strength and protection. Ionian runes were employed by the majority of spaers working in Scotland and it is these which we find in *This Iron Race*.

According to James, the Ionian runes developed from the Northumbrian runes early in the ninth century and they have much in common. In particular, the Ionian Futhorc includes the Calc, Gar, Cweorð, and Stane runes not found in the earlier Anglo-Saxon Futhorc. In common with other forms of religious and educational establishments, each Fellowship of Grace developed its own traditions, and this extended to the runes; hence the differences between the Ionian and Northumbrian futhorcs. Despite these variations, comparisons of runes from the Fellowships of Grace at Mannin, Iona, Tara, Lindisfarne, and the Écoles des Etudes Esotériques at Mont Dragon in Brittany, shows a clear line of descent from the Elder Futhark of Scandinavia down to recent times.

In the Northern Tradition rune stones are primarily for divination but they can also be used for protective and malign purposes, and a few have even entered popular culture in the form of hand-casting. Few realise that crossing their fingers for luck invokes gyf, the rune of generosity, while the vulgar 'two-fingered salute' invokes arbh, the rune of the wild bull.

Chapter Six

Portree

The bright and modern interior of Edenborough's Registry House is a far pleasanter place to work than the Reserved Manuscript Depository. Your editor called at Registry House last June to research his biography of Sir Tamburlaine Bryce MacGregor—a work temporarily on hold while he edits *This Iron Race*—and while the focus was on papers directly related to MacGregor's life and works there was opportunity to examine the census records for several of the locations of MacGregor's novels to see how well MacGregor's description matched reality. Among them was Portree.

Portree's entry in the 1860 census, the nearest we have to the date of the novel, is illuminating. The previous decade had seen much new building with a number of well-built terraces in the centre of Portree replacing the earlier hovels. One might therefore assume the lot of the town's inhabitants had improved considerably, but the census reveals astounding levels of overcrowding with several generations of entire families crammed to each floor. This is shocking enough, but further enquiry proved conditions in the surrounding townships were far worse. This suggests MacGregor toned down his descriptions lest the reader think he was exaggerating the misery.

What did accord was MacGregor's description of Portree's change from a town of Gaelic-speaking labouring people to an English-speaking town of shopkeepers. Comparison of the 1850 and 1880 census returns shows the weavers, cobblers, and other craftspeople living in Portree in 1850 had by 1880 been pushed to the margins of town, such as Stormy Hill where Tearlach M'Leòid clings to the old ways and sells a sheep carcass no other butcher would touch. Their place in the centre of Portree had been taken by fish merchants, tailors, grocers, and pharmacists. Fancy Hill, where Màiri and Rosie gather herbs, is another example of Portree's changing fortunes and it remains a pleasant civic park quite at odds with the wildness of its surroundings. Comparing MacGregor's descriptions of Portree with the recorded history of the town proves the accuracy of MacGregor's observations and his willingness to be critical of society.

Medicine & magick—rivals or complementary?
If Eolhwynne portrays the spaewife in the first flush of her abilities then Màiri Mulcahy shows her at, or near, their end. Indeed, the juxtaposition of this chapter with the previous is one of the rare occasions when MacGregor's declaration, "the chief concern of this novel is magick" becomes explicit and Eolhwynne and Màiri Mulcahy can be read as portrayals of the same character separated by time.

While Dr Ramsay and Màiri Mulcahy respect each other's talents and even show some knowledge of the other's sphere—especially so in the case of Dr Ramsay—MacGregor is depicting what he regarded as an ideal. In reality, outside-women served those who could not afford the doctor's fees while the doctor practised medicine to those who would not dream of calling on an outside-woman. Only if the doctor's remedy proved ineffective—common in an age when medicine was primitive—or in cases of unwanted pregnancy would a self-professed 'decent' person consult an outside-woman.

At the same time, far from regarding outside-women as equals, many doctors, perhaps objecting to the loss of potential patients, claimed their potions ineffective or even harmful. This was the view for over a century and only in recent years has science tested the herbal remedies, charms and potions of outside-women and verified that many of them are as effective as modern medicine. Your editor discovered this recently when a simple copper bracelet bought at the village shop cured the rheumatism in his fingers, proving nothing is more effective than direct experience to convince a man there is truth beyond our philosophies.

Màiri Mulcahy's book

> The type was small and hard to read. He did not bother beyond the first few words if he did not think it useful. There were a great many forms of wandering spirits, and it was curious such a thin book should have so much to say on them.

Dr Claude Crabtree, writing in 1930, suggested this apparently casual remark alludes to the common belief that books of magick, as opposed to books about magick, were panaceas, literally 'all things to all men' and could, in effect, answer any query given to them regardless of its obscurity. From the description of the book Bheathain reads it seems unlikely it is anything other than a simple guide to common magickal practice and phenomena—genuine books of magick being rare and expensive—therefore, accepting the remark is without obvious narrative context, we concur with Dr Crabtree it probably refers to a text outside the narrative.

MacGregor wrote considerably more on the nature of books of magick in his last major work; *The History of Scottish Magick* (published posthumously in France in 1899 as *L'Histoire de Écossais Magie*) and this brief extract may be of interest:

> Ordinary books suffer from a requirement to contain in one volume all that reasonably falls within the remit of their title. Thus, even books of seemingly modest scope weigh heavily in the hand and by their length obfuscate and conceal the seed within an immensity of chaff; notwithstanding the uninteresting chaff will contain one or many seeds suiting the enquiry or enquirer of a different time or place. Books of magick, necessarily containing magick need not suffer from this but may reveal to the reader exactly what he sought (whether he knew it or not) without the pain of always carrying and periodically winnowing the chaff. That books of magick go to such pains to please the reader may be the reason they become curmudgeonly when treated in a careless or unappreciative manner.

How such books might materially function is another matter entirely. The best explanation argues they are palimpsests with multiple layers of writing any one of which may be superimposed to suit the needs of the moment. Hendryk van Zelden, a man whom, despite our disagreements, we allow is an excellent communicator, has said in an interview that books of magick are akin to the hyperweb in containing a vast amount of immediately accessible knowledge whose exact whereabouts and provenance are almost unknowable.

Chapter Seven

The Hanseatic League

The Hanseatic League developed from a trade federation of north German towns and ports who used their superior maritime expertise to monopolise trade in the Baltic and much of the North Sea and who then expanded east to Russia and west to France and northern Spain and eventually to the area north of the Canadian

Great Lakes where they controlled the trade in beaver fur. By the early years of the seventeenth century the Hanseatic League had lost its dominance in Europe as a result of nation states establishing their own merchant shipping fleets, such as the Merchant Adventurer Companies of Lunden, Antwerp and Edenborough. It responded by following the example of the Dutch East India Company and reformed its financial and trading structures to emerge as a chartered company, while retaining the majority of its historical privileges. In this form it survived into MacGregor's time, only to have its activities drastically curtailed after the unification of Germany in 1872. It ceased activity altogether during the Great European War of 1915–1921.

In character the Hanseatic League combined monasticism with ruthless business practises such as bribery, black propaganda, and the encouragement of piracy against rival shipping companies. Its Aldermen were always German-born Catholics, while Housemen acted as unpaid apprentices until such time as they had sufficient experience and influence to buy themselves an aldermanship. Their 'monasteries' were German-speaking walled enclaves within foreign cities, containing a chapel, refectory and dormitories, along with warehousing and wharves to service shipping. Known as 'kontor' (plural kontore) the principal ones were at Antwerp (originally Bruges), St Petersburg, Bergen in Norway, and Lunden and Winchester in Anglia. In addition, smaller depots developed along the Baltic and North Sea coasts and as far south as Bilbao and across the Atlantic in Wittemborg Bay in Canada. Everywhere it went it had a reputation for sharp practice and was universally loathed. MacGregor, writing in his history of the Merchant Adventurers Company of Edenborough, described them thus:

> Prior to 1630, Aldermen and Housemen of the Hanseatic League were required to abstain from alcohol and the company of women, thus obliging the more enterprising of them to acquire skills at deception, duplicity and opportunism naturally complementary to their mercantile activities. Although the restrictions on their habits have become more liberal of

late, their culture remains inured and there are few sights more likely to encourage a man to despair of the Human Race than a Hansard 'on the make.'

Finland

Finland is one of Europe's youngest nations and has only recently celebrated the centenary of her independence, which she won, somewhat by default, when Russia imploded in revolution and civil war at the beginning of the twentieth century. Russian rule in Finland lasted most of the nineteenth century but in the centuries before, back to medieval times, Finland was ruled by Sweden.

In the eighteenth century Sweden and Russia had vied for supremacy in the Baltic until a series of bad harvests and defeats ended Sweden's golden age. For the Finns it was a period of unrest and insecurity, and peace was welcomed. Unfortunately for them, while Stockholm's rule had been relatively benign, rule by Russia brought tax increases and land seizures by favourites of the tsar. Russia made Finland a Grand Duchy in its empire and appointed a governor who ruled according to the tsar's edicts. This injustice should have provided fertile ground for unrest, but opposition to Russia came slowly and from an unlikely quarter.

Finland was essentially two nations in one: a Swedish-speaking gentry and mercantile class in the west of the country and a majority peasant class of Finnish speakers in the centre and east. The Swedish speakers had been the elite under Swedish rule, and it was they who fomented opposition to Russia by promoting the native Finnish culture. Among their endeavours was a printed text of Finland's national epic, the *Kalevala*, compiled by Elias Lonnrot. The *Kalevala* is the Finnish equivalent of our Arthurian legends, but until Lonnrot it existed only as orally told fragments. Other poems and texts, usually written first in Swedish and then translated into Finnish, soon appeared alongside the *Kalevala* creating a Finnish national literature and cultivating a sense of national identity and the belief they had a right to self-rule.

Russia's reaction was brutal and typical of empires sensing a threat from within, but that sorry history lies outside the bounds of *This Iron Race*. Suffice it to say Paavo Jukola's possession of the *Kalevala* would have earned him a lengthy spell in Helsingfors prison.

So much for the historical background to this chapter, all of which MacGregor could have learned from texts held at King James University. However, accounts of Finnish peasant life under Russian rule were rare and none were translated into English. Fortunately, a German edition of Johan Runeberg's poem 'Farmer Paavo' (In Finnish, 'Bonden Paavo') had been published a few years earlier and while it provided MacGregor with little more than the first name of his character, he began a lengthy correspondence with the poet. Runeberg, delighted at the attention shown by MacGregor, was happy to answer enquiries on language, rural settings and customs, and even the uniform of the Russian soldiery. In return, MacGregor translated 'Bonden Paavo' into Scots and wrote a piece championing it for the Edenborough Review, which concluded with this statement in support of Finnish nationhood:

> It is said Tsar Alexander the First ennobled himself Grand Duke of Finland to placate Finnish desire for self-governance. Happily, in spite of (or as a result of) being dominated by their neighbours for centuries, the Finns are a plucky and shrewd people and, except for the most credulous and those with money to lose by disturbing the cast of power, they have not been fooled by their Emperor's new title.

It is unclear if MacGregor took the name *Jukola* at Runeberg's suggestion, but in a curious coincidence Alexis Kivi (1834–1872) also chose Jukola as the family name of his *Seven Brothers*, the first novel written in Finnish and published a few years after the first volume of *This Iron Race*.

Maimed heroes

What do we mean by a maimed hero? First, a hero is not necessarily a creature of action or heroism; rather, the hero is merely the centre of his or her story and Paavo Jukola, for all his failings, is the hero of this chapter. Second, the maiming need not be physical for a metaphysical or psychological injury will suffice.

To qualify as a maimed hero the injury or condition must be chronic. That is, it is persistent and will not mend by itself. It may originate in a single event or it may develop gradually, as happens in a deprived or emotionally unstable childhood. However, unlike the flawed hero, typified by Achilles, who is always undone by his weakness, the maimed hero can overcome their injury and achieve success.

Sometimes, as here, the hero is wholly to blame for their condition. It is a harsh judgement but had Jukola not beaten the old horse he would not have encountered Lieutenant Zhulpa, Lauri would not have run away to join the army and, we assume, Jukola would have stayed on his parent's farm.

Bheathain Somhairle and Eolhwynne also qualify as maimed heroes for both were orphaned in dreadful circumstances, though quite how dreadful we have yet to fully discover. Lord MacDonald's circumstances are different again: the most obvious tragedy in his past is the death of his first wife, but what truly maims him is the crushing responsibility he bears for his failing estate. All three are maimed heroes because they are unable to reconcile what they happened to them and find happiness.

Captain Wolfe's injury is metaphysical but equally damaging, for his inability to reconcile his self-image with his inner nature leaves him incapable of being either.

In classical literature the maimed hero is not nearly as common as the orphaned hero we discussed earlier. Samson, of Samson and Delilah, is an easy to understand example, albeit his recovery from the injury done him by Delilah requires only time so cannot be said to be chronic. A better example is the Fisher King of Grail legend whose wound is both physical and metaphysical. An injury to the thigh or groin has left him lame and, it is inferred, impotent. Mirroring his infertility, his land is wasted and barren. We see the connection here between the Fisher King's wound and our characters' situations: unless they can find a cure for their injury, Bheathain, Eolhwynne, and the rest, cannot prosper. However, unlike the true maimed hero, the Fisher King's cure is dependent on a conventional hero, Sir Galahad, noblest of King Arthur's knights, whereas a maimed hero must be cured from within.

The Beast, from *Beauty and the Beast,* is a perfect example.

In part, the Beast is maimed by an enchantment leaving him seemingly more animal than man. The true wound, however, is to his self-perception for he believes himself unlovable, even though he is unchanged beneath his rough exterior. It is a conundrum faced by every middle-aged man when he stares in the mirror and wonders where his youth went.

The Beast resorts to trickery to gain a bride, the Beauty of the tale, but her initial reaction only confirms his self-perception for she is repulsed by him. However, as time passes, she grows to see the true man within The Beast and falls in love. Once The Beast realises this the enchantment is broken and he regains his handsome appearance. Leaving aside the element of magick, the real change is to his self-perception, for he can only return Beauty's love when he accepts he is lovable.

In *This Iron Race* we see characters reliving in thought and dream the origin of their troubles. In part, this is necessary to the narrative for it is there the curse is most likely to work its blessing, but it also reflects life, for those who have suffered a traumatic event return to it again and again, replaying it in their minds as though hopeful of a different outcome.

There are two possible explanations for the emphasis on maimed heroes in *This Iron Race*: one is intratextual while the other is extratextual. The former is a manifestation of the Curse's wish to bring about a blessing and so end its existence. Inevitably, this exposes the character's regrets and bad experiences but often it discovers they have become so embedded in the character's identity it cannot alter them, as with Eolhwynne when it admits:

> Her grief, like the shipwrecked reef
> Lies hidden at high-water.
> Grace was met with tragedy
> And she has built her house upon its rock.

The extratextual explanation lies in MacGregor's profound grief following the death of his first wife for there is a clear parallel between his two years of creative silence and the wasting of the Fisher King's lands. Fortunately for him (and for us), and unlike Sir Galahad, Lady Helena Northwood succeeded in restoring her 'Fisher King' to vigour.

The compass as metaphor

Commodore Walter Huygens of the Solent Coastguard has confirmed MacGregor's description of operating the compass is correct in all detail, even down to the name of the manufacturer.

This should not surprise us: MacGregor often took pains over apparently minor details and among the mariners of Leith he had plenty who might advise him.

The title of the chapter and the detailed description of the compass indicate it is more than simply a prop within the drama. Rather, the care Jukola takes to make an accurate reading with the compass contrasts with the waywardness of his life. The proof of this lies at the end of the chapter in the line, "Hate takes its bearing from a wrecker's light," but to understand the proof requires a little maritime history.

The wreckers were never as numerous as folk history suggests, but nor were they wholly legend. In parts of south west Anglia a handful of villages and parishes profited from luring ships on rocks and plundering the wrecks. A diligent navigator sure of his position would not be led astray but, especially in poor visibility, the incautious could mistake a wrecker's lantern for a beacon and set a fatal course. Jukola's course has been set by his hatred of Russia but hate, MacGregor states, is a false light, implying Jukola's employment by the Hanseatic Company will not end well.

MacGregor & the sea

In 1819, aged eight, MacGregor sailed with his father aboard the *Arcturus* of the Edenborough Merchant Adventurers, on the crossing from Edenborough to Tromsø, in Norway. Remarkably, the ship's manifest survives in the archives in Edenborough, revealing the ship offloaded coal and woollen goods and returned with Norwegian spruce and had one T B MacGregor listed as "cadet seaman". There were no passengers aboard so we can assume this was the young MacGregor. An eight-year-old serving on a ship may seem extraordinary to us but it was not unknown for children as young as seven to serve in the Scottish Navy. However, it is doubtful MacGregor's rank was more than an honorific and most likely, he was brought along purely to get a taste for life at sea and to see his father at work.

His bout of polio a few years later ended any prospects of a career with the Adventurers, but their loss was literature's gain.

MacGregor never lost his love of the sea. Aged twelve and accompanied by his aunt he took a voyage from Edenborough via Ostend to Calais before travelling overland to take the water cure at the French spas. The treatment proved ineffective. In his early twenties, shortly after his first literary success, he sailed again, this time on a European tour that included the German-speaking lands, Switzerland, Italy and Greece. There were also numerous passages from Edenborough to Lunden and Winchester to promote his works and in his capacity as Master of Revels to King Charles. Then in the summer of 1861 he and Lady Helena took a cruise aboard the *Caledonia* to Skye.

The latter is the most interesting of these voyages as it is nearest to his commencing *This Iron Race*. Marine technology advanced rapidly in the mid-nineteenth century. The increased reliability of engines and the building of lighthouses made shipping safer and faster and a sailor's life in 1861 was markedly different from that of 1819. MacGregor took a keen interest in the *Caledonia* and saw the engine room, bridge, and even the crew's quarters. An advertisement for the shipping company shows a two-masted schooner with paddlewheels, similar to the fictional *Dundalk*, and it is likely MacGregor's time aboard the *Caledonia* informed its depiction. His fame also bought him a place at the captain's table, though it is clear from his favourable impression of Captain Cockburn he was not the inspiration for Tynan Loveless.

The allegation of horse cruelty

As mentioned on page lx MacGregor was no horseman but while your editor considers this a mere curiosity, other critics have seen something sinister behind it.

The first allegation came from Humphrey Doolittle in, 'Equus: equinophobia in the works of Sir Tamburlaine MacGregor,' published in the September 1957 edition of Psychology Review—MacGregor's *Edmund Pevensie* had recently been reissued for its centenary—which listed in exhaustive detail the fate of numerous horses in MacGregor's work. We have just seen the sufferings of poor Minna and you will recall the death of a horse in chapter five. They are not the only horses to suffer in *This Iron Race* and there are many more in the whole of MacGregor's works. However, Doolittle—who was clearly a horse lover—is unjustified in claiming MacGregor had an obsessive hatred of horses.

A similar allegation appears in *The Wizard of the North* by Dr Claude Crabtree (King James University Press, 1930), except Dr Crabtree argues the root of it lay not with MacGregor's antipathy towards the horse, but their antipathy towards him. For evidence he gave the testimony of the son of MacGregor's coachman at Arbinger and a letter from MacGregor to Sir Charles Palliser stating, "I cannot say who or when, but it appears an ancestor of mine has offended the entire equine race for none will bear me". Dr Crabtree then referenced a folk belief that no horse will abide on its back one who practises magick, his inference being, as you understand, MacGregor was such a person. Although an admirable scholar, Dr Crabtree was an ardent socialist and in sympathy with the anti-shamanic pogroms of communist Russia he made allegations of witchcraft against a number of literary figures in Scotland and Anglia, none of which have been proven.

As for MacGregor and horses, it is perfectly true that there are people horses do not get along with—indeed, a horse would rather bite your editor than take an apple from him—but a surprisingly large number of people are simply allergic to horses and it is probable MacGregor was among them.

Digression
The purpose of the digression
MacGregor informs the reader *This Iron Race* will be very different from his earlier work and from the great majority of his contemporaries. Radically for its time, and unusual even for now, *This Iron Race* has no heroes or villains and no single character leading the narrative. While Bheathain Somhairle, MacGregor's "Man of Skye", is the most significant character, he is absent from some two thirds of the novel. Moreover, MacGregor rarely shows Bheathain acting like a conventional hero and instead of being master of his narrative, he frequently displays a stoicism bordering on inertia.

Crucially, however, the need for Bheathain's curse to redeem itself by finding "one for whom it is a blessing" allows MacGregor to expand his scope far beyond Bheathain's world. Thus far we have seen glimpses of Winchester, Highland and Lowland Scotland, Eireland and Finland but in the next volume MacGregor's scope extends east to the Black Sea and south to Equatorial Africa and encompasses the full spectrum of human society from the highest to the lowest, regardless of geographical and, albeit limited by the span of human memory, temporal boundaries.

None of the characters MacGregor gives us is remotely a conventional hero or villain; however, Louis S Robertson writing in *A Literary History of Alba vol. ix* (Pembury Press, 1911) convincingly argued that MacGregor's true hero and true villain in *This Iron Race* was humanity itself because the novel displays both the very best and very worst of human character.

Veracity?

To what degree can we trust the text? It is an unusual question to ask of a work of fiction but here we have MacGregor delivering the amended proofs of 'Lays of Brigadoon', to Sir Sidney Beresford at his offices in Edenborough, an event which we know took place on the afternoon of April 23, 1862 from Sir Sidney's letter to MacGregor a few days later.

Thus, if the meeting took place for the purpose MacGregor states in the text, then we can reasonably ask how much else in the text is true and how much is elaborated. But first, some background on MacGregor's visit to Edenborough.

Lady Helena did not accompany her husband: she was some five months pregnant with their first child, Lorcan MacGregor, at the time and remained at Arbinger. Her diary states MacGregor was away for the nine days, 21 April to 30 April which, allowing for a day's travelling each way, gave MacGregor a week in the city. His whereabouts beyond his meeting with Sir Sidney are something of a mystery. His journal, usually a reliable source for his activities, was subsequently mutilated and the pages excised between the 22 and 28 April. The excision was deliberate and neatly done, leaving only a knife indent on the next intact page. Who removed them and when is unknown, though MacGregor is the most likely culprit.

However, the text of "The Nature of the Tale" is false in one crucial aspect for we know MacGregor began *This Iron Race* at Christmas 1861, almost four months before he handed Sir Sidney the amended proofs for 'Lays of Brigadoon'. Not only does this show the work was considerably advanced by April 1862, but it suggests the reason MacGregor remained in Edenborough.

We have noted that he conducted considerable research into shipping and especially the Baltic Trade in connection with Paavo Jukola's character and, going to the very heart of *This Iron Race*, he needed first-hand knowledge of the practice of magick and the most obvious source was the booth-scryers operating in Edenborough's Old Town. It is wholly speculation on your editor's part, but it is possible the pages missing from his journal included notes taken when he visited booth-scryers and their removal was either for ease of use or perhaps to protect the identity of his sources.

Having shown MacGregor's account of spontaneously conjuring *This Iron Race* is false we must also disprove the loss of the emigrant ship. Firstly, *The Times* for April 23, 1862, did not report the loss of any emigrant ships. Secondly, Lachesis, along with Clotho and Atropos, was one of the three Fates of Greek mythology tasked with spinning the thread of life and determining its length and it is unlikely any ship has ever borne such an unfortunate name.

It seems clear a meeting took place between MacGregor and Sir Sidney at the place and time indicated, but much, if not all MacGregor depicts in this scene comes from his invention and intended to inform the reader of the nature of this novel. On that account, the text is entirely honest.

Lays of Brigadoon

Published on 21 June 1862, 'Lays of Brigadoon' was MacGregor's first completed literary work following the years of silence brought on by the death of Madeleine MacGregor. It is a narrative poem in thirty-six stanzas concerning the inhabitants of Brigadoon, a Scottish village fated to appear in our world only on midsummer's eve once in a hundred years.

The opening stanzas show an idealised medieval Scotland unchanged by several hundred years of our history and in the fifth stanza a young newly engaged couple from our world, Peter Cavendish and Susan Orne, stumble on Brigadoon during one of its rare appearances. Initially, there is comic confusion between the nineteenth century sensibilities of Peter and Susan and the archaic-seeming Brigadoon, but the village begins to work its charm on the young couple and presently Peter falls in love with Fiona, a maiden of the village, breaks his engagement with Susan and declares he will remain in Brigadoon forever. Susan, meanwhile, has fallen in love with the mysterious Laird of Brigadoon, but at the last she cannot bear to be parted from *Edenborough's pairties and courts and lichty streets*, and returns to our world alone. In the penultimate stanza we learn how she did not find happiness in our world and regretted leaving Brigadoon and in the last stanza when Susan is dying of old age a doorway opens between the worlds and she returns, youthful once more, to marry the laird.

It was not a wholly original concept, having much in common with *Germelshausen*, a German novel of 1860 by Friedrich Gerstäcker, itself based on a folktale.

The name Brigadoon probably derives from Brig o' Doon, a supposedly haunted bridge over the River Doon in Ayrshire, but the village's mysterious appearances and the rule a human may only enter under special condition and no native of the village can ever leave, identify both Brigadoon and Germelshausen as 'Elfhame', or Faerieland. Elfhame, the land of the elves, appears in numerous Scottish ballads, including the well known 'Thomas the Rhymer' and 'Childe Rowland'. Elfhame may also be the mysterious land ruled by the lamed Fisher King in Arthurian legend. The correlation between Brigadoon and Elfhame is confirmed by the attributes and character of the Laird of Brigadoon who rules the village and is responsible for its suspension out of time. Although never named, reference to his magickal powers, such as speaking to animals and possession of a cloak of invisibility whereby he eavesdrops on the conversation of the incomers to the village, tells us the Laird of Brigadoon is Oberion, King of Faerie, and places 'Lays of Brigadoon' firmly within the tradition of journeys to the otherworld.

'Lays of Brigadoon' is of particular interest to us for a number of reasons:

It is common today for authors to keep their readers waiting years, even decades, for new works, but demand from readers in the nineteenth century was rapacious and they would have lost patience at such dilatoriness. Earlier in his career MacGregor excelled at satisfying this demand, maintaining an average of one novel every ten months for eighteen years, but the four year gap between publication of *Edmund Pevensie* and 'Lays of Brigadoon' left MacGregor and his publisher uncertain whether he still had an audience.

In form and tone, 'Lays of Brigadoon' was a return to MacGregor's early minstrel poems and although a backward step in terms of the development of poetry, the combination of minstrelsy and the quasi-medieval setting met with broadly positive reviews. The lightness of tone also disguised the content of the poem, which was darker and more visceral than anything he had written before. We cannot conclude 'Lays of Brigadoon' was a deliberate exploration of the limits of public taste, but its acceptance by his publisher and readers (albeit sales were slow) surely encouraged MacGregor to continue and deepen his exploration of the darker and more physical side of human nature in *This Iron Race*.

A second aspect 'Lays of Brigadoon' shares with *This Iron Race* is the dominant role given to magick. However, MacGregor failed to appreciate traditional Scottish poetry has its share of otherworldly beings and magick, whereas the Scottish novel was predominantly realist in subject and what was acceptable in poetry may not be, and in the event would not be, acceptable in prose.

Reading 'Lays of Brigadoon' alongside the first draft of *This Iron Race, volume one*, reveals a continuum in MacGregor's study of the darker, less seemly side of human nature, and a harking back to his earliest literary endeavours. For that alone, regardless of the merits of 'Lays of Brigadoon' as an independent work, it should interest any reader of this volume.

"Clouds of my own making"
Dedalus Le Pilote was born Claude Villon, in Montpellier, France, in 1809. The eldest son of a circus owner, Villon found fame in France as an early exponent of hot air ballooning, before exhibiting under the name Dedalus Le Pilote in the Low Countries, Anglia and Quebeck. In spring 1855 he sailed for the Crimea in an attempt to convince French High Command of the practical uses of ballooning but was fatally injured by Russian artillery while observing enemy positions, earning him the distinction of being the first, and for over thirty years, the only casualty of aerial warfare.

This much appears in *Encyclopédie Français*: less clear, if not obscured in cloud, is why MacGregor references him. We have established MacGregor began writing the first draft of *This Iron Race* some four months before meeting Sir Sidney; therefore, his account of departing "trapped in squid-dark clouds of my own making" must be false. Indeed, from the dates marking the commencement of each chapter, it appears he was already writing chapter four when he met with Sir Sidney and it is inconceivable major aspects of the plot, such as the purpose of the curse, escaped him at such a late point. However, the survival of numerous, and sometimes conflicting narrative outlines—many of which were never carried into the finished text—scribbled in the margins of the first draft suggest a remarkable amount of the narrative, if not the raw fabula, was developed in medias res, which is to say in the act of composition or shortly before.

We must allow, therefore, MacGregor's account of creating the story out of thin air is exaggeration, rather than a complete falsehood, for the shape of the story was indeed, as he states, "slowly revealing itself, like Salome through her veils, or as a landscape through clearing mist" as he worked on the text.

This brings us to another question: to what extent did MacGregor fear failing in his self-appointed task? He says had he appreciated its magnitude he should "have written his publisher advising he had condemned the scheme as out of all proportion to his abilities," which implies all that prevented him giving up the novel was ignorance of its scope.

There are arguments either way. On the one hand, by this stage in his career he was an immensely experienced novelist with over a score of titles to his credit, most of which he had completed in something less than twelve months. Admittedly, there are many examples of writers who had written themselves out after such a prolonged period of activity, but it does not apply here: MacGregor's most famous, and in some ways best novel, *Edmund Pevensie*, was the last to be completed before the death of Madeleine Nicholson and the beginning of his long silence. On the other hand, we must allow *This Iron Race* was a major departure from all his earlier work (indeed from *any* previous work) with a new style of writing more permissive than anything previously attempted, with considerable narrative complexity and a multitude of characters, each demanding a unique voice. As if this were not enough, he attempted it following a depression so severe he contemplated suicide and surely thought he would never write anything of consequence again.

In the event, MacGregor's skills as a writer came back to him and served him well, but there is no reason to suppose he ever took this for granted. *This Iron Race* would be, in your editor's opinion, a remarkable work by any writer, but after the trials MacGregor suffered it is little short of a miracle, not least for the courage of his convictions in the face of the implacable Messrs Beresford & Lucas who did their best to ruin all he set out to achieve.

Chapter Eight

The lost prince

As we saw earlier, stories of orphans and abandoned children raised in ignorance of their highborn birth are a staple of mythology and faerie tales and 'the lost prince' is a particular example of the motif.

In the majority of lost prince narratives, the prince is an outcast unaware of his birthright. He may be like Heracles, a feckless wanderer engaging in adventures when it suits him but never approaching his true destiny, which is to be acknowledged as the son of Zeus, the greatest of the gods. Alternatively, he discovers his true heritage only after bringing ruin on those who rejected him, usually by fulfilling the prophecy that led to his abandonment. Examples include Oedipus, who we met earlier, and Paris, the son of King Priam of Troy whose abduction of Helen is the cause of the Trojan War in which Priam is killed and Troy falls.

In other examples the prince is aware of his status but through war or usurpation has lost his place in line to the throne. Edgar the Atheling was such a prince in MacGregor's *Dragonships* after the death of Harold Godwinsson at the battle of Lincoln in 1072. Another example is the unnamed 'Man in the Iron Mask,' alleged to be the illegitimate elder brother of Louis XIV of France and made famous by Alexandre Dumas's *Le Vicomte de Bragelonne* (1847).

This Iron Race combines both fabula by featuring two lost princes. Bheathain is ignorant of his royal parentage but otherwise content, while Prince William is lost between the lands of the living and the dead. The manner in which both are lifted from or reconciled to their state forms the substance of MacGregor's narrative.

Wards & talismans

At the simplest degree a ward or talisman may be a humble four-leaf clover or a rabbit's foot or the lucky bandana worn by a successful sportsman; however, in general these are only as lucky as the holder believes them to be: which is to say, their effect is wholly psycho-suggestive. Bheathain's hurriedly scratched rune-mark in chapter one is such a psycho-suggestive object and while there is something in the idea that a man is more inclined to good fortune if he believes himself fortunate, the object itself has no power. To create a ward or talisman with genuine power one must have the gift of clearsight or the skill to draw upon one or more of the five elements, earth, air, fire, water, and ice. Màiri Mulcahy uses fire in this chapter. Copper smelting, as with the processing of all non-ferrous metals, releases considerable quantities of auric energy along with heat radiation and some of this auric energy can, so it is said, be channelled into the artefact during the casting process. Thus, the talisman Màiri makes for Bheathain retains within it a portion of the auric energy created during its making and this provides protection for the individual wearing it.

At least, that is your editor's limited understanding of the process as he prefers a silver crucifix. Instead, we rely on the *Manual of Magickal Practice* by Guido Vincenza, (Brimstone Press, 1959) without means to test its veracity. The key point, so far as we can establish, is a ward or talisman made in a transformative process, such as smelting or casting, by one who knows what they are about is infinitely more capable than something you or your editor might fashion out of a bit of stone or a few sticks. It also follows, one supposes, that the runes Màiri carves into the emigrant's ship are merely psycho-suggestive since there was no transformation involved in making them.

Jo Pogle, Avebury's very own blacksmith and farrier, advises us the description of Màiri Mulcahy's forge and the smelting is accurate. Like the description of Paavo Jukola taking a compass bearing in chapter six this is an example of MacGregor making everyday actions heroic. However, Miss Blackman believes the scene insufficiently detailed to allow its use as a guide and an amateur attempting to cast magickal objects is certain to fail and quite possibly suffer grievous injury.

Referring again to Guido Vincenza's work, the complex hierarchy of materials suited to making wards or talismans is similar to that for making rune stones, with the proviso the materials for wards and talismans are generally more robust since they will not be cared for by a spaewife and are liable to be attacked by the malevolent forces seeking to harm the wearer. It follows wood is seldom used owing to its susceptibility to water and fire, two of the elemental forces, except when only a short period of useful life is required: examples being the protection of an unborn child or alleviating pain during an illness. Unlike in runes, human and animal bones are never used for making wards because one cannot guarantee the original owner of the bone did not bear ill thoughts toward the wearer.

Amber, because of its electrostatic properties, is highly prized despite its lack of durability, and is followed in precedence by the noble metals and various gemstones. Copper is the second lowest of the noble metals, with only lead of inferior status, however there is an accepted rule the substance should be obtained close to where it would be utilised, hence Màiri's desire to source copper on the Isle of Skye. Until recent decades gold was the noblest of metals but recent improvements in metallurgy have brought platinum into favour.

Folklorists claim an echo of this ancient hierarchy of materials survives in the traditional metals used for engagement and wedding rings and in the names of wedding anniversaries, such as tin, silver and gold. Your editor recalls had Edith not left me for the charms of her riding instructor this year would be our silver anniversary. Everything to do with horses is bothersome and expensive.

Chapter Nine

Herr Danneberg

Aside from the offstage presence of Kpt. Hausmann in chapter two, Otto von Danneberg is the first member of the Hanseatic League to appear in *This Iron Race*, giving a human face to what had previously been abstract.

His character has divided critical opinion. According to Dr Claude Crabtree in *The Wizard of the North* (King James University Press, 1930) he is "the personification of an antiquated medieval past," while Louis S Robertson in *A Literary History of Alba vol. ix* (Pembury Press, 1911) argues Danneberg preys on Jukola's naivety and inveigles him further into the league's criminal activities.

Either interpretation is plausible and, more importantly, they are not contradictory. One can believe Danneberg cares for Jukola and rather than abandon him, his offer of a letter of introduction to Friedrich Diesler is a kindness. However, while it is unclear what this new role will entail, Danneberg intimates it will require more than a little espionage.

With this reading it is possible to judge Danneberg as a man whose moral compass has been distorted by decades of service to the Hanseatic League and though he genuinely believes he is helping Jukola he is further corrupting him. MacGregor's refusal to depict moral absolutes at a time when literature principally portrayed an idealised and untroubled social dichotomy where everyone knew their place is one of the more remarkable and surprisingly unsung aspects of *This Iron Race*.

The booth-scryer

The Booth-Scryer had been a stock character of Scottish literature from the times of the medieval makar poets, such as William

Dunbar and 'Black' Campbell, through to the poetry of Robert Fergusson (1750–1774). Fergusson's celebrated 'Mab of Cock Wynd' (1772), telling of the wickedness of Fionnghuala Tanttrum whose misdeeds led to her execution by hanging outside Edenborough's Old Tolbooth, is only the most famous of a rich vein.

A booth-scryer first appeared in what we would recognise as a novel in James Dalziel's *Dunedin Fayre* (Qualitie Books, 1749) and soon after they were an established part of any sensationalist or Gothic novel set in Edenborough. Their role was to lead the hero astray with false prophecy or foreshadow some peculiarity of their fate. Booth-scryers, or perhaps women in general—certainly ex-wives—rarely give a definite answer to a question, but always leave one feeling anything might be inferred from their reply. Of course, when whatever they alluded to finally occurs, they claim you were told it would happen and it's your fault for not avoiding it. One presumes the Oracle at Delphi was equally vague.

In reality, most booth-scryers had only a rudimentary knowledge of magick: enough to tell a man's fortune with cards or dice or diagnose if his wife was faithful or deceiving, while charming silver from his purse. Few possessed clearsight or genuine intuition into magick, though public opinion—in part encouraged by the booth-scryers themselves—exaggerated this number. Though this brought increased demand for their services, it also brought unwelcome attention from the church which periodically demanded the town clerk and the magistrates remove them. Thus, booth-scryers, like prostitutes, were in the unfortunate position of being publicly condemned and privately employed. Generally, however, save for occasional sweeps through the wynds and closes by the town's auxiliary justices (later known as the Dunedin Nobblers from the truncheons they carried) little was done to deter them and unless a booth-scryer became particularly prominent or transgressed, as did Fionnghuala Tanttrum, they were tolerated until the early years of the twentieth century when the terminal decline in magick saw them at first marginalised and then wholly ignored.

At the time of writing the first volume of *This Iron Race*, MacGregor would certainly have been at least as familiar with the booth-scryers as any other resident of Edenborough, and likely more so, for the booth-scryer encountered by Jukola is not the first to appear in his work. At the beginning of his best known novel, *Edmund Pevensie* (1857), a young Edmund encounters a booth-scryer who plies him with sweetmeats and attempts to kidnap him, and in *Camberwick* (1842) Ben Camberwick's horse accidentally tramples a booth-scryer whose dying curse haunts the Camberwick family for three generations. Booth-scryers also appear, either directly or in passing, in three of the poems collected in 'The Border Minstrel' (1837) and several more in 'A Basket of Balladry', a collection of traditional Scottish verse which MacGregor edited and compiled in 1839. However, whatever he may have known of booth-scryers while writing *This Iron Race*, he would later become much more knowledgeable for *A History of Scottish Magick* (Posthumously published as *L'Histoire de Écossais Magie*, Paris, 1899) includes an entire chapter on their history and practices, together with a dozen pen portraits of individual booth-scryers.

The evidence shows the great majority of booth-scryers were destitute women drawn from a variety of backgrounds who were one step from prostitution and two steps from the grave, with many pursuing the oldest profession by day and the second oldest by night and often to the same customers. Undoubtedly, among their number were a handful who genuinely possessed and employed magick, both for good and ill-purpose, but compared with Edenborough's resurrectionists and vivisection men who preyed on graveyards and workhouses for dead and infirm bodies to provide specimens for apprentice surgeons in the early decades of the nineteenth century, the wickedness of the booth-scryers has been greatly exaggerated.

Chapter Ten
Degrees of separation

An anonymous piece in the fall 1864 issue of the Edenborough Review welcomed MacGregor's return to writing and then lambasted volume one of *This Iron Race* for:

> ...the remorseless misery of its leading characters, of whom there are so many the reader might be forgiven to understand he is to act as their shepherd and herd them into order, engenders a sense of despair out of keeping with an activity chiefly undertaken for pleasure.

> What is MacGregor trying to tell us
> in his earnest new voice? Are we each
> entirely alone, whether from choice,
> vocation, or misfortune? Is there no
> joy in company or are we islands,
> distant one from another? The won-
> der is not MacGregor spent two
> years cloistered in his abbey but that
> on rejoining society he should give us
> such a parade of unhappiness. It is as
> though a castaway newly removed
> from his desert strand has neither a
> good or a kind word for anyone.

Employing the then infant science of textual analytics, Dr Claude Crabtree, in *The Wizard of the North* (King James University Press, 1930) concluded this unenthusiastic review was penned by MacGregor himself out of pique at the bastardisation wrought on the novel by his publishers.

Although not expert in textual analytics we cannot agree with Dr Crabtree; MacGregor had a family to support and no matter how frustrated he was with Beresford and Lucas, the first volume of *This Iron Race* had to sell, and critical reports in the Edenborough Review would hardly assist.

Leaving aside authorship of the review, it does make a serious point; all the main characters in volume one, and in the successive volumes, are to some degree set apart from those around them and this separation is a source of unhappiness. Psychologists would properly term this 'alienation' for the true source of each character's isolation is the perception they are unlike those around them and must carry their burden alone or suffer from those perceiving them to be different, for example: Captain Wolfe; or their difference defies description, as Eolhwynne tells Lord MacDonald.

Alienation in particular is at the heart of Bheathain's circumstances and explains his hostile reaction to Màiri informing him he is acquiring the gift of Grace. Already stigmatised by the mark on his face he can only see Grace as a second cause for people to disassociate from him.

Lord MacDonald also suffers from alienation but here the cause is his position in society. The finances of his estate depend on good governance, and he feels responsible to his clansmen—two forces not easily reconciled. Murdo Dixon ably assists him, but Dixon is primarily his servant and not someone with whom he can fully share his burden. Those with whom MacDonald might share it, namely Sir David Mackenzie and the Commission Men, have a very different attitude to the care of an estate and he cannot take any comfort from them.

Paavo Jukola has, although he is almost certainly unaware of it, chosen alienation for he is a spy for the Hanseatic League, which, he erroneously believes, supports his hostility toward Russia. His alienation may have a moral standing, for he believes he deceives for a higher purpose, but his acceptance of a continuing role in the league after Danneberg has explained their true position to him, shows Jukola actively thrives on his sense of alienation.

Initially, Sir David Mackenzie may seem the exception to the alienation of other characters, but this is a misreading. Although surrounded by his loving wife and family, his concern for them, expressed in the finery of his household, comes from depopulating his estates and alienating those who look to him for care.

There is one exception among the major characters. Màiri Mulcahy has not chosen or had reason to be alienated from those around her. Freed of the isolation clearsight brought her, she initially continues her isolation by setting up home on Haelda's Island but now recognises she wants acceptance and a position where she can be of greater use to those around her. Chief among the people she seeks acceptance from is Bheathain Somhairle, provided he can meet her reasonable conditions.

Why might MacGregor have chosen to give his reader so many characters alienated from those around them? There are two possibilities, though they are supportive rather than competing.

Firstly, the subtext of *This Iron Race* is acceptance and toleration, most obviously of those with Grace.

Secondly, MacGregor began *This Iron Race* after enduring two years of isolation at Arbinger Abbey following the death of Lady Madeleine MacGregor. Though his isolation was, one presumes voluntary, it was also a response to grief and despair, and perhaps the belief he was unworthy of good company. His journal makes it clear he took some of the blame for Madeleine's death on himself as he was aware of her unhappiness at Arbinger and believed he had failed in his duty as a husband and father-to-be.

Grief especially isolates us because the grief-stricken believe no one can fully understand their loss. This was confirmed for MacGregor by his own father's brusque (though well-intentioned) advice to "get over it swiftly or lose all position in society," as quoted by MacGregor in his journal. Thus, MacGregor chose to depict alienation as a plea for the toleration of magick and those who practise it and because he knew how terrible it could be.

If your editor may speak of his own circumstances, he has some personal experience of MacGregor's motivations. No blame attaches for the death of his father, the poet, Thomas Warbrook, but he is cruelly aware he has not lived up to his father's expectations or those who expected him to follow his father's illustrious career. Comparison with one's father's work always inspires gloom and, of course, one misses his company and advice dreadfully. Your editor is also father to his own son, Gerald, yet there lie more degrees of separation. It is not that we do not get on, but Gerald is so distant. Presently he is working for some charity in Sumatra. Quite literally, we must turn half the globe to find him. Of his ex-wife, Edith, your editor shall say nothing. In his cups but honouring the near completion of work on volume one, he has opened a bottle of Châteauneuf-du-Pape. Sometimes we wonder if all we have for company is Tam MacGregor and that damn fool Hendryk van Zelden.

And the cats of course. Though Boris and Tusker are probably next door at Mrs Pumphrey's; she spoils them dreadfully.

Marxist Alienation & This Iron Race
Dr Claude Crabtree was the first to apply Marx's 'Theory of Alienation' to *This Iron Race*. Dr Crabtree was a member of the Communist Party from 1931 until his suicide in 1957 shortly after the Russian invasion of Hungary. While accepting he had the courage of his convictions and the decency to know when he was betrayed, much of Dr Crabtree's analysis of *This Iron Race* is biased. However, it has gained considerable traction in certain left-wing Oxford institutions so we must counter it as best we can.

We shall take the obvious point first: Marx's 'Theory of Alienation' was written in 1844 when he was still a young man, but did not appear in print until 1927, half a century after MacGregor's death. It follows whatever connection *This Iron Race* may have with Marx's 'Theory of Alienation' there was no direct influence. It is true MacGregor read Marx's *Communist Manifesto* shortly after its publication in Germany in 1848 and acquired a copy in translation for his library at Arbinger; however, despite recognising many of the same ills in society, MacGregor was not sympathetic to Marx's theories, as proven by the criticisms MacGregor wrote in his copy of the *Manifesto*.

First, we must describe Marx's 'Theory of Alienation' as it is unlikely to be familiar to many readers. Essentially, in an industrial society the majority of workers are alienated from their own labour: that is, there is no natural connection between labour and livelihood, such as exists in an agrarian society where food production is the primary employment. Instead of acquiring through labour the means to sustain himself, the worker is paid in money. This he exchanges for the material goods he needs to live, or rather, survive, since in Marx's view the necessity of labour means the individual is no longer a free man but a waged slave without an independent life of his own. Moreover, at no point does the employed man own the thing he makes, either in a legal, moral, or artisanal sense, or receive its full value in his wage. Rather, it remains the property of the owner of the land, machinery, or materials with which he works. Your editor confesses sympathy with this aspect of Marx's theory though it is rather more pertinent today than in Marx's time. One cannot imagine, for example, the staff at a call centre or a supermarket enjoy rich and satisfying employment compared to the farmer or woodsman working on the land; however, I believe Dr Crabtree was mistaken to see much of Marx's 'Theory of Alienation' in *This Iron Race*.

The principal conflict for the characters in *This Iron Race* is not concerned with their employment; rather, the character's natural abilities or inclinations conflict with their expected role in society. Thus, Captain Wolfe, Bheathain Somhairle, Lord MacDonald, Sir David Mackenzie, and Paavo Jukola are in some degree conflicted between what they are or wish to be and what society requires of them. Only Eolhwynne and, to a lesser extent, Màiri Mulcahy, have reconciled their nature with their role in society. At this point we must recall Marx's famous maxim "From each according to his ability, to each according to his need," for several of the characters in *This Iron Race* are unwilling to use their abilities and therefore do not have what they need. However, as in a number of cases these abilities are supernatural in nature, they hardly fall within Marxist Theory which regards magick, along with religion, as "the opiate of the people".

There is, however, one character in this volume to whom

Marx's Theory of Alienation applies very well: the admirable Uilleam M'Illathain, the last kelp gatherer of Staffin Bay. Rather than using kelp to manure the land, M'Illathain burns it to make soda ash, a substance used in glassworks and soap manufactories. He has no direct use for soda ash—it is in fact toxic—nor does he own what he produces since the greater share of its value goes first to the estate and then to agents who broker it to industry.

The kelp industry was a major source of employment and profit in the Highlands and Islands during the Napoleonic Wars, but the end of the war brought access to better sources of soda ash overseas and the value of kelp dropped by a quarter in the following decades, bringing mass unemployment to coastal communities. It seems likely M'Illathain personifies MacGregor's oft-stated criticism of the management of highland estates, but we cannot conclude MacGregor was sympathetic to Marxism. After all, one can acknowledge society's ills without seeking to overthrow the established order and nothing in MacGregor's writing indicates he harboured revolutionary ideals. Rather, he wished the existing order had more compassion and took it upon himself to indicate where it was most needed.

Bheathain as Christ figure

The Sacred Vine by Mrs Merriel Shepo (Advent Press, 1957) is a work of extraordinary literary and theological research purporting to prove all stories, whether from myth, religion, the biographies of the famous and even the lives of fictional characters, ultimately derive from the life of Jesus Christ as recorded in The Gospels.

The first part of *The Sacred Vine* constructs the life of Christ from Matthew, Mark, Luke, and John, ancient papyri texts then recently discovered at Khirbet Qumran in Israel, the Gnostic Gospels, and the Apocrypha. It then examines the lives of some three hundred real and fictional individuals from the Buddha, through Louis XVI of France, to Pinocchio, and attempts to show how the key events in the life of Jesus are echoed in the lives of these individuals. Majestic in its scope and ambition, *The Sacred Vine* reveals patterns of narrative many have overlooked but ultimately it fails to prove the life of Jesus is the *fons et origo* for every story ever told and many of its conclusions are, frankly, bizarre. Nevertheless, Mrs Merriel Shepo's concluding statement, "We are all Jesus; chosen by God, scourged, denied and crucified by man, we shall all sit at His right hand in heaven," is, in your editor's opinion, one of the great closing lines in modern academic literature.

Among the lives of the fictional characters examined by Mrs Merriel Shepo is Bheathain Somhairle, the hero of *This Iron Race,* and, although her conclusions are flawed, her depiction of Bheathain's character and story is intriguing. She begins with his birth, noting his cursemark immediately set him apart from others, and then compares an early attempt on his life with the Massacre of the Innocents, described in Matthew 2:16–18. Later, once he is on the Isle of Skye, Mrs Shepo notes the man Bheathain calls his father is not his birth father as Joseph is not the birth father of Jesus, and when we first meet Bheathain he is, as Jesus is so often portrayed, a shepherd rescuing a lamb. Bheathain, as we have seen, rejects Màiri Mulcahy's claim he has acquired the gift of Grace and Mrs Shepo compares this with an event in the little known Infancy Gospel of James, an apocryphal second century text purporting to relate the childhood of Jesus.

As Bheathain discovers, children are cruel to those who are different from them, and the infant Jesus suffered likewise. Eventually, unable to bear it any longer, Jesus reacts to the taunts and beats a boy to death with a stone. Regretting his wickedness, Jesus prays to God and begs release from the burden of being His son. Instead, God reveals to Jesus how to use his gifts to good purpose, beginning with restoring the life of the boy he murdered. Bheathain will also ultimately learn to use his gift for the benefit of others.

Another parallel between Bheathain's story and Jesus is Bheathain's relationship with Màiri Mulcahy. This, as you may guess, Mrs Shepo compares to the relationship between Jesus and Mary Magdalene, as depicted in the gnostic text, the Gospel of Nicodemus. However, at this point we must cease comparisons or risk revealing too much of Bheathain's future and spoiling the tale.

The Sacred Vine is an enlightening and entertaining read: who would ever have thought of comparing Pinocchio with Jesus Christ? The one crucified upon a wooden cross, the other whose burden, or cross, it is to be made of wood; both the 'sons' of woodworkers; both reborn after death, Pinocchio as a real boy and Jesus as the resurrected Christ; and both one part of a trinity, the roles of The Father and the Holy Ghost taken in Pinocchio's story by Geppetto and the Fairy with Turquoise Hair. Moreover, in attempting to prove the unprovable *The Sacred Vine* touches on a great truth. Jesus' story is not the template for all other narratives;

rather, it follows a pattern common to all narratives, whether from myth, fiction, or history, and reveals the mythic in the flesh and blood of real people and real events.

Thus, Bheathain's story does not lie in the shadow of Jesus Christ but follows a universal pattern much, much older, perhaps dating back to the first story ever told. Humans are, above all, storytellers and the story is how we make sense of the world.

Sense of an ending

The first volume of *This Iron Race* was published on the 17$^{\text{th of}}$ May 1864, volume two some ten months later, and volume three in January 1866. Collectively they were titled *Acts of the Servant* and would be followed by the first volume of *Works of the Master* in late 1866.

Modern reading habits are quite different from those of the nineteenth century. Novels then were likely to be read many times, either passed between friends or lent out by circulating libraries: a stark contrast with our culture of disposability. It follows novels had to be durable and unfortunately animal or fish glue and cotton binding was inadequate for large works. Commercial and practical concerns thus favoured the division of novels into two or three volumes and many nineteenth century titles began life as 'triple-deckers'.

Of course, some nineteenth century books, such as Bibles and Atlases, were immense but the techniques involved were enormously expensive and unsuited to commercial fiction with its competition and tight margins. Modern glues allow the binding of much longer novels and titled *Acts of the Servant* the first three volumes of *This Iron Race* have been reprinted several times as one text. However, for the release of this new edition Hare & Drum have reverted to the format of the First Edition and books two and three of *This Iron Race* will appear in due course.

The book's binding was not the only concern to the nineteenth century publisher: the reader must also be protected from strain. Throughout much of the nineteenth century, novel-reading was a feminine pursuit and male society regarded it with contempt, albeit it was popular in serialised form among literate lower-middle class males. MacGregor references this attitude in an exchange between Lord MacDonald and his wife in chapter two:

> ... he dropped the book on the seat
> and quite intended leaving it there,

having never read or considered reading, anything by MacGregor, or Copperfield, or Thaxstead, or any other manufacturer of novels.

Frequent articles in medical journals—the profession was exclusively male—blamed novel reading for various disorders to the female constitution, including hysteria, mood swings, improper desires, listlessness, agitation, and injury to the wrist. The wrist in question belonged, of course, to upper and middle class ladies who might afford a novel and the time to read it, and not to the working woman whose wrists were capable of hauling coal tubs in the mines, animal husbandry, and all manner of heavy labour. In any event, while a novel in the hand of a woman invariably met with male disproval, a slim volume met with rather less than a large one.

For publishers, the chief advantage of producing a novel in two or more volumes was cost. Not only were printing costs much lower for a small volume, but spreading the expense of a novel over a number of volumes made it more attractive to readers. In addition, if the first volume failed to sell in the expected numbers the print run for the second and third volumes was reduced accordingly.

For marketing and pricing purposes the separate volumes of a novel were of approximately equal length, but this took no account of the natural divisions in a narrative and the first and second volumes merely ended at a convenient chapter break. Indeed, the modern reader of a novel originally published in three volumes is hard pressed to know where one volume ended and the next began. Similarly, the volumes of a triple-decker were never intended to stand alone but were always read in sequence.

However, while book one of *This Iron Race* does not stand alone, MacGregor has broken Bheathain's narrative at a natural pause. Bheathain's life has changed: he believes he is in love and has acquired the gift of Grace yet is obliged to return to his former life as though nothing has happened. He is reluctant and out of sorts and we sense he will be sorely tested, if not how matters will resolve.

In the narrative with the wandering curse, we might assume, based on precedent, its next host will be drawn from those Jukola encountered on The Shore in Leith. Whether it will be Frank

Farron, the young man who assists Farron, or even the man's wife, whose mistreatment caused a moment of pity to enter Jukola's heart, is for the moment unknown, but we know its search for one to bless will continue. Furthermore, it seems unlikely we are quite finished with Lord MacDonald and his party.

Regardless, Bheathain is at the heart of the narrative, even if he does not dominate it, and his story will bring the majority of readers back for volume two. Accordingly, I look forward to renewing our acquaintance in the near future.

Nevil Warbrook, Avebury Trusloe.

Bheathain Somhairle will return in the summer of 2024

COMING SOON

The Reluctant Ascent of
NEVIL WARBROOK
In his own words

Volume One

INTIMATIONS OF MORTALITY

Published by

AVEBURY PRESS

Foreword

Intimations of Mortality is the first of Nevil's Warbrook's journals to be published The title was chosen in consultation with Edith Warbrook, Nevil's ex-wife, and with Deedee Bowbells, Nevil's colleague at Creative Havens and the acclaimed author of *Calypso and Wine*.

Nevil Warbrook is best known today for the restoration of Sir Tamburlaine Bryce MacGregor's *This Iron Race*. Originally published in the 1860s, MacGregor's work was subjected to extensive censorship by his publishers and Warbrook's revised and restored text was an attempt to recreate the text as MacGregor intended for publication by Hare & Drum of Edenborough. *Intimations of Mortality* serves as a companion to Warbrook's restoration of Sir Tamburlaine Bryce MacGregor's text and ideally should be read in conjunction with book one of *This Iron Race*.

Avebury Press wishes to express its profound gratitude to Eurydice Glendale, and Sister Ethelnyd of the Iona Fellowship of Grace for saving Nevil Warbrook's journals from destruction, and to Nevil's son, Gerald, for agreeing to their publication. We also extend our gratitude to Hendryk van Zelden for his advice and constant support; thank Nevil's agent, Desmond Catterick and Associates; his friends at Avebury and his colleagues and acquaintances at Creative Havens and Belshade College for excusing the sometimes unflattering opinions expressed herein. To all others mentioned we request your tolerance and understanding.

DOCTOR'S ORDERS
6 February; White Bear, Devizes

It comes down to this: if I do not lose weight, I shall die; if I do not curb my drinking, I shall die; if I do not take more exercise, I shall die; and according to that ghastly inflatable contraption that measures your blood pressure, if they don't get me a burst artery will.

Sobering news on the eve of a chap's fifty-eighth birthday, and especially so when Daddy didn't live to see his fifty-ninth.

"Wasn't your father a poet?" Dr Saunders asked from behind her black-rimmed glasses.

"He was. Tom Warbrook was rather well known in his day."

"Died young," she said, and just as I thought Dr Saunders might have an interest in poetry, she said the date of death was in my patient notes.

I said my father's early death had robbed us of a significant voice among the late-twentieth-century poets, and we could only guess at what he would have written had he lived another decade or two, but my thoughts were already elsewhere.

Eleven is the age at which a child (boys, anyway) realise their happy state cannot last forever. Perhaps it's the acquisition of that second digit (the zero in ten not counting); or wearing long trousers with attendant restrictions on boisterous activities that might scuff one's knees; or that schooling suddenly seems to have a purpose, like a train with a destination and not a nice destination at that. Anyway, at age eleven I became aware of my waning childhood and symbolising that awareness was my father's French, eggshell blue Aller motorcar.

I don't suppose I ever thought of it as *eggshell* blue. Not then. If I apply an adjective I learned much later to a childhood memory then what exactly am I remembering?

Stick to the facts. A blue Aller parked at Camber; a tartan travel rug spread on the sand (Mummy was proud of her Scottish heritage) Mummy and Daddy sitting on said rug; Mummy with her sunglasses on, even when it was cloudy; Daddy taking off his jacket and hat, though never his tie; and me playing on the sand and wishing it was Cornwall where there were rock pools to play in.

The only queer note in the whole day (apart from being dragged round Rye's antique shops where Mummy's eye for a bargain was matched by Daddy's concern for expenditure) was Edwin, my imaginary friend, who refused to *aller* from the Aller and sat on the back seat waiting to go home. He was afraid that if he joined me on the beach we might hurry away and forget him.

The seats were a dark blue, plasticky material. Absorbing the sun during the day they roasted the back of my legs all the way home.

I lost Edwin in Tonbridge when I was twelve. Probably that's about the age all children lose their imaginary friends. Apparently, it's something to do with the growth of neural connections between the left and right hemispheres when the brain stops being two communicant halves and becomes one. I recall we had travelled by train to see Auntie Eileen— Daddy had had a bad year and the Aller was *allering* another family—and Edwin stayed behind on the train when we got off at Tonbridge. I think he was expecting us to return to the train later, as we always had to the Aller, and I last saw Edwin with his face pressed against the carriage window en route to Dover.

Dr Saunders was staring at me.

"Sorry. Mind wandered," I said.

"According to your Well Man appointment six months ago you drink approximately twelve units of alcohol a week. Has that changed at all?"

I admitted to confusing units with pints.

"Still," I ventured, "twenty-four is hardly excessive."

"Almost everyone," Dr Saunders said, "underestimates their alcohol intake, but even twenty-four units is considerably above the recommended limit. Do you drink alone, Mr Warbrook?"

"Not in the pub," I said.

"And at home?"

"Only a night cap before bed. And sometimes a glass of wine with dinner. So, what's the verdict? You make it sound like I'm at death's door."

It was then she delivered the bad news which I paraphrased at the top of the page and having, somewhat tactlessly, said that if I didn't take better care of myself I would soon be following my father, she instructed me to keep a daily record of my alcohol consumption and weigh myself weekly; both accounts to be presented at my next appointment. In the meantime, if I experience tightness about the chest or dizzy spells, I should call the emergency services.

I have never met a women less ruffled, or more in need of ruffling, than Dr Saunders whose starched white blouse is so unyielding it wouldn't look out of place in the sculpture gallery at the Ashmolean, but her instruction had the desired effect and I walked straight into W B Jones, stationers and bought this journal. The cover is faux leather in a shade of terracotta and each day occupies a generous two pages. That is far more than Dr Saunders requires, but it has reminded me of a conversation with Elfa Jonsdottír at last October's Exmoor Haven.

The weather that week was delightful, and it had prompted Elfa to be particularly adventurous with the Inspirational Walk, intended to get our Castaways that week inspired and writing. Icelanders are extraordinarily strong-willed people, and one does not say no to them. Hence four hours on the moor had left me footsore and stiff in the saloon of the Withered Arm in Porlock.

Elfa, who is half my age and frightfully outdoorsy, took pity on me and began rubbing my calf muscles whereon I mentioned that I was soon to be fifty-eight, the very age my father was when he passed away.

"Anything more will be a bonus poor Daddy never enjoyed," I said.

Elfa paused massaging my aching calf, my stockinged foot resting snugly in her lap, and said, "You should make a saga. You can call it Nevil's Saga and in it you must write all you do. Then you see what you do in the years denied your father. Yes?"

Elfa is probably the sanest and most down-to-earth of all my colleagues at Creative Havens—even if her crime novels are far too macabre for my taste—and, as I said, one does not say no to an Icelander, but I had put her suggestion aside until Doctor Saunders' prophecy this morning.

And so the page fills.

Postscriptum: two glasses of house Merlot with lunch.

Post-Postscriptum: I miss the eleven-year-old me. I miss Edwin. I even miss the Aller.